BLACK WATER WELL

The Dark Arrow Trilogy #3

MATHIAS G. B. COLWELL

BLACK WATER WELL
THE DARK ARROW TRILOGY #3
Copyright © 2018 by Mathias G. B. Colwell

ISBN: 978-1-68046-629-4

Melange Books, LLC
White Bear Lake, MN 55110
www.melange-books.com

Published in the United States of America.

Cover Design by Stephanie Flint

Dark Arrow Trilogy

Dusk Runner
Entrance to Dark Harbor
Black Water Well

PROLOGUE

The inky-black water beckoned Half-Mask's ship as he sailed into the protected waters of the Midnight Cove. This was as close to home as he ever felt. Half-Mask wasn't quite sure he understood what others meant when they spoke of home, didn't quite understand the warmth in their tones or the joy on their faces. But maybe this feeling of rightness he felt as the prow of the ship cut through the dark waters was something like what they were speaking of when they thought of home.

Black water met light in a familiar way where the cove and the surrounding sea collided. Clear blue and green waters had been left behind as they entered the Midnight Cove, named for the dark water that contrasted so sharply with the rest of the seas around the Enclaves. This particular Enclave and the fortress on the shore called to him. Half-Mask smiled to himself, tongue idly touching the points of his needle-sharp teeth. The King of the South would be pleased he had arrived. His father was impatient and not one to be kept waiting for overly long.

The warship dropped anchor near to shore and Half-Mask disembarked onto a skiff rowed by slaves. A few trusted nobles accompanied him but, in anticipation of the meeting with his father, it was difficult to even remember their names.

"Row faster!" The Prince of Darkness grimaced as he watched the shore inch nearer. Half-Mask cursed and cuffed the slave nearest to him.

1

"I said row, damn you!" A few of the nobles looked at the prince nervously, sensing his changing mood.

The closer he came to the fortress and the King of the South the more anxious he became. He would have to tell him—his father—what he had done. He would not be pleased.

The next few minutes were a nervous blur, and Half-Mask hated it. He should not be nervous. He was the Prince of Darkness, after all! Was he not as powerful as his father? But, then again, had his father ever made a mistake like this before? He angrily shook away that thought. It made no difference: what was done was done. The boy was what he was now, and there was no changing the past. Not even Half-Mask or his father could do that. Even a Spectralist had limits to his power.

Before he knew it, Half-Mask was striding through the small throne room, or as close to a throne room as existed here at the Midnight Cove. This wasn't exactly a royal palace. The fortress was a refuge, a haven, a special place for Half-Mask and the king. It was where his father had first discovered the darkness so many years ago. It was a place to create, to replenish, to retreat, and to reemerge stronger and better and more powerful. It was not a place from which to rule—that was the purpose of Dark Harbor. The grand southern port was the hub of all life in the south. Merchants came and went; slaves arrived, worked, and died; and the nobles competed in their petty politics. But here at the Midnight Cove was where the true power lay. The well was here.

Half-Mask crossed the throne room and went to open the oak door on the far side. It was a strong slab of wood bound with iron. He glanced around as he pulled it open. At some point, everyone had left him. He was now alone. *Good*, he thought, for if they'd had the temerity to follow him to his private quarters they would have been chastised. It was a small pleasure that his slaves and attendants knew him well enough to anticipate his desires. Yet it was not a big enough pleasure to squelch the growing anxiety he felt as he climbed the stairs. The feeling made the Prince of Darkness angry, angrier than just about anything since Silverfist had died. At the top of the stairs, he pulled open another oaken, ironbound door and stepped into his chambers. His father waited within.

"It took you long enough to arrive," the King of the South said in his dead voice, disinterest in all activity around him seeming to overwhelm nearly every other attribute he possessed. But one did not make the mistake of believing the façade. He might seem disinterested, but Half-Mask knew his father was keenly invested in the events that had been transpiring these past decades. He would not appreciate the wrinkle

Half-Mask had created, but maybe he wouldn't know it was Half-Mask's fault. Just maybe.

"I had matters to attend to in the capital," Half-Mask responded.

The king ignored his comment except for a scornful glance. "Did you feel it?"

"What?" Half-Mask asked warily, testing the waters to see what his father really knew.

"Don't play games with me!" The disinterest was gone and even under the darkened cowl of his father's cloak Half-Mask could see his anger flashing. "I am speaking of the only occurrence worthy of notice these past weeks. Did you feel the *Becoming*?"

The Prince of Darkness couldn't help but grimace. "Yes, of course I felt it."

"Yes, of course you did," the king said slyly.

He knew. Half-Mask wasn't sure how he knew, but there was no doubt his father knew. He didn't respond, just stared at the king.

"Well, boy, answer me!" he barked.

Half-Mask hissed convulsively. His father hadn't dared call him 'boy' in more time than he cared to remember. "Call me that one more time," he warned with quiet anger. Nerves were gone now; he would not stand to be disrespected, not even by the king. Perhaps the time had finally come.

The King of the South was across the room in a flash, faster than Half-Mask had expected, clothed as he was in a heavy black cloak. The king's hands closed around his son's throat, constricting like a snake, powerful and furious. His father's black eyes burned into his.

But Half-Mask was not to be underestimated, either. A knife was already in his hand and held to the king's groin near a major artery. "Do you really want to do this?" the prince gasped out angrily.

His father's hands did not lessen their grip. "Tell me. Admit what you have done."

"What do you mean?" Half-Mask wasn't quite ready to give up the act yet. Perhaps he could yet shift the blame.

The king shook his head scornfully. "I know you must have done it. Only you or I could have, and *I* did not."

Fine, so the game was up. Half-Mask had to concede at some point. He might as well answer. "It was not intentional," he muttered stiffly as his father finally loosened his grasp on his throat.

The King of the South shoved his son away in disgust. "Another one of your games?"

Half-Mask sucked in air greedily as he ignored the jibe. "Relax Father, it will be fine."

"Will it? Do you really think so? Another Spectralist exists. Perhaps something more than a Spectralist, as his presence feels slightly different. I would not doubt it if he has the powers that the rumors claim in addition to what you gave him. It was the boy from the north, was it not? I can only assume that it was."

"It was. It was only supposed to make him an Unsired, nothing more," Half-Mask explained sullenly. He immediately loathed the tone his voice had assumed. He hadn't sounded like that since he was a child.

The king shook his head. "This must be fixed. We cannot allow it to just 'sort itself out'."

"What do you propose?"

Again the king assumed a sly expression. "There was once one who was quite useful. One who could be counted upon to carry out dangerous and difficult tasks. Even you counted on him at times. And you hardly ever rely on anyone, my son."

Half-Mask thought he saw where this was going. What was his father thinking? The amount of effort would be colossal.

"He couldn't be trusted then, and that won't be any different now. I wouldn't pay two rakkas for him," he argued.

His father stared at him with those piercing, black eyes, dark hair shaved on the sides of his head in warrior fashion just as Half-Mask's own locks were shorn. "But still...he *was* useful."

"He was weak," the Prince of Darkness exclaimed. "He allowed himself to be killed!"

"Utility outweighs all," the king replied. "Besides, he will be more trustworthy in his future state. They are never quite the same after rising."

Half-Mask sighed angrily. He could tell there was no arguing with his father in this case. The king took his silence for acquiescence, which perhaps it was, grabbed a bell-pull, and yanked. A few moments later, a slave could be heard laboring quickly up the stairs. He knocked and entered upon command.

"Fetch him," the king said tersely. The slave bowed and exited.

"Who?" Half-Masked asked.

"You will see. When we raise him, he will need a companion, someone who is not so...*odd* in appearance."

The slave returned accompanied by an extra set of footsteps. The knock sounded again.

"Come," Half-Mask commanded angrily. He didn't enjoy the fact that his father had clearly made plans without consulting him, taking his agreement for granted.

The door opened, and the slave entered with a traitor in tow. Blond, with the red Traitor's Tears tattooed upon his cheeks, Half-Mask could see what had once been anger faded to bitterness finally to be replaced simply with fear. Fear always ended up replacing whatever emotion preceded it, at least when one associated with the Prince of Darkness and his father.

Half-Mask's eyes narrowed. He knew this one. He had been present when this mess began. "Borian, right?"

The traitor nodded and then answered, "Yes, Prince." When he spoke, Half-Mask could see that his teeth had been filed to points like those of the south often did. Similarly, the sides of his head were shaved. Half-Mask was almost surprised he'd remembered the name. But then, it had been an eventful night. He remembered with joy the feeling of pinning Wintermoon to the wall with his sword.

The king spoke. "Borian, we have a task for you. We will be attending to a matter of dire importance. Directly after, you will be given orders to meet with and then accompany a subject of ours. Would you like the chance to kill a Wintermoon?"

Borian's fearful eyes lit up for a moment with old hatred. So, the traitor wasn't completely cowed yet. Half-Mask thought it boded well that the boy could be counted upon to hate his foe.

Borian bowed. "Yes, my king."

"Leave us," the King of the South said haughtily as soon as his command had been heard by the traitor. The boy bowed again and then exited the room alongside the slave.

"You hardly needed to bring him in. You could have simply told me the plan," Half-Mask said in annoyance.

"I suppose that is true. But these days I worry that I need to spell things out for you, especially after the mess you have made."

Half-Mask gritted his teeth—the unfiled molars, not the sharpened front row—in frustration but declined to respond. Instead, he walked to the door and grabbed the handle before looking back at his father. "Well, we may as well get on with it."

Finally, the king smiled at him. "The first sensible thing you have said yet."

They walked down the stairs, back through the throne room, and into the bowels of the fortress. They walked past torches in sconces which lit dingy tunnels as they reached the heart of the fortress. Half-Mask and the King of the South entered the cavernous room where the well lay. The black well; the well for which this fortress had been named. Black Water Well. Its name was spoken with fear by all those who had heard of it. Even the most seasoned Departed grew nervous at its mention. As Half-Mask approached, he stared into the pure contents, the core, the contained essence of the substance that seeped through the ground, through the rocks, to reach the waters of the cove and leak out to the sea, giving it the name the Midnight Cove.

"It is the one truly beautiful thing in this world. Is it not? They have their Source...and we have ours." The king sighed almost lustily as he dipped his hand into the inky depths, cupping some of the water to his mouth and drinking. Half-Mask did the same.

The drink burned and cooled, invigorating and sapping all at once. It was the energy of death in liquid form. The prince could not help but agree with his father. Still, he contained his pleasure and returned to business. "You know how much energy this will expend?" He leveled a steady gaze at the king.

"Who taught you? Of course I know. But it will be worth it. *If* he accomplishes his task, of course."

Half-Mask nodded. "Then we must drink. We must drink as much as our bodies can hold in order to accomplish it."

They dipped their hands into the well in unison, cupping the dark liquid to their lips, greedily at first and then with less urgency as their bellies filled. Then, at the last, they drank only what little bit they could force themselves to consume, so bloated with liquid were they. They were bloated with power, as well. Half-Mask could feel it in his veins. He could feel it pulsing through his body, radiating with all the power of lightning and thunder in a winter storm. He could feel the swell of energy, the flood rising in him like high tide—like a tide that could never be stopped.

He knew his father must feel it, too, because the king reached out and clasped his hand. They joined their powers and reached out. They stretched out their wills. They called. And called. They called beyond the tainted veil, beyond the wall between the living and the dead. Exhaustion filled Half-Mask's limbs almost immediately. It was difficult. Much easier to simply create an Unsired from a living elf. All the power Half-Mask had felt after guzzling the black water from the well began to drain from him almost immediately, but he pushed through. Once committed there would be no stopping. Even with the ebb in their strength, with the magnitude of the task, Half-Mask and the king working together were strong enough. They sought their target in unison. They called his name and knit him back together. Bones joined and muscles regrew. Skin reformed—at least partially, as nothing could ever be completely made as it was. There were holes, of course, gaps in his body that would look hideous upon completion, but they wouldn't slow him down. Enough had been restored. Half-Mask and his father willed purpose, imbued his new consciousness with it. It was enough. It was time for him to rise.

———

HE GASPED WITH LIFE, but soil filled his mouth. He needed air, but only loam greeted him when he tried to breathe. He clawed his way up—or, at least, what he thought was up. And all the while a burden of purpose weighed upon him. He fought his way upward for a reason, for more than air, for more than breath. He clawed and scrabbled his way up from the dirt in order to find *him*. He had to find him. That was all there was, all there ever would be. It was impressed upon his consciousness.

His hand finally broke the surface and felt the cool air of late autumn. His head and body followed. He fought to free himself from the earth, from death. Finally, he broke free and heaved himself out of his hole onto the mossy forest ground. He lay on his back and stared at the green that had replaced the void, wiggling the toes on his feet and the fingers on his hand. He smiled a contorted smile then, a hideous smile as only half the flesh on his face was still there, leaving partial skull and cheekbone poking through. But he was alive. And he had a purpose. He was to be granted revenge.

He clenched the fingers of his right hand into a fist and felt power there, strength that could not possibly have existed in the void. Glancing to his left, he saw that the metal was rusted and covered in moist earth. He brushed it off as best he could. It was still grimy, caked in dried blood and muddy moss, no longer shiny, but it looked a little more as it once had.

It was unmistakably a silver fist.

CHAPTER ONE

The clash of steel rang familiar and comforting in the air, as was the feel of a blade in her hand. Rihya ducked a slash and rolled to one side—heart pounding, blood pumping—and bounded back to her feet in a half-crouch. She was wary. He was not to be underestimated. Rihya tossed her dyed-green hair in annoyance, switching her sword back and forth between hands in what appeared to be a careless manner. All the while, she and Aldashir circled one another. He feinted, she reacted, and vice versa. It was their daily duel. Practice swords. The prince hadn't quite relented full-edged steel yet, but it still felt good to hold a weapon in her hands.

They came together again as they locked blades, her lithe, willowy frame pressed against his swarthy, thick one. Rihya felt him press down as the hilts of their swords locked, felt his strength as he bore down upon her. She spun away in a shower of sparks. It was not to her advantage to get into a contest of muscles with her captor. He was her enemy, but he was good. There was no doubt about his ability. He was nearly as good as Elliyar, perhaps even better—when Ell wasn't tapping into his powers as a Water Caller.

Rihya's feet slipped on the sandy practice field as she spun away, and Aldashir permitted his mouth to rise into a small smirk. She yelled curses in her head at his damned satisfaction, but she kept her lips shut and focused on the bout. He'd won more of these duels than she cared to admit. If Rihya was being honest, she'd probably only won maybe a quarter of their fights, but she was determined to win today.

She stepped back and let the tip of her sword dip down to rest upon the sandy earth. Shoulders heaving up and down, she caught her breath. Aldashir smiled for real this time, revealing his unfiled teeth. Most Departed warriors filed their teeth to points, but he and his men did not; it was one of the first things she had noticed about them after they had pulled her sodden body from the shore where The Point met the southern seas. Aldashir's head was unshaven at the sides and his hair was pulled back into a long tail, another difference from most of the Departed warriors outside The Point who looked more like gruesome beasts.

"Do you concede?" he asked in that annoyingly haughty tone he always used.

Rihya just stayed silent. *Let him come to me.* She leaned forward onto the hilt of her sword as if exhausted from the heat. Even in late autumn, the south could have days hot enough to sap a person's energy.

He took one step forward and then one more. "I said, do you concede?" The smirk was back. He knew he was good, and she hated that about him. He took one last step, putting him within range. It was enough.

Rihya swung the tip of her sword up, almost like a shovel, bringing with it what amounted to a handful of the practice sand. It sprayed upward as the point rose, showering the prince's face. He swore and blinked his eyes furiously, even risking his free hand to try and clear them of the blinding sand, but it wasn't fast enough. Rihya was a good fighter; she was death with knives, as her family knew, and decent with a sword. But most of all she was fast. In a heartbeat, as Aldashir struggled to clear his eyes, she had closed the distance and snaked the tip of her sword up to kiss his throat.

"The bout is mine," she said calmly. Then, just to throw it in his face a little, "Do you concede?"

The prince finally cleared his eyes enough to return her stare. He glowered angrily, so she pressed the tip of her sword a little more firmly. It was only a practice sword, mostly blunt, but it still had enough of a blade to cut if pressed hard enough.

"I said, do you concede?" She pushed the tip against his throat until a tiny trickle of red-brown blood appeared against the dark skin. His soldiers, who were watching the bout, murmured and made to step forward, but the prince flung up one hand to stop them in their tracks. His glare made it clear that he was the ruler here; *he* was in control, not she. Aldashir stared hard at Rihya with his dark eyes before leaning into the blade slightly, increasing the flow of blood. He leaned in enough to get close to her, almost close enough to kiss. *Now why did I think that?* Her thoughts skittered awkwardly away from that thought. She wasn't one to chase boys, especially not her enemy.

And then, before she could sort through those thoughts more thoroughly, Aldashir smiled a brilliant, white-toothed smile, and she heard the thump of his practice blade as he dropped it to the sandy ground.

"I hate losing to you!" He shook his head in annoyance, but the smile was still on his lips, contrasting his words.

"Well, you beat me more often than I you," she muttered back, surprised at her own forthrightness.

Aldashir cocked his head at her as if he, too, was surprised that she had admitted it. "That is...kind of you to say. Although, it was a dirty trick." The smirk lingered.

Rihya snorted. "I learned long ago that a fair fight is a fight I don't want to have. You should know that by now as a commander of troops."

The prince stared at her but did not answer immediately. "A duel is different, though. There is honor to be found in a duel in a way that you cannot find on the battlefield. This is a contest, not life and death—not like it is with war."

It was Rihya's turn to shake her head as she quipped back, "I am always at war, Southerner. If you forget that fact then you are not as smart as I thought." Again her thoughts grew confused. *Why did I say that? It was almost a compliment.* She bent over to begin post-duel stretches to keep her muscles limber, but she appraised her captor out of the corner of her eye. A sidelong glance was enough to see him staring at her openly, a slightly bemused expression on his face.

As Rihya stretched, she remembered one of their first conversations after her capture, nearly a month and a half gone now. On her second day at The Point, Aldashir had strolled up to her in her chambers—much nicer chambers than she would have expected for a prisoner—and asked her politely if she'd like to spar. She remembered the conversation like it was yesterday.

"Care to spar?" he'd said in that haughty voice, a voice full of ancient entitlement, a voice that could only belong to a noble. But she'd heard an undertone to it, as well. It possessed a sadness, and it was enough to perk her interest. Besides, she couldn't really have said no to him. Prisoners didn't make demands.

Instead, she'd responded in typical Rihya fashion with a fiery, "You would fight a female?"

"The females in the south rarely engage in combat, but I have heard tales of you wild northern dames and your aptitude for battle. I would see it for myself."

"Very well."

The prince had led her from her plush quarters, a room with a canopied bed, tapestries on the walls, plush rugs on the flagstone floors, and a window with a view like few she'd ever seen, one overlooking the southern seas. They'd descended from her chambers and walked through the fortress filled with Departed soldiers. Her skin had crawled to be among so many enemies and without a weapon. They eventually reached the practice yard and approached the weapon rack.

"Weapons?" the prince had asked.

"Blades," she'd volunteered without hesitation. The prince nodded and reached eagerly for a sword. "No, I meant knives," she'd corrected.

He'd turned back to her, disdain written clearly on his face. "Brawlers tactics."

Her insides had clenched up at his obvious distaste. How dare he judge the weapons that had kept her safe—well, not 'safe', maybe, but alive—her entire life? Knives be damned, she would show him what she could do with a sword! Rihya had reached for the practice blade, felt its comforting weight as she'd hefted it.

"I guess it's lucky you aren't meeting me in a tavern, then."

He'd smiled at her for the first time then, dark eyes lighting up with intensity, interest, and an eagerness that had to be about more than just sparring. An eagerness that had to be curiosity.

Aldashir had grabbed two knives off the rack and handed them to her. Rihya had looked at him quizzically. "I thought those were brawlers tactics," she'd said in a mocking tone of voice.

"I did not say I was not adept with them," the prince had answered.

Rihya had taken the bait. She'd put the sword back on the rack and grasped the two knives, feeling the rightness of them in her hands. The prince had picked up his, as well, and they proceeded to have their first bout, a bout that Rihya had promptly won. She really was the best with knives of anyone she'd ever met with the exception of her brother, she had to concede. Rihya had seen the surprise and respect bloom in Aldashir's face as she beat him.

They sparred once more that day, a closer match, but still she won. In the days that followed, they began sparring every day, often with swords instead of knives, but really with any weapon at all. She won most of the bouts fought with knives, but Aldashir often won just about everything else. She hated the smug look on his face whenever he beat her, conveniently ignoring the fact that she must possess the same look when their roles were reversed. Her disgust for the enemy had given way to a grudging respect. Aldashir was proud, he was a noble to his core, but he was also a good leader. She could see that by the way his warriors looked at him. He was strong and physically imposing, and most of all he and his people were not modified. That alone was the one thing that allowed Rihya to relax just the tiniest bit in their presence during her captivity. She had not seen one of the Unsired nor even a modified Departed amongst their ranks. And, if she was being honest, she had been treated well, more like an honored guest than a prisoner. But she was still a captive: the guards on her doors and the ones that followed her everywhere made that abundantly clear.

Rihya flashed back to the present. She finished stretching her muscles and sat in the sand of the practice yard. It was warmed from the autumn sun and felt good against her body. She looked up at Aldashir, eldest prince of the Southern Kingdom, older brother to the feared and terrible Half-Mask, Prince of Darkness, and she simply could not figure him out.

"When we first sparred, you said you had heard of the females in the north and their—*our*—battle prowess. Have you never been to the north yourself?" Rihya asked tentatively, unsure if he would admit to raiding her homeland, unsure what she wanted to hear.

"No," the prince responded almost harshly.

"Why not?"

"I have duties that keep me occupied here." A snag in his voice hinted at a dislike for something. Was it the dislike of her people, of Andalaya, or was it a dislike of slaving and raiding and war? She wished she were brave enough to ask, but for some reason the words stuck in her throat as she tried to speak them.

They sat in the autumn sun for some time, speaking of tactics and fighting. Aldashir picked her brain on northern strategy, and she talked around the subjects as much as her honor would allow her. Rihya would never answer a question that might betray any kind of secret belonging to her kinspeople still fighting far to the north.

Suddenly, a desperate ache filled her chest and her throat constricted.

She'd never been away from family for this long, never been this far from home, never been this alone. *I will not shed tears, not in front of him, not in front of my captor.*

She was surprised when he said, "You miss it, don't you? The north."

Rihya nodded. "It is green. I haven't seen anything green in what feels like forever." She motioned around herself to the dusty, sandy practice yard, to the golden-yellow rock of the fortress and the sun beating down on their heads—too hot by far for this time of year—to the dry beaches and land beyond the fortress at The Point.

"I would...like to see that someday." Aldashir's tone told her he never expected that to actually happen.

"Why do you stay here?" Finally, she asked a forthright question.

"Why do you care?" he shot back quickly, defensively.

She softened her tone somewhat and asked again, "Why?"

"It is the only place left for me to find honor," the dark prince murmured.

"What do you mean?" She picked up a handful of sand and let it trickle out of her fist as she held it above her other hand.

Aldashir sighed. "There is no honor to be had by turning my back on my own people, and there is no honor to be found in hunting yours. But this is the one place I may defend my people against the only foe not of my race: the humans. The hill forts protect us by land, and my soldiers— my company of The Thousand—and I protect Dark Harbor by sea."

And there it was, the question she'd been dancing around for weeks, what she'd wondered regarding his opinions of her people and the war. It was not a full discussion, not a clear explanation, but it was a more open conversation than they'd ever had before. Previously, they'd restricted their discussions to safer topics—him not wanting to divulge too much of himself to a captive, and her the same in addition to not wishing to divulge any secrets of her kind and their resistance to the enemy.

For some reason, she almost reached out and took his hand. *How strange would that have been?* But although there was pain on the prince's face, it flashed across his visage quickly and then it was gone, replaced again by the haughty gaze he adopted most of the time.

"I notice none of your warriors are...different," she said cautiously, assessing the lack of Unsired in the fortress.

Aldashir's eyes narrowed. "I think we are approaching one of those topics we have both tried hard to avoid these past weeks."

She stared back at him. "Are we? Well, maybe we shouldn't." Something about him made her want to trust him. She shouldn't. She knew it. But, just maybe, if she could just figure out where he really stood. He clearly bore no love for his family, regularly muttering things about Half-Mask and the King of the South that Rihya wouldn't have expected anyone in the south to be brave enough to say aloud, let alone *want* to say. But it rarely went farther than that.

The dark prince leaned back, his hands behind him propping him up. He shook his head, his mane of hair waving slightly with the motion. "It's not a good idea. You're a prisoner, and I shouldn't speak of such things."

"Why shouldn't you speak of the...Unsired?" There. She had finally said it.

He cocked his head, unsure of what she meant. Then realization dawned on him, followed by pain and a grief more real than any she'd seen cross his face before. "Ah, you mean the Blackness."

"'The Blackness'?" Rihya probed.

"When my people become different, when they lose themselves to the new plague—the transformation we cannot fight. We call it the Blackness here. None of my men have it; I'll not stand for it within my walls." Iron entered into his voice, enough to make her shiver. Rihya suddenly realized that she very much hoped she would never truly be on his bad side. She might be a prisoner now, but she rarely felt it in any real way. If that changed, something told her he'd not be a foe she would want to have.

He stared at her for a moment longer. "You have encountered the Blackness? Of course you have, you have been fighting your entire life." Aldashir spoke the last bit almost with wonder. It still surprised him that females almost always fought alongside their male counterparts in Andalaya.

She nodded her agreement. "I have seen them, those possessed by the Blackness, although we don't call it that. We call it what it truly is. It is a disease upon the land. It is the First Days returned to haunt us once more."

The dark prince scoffed slightly. "Stories, nothing more."

"You cannot really believe such a thing? Have you not seen what your brother and father can do?"

Aldashir swallowed and looked away.

Rihya continued, "The Blackness is just another word for the Unsired —a disease on the land, on all Creation." Impulsively, she put her hand on his wrist. "You don't have to sit here and fight the humans all alone, you know."

He looked at her hand on his arm and she took it away, uncomfortable. "I am not alone. I have my warriors. They're family."

Rihya made a frustrated sound in her throat. "That is not what I mean. There are those who fight the Unsired—the Blackness—with every breath, with every ounce of strength in their bodies. You could fight it, too." Suddenly, she wasn't sure why she wanted him to fight the Unsired in the first place. She just knew that she did, and she wanted it badly.

"I cannot, Valerihya Wintermoon. I am honor-bound to defend my people."

"Damn your honor! Protecting your people means more than just defending them from the enemy without. Sometimes it also means defending them from the enemy within."

Aldashir, Prince of the South, elder brother of The Prince of Darkness, cleared his throat awkwardly. "We should freshen up before the midday meal."

He stood and walked away, silent and without responding to her statement. Yet there had been a look in his eyes as he'd stood, a tenseness in his muscles, in his gait, as he walked that made Rihya think Aldashir was considering her words more than he let on.

CHAPTER TWO

They had been heading southeast for weeks now. Iyonei had lead ambush after ambush, raid after raid as they escalated the violence against their human enemies to the east, and all the while they made their way south. Their direction was Miri's doing. Over a month had passed since the day she had accessed the Graft into Ell's mind and experienced a battle through his eyes, felt his emotions as he'd fought and killed. But everything had felt wrong—more than wrong. Ell was good. Miri knew that to the core of her being, but there was a darkness clouding his thoughts and directing his movements, a darkness that he was only barely—just barely—keeping in check. She needed to find him and find him fast. It hadn't taken her long to impress the same need upon Arendahl. The old elf seemed nearly as keen to reach his pupil as Miri, although for slightly different reasons.

And so it was that they were heading south. Miri accessed the Graft into Ell's mind multiple times a day now. She was growing more and more adept at the skill. It rarely eluded her now. She knew that he was on a ship sailing west and, after seeing the nighttime sky through his eyes, she had relayed the star patterns she'd seen for Arendahl. Versed in all manner of knowledge as he was, he had been able to discern their relative course. Miri hoped that by the time they reached the coast Ell would be waiting for them. She couldn't bear to be separated any longer, especially when he was so clearly in need of...well, in need of *something*, that was certain. Miri didn't know why, but she was fairly sure that whatever it was he needed only she could give.

"Stay to the back. It isn't a big company, but I'd rather not take any chances." Iyonei, the one-eyed warrior elf, tussled Miri's hair with her strong, callused hand.

Miri almost argued. She'd been participating in some of the raids they'd been doing over the past few weeks now, but she closed her mouth as soon as she opened it. It was true: she may have been participating, but that was only out of necessity. Arendahl needed her to guide his course. Besides, Miri wasn't waiting a moment longer to steer her path toward Ell—and that meant she must accompany them. But they were moving south, along the eastern front, near enemy territory. Skirmishes were bound to happen, and happen they had. Miri had fought as best she could, firing arrows from the back of the band, making sure to stay out of the thickest fighting. Briesom—or Brie, as most people called her—was Miri's ever-present guardian.

She knew Brie must long to join the melee with her small hand axes twirling dangerously, to fight her foes like she'd been doing most of her young life, but the pixie blonde elf stayed right by Miri's side. She fought her urges and kept Miri safe. They were friends, and friends looked out for one another. The closest of friends—especially close since that one day months ago when Miri had experienced the vast numbness seeping through Ell's mind through the Graft. Only one thing could have caused that, and Miri was fairly certain that it meant his sister had died. It was the only thing she could imagine sending Ell into such an emotional downward spin. He'd eventually shaken it off, snapped out of it, but it still left her feeling a tiny bit dead inside. She and Rihya had been fast friends, opposite like Miri and Brie, yet friends all the same. It hurt that she would never see her again, but Brie's close friendship had helped to assuage the pain.

"Stick by me, Miri. It'll be over before we know it." Brie flashed her an excited grin.

Arendahl grunted his approval and shot her a cautionary glare, as if he expected her—crippled and all—to ignore their warnings and thrust herself into the midst of the fray. Miri unlimbered her bow and nocked an arrow.

"The humans are not far ahead of us," Iyonei motioned with one muscled arm to the grassy hill rising ahead of them to the southeast. "We'll wait here, where we still have tree cover, and ambush them as they come our way. Nice and simple. Any questions?"

There were murmurs of assent, but no questions. Iyonei's band of almost all female warriors—except for the short and incredibly stout half-northern Yendil—had been fighting most of their lives. The extra elves who now accompanied them under Arendahl's direction also numbered themselves with many warriors. Some might not have fought for some years, but they were quickly recalling the use of weapons and the skill with which they had defended Andalaya in their youth.

Miri leaned next to Brie against a spreading oak tree. Her breath came in short, quick gasps; she always got nervous before a fight. She wasn't a particularly good fighter, and the old injury to her leg, the one leaving her lame since childhood, did little to help. Brie nudged her and flashed another smile. "Like I said, stick close to me and it'll all be fine." The tiny elf, her hair in braids, twirled her hand axes almost lazily.

The rest of the Highest—the fair-skinned northern elves—hid themselves behind trees and assumed ready stances. One-eyed Iyonei, fierce and tall, was flanked by Satiri who was nearly as tall, just as strong, but with both her eyes healthy and whole. They stood side by side at the front, determined to lead the ambush. Iyonei, her hair divided into one long braid that draped down around her shoulder and another short braid on the opposite side of her head, would allow none other than herself to lead them into the fray. She was quite possibly the boldest elf Miri had ever known. Well, with the exception of Ell, perhaps. But she had none of Ell's Water Calling powers which, in many ways, made her courage all the more remarkable.

The scout shimmied back down from the crest of the hill and sprinted quietly back to the tree cover. "It won't be long now, just a few more minutes," she reported.

Iyonei turned to look at Arendahl, her gaze asking silently if he had any last words of instruction. She'd probably never admit that, not liking to be under anyone's direction, but Arendahl just stared back silently, as well. He knew there was no need to guide her in battle tactics. She had fought on the walls of Verdantihya two decades ago and had been fighting ever since. The elf knew what she was about.

And then the humans came. A group of them, smaller than the last company Miri and her friends had faced, trotted toward them. They were raiders themselves, heading northwest toward the Lower Forest in hopes of capturing slaves. The Departed—the dark-skinned southern elves—had ceased their slavers raids over the past weeks; some kind of breakdown in the alliance between the humans and the Departed had occurred. It bode well for Andalaya and her people, but it meant that the humans had increased their raids now that they couldn't count on the southern elves to plunder their northern cousins and send a steady stream of free labor their way.

The humans moved in light chain mail with swords in sheathes at their hips and axes or spears resting upon their shoulders. The armor might protect them, but it also slowed them down. They were in for a surprise. As the humans entered the tree line, Iyonei burst from the side of the trail screaming ululating war cries and burying her sword in the heart of the soldier nearest her. The rest of the company began loosing shaft after shaft, feathering the humans with arrows while many also rushed forward to engage them in hand-to-hand. Miri loosed her own shafts with the rest of her company. One of her first three arrows struck home, the sharpened head burying itself in the throat of an oncoming soldier. Miri felt a fleeting moment of disgust at herself for killing, but the thought skittered away as she loosed another and another shaft. This was war. This was a three-way war now, since the alliance between the humans and Departed had splintered, and Miri and her people were doing everything in their power just to survive. It had to be this way, at least for now.

Brie was jumpy to her right, clenching her hand axes tightly, wishing to rush forward and join the fray, but she stayed where she was right next to Miri as she continued to fire arrows.

"Just go," Miri grunted between shots. "I'll be fine."

Brie's eyes flickered back and forth between Miri and the skirmish that was boiling in front of them. "Are you sure?"

"I said go!"

Brie grinned and sprinted forward into the melee as Miri continued her volley. Arendahl, a Water Caller in full force, spun about with his sword, dealing death with every swing. Iyonei, Satiri, and Brie fought with impeccable skill and timing, their slashes eviscerating foes and hamstringing their enemies. Yendil, shave-headed like his distant kin to the south—born from the ravages of southern raiding in the north— fought like a boulder, plowing through the hips and knees of his foes with hammer and axe, broad-chested and bold like any warrior of Andalaya should be.

Miri loosed her shafts, picking targets until there were too many of her own people amidst the crowd to fire safely any longer. She didn't have the accuracy of one who'd been fighting her whole life and wouldn't risk feathering her own people in a failed attempt to kill one of the humans. She grounded the end of her bow and leaned over on it wearily, using it as a resting stick. The fight would not last long now. Already the elves were swarming the humans. This was as big a raiding party as had ever been seen this far south in the past two decades. Arendahl had been garnering support for Ell and for all of Andalaya's cause these past months, and many of those supporters had followed them south. They were too many for the opposing force.

Miri slung the bow back over her shoulder, done firing as she was, when an enraged human burst from the pack straight toward her. He was berserk with anger and more than anything with fear, a wild animal that knew when death had come. He sprinted toward Miri, his chain mail not slowing him down as much as she would have expected. She fumbled for her bow but it was already looped over her shoulder; she wouldn't have time to remove it. Instead, she reached for her belt knife just as the man tackled her.

Her weak leg gave out immediately as his body collided with hers, and she crumpled to the ground beneath him. He must have lost his sword in the skirmish and, crazed as he was, he simply grasped her throat with his ham-fisted hands and squeezed. She felt her air constricting and smelled the stale odor of dried sweat and dirty beard caked in old grease from food as he pressed his face close to hers, eyes lost in the mania of battle. Miri freed her belt knife and plunged it into his side, just above the hip, where there was a gap in the chain mail. She stuck and twisted, and though the human grunted and screamed in pain he only tightened his grasp on her throat, determined to take one last elf with him to the grave. Her vision faded and blackness edged around the corners of her eyes.

She stabbed him one last time but to no avail. It was almost over now. But then a hand axe buried itself in the man's head and Brie wrenched the human off of Miri as she pulled her axe free, bits of blood and gore spraying as she did so.

Miri gasped for air and scrambled away from him as he died, shuffling until she leaned back against the trunk of a nearby tree.

"It's different when they die close up, isn't it?" Brie said matter-of-factly. "Not like filling them full of arrows."

Miri swallowed and nodded. She'd fought before, but nothing like what had just happened.

"I shouldn't have left you." Brie's voice was clouded with guilt. "It wasn't really needed. The fight was over, and I just wanted to join in. I should not have left."

"I'm fine," Miri rasped. And she was. She really was fine. She shouldn't be, but everything since she'd met Ell in Little Vale seemed to have been leading her down this path.

"Well, at least you got your first hand-to-hand kill," Brie muttered with false brightness, eager to bury the guilt she clearly still felt.

"What?"

"That kill was yours. I might have finished him off, but he was already a dead man after the work you did on his side," the pixie blonde elf explained.

"Oh, right," was all Miri could muster.

Brie was worried now. "Look, are you sure you're all right? Should I get Arendahl? Are you hurt?"

Miri shook her head. Her first real kill. It felt surreal, ugly, and meaningless, especially considering she'd be dead herself if her friend hadn't showed up to keep the dying human from strangling her. "No, I'm fine. I promise."

Brie relaxed some after hearing Miri's reassurances. "Good. I'd hate to have to explain to the big, bad elf why I left you alone during the skirmish and let something happen to you." Brie giggled. She had kept up a running string of irreverence directed Arendahl's way ever since they'd met.

Miri smiled. "No need to tell. Like I said, I'm fine." She extended her hand to Briesom, asking for help up. The little elf grasped her hand with a strength that belied her size and yanked Miri to her feet. Her bad leg wobbled slightly and she almost lost her balance again, but Brie steadied her.

"Easy there."

Miri smiled her thanks and tried her best to avoid looking at the human she'd killed as they walked back toward the rest of the group. They drew close enough to hear the conversation between Arendahl and Iyonei.

"See, aren't you glad you abandoned the war in the north to fight with us in the east?" Iyonei ribbed the old elf.

Arendahl stared at her with grim eyes. "The alliance between the humans and the Departed might be crumbling, but who knows if it will coalesce again? If that happens, then the dark creatures in the north will be controlled by the Unsired in the south and aligned with the humans to the east. It is all one war now, or close enough that it makes no difference where we fight. The return of the Unsired saw to that. It changed everything; it remade this new war into the ancient war of old, the one from the First Days."

Iyonei rolled her good eye. "Learn to laugh at a jest, old one. I know this the same as you. I was only seeking to lighten the mood."

Surprisingly, Arendahl did smile. He even barked a short laugh. "I haven't forgotten how to laugh, girl. Nor will I. It's what we are fighting for."

And then, even more surprisingly, the old elf cupped her cheek, thumb brushing the patch that covered her long lost eye. "You fought well, Iyonei. As always."

The warrior elf flushed, then smiled, and then of course scowled. "I don't need the flattery of an old teacher, Arendahl. I know my business, I know what I am about."

Arendahl smiled again, this time wolfishly. "I know you do. It's why they're all dead." He swept his hand toward the humans littering the ground.

Miri wished she could pity the dead. She wanted to return to the old her, the one who could look at the carnage with nothing more than disgust. But she had been a captive herself; she had seen what slavers did to her land. And these humans had been traveling north, heading for Andalaya to do more of what the Departed had been doing for decades. She couldn't help but feel a savage sense of satisfaction that they were dead, even if that satisfaction conflicted with her softer side at times.

"All well, girl?" Arendahl asked Miri as he saw her and Brie's approach.

She nodded to him. "Of course."

"What of our young friend? Any changes?"

She knew Arendahl was referring to Elliyar. "No, his course seems the same as it has been." Miri had tapped into the Graft just before the skirmish. It calmed her to be inside of Ell's mind, especially before a battle. Even if there was something off about him, it was still better than nothing.

Arendahl nodded. "Good. We'll hold course, then, and kill any who cross our path," he said in his stilted voice as he nodded to her, Brie, and Iyonei. The two warrior elves flashed him fierce grins. He continued, "If we hold our course much longer, we'll reach the ruins of Akan Deraiya."

"What's that?" Miri asked.

"It was once called the Shining City for its white marble and the pearlescent shells that lined the fortress walls, glimmering in the morning sun."

The Shining City. If Ell was truly headed there, then Miri couldn't help but think that the name made it seem like there couldn't be a more fitting place to reunite.

CHAPTER THREE

Rihya strode idly through the solitary patch of garden at The Point. Most of the thick-walled, yellowish stone fortress was devoted to defense. At the very tip of a narrow peninsula jutting out into the southern sea, The Point was surrounded on three sides by water and, as such, needed to be defensible on those sides. But the dark prince, Aldashir, had reserved a tiny corner of the grounds for a garden. Rihya had never really been in a garden before. Things simply grew in the north, and Verdantihya—the ancient, ruined capital of Andalaya—was a mixture of architecture and creation woven together. It was difficult to discern where the green life ended, and the ruined stones of the city began. Things were not so in the south. Buildings were constructed for practicality. The Point was built to withstand siege. In truth, Rihya understood that. Her life had been one series of practical decisions after another—when at war, any other type of decision would get her killed. Yet Rihya missed the green. Her hair wasn't enough to tide her over until she someday returned north. She promised herself that she would return to Andalaya, some way, somehow.

But as Rihya walked through the perfectly even, straight rows of plants, she found herself drawn not to the greenest of growing life but to something a little bit different. She meandered toward the far end of the garden, passing all manner of flowers in bloom. Green stalks gave way to everything from yellow to red to blue petals. She passed vibrant, fresh herbs grown specially for the prince's private cook to use in preparation for his meals. Eventually, she came to rest in front of a particularly odd and riveting cluster of roses.

These were not red roses, nor were they even the white or yellow buds she had sometimes seen growing amidst the wild, thorny patches in Andalaya. No, these roses had dark green stalks leading up to plush, black petals. Black roses. She should have known that the south, the Departed, would have a species of black rose. She began to turn away in disdain, but they pulled her back. She felt her gaze caress them again, swallowing up their glossy sheen in the morning sun. They were so dark as to swallow the light, yet they reflected it, as well. She could not pull her eyes from them; as much as she wanted to, she could not. They were riveting.

"Impressive, are they not?" Aldashir's voice startled Rihya enough that she jumped and immediately felt for the belt knife that was no longer at her hip. Reality crashed back in on her. She was a prisoner. A comfy, cozy captive, but a captive all the same.

The southern prince looked proudly at the black roses, petals shimmering in the hot sun. In fact, he seemed inordinately pleased with them, more invested in their upkeep than a warrior normally would be. The prince reached out and almost fondled the stem of one, his swarthy fingers reaching up as if he wished to caress a sable petal before realizing he should not and placing his hands behind his back to make sure he did no harm.

Rihya made a noncommittal grunt meant to fall somewhere between agreement and dissent. Aldashir flashed her a knowing smile and shook his head at the half-remark.

"They are strong, for flowers. They are rare, but they can still grow in many circumstances if given the proper care. Once planted, they do not often wither." Aldashir smiled faintly again.

Rihya peered at him with a sidelong glance. "You really love these roses, don't you?"

"'Love'?" He cocked his head, sun glistening off the sweat on his brow in the unseasonable heat—well, unseasonable for her. "I do not know if that is exactly what I feel when I look at them. But I do find them...comforting."

"How so?" she prodded.

The prince cast his own sidelong glance her way as if wondering whether to divulge his meaning. He seemed to reach a decision as the set of his face firmed. "They are attractive flowers. They remind me that we can be more than what we seem, more than what is expected of us."

"They are not really to my taste," Rihya murmured as politely as possible, not wishing to dissolve the good will she was shown here, even as a prisoner.

"No?"

She shook her head in response. "They are a bit...*dark* for my taste."

Understanding crossed his face. "Ah, but not all things dark are ugly. Sometimes dark can be beautiful—stunning, really. These roses remind me of that fact."

His comment gave Rihya pause, and she was forced to admit, at least to herself, that perhaps he might be right. Maybe the roses were beautiful, only in a different way to the one she was accustomed to. Suddenly, she flashed back to another conversation from months ago between Ell and Dacunda when they were about to steal Captain Piripeos'—the smuggler Rimmer elf from the Outer Rim Islands—ship to sail out of Dark Harbor. Ell had argued not to kill the guards whenever possible, saying that not all those in Dark Harbor and the south were their enemies.

"My Prince!" A warrior dashed up and stood to attention as soon as he was close enough to Aldashir.

The prince was all business now, metaphors and musings behind him. "Report."

"A pigeon arrived from our scouts to the east. The humans are sending ships into the southern seas."

"How many? A fleet?" the prince barked, one hand already clasping the hilt of his great war sword.

The warrior shook his head. "Not even close to that many. Only a few ships, but still, it is more than they have sent in years, Highness."

Aldashir nodded his agreement as he paced and pondered the news. Rihya watched questions and decisions flicker across his face faster than even Dacunda when he'd led them for so many years. The prince was decisive, and she knew that decisive people were often good leaders.

The prince began muttering to himself, enough that Rihya could hear what he said. "Relations have been strained ever since word of that revolt in their land spread and reached us. My brother is ambitious, and he'll look to gain from the humans' weakness. Tensions and scuffles are reported in the lower forest between Departed and humans. The alliance is all but broken already." He paused as if first realizing he'd spoken aloud, and in front of an enemy captive, no less. Aldashir cleared his throat awkwardly and continued pacing a moment longer before speaking again. "We'll meet them," he said without too much delay.

"Should we send word to the capital?" the warrior asked uneasily.

"No, I have been placed here by my father and younger brother for a reason," he said almost bitterly. "They trust me enough to do my job—protecting the southern seas. This decision is mine."

A calm and sure smile crossed the warrior's face. Not for the first time, Rihya was surprised by the lack of regard given Half-Mask and the King of the South here at The Point. Yet it was clear they were still the authority, or at least *an* authority, even if the common soldiers under Aldashir's command clearly preferred their local prince's decisions to those stemming from the capital.

The prince turned to stride away back through the garden, giving instructions to the warrior at his side. "Prepare ten ships. That should be enough. My personal warship will lead them, and of course I will command it. Have my servant ready my things, oil my weapons not already in my possession. We leave at the evening tide—early enough to head them off before they delve too far into southern waters. These waters are *ours*," he growled the last bit with a clenched jaw. "Perhaps we can even head them off and force them back to avoid outright conflict."

The warrior ducked his head and turned to sprint away. Rihya had to take long, quick steps to try and catch up with Aldashir. The guards who had been discreetly following her all morning quickened their pace, as well.

"And what of me? Shall I stay here?" she asked when she reached his side.

"What?" He seemed lost in thought, shook his head slightly as if to clear it, and peered at her closely again. "Oh, I suppose. What else can I do with you?" he asked distractedly.

"You know, I have been known to fight humans from time to time myself," she told him in her most persuasive, wheedling tone that she always used when wanting to get her way; the tone that always made Elliyar roll his eyes in annoyance.

The dark prince narrowed his eyes and a smirk lined his haughty features as if he saw right through her. A flush crept into her cheeks, but she kept her gaze steady and strong.

He tilted his head as he stared at Rihya and then said slowly, "On second thought, we are sending out a half-fleet of ten ships, and many of the rest of my warriors will be busy patrolling the southern seas and even the waters back toward the Enclaves and Dark Harbor. Not to mention defending this fortress, obviously. I cannot very well spare any soldiers to care for a captive. Neither can I, in good conscience, send you along to Dark Harbor. That would be most unpleasant."

For a moment she saw that he really did not want her to experience the horrors of servitude in the southern capital. She softened slightly toward him. "Well?" she prompted, hardly able to contain the giddiness she felt at the prospect of finally doing something rather than strolling in gardens and participating in mock duels all day long.

He shook his head in annoyance at her prodding, but a deeper smile crossed his lips all the same. "I am honor bound not to set free an enemy captive, and I have established that it would be a waste of resources to keep you here. I guess the only recourse is to take you with me."

Rihya finally let a grin flash across her face. "I've killed more humans than you, probably."

He thought for a few silent seconds before answering, "I do not doubt that, Valerihya Wintermoon. But would you really raise arms on behalf of your enemy? Would you really fight with the Departed?"

She peered at him just as intently as he stared at her before tossing her green hair and answering finally, "Do you really believe that we are enemies?"

It was the first time she had voiced the sentiment out loud, the first time its surprising implication had crossed her lips. It did surprise her, but the surprise was mostly in how right it felt to say it. She could see the gleam in the prince's dark eyes as she said the words, saw the uncomfortable way he realized how much he wanted it to be true.

He stared at her a moment longer. "Come, Wintermoon, we have preparations to make."

———

TEN SHIPS WASN'T an entire fleet, at least not according to Aldashir, but it felt like one to Rihya. She stood at the prow of the foremost warship as it sliced through the waves, setting a course due east. Spray came up in flurries, carried by gusts of wind that foreshadowed winter squalls. It was still unseasonably warm, but Rihya felt it less when on the open ocean.

"The Thousand is the number of warriors I command. It fluctuates, of course, but stays near enough that it proves a suitable name." Aldashir was obligingly addressing some of her idle curiosity about his life and duties at The Point. They'd spoken daily since he and his soldiers had pulled her from the surf after she'd sunk another of the fleet's warships, enabling Ell and the rest of her family to press on. Had they rescued her mother and sister? She didn't know, but lately their conversations had become something different. Somehow...more. They both danced around subjects less often, one laughed when the other joked and, in truth, Departed or not, Aldashir was quite funny. Nothing compared to her enormous and ravenous cousin Ryder, of course, but still, funny was funny. She found that she actually enjoyed Aldashir's company. It was strangely exciting, but also very frustrating. She should be planning escape now that she was away from the walls of the fortress, but all she could manage to do was ask yet another in a long string of questions.

"And none of your soldiers have the...the Blackness?"

He pursed his lips at her. "I told you already, no. I'll not have it."

She nodded silently, remembering him saying that he would not tolerate it. Still, it was an important question, important enough to merit more than one brief query.

"And why not?" she pressed.

Aldashir sighed. "You wouldn't believe me if I told you."

She cocked her head and waited. The silence between them dragged on, punctuated by the curses of sailors and the creaking of ropes, sails, and the mast.

"Fine. I will not allow the Blackness among The Thousand because— whether you believe it or not—my company is *good*." He said the last word almost fiercely, daring her to disagree. Once, she would have. When he'd first hoisted her sodden body up from the wet sand that day, she had seen him as only an enemy. And, for the first couple of weeks, she had held the same countenance. But that had begun to change. Speaking with Aldashir, she had seen an elf in as much pain as any of the Highest. He felt he'd lost a homeland just as they, only for him it wasn't a coalition of enemies that had stolen his home, it was the enemy within— his own family. And there was nothing he could do about it. Oh, he never quite came outright with it, but Rihya was clever; she could read between the lines of everything he said.

"I can see how you would think that," she responded softly, almost gently. Aldashir's face at her response was possibly the most vulnerable she'd ever seen on him. Relief plastered his features. High cheekbones, tanned and dark, his long mane whipping in the wind, he looked nothing so much as like a little boy begging for someone to believe that the terrible thing that had happened had not actually been his fault.

"You cannot possibly believe me," he muttered. "Not after everything my people have done...not after what we've become."

"Not all of you," she murmured. "It's not too late." Her words were barely loud enough to be heard over the sound of the waves crashing against the prow.

They stood in silence side by side as they watched the sea ahead. Rihya broke the peace first. "So, are you ever going to give me back my blades? I mean, I'll need them if I'm going to fight the humans with you."

"Whoever said you were fighting?" the dark prince asked with mock incredulity. And yet, Rihya was nervous that he really wouldn't let her. Her fingers itched to hold a knife again. He seemed to notice her twitchiness and risked a smile. If only she had her knives, she'd mark him for that impertinence. Instead, Rihya settled for tossing her hair even more haughtily than Aldashir could normally manage—and he was a noble!

The prince glanced at her from the corner of his eyes, and a small grin played across his face. "Well, I could, perhaps, be persuaded, just maybe, to allow you one small blade. Not to fight, mind you—just to clean up the mess after my warriors and I do the real work. You know, I could allow you to make sure the dead are really dead."

Rihya gasped in annoyance. "I'd never be left behind to do the dirty work!" she exclaimed. He chuckled as if anticipating her remarks, and she whacked him in the arm in response. Somehow, this all felt very... right. Even though it shouldn't. Even though she was weaponless in the midst of an enemy armada, she felt...*what? Safe? Yes.* Safer than she'd ever felt, maybe. If that wasn't irony, she didn't know what was.

The next few days passed quickly. They sailed east with no sightings of ships, but that wasn't surprising. A homing pigeon traveled faster than a ship on the waves. Her days were filled with more mock duels—the only times she was allowed a weapon—wave upon wave upon wave, and seemingly endless banter with Aldashir.

When finally ships were sighted on the distant horizon, their blocky make and wide sails marking them as human in origin, Rihya felt an excited shiver travel down her spine. A fight was brewing; she could feel it. Aldashir may not have promised to allow her to fight, but she was fairly certain she could win him over. And who better to test her blades against than her age-old foe, the humans? The anticipation practically made her quiver. She was a warrior born for the fight, and if Aldashir didn't yet know that fact, then he soon would.

But something else was different, too. There was a new excitement bourgeoning within her. She looked at the prince standing next to her on the deck, his tall and proud form silhouetted against the setting sun. A different tingle ran down her spine and through her limbs, out to her very fingertips. She'd fought back-to-back before against all manner of foes—humans, Departed, and dark creature alike—so that couldn't be it. Fighting side by side with Aldashir as she was almost certain he was willing to allow wouldn't be all that new, would it? She struggled to put her finger on the feeling. Yes, she'd fought side by side with her family before, all her life actually, but never side by side with someone she...*what? Wanted to kiss?* The thought was almost too wild to imagine. Her with a Departed. It just couldn't be. But almost as if reading her mind, Aldashir turned toward her, still darkly silhouetted against the falling sun, dark enough that all she saw were his glittering eyes as he stared hard into her own, a hungry expression on his face.

She swallowed. Ell might be younger, but in this he was the more experienced, Joined to Miri as he was. Rihya had hardly spent any time alone away from her family with other elves her age. Aldashir closed the distance until only a few breaths separated them. He reached up to touch her arm, or maybe his hand was halfway to her cheek before he nervously let it fall back to his side. A withering sensation hit her then, and she realized how badly she wanted his touch, how much she wanted to feel his hand on her skin. He seemed to sense it and nervously reached for her again, almost jerkily, as if afraid he'd not do it at all if he didn't do it fast. All at once, his hand was on the back of her neck and they were together, his lips on hers, her hands groping against the ropey muscles of his back. The world swam and somehow she grew dizzy even as she closed her eyes and lost herself in the kiss. And then it ended as suddenly as it had begun, and Rihya was left more breathless than ever before in her life.

The prince pulled away and stammered half an apology. "I shouldn't have..."

"Why not?" she asked, still breathless.

"Because..." Again he trailed off, his tall, strong body still looming close to her.

This time, it was she who pulled him close, and they lost themselves in each other once more until finally they broke apart, lungs straining for air.

They gazed at each other for a moment before Aldashir gave her a quizzical look, feeling at his hip. "You didn't."

"Didn't what?" she quipped, assuming her most innocent expression.

"Give it back," he chided.

She assumed a blank, straight face. "No." She produced with a practiced flourish the knife that she'd managed to palm from his belt.

"Valerihya," he warned, but there was a half-smile on his face.

"What? I'll need it if I'm going to fight. If I'm going to fight...with you."

He stared at her for a long time then, as if weighing every single one of her words carefully. It made her more nervous than the moments leading up to the kiss, as though he saw more in her words than even she knew. "Very well," he said with a small nod. "Keep it."

And keep it she did. They set their shoulders and stared at the enemy sails ahead. The humans aboard their ships must have recognized a superior fleet in both size and quality coming their way—the Departed were the terror of the seas, and the humans stood no chance and knew it—because they had turned sails and were attempting to run back the way they had come. They wouldn't be able to. They weren't fast enough. And so Rihya kept the knife. She would need it in the battle to come.

CHAPTER FOUR

"Have you ever been this far south?" Brie asked as they made their way east and out along the peninsula that led to Akan Deraiya. Her bright eyes were curious as they surveyed the land with a cautious warrior's gaze.

Miri shook her head. "Never."

"Me neither. We usually raid farther north. You're sure your Elliyar is heading to this place, this Akan Deraiya?"

Miri was sure of nothing. All she did was relay information to Arendahl, information that was gleaned from the Graft she had forged into Ell's consciousness. The old elf deciphered what it meant. "That's what Arendahl thinks. I trust him."

Brie grunted as if she weren't sure. The company of elves was about a hundred strong—Iyonei's small band, plus Miri, Arendahl, Artorious—or Art, as everyone called him, the young boy Ell had rescued from the Pillar at the same time as he'd rescued her—and then a host of other northern elves able and ready to take up arms at Arendahl's request. There were many more of her people amassing in the north. They moved at an average pace, slowed by their larger numbers. It was a relief that Miri was not the sole reason for their less than rapid travel speed.

"They say it glows—its walls, that is." Brie chatted with a toss of her blonde hair. She nevertheless kept one hand ready to draw a weapon at all times. It was a habit forced from years of combat readiness.

"We'll soon find out, I suppose," Miri answered. The sun was low in the sky and soon to sink. If the rumors were true, they'd reach the ruins around sunset and would see whether the fading light really did illuminate the walls.

Miri and Brie passed the next few hours in easy conversation. Their time together had been wonderful. Miri missed Ell fiercely and could scarcely contain her excitement at the prospect of reuniting with him once again, yet she had to admit she would not likely have grown as close to Brie if she had been with Ell these past months, and she valued Briesom's friendship greatly. Miri supposed most negatives came with a positive twist to balance them out.

Arendahl checked in briefly every hour or so to see what she was accessing from the Graft. Nothing was changing, but he seemed more eager and agitated the closer they were to seeing Ell. She rarely saw him this frayed. Perhaps her warnings about the changes she'd sensed in Ell had worried him more than he had let on.

Soon they crested a rise on the peninsula and, sure enough, the stories were true. Fading light struck ruined walls and reflected off them in mesmerizing fashion. The walls were pocked and scarred, much of them having been stripped of their shiny substance years ago, but there were still significant enough patches intact to demonstrate what the legends spoke of.

"It's thousands of shells mortared into the rock, shell-side out, to catch the light," Arendahl murmured with as close a tone of wonder as Miri had ever heard from him. "The rest of the gleam comes from the white marble. Both substances reflect the light better than normal stone. Much of it's been stripped over the centuries, sacked by various elf and then human factions. But there's enough left."

"Enough for what?" Iyonei asked as she stood side by side with Arendahl at the head of the company. They had effectively shared command, Arendahl deciding the important details and Iyonei handling most of the rest.

"Enough to show why it was called the Shining City," the old elf sighed wistfully.

Miri cocked her head to the side as she stared at his regretful expression. "Is there something else, some additional sad story about this place that you aren't telling me?"

Arendahl looked at her briefly then turned his grey-eyed stare back toward the broken-topped towers that dotted the sprawling city before them. "Nothing more than the rest of our race's history. Akan Deraiya was a jewel of the ancient age. Not the center of learning like Riora, but it was still *a* center. Culture, society, art, craftsmanship—all things gravitated to Akan Deraiya like the very sun seemed drawn to its walls. I suppose my sadness is just the melancholy of an old loremaster wishing the past had not occurred in the manner that it did."

A broken society fractured down the middle, north and south. That was what the elves were. And that fracture had caused the ruin of their people. Everyone seemed to be considering Arendahl's words.

"Enough talk. We should get on with it and find a defensible spot within the ruins to make camp." Iyonei's brisk voice snapped them out of the thoughtful moment.

Arendahl nodded sharply, back to his usual, abrupt self complete with stilted speech. "Near the port. The boy will arrive by ship."

The company of elves cautiously made their way into the city, heading through the doorless gate and then the empty yet still-cobblestoned streets. It would have been a perfect place for an ambush, with vacant windows and dark doorways aplenty overlooking the streets. The company kept a keen eye, but there were none to bother them other than the ghostly memories of a fading race.

When they reached the quarter of the ruins near the port, Iyonei sent out scouts and posted sentries. The rest of the company set about making camp and cooking food. Small fires were permitted since they hadn't passed anyone since their last skirmish.

"Any change?" Arendahl asked Miri for what felt like the hundredth time that day as he sat next to her on a toppled statue of some ancient noble.

Miri gave a vexed little sigh. "I checked no more than a few minutes ago. He's holding the same course—I think. And he's close. I can somehow feel his nearness. But I don't have much else to say."

Arendahl gave her a pat on the shoulder. "I wasn't trying to pressure you. Just on edge, I guess." He peered around the ruins.

"We all are," she replied.

"Not like me. There's this prickly feeling I usually get right before a Ghoul tries to take a bite out of me. Can't shake it." He continued to glance around.

"Well, you trust Iyonei's sentries, don't you?"

The old elf snorted. "Of course not. No offense to them, but I rarely trust anyone other than myself to do a job right."

She laughed quietly. "Relax, Arendahl. Ell will be here soon, and then we can plan for whatever comes next."

"If only I had the faith of youth to help me relax when my senses are telling me otherwise." He shook his head at her, but his expression was not unkind.

Miri felt a chill at his words but shook it off. No, Ell was almost here. She could hardly bear to wait any longer now that they were nearly reunited. Nothing was going to ruin their reunion. Not if she had anything to say about it.

———

As it turned out, Miri did not have to wait long.

"Ship sighted!" a voice called out from one of the sentry posts on the wall above the courtyard in which they had made camp.

Miri along with the others rushed to open vantage points to catch a sight of the harbor and the Fracture beyond. A lone ship was charting its course straight for their location.

"Calm water, full sail, and the wind at their back. They'll be here within the hour," Arendahl muttered.

Miri's heart fluttered. She would see Ell before the sun would set. Twilight was poking its murky fingers through the ruins as shadows grew and lengthened, but it was still light enough to see. She could not wait to gaze upon her mate's face again.

Brie hugged her, clearly sensing her excitement. "I'll have to spar with Ell sometime soon, see if he's as good a fighter as you claim," she joked.

Miri laughed giddily. "Spar all you want, but only *after* I'm done with him!" She felt a blush rise to her cheeks at the forthrightness of her comment but did her best to ignore it. Brie merely laughed along with her and took her hand.

The next hour felt like the longest in her life even though Miri knew it must have passed at the normal rate. The ship crept closer and closer until it was only minutes away. Miri, Arendahl, Art, Brie, and Iyonei descended the steps leading down to the quay to be ready and waiting for Ell's ship when it arrived. She accessed the Graft one more time, just briefly, and saw the ship's-eye view of Akan Deraiya from the opposite direction rising strong and white from the water's edge. She quickly let the link go. She wouldn't need to access it as much now that they were about to be together again. It would be strange to stop; accessing his mind whenever she felt like it had grown into such a habit.

The ship docked, and a flurry of activity occurred as Departed sailors —Miri and the others would have been startled by this if she had not already relayed this information to Arendahl at an earlier stage—began fastening the ship, anchoring it to the quay at the docking points with rapidly-tied sea knots.

And then the passengers were disembarking. Miri saw Dacunda as he strutted down the boarding plank followed by his Ryder. Both of them had light-brown hair braided down their back. They were tall and powerfully muscled while still maintaining lean forms. There were new faces, as well. A plethora of swarthy sailors continued with their business, some disembarking with the rest. A few other fair-skinned elves, unknown to Miri, descended as well, faces looking haggard as if they'd been worked half to death for years. Yet the light of victory and joy shone in their faces. Finally, last to descend the boarding plank, was Ell.

Elliyar Wintermoon, love of her life, light of her soul. She savored the sight of his wavy blond hair as it hung loosely around his shoulders. His eyes—blue like crystal waters—chiseled features, and lean, toned body. But there were differences she noted as he descended toward her, framed by the falling light. There was a weariness about him, a worried cast to his face and shoulders that was new. There was also a small, blackened scar under his eye, a blemish on his otherwise perfect face. She swallowed, wondering what had happened to him to leave such a mark. She thought she might have an idea, having witnessed some of his duel in Dark Harbor through the Graft.

He caught her gaze and paused a moment, as if surprised to see her waiting there for him. People were clasping forearms and making necessary introductions on the stony quay around them, but Ell had eyes only for her. His pause lasted only a moment, and then he seemed to snap back to reality or out of whatever astonished reverie he'd been in whilst staring at her. He burst forward, sprinting in her direction, closing the distance between them in a handful of heartbeats.

Ell reached Miri and crushed her in a fierce embrace. He held her so tightly it hurt, but she wouldn't have had him loosen his grasp for all the world. She held him just as tightly. They finally broke the embrace but stayed close. His lips found hers, their eyes closed, their tongues touched, and their hands strayed across each other's bodies feverishly as if memorizing every contour of their shapes, as if it was the first and last time they would ever see one another and needed to store up every memory possible for a lifetime apart. Thankfully, that was not the case.

They pulled apart again and just gazed silently into each other's eyes.

How much she'd missed Ell came crashing in all at once. Tears formed in the corners of her eyes as she cupped his face.

"Never again. Don't you ever leave me again," she whispered fiercely and kissed him one last time.

She felt him smile through the kiss. "I promise," he said eventually when they'd finished. Those first words spoken in months felt like an oath from both of them. Miri could feel the strength of the promise, knew that it was true. They had to be together. Life just made more sense when they were.

A throat cleared, and Miri turned toward the rest of the group who were staring pointedly at the two of them as they had been lost in the passion of their reunion, waiting to move away from the port and back to the camp proper. She couldn't even muster any embarrassment. She was just too happy that Ell was back. What did it matter if people had been watching their displays of affection?

"You did it," she exclaimed to Ell as she surveyed the small crowd. "You rescued your family!" She knew the aged northern elf standing near to Dacunda could only be Ell's father. The resemblance was too much for him to be anything else, and the way he held the hand of the female next to him had to mean she was Ell's mother. Miri felt a flash of nerves at the thought of meeting his parents. And was that his sister standing next to his mother and father?

Sister.

The thought crashed home like a landslide.

She turned to Ell. "Rihya..." she mumbled without really wanting the answer.

Ell's face crumpled at the mention of his sister's name. His expression said it all. Miri wanted to cry, wanted to bawl upon getting the confirmation that what she feared was true, that Rihya really was gone. Dead. But, looking at Ell, she knew that he needed her to be strong. Something about his visage told her that he was barely holding it together. Impulsively, she accessed the Graft and felt a swirling tumble of emotions in him. Confusion and anger, worry, fear, and even hate bubbled around the joy and overpowering love he felt at seeing her once again. Through it all, there was a dark undercurrent of...something. Something she couldn't put her finger on. All she knew was that he needed her right now. She could be strong. For him, she could be anything.

Miri pulled him close and murmured quietly in his ear as he let his tears fall.

"It's my fault she's dead," he wept brokenly.

"Shh," she consoled and stroked the back of his head as he cried even harder, hard enough that she wondered if he'd even allowed himself to cry since it had happened. And then even after her promise to be strong for him she couldn't quite hold it together either. They cried in each other's arms for an indeterminate length of time, going on until they were both cried out. When she opened her eyes to look around, she guessed that the rest of the group must have gone back up the steps to the camp, leaving them in their grief.

"Ready?" she asked, tilting his chin up, forcing him to meet her watery gaze.

He wiped his eyes and nodded. Without thinking, she lightly touched the blackened scar on his cheek. He flinched, shying away from her touch.

"I'm sorry, is it tender? Did that hurt?" she asked worriedly.

Ell shook his head. "No. I...I just...never mind. We should get back to the group." There was a conflicted look on his face, and not for the first time Miri felt a tremor of fear as she thought about what that dark undercurrent in his consciousness might be. She ignored it for now, grabbing his strong hand in hers and leading him back up the steps to the camp.

Suddenly, another horrible thought crossed her mind. "Wait, where is Dahranian? Did he also...?" She couldn't manage to voice the question.

Ell looked at her sharply but then understanding crossed his face. "No, he stayed behind." Miri stared at him, confused, eliciting another response from him. "He's fine, don't worry. Or, at least, he was fine last I saw him. He and Kalabi both stayed to help with the uprising. They are going to try and help the slaves fight their way north and then across the Great Bridge to Andalaya. Dahranian with his sense of duty and honor couldn't leave the slave army we'd just created to their own ends. He felt responsible." Ell shook his head in annoyance at his eldest cousin. Dahranian's almost self-righteous sense of duty could sometimes be a sore spot for Ell, yet Miri noted the hint of admiration in his tone and his expression as he spoke of it. He continued, "We couldn't find enough ships for all the slaves we set free and, even if we could, they wouldn't have been able to cross the Fracture without a Water Caller to guide their way. I'll explain it more later. Come on—let's get back to the group."

Despite Rihya's passing, there was a celebratory air within the camp. Fires cheerfully roasted skewers of meat, conversations were happy and animated. Miri supposed that it made sense. They'd had over a month to adjust to Rihya's death, plus Ell really had, somehow and against all odds, managed to rescue his mother, father, and older sister after they'd been lost to slavery for the past two decades. It was remarkable.

Ell had calmed as they walked back up and had on his usual serious expression by the time they reached the others. He led Miri straight to his family.

"Love, this is my father, Adan, my mother, Lliaria, and my sister, Delle. Everyone, this is my mate, Miriyah."

Miri smiled and nodded her head to each of them, nervous to say or do the wrong thing. Lliaria stood and embraced her without a second's hesitation. "My son does little but speak of you. It is wonderful to meet you, Miriyah."

"Miri is fine," she mumbled.

Lliaria was clearly aged by bondage, weary and with more grey than most elves her age. She was weathered, but there was a sweetness in her aspect that even decades of servitude could not erase. Delle seemed the same and hugged her, as well. Adan stood and clasped her forearm a bit more formally. He was powerful in the way that Dacunda was and had hands that were rough from holding tools and working from sunup to sundown. He smiled, too.

"It is an honor to be introduced."

"Likewise," Miri said, still at a loss for what more to say.

Chatter from around them drew her attention and she sat, listening to everyone converse while accepting a small skewer of meat that Ell had taken from the fire.

"Tell me, what was Dark Harbor like? Was it hot? Was it scary? Did you kill anyone? And what about the human continent? Do the rulers of the humans have horns on their heads and hair that grows from their faces all the way down to their feet like the stories say?" Art was peppering Ryder with one question after another, too quickly for Ell's cousin to respond.

Finally, a break in the young elf's questions came, and Ryder put up his hands in defeat. "Enough, lad. I'll answer them all if you give me a chance. And, by the way, when did you start speaking?" The boy blushed slightly as Ryder ruffled the hair on his head, but then he recovered and continued to gaze boldly at the older elf, demanding answers.

Miri thought back to the haunted boy that Ell had rescued from the Pillar last spring along with herself. Who knew what trauma Art had experienced at the hands of their enemies? All they knew was that his family was dead, and he had been a captive. Artorious had only spoken in one word or very short sentences, if at all, for months after joining them. Only recently had he begun to crack open the shell formed from the suffering of his past. But tonight was exciting, the company was back together, and Miri had a sneaking suspicion that the brash and boastful Ryder who told more jokes and stories than ten elves combined was a favorite of Art's. Sure enough, the young elf stared adoringly up into Ryder's eyes as he regaled the boy with no doubt exaggerated tales of all that had transpired abroad.

Snippets of other conversations wafted around the fires in the not yet fully dark evening. Iyonei had taken a seat on a stone next to Dacunda and was doing her best to antagonize him.

"Thought you'd leave the fighting to us, eh? No matter, we've killed enough humans and Departed in raids these past months to make up for your lack of effort," she teased.

Dacunda stared at her placidly before responding, "You are aware we started a revolt back on the human continent. Aren't you?"

She waved her hand. "Pssh. Hearsay."

Her comment surprisingly managed to draw a small smile from Dacunda. But Miri's attention was soon drawn away from Ell's uncle and Iyonei and back to Ell and his parents. Someone had said her name. She looked at Lliaria.

"I asked where your parents were," Ell's mother repeated the question as she sat next to Miri on a fallen column.

"Oh, they—they died a long time ago," she said as quickly as possible to take the sting out of saying it aloud.

Lliaria saw through the façade and put her arm around Miri's shoulders. "Well, you have a new family now." The motherly way she said it warmed Miri more than most things she'd experienced in her life.

"Thank you. I already feel that way." She smiled at Lliaria. "Ell, Dacunda, and the rest took me in immediately and without question. Rihya and I were practically sisters from the start!" She bit off the last portion of her statement, wishing she had not said it. Tears formed at the corners of her eyes at the thought of Rihya. Ell's green-haired sister really had been a sister—a real sister in all but blood.

"My daughter was special, wasn't she?" Lliaria commented proudly. Miri nodded, unable to speak past the lump forming in her throat. "I wish I could have known her," Lliaria sighed mournfully. "Perhaps you'll tell me about her. It is hard to get Ell to speak of her. He blames himself so."

Miri smiled a watery smile. "Of course. I'd love to tell you all about her. She was incredibly brave and fiery. Fiercer than almost anyone I've ever met."

"So I hear," Ell's mother said.

Miri glanced around the camp. Adan was engaged in a serious conversation with Arendahl while Dacunda and Iyonei were still bantering back and forth. Ell was deep in discussion with his eldest sister, Delle, and Ryder was entertaining Art and Brie with more stories. The Departed sailors had set up their own small camp just within sight, and while things between camps were just a hint of tense, they were about as good as could be expected. All felt right. Other than Rihya and Dahranian being absent, things hadn't felt this right in who knew how long? Fires crackled merrily, larger than was normally allowed when away from Andalaya, but nobody had the heart to question the desire for hot meat and a warm, cheery camp. Honey mead was passed around in drinking horns, and laughter rose into the evening sky.

"Ships! Of human make!" The sentry's cry cut through the cacophony of sound, silencing the merriment. "A few of them, and they'll be here in less than half of an hour. It was too dark to spot them any sooner."

"Are there more with you?" Iyonei asked Dacunda tensely, one hand already straying to her sword hilt. Dacunda shook his head grimly.

Ell's uncle swore. "These fires are too big. They'll have been seen for miles. Whoever they are, they already know we are here. We should leave."

Iyonei shook her head. "The nearest cover, forest or otherwise, is days to the north. This is the only defensible position in the region. Our best and only chance is to stay, dig in, and defend."

"You always advocate action even when it is not sensible!" Dacunda shot back.

Arendahl interjected himself into the conversation. "This time she's right, Dac. They've seen us, and both humans or Departed are bound to follow us. They've got the numbers on us with multiple ships. Fighting where we have a chance is our best option."

Adan pulled a sword from his sheath and grimly began sharpening it with a whetstone. Miri took one look at his face and quickly realized she never wanted to be on the other end of his anger. Everyone began preparing weapons. Iyonei and Dacunda barked orders and warriors started prepping defenses. The ships crept ever closer.

It isn't fair, Miri thought bitterly. She'd only just reunited with Ell and within hours a battle was already brewing.

"The numbers are not with us," Iyonei told Arendahl, glancing out at the approaching ships.

Arendahl grinned wolfishly. "But we have not one but *two* Water Callers on our side. That is more than enough to even the scales."

Still, even as the greying elf said it, the sentry hooted again to call attention. "More ships sighted! Departed warships. Looks like a small fleet closing in on the first set of ships, and not far behind."

Everyone stared around at each other. The first set of ships were minutes from landing. It was too late to run, but a whole other armada of feared southern warships were hot in pursuit and likely to land not long after.

What had they gotten themselves into?

CHAPTER FIVE

"Fortify that gap in the wall!" Ell called out forcefully. He pointed to a pile of rubble, and a handful of elves quickly scampered over and began plugging one of the gaps in their defenses. It was makeshift and probably wouldn't hold for long, but it was better than nothing.

Ell had left Miri's side and was striding around issuing orders left and right. "I want all archers elevated and behind. Miri—you, Lliaria, and Delle join them." He didn't pause to see if they listened. "Piripeos!" he called to the Departed camp just a stone's throw away, "I want your pirates to hold the right, Iyonei and Dacunda will command the left while myself, Arendahl, and my father command the force in the center."

The Rimmer captain nodded tersely. He was from a ring of islands far to the west, so far into the western ocean that legend said they were the last stop before the world ended. He had every reason not to want to get caught in the middle of a struggle between humans and his northern and southern kin, but here he was all the same. He could be counted on. Surprisingly, Ell found he trusted Piripeos about as much as he could trust anyone who wasn't family.

"Boy, I hardly know you, and I'll not take orders from a stranger." Iyonei thrust a belligerent face in front of Ell's. He'd just met her and, perhaps a year ago, her scarred and one-eyed face—firm and hard from years of fighting—might have given him pause. But he was not that young elf any more. He'd done things, experienced things, and they had set him apart whether he wanted them to or not.

"Stand down, Iyonei. We don't have time for this." Ell's voice crackled with authority, enough that he could see his tone had given the warrior elf pause. She grimaced, and Ell continued, "We have minutes before battle breaks loose. I'll not have my command challenged at a time like this."

"*Your* command?" she murmured softly, almost thoughtfully. She still looked like she was swallowing something bitter, but after sharing a meaningful glance with Arendahl she nodded to him. Ell didn't have time to ponder the meaning of the interaction; he simply wanted them ready and prepared for battle. They had just under two hundred fighters and easily double that number were bearing down on them in the human ships about to make port, not to mention the Departed warships that were following.

Iyonei turned to Dacunda. "Well, it looks as though we've been given our orders." The sour look on her face had not quite faded.

"You'll get used to it," Dacunda said ruefully with a half-smile. The two of them began efficiently marshaling their warriors on the left. Piripeos was already organized on the right. Kester the half-mad pirate was whistling as she sharpened her cutlass. Baerg and Rikiol, fierce and inseparable, stood just beside them, and the rest of the pirates followed their lead. Ell turned his attention back to those under his direct command at the center of their defense.

Arendahl was looking at him with a keen, thoughtful gaze, while Miri was staring at him as if he were someone else completely. He'd only just been growing used to being in command when she'd left with Art and Arendahl months ago. Command had come to feel more normal to Ell now. It still had weight, the responsibility for the survival of people he loved, but the feeling was settling in better now.

He glanced at his father who was busily working along with a few other elves to shore up the hole in the center of their defenses. Trust Adan to find where the labor was needed. Twenty years as a slave had drilled into his bones the need to keep useful and busy. Ell stepped forward and surveyed their defenses. The ships would make port at the quay below. The only way they could make their way through the city was to fight their way up the stairs and through Ell and his company's position. There was a long wall the height of an elf that would provide defensible cover. It was shaky, but they had plugged its gaps as best as possible. However, the gate in the middle where the stairway passed would be the weak point in their defenses. There was no door to close, having long ago disappeared from these ruins.

Arendahl seemed to follow his line of thought. "The two of us together should be enough to stop the flow, to keep that hole in our defenses firm."

Ell grunted agreement. "It'll be hard to do with arrows flying our way. You know they'll focus their attention on those of us holding the empty gateway."

"Change of tactics?"

"Change of tactics," Ell agreed. He turned to the archers who had taken up elevated positions behind him. Thankfully, Miri had listened to him and was with them. "Archers, I want you to target *their* archers first. Understand?" he cried to those above. Confused nods answered his call, but they were nods all the same. Usually, archers picked off those of the enemy who were first in line to attack a position, thinning the ranks for their comrades on the front lines. This time, though, with such a gaping hole needing to be covered in the middle of the empty gate, every measure had to be taken to prevent the enemy's archers from pinpointing the two Water Callers and exploiting that weakness.

Preparations finished, Ell stood in the gateway beside Arendahl, elf warriors at his back as he stared down at the ships that were just now making port. Humans began streaming down ropes and disembarking by use of planks to the stones of the quay. For a moment, Ell imagined this must have been what it was like once upon a time. He felt transported back to another century, a time when Akan Deraiya wasn't ruins and elves had fought and died and bloodied its gleaming walls to protect the city they loved. He fondled the black Dreampine arrows in his quiver. His people had adapted; they had learned to fight from the shadows, to strike and slash in cut-and-run tactics, but it had not always been so. Once, they had stood shoulder to shoulder and faced their enemies in an army. Ell felt a sense of satisfaction in this return to the old. Less than two hundred elves did not make an army, but neither was it a pittance. Damn their enemies, damn the humans and the Departed who wanted their blood! Ell screamed his defiance as the humans began rushing up the stairs to the courtyard in front of their defensive wall. The elves behind him echoed his ululating war cry. He felt the blood rush to his head and, without difficulty, Ell tapped into his Water Caller powers. Arendahl knelt beside him and touched his hands to the ground to do the same thing, something he'd keenly forced Ell to learn to do without.

Ell felt the salty sea water in the ocean before him and in the air around him. He reached out his consciousness into the land, into creation, and then pulled upon every droplet of water he could feel. He felt the power swell like a deep reservoir in his chest. The air misted up around him, and dew-like droplets clung to the dueling daggers he had drawn from their sheaths. His eyes clouded over in that foggy way that made it harder and yet easier to see all at the same time. Then he instinctively did something else. He tapped into the dark undercurrent in his consciousness—that *something* that had been swirling just under the surface since Dark Harbor and his defeat to Half-Mask, the Prince of Darkness.

Ell felt another power swell within him. A dangerous power, a cry for blood and death and victory at all costs. He bared his teeth in a grimace as he struggled to corral that dark power. But it was a part of him now, and he might as well use it.

And then it began.

The humans rushed, and arrows started flying in both directions. Hundreds of enemies poured in Ell's direction, and the wall the elves defended was soaked in blood within minutes. It was a vicious fight. He stayed close to the gate to defend their weakness, as did Arendahl, but the humans devoted most of their numbers toward the two Water Callers and the elves they commanded, trying to break through and exploit the gap.

Ell fought like a whirlwind. He smoothly avoided axes and swords, dodged arrows, all the while leaving a bloody trail in his wake. He eviscerated human soldiers, hamstrung them, cut throats and loosed hands from arms. He fought with reckless power that came from tapping both powers that lived inside him. The mist danced around him as he fought, swirling as it always did around a Water Caller of his magnitude and power. But a few wispy, black tendrils wafted up from the tips of his fingers, as well, and a ghostly black cloud of…what? Smoke? Ell didn't know. But he felt the surging power that the blackness gave him. He lusted after the blood of his enemies.

Arrows whizzed by him and one struck him in the meat of his left shoulder. For a moment, the impact threw him backward and off course, but he snarled and snapped the arrow off, leaving the head in and a few inches of wood protruding from his arm as he went on. It was a hard-fought battle. The humans had at least twice their numbers, but they had no Water Callers—or whatever Ell was now. Still, they fought with desperation. Elves dropped all around Ell, falling to axes and war hammers. Oh, they took humans with them, but the war of attrition hurt the elves more. Ell shared a worried look with Arendahl. The old elf grimaced.

"Nothing for it but to fight boy, fight to the end," Arendahl grunted between gritted teeth as he parried a sword stroke and then smoothly ran his opponent through with his own weapon.

Ell hefted his dueling daggers, feeling the familiar buzz they created when used together: two halves of the same blade forged as one then split into two twin blades. They had a power all their own. Ell would take any edge he could get. He bloodied more and more of his enemies, dancing a trail of death through them, leaving bodies gutted and skin diseased wherever he touched it with a blow. Ell didn't even pause anymore upon seeing that. Death was death, wasn't it? What did it matter which power inside him allowed him to defend his people? And so he fought on, brutally, forcefully, and with every shred of power he possessed—dark or light.

Then the Departed landed. A mini flotilla entered the harbor and began disembarking. They hit the humans from behind with double, even triple the humans' numbers, and all of a sudden Ell understood why the humans had landed and fought so desperately. They were fighting for their survival. Had the alliance completely broken down between them and the Departed? Had Half-Mask finally severed connection with the east?

Ell didn't have time to wonder because all it meant was that his people had even more enemies to fight. The Departed might be killing the humans now, but when they were finished they would turn to the Highest and pirates who stood in their way. The numbers were overwhelmingly against Ell and his people. He cut and slashed and fought his way forward, somehow winding up with enemies on every side. Screaming his defiance, he took wounds from weapons that found their mark simply due to the fact that he could only block so many blades. The humans were falling now like harvested grain, and Ell fought his way ever forward. Something in him wanted a chance to cross blades with at least a few Departed before it was over. As Ell fought, he tapped deeper into the blackness inside him. He saw the mist around him darken slightly in the moonlit air, like smoke and mist combined. His blows dropped humans at one touch, sending them into diseased throes of agony. He couldn't find it in him to care.

And then it happened. He finally saw a Departed close enough to fight. He lunged toward the warrior, dueling daggers flashing in the moonlight. He crossed his blades with a regal-looking dark elf wielding a longsword. The Departed fought to defend himself, and he did so admirably, considering that Ell was a Water Caller—or more—facing a paltry, lone warrior. Ell toyed with him, moving too quickly to be stopped. He flicked his daggers and inflicted a shallow gash along the Departed's ribs. The southern elf grimaced in pain but fought on to defend himself. Strangely, he didn't attempt to attack. Perhaps Ell was simply too much for him. A clamor grew in the background, but Ell ignored it, so focused was he on the fight, on the eventual kill. He flurried forward in a whirl of blades and a look of fear crossed the dark elf's face. Ell could feel the kill coming; it was almost time to stop playing with his food. He wanted to devour the very soul of his enemy. He could smell a whiff of something rotten and dying, a stench of Bonewinds filling the air, but he ignored it. All he could feel now was the lust of the kill, and it gave him tunnel vision, not allowing him to focus on anything else.

Almost over now. He moved like lightning and sent the sword flying out of his enemy's hand with a particularly clever and powerful maneuver. He kicked the Departed's knee, and the dark elf fell to the ground before struggling to his knees. Ell panted with delight as he lunged in for the kill, a spider about to finally consume his prey. The dueling daggers descended, and a shriek resounded through the air.

Finally, words pierced the fog that was clouding his brain. Something familiar about them gave him pause, arresting his downward stroke in midflight.

"Elliyar, no!"

He froze. The familiarity of the voice struck a chord in him. It snapped him out of the darkness that had been consuming him and pushing him further into battle-madness than he'd ever been before.

Green hair flitted toward him, and the moonlight illuminated what could not be.

"Stop, brother," Rihya said again, even though his daggers had already clattered to the cobblestones around him in shock.

"But you're..." He couldn't finish the sentence. Clearly she was not. She cupped his face.

"What is wrong with you? What has happened to you?" she murmured almost tearfully, worry clouding her features.

Ell glanced around and realized that the battle was over. All of the humans were either dead or captured, and the Departed who had arrived had not tried to attack the Highest or the pirates in their defensive positions on the walls. All eyes were on him, the lone antagonist trying to kill the leader of the army that had just saved their lives.

He stumbled backward in a daze, not wanting to see the look of disgust written plainly on Arendahl's face or Miri's frightened visage. He didn't even look at his mother or father, not wanting to see what they thought of him.

Ell swallowed, gathering himself and picking up his dueling daggers, sheathing them in one fluid movement born of habit and many years of practice. He stepped forward toward his not-dead sister and the Departed he had almost killed. The dark elf had gotten to his feet, reclaimed his sword, and was now hovering protectively behind Rihya as if he needed to defend her from Ell.

Ell took a hesitant step forward, and he couldn't have expressed the relief felt when Rihya didn't back away in fear. She stood calmly, looking at him.

"You're alive," he murmured.

"I am," she said somewhat saucily, a twinkle returning to her eyes, "and you are stating the obvious."

He laughed then. He had missed her teasing these past months. Ell gathered her in his arms and held her tightly.

"Are you all right?" he heard her ask in a muffled voice as he pressed her face to his chest.

"I am now," he said fiercely. "I am now."

CHAPTER SIX

"Elliyar!" Adan called out from the other side of the courtyard that had been the scene of the battle.

Ell turned his head away from Rihya and broke their embrace. "What is it, Father?"

"A prisoner. Do you wish to interrogate him?" Adan was holding one wounded human by the scruff of the neck, using a fistful of the man's chainmail collar to drag him toward Ell.

"Duty calls." Ell tilted his head ruefully toward his sister.

She winked at him knowingly. "Don't act like you don't enjoy it, little brother. I saw how hard you fought for command last summer. Just admit it suits you."

He smiled sheepishly at her. "All right, I will concede that on some days it feels right. But on other days, like when you..." he broke off, unable to finish right away. "Well, on those days, I wonder why I ever wanted to lead in the first place." He turned to walk toward his father, but then half-turned back toward Rihya, loathe to leave her side after so long apart and thinking her dead.

"Go on," she shooed him. "I'm not going anywhere."

He nodded and turned toward his father but was again arrested in his tracks by a voice crying out, "Valerihya?" Ell saw his mother, Lliaria, descending from the archers' positions. "Valerihya!" she called again, this time with more urgency.

"Mother?" Rihya whispered, incredulity staining her voice. She turned to Ell. "You really did it? You crossed the Fracture and saved mother?"

"And Delle, our sister," Ell said with satisfaction, and for the first time in a while he felt pride in what he had done. He'd been so worried with what was happening inside of him that he'd lost sight of all he had accomplished. He waited for Rihya to compliment him or even tease him about what he'd done, but she was already sprinting across the courtyard toward Lliaria.

"Mother!" She wept as they came together, flinging herself into Lliaria's arms. They were nearly the same height—Rihya just slightly shorter—but the resemblance faded there. Rihya was green-haired and feisty whereas their mother appeared placid and steady. Lliaria was aged for an elf, with weathered features compared to Rihya's youthful vitality. Nevertheless, they molded into one body for a matter of minutes as they clung to one another. *Of course*, Ell thought, *Rihya remembers her in a way I don't.* She was just old enough to feel their parent's loss more keenly. He smiled one final smile at the scene, again feeling pride at the fact that he'd made their reunion happen, and then officially turned his attention to Adan and the prisoner.

His father was waiting patiently, a longing look on his face as if he, too, wished to embrace Rihya and never let her go. But he was like Dacunda, always attending to duty first.

"He's one of the few survivors. They were crushed between our forces like a hammer and anvil," Adan stated coldly.

Ell stared at the human who carried a nasty wound in one leg but, to his credit, still managed to throw a scornful expression in his direction.

"The Grand Marshal is coming for you," he spat bitterly, angrily.

"That is the commander of your forces on our continent, yes?" Ell questioned.

The prisoner nodded jerkily, his black beard wobbling with the motion. "You pointy-eared bastards attacked our homeland, and that really stirred the pot. You'll not last long once reinforcements arrive!" The man smirked, clinging to the last shred of purpose he had left: his satisfaction at what he perceived to be his captors' future misfortune.

So, the humans were already reacting to the rebellion that Ell and his company had begun in Lu Fang. "When will these reinforcements arrive?" he asked.

The human clamped his teeth together as if realizing he'd already divulged too much. He glared at Ell and Adan.

Arendahl strode up purposefully. "We have ways of making your kind talk." His piercing, grey eyes made the human shrink back before them.

The man gathered his courage and sneered, "Do your worst." The fear in his eyes belied his words.

Arendahl put one hand firmly to his belt knife as if to draw steel, but Ell quelled him with a simple touch to the arm. "It's not worth it, Arendahl. The humans are coming, we know that now. They already have numbers in our land, and even if those numbers swell, it does not change what we must do. This war is inevitable. We either fight and win our freedom—win our land back—or we fight and die. Those are our options."

The old elf grunted. "What do you plan to do with him?" He motioned toward the prisoner with his hand. Ell couldn't help but hear the implicit 'to' in that question in place of 'with'. *What do you plan to do to him?* He swallowed. He'd nearly succumbed to his darkness today, and he couldn't let that happen again. He had to fight the darkness for as long as possible. Torturing or executing a prisoner of war wouldn't help his inner struggle.

"Let him go," he murmured. "We won't be staying here long, so he can't give our location away. Besides, he won't be moving anywhere very quickly with that." Ell inclined his head toward the wound on the prisoner's leg.

"Are you sure?" Adan asked carefully.

Ell nodded again. "I am." This time, he said it with more force: "Let him go."

"Very well." Arendahl mused and shared a covert glance with Ell's father.

Adan let the prisoner drop to the ground. The human scurried backward, away from the three of them as if unable to believe that he had been given his freedom.

"Go on. You have a matter of minutes to be out of my sight, lest I change my mind," Ell said with much more threat than he actually felt. He didn't want to execute the soldier given his inner condition, but neither did he want the human to think him—and, by extension, the elves he commanded—weak. It wouldn't do for that information to get back to the Grand Marshal and embolden the human commander further.

The man didn't need another comment to elicit his flight. He struggled to his feet and hobbled through the remains of his comrades. Elves glanced his way, casting scathing looks as he made his way away from the port and up toward the rest of the city ruins, but no one made a move to stop him. The elves realized that if Ell, Arendahl, and Adan had let him rise and walk away, then he wasn't to be stopped. Besides, with the wound in his leg continuing to leak blood, he wouldn't make it far. *Perhaps*, Ell thought, *it would actually be a kindness to kill him here and now*. Then again, perhaps not. With some fortune, he could make his way far enough north along the coast to reach the human encampments. Maybe. But Ell wouldn't bet on it.

Ell pushed the fleeing human from his thoughts and focused his attention on the rest of the elves in sight. Tensions were high, as they were certain to be when an army of dark elves met a smaller army of the Highest, but that tension did not seem on the verge of boiling over. The Andalayan elves recognized the aid given them by their southern cousins, and though they were eyeing them carefully it was with a certain respect.

"Who would have thought my daughter would save our skins with a Departed army at her back?" Adan asked, a note of wonder and pride in his voice.

"Who, indeed?" Arendahl muttered much more circumspectly.

Ell glanced at his sister. She had finished her reunion with their mother and Delle, as well. He saw her hugging Miri fiercely. Those two had grown close almost immediately last summer after Ell and Miri's Joining. Rihya was wiping a few happy tears from Miri's cheeks. Ell's mate said something, and they both giggled and then looked his way. So that was beginning again already. They had a habit of talking about him within eyesight but out of earshot. It used to annoy him to no end, but he just couldn't muster the same frustration with it now. Rihya was alive, Miri was by his side again. All was as well as it could be. A cloud of doubt filled his mind. *Was it? Was all really as well as it could be?* He had a pit of darkness buried in his soul, put there by the Prince of Darkness himself. *Would anything ever truly be all right ever again?*

Ell's thoughts seemed to coincide with the cautious approach of the leader of this army of Departed. Rihya noticed him striding toward Ell and broke away from Miri to flit over and introduce them.

"Ell, this is Aldashir." She indicated the proud, southern elf who had stopped in front of them. Ell reached out to clasp his forearm, and the elf reciprocated the gesture, again cautiously. Ell couldn't blame him. After all, he had nearly killed him a matter of minutes ago.

"He is prince of the Southern Kingdom," Rihya continued.

Ell dropped the dark elf's forearm as if it were red hot, taking a startled step back. "Are you insane!" he exclaimed in Rihya's ear. "Half-Mask's brother, here? With us?"

"So you know my brother, I see," Aldashir said almost bitterly.

"We've met," he answered, iron in his voice. "He gave me this." Ell pointed to the blackened scar on his cheek.

Aldashir's eyes widened slightly as if truly seeing the scar for the first time. "Black..." The prince's eyes roved Ell's body, touching upon the various wounds he had sustained in the battle—none of them were more than shallow grazes. The prince spoke again. "Black scars and black...blood."

Ell really looked at his wounds for the first time since the battle had ended and realized that some of the blood seeping from the shallow cuts was, indeed, black. Not all of it—there was red swirled in, as well—but there was unmistakably black blood dripping down his skin. He swallowed nervously, but then anger welled up in him. This was Half-Mask's brother, a relative to evil incarnate. Who was he to judge?

"Let me worry about my blood. It's none of your concern," Ell answered stiffly.

Aldashir nodded just as stiffly, but he was staring at Ell as if looking at an adder that might strike at any moment. That this Departed had the nerve to look at him as if *he* were the dangerous one made Ell seethe. *Aren't you, though?* a small voice murmured in the back of his head.

"Ell, calm down. Aldashir is a friend." Rihya placed her hand familiarly on the prince's shoulder.

Ell narrowed his eyes. She couldn't have...could she? But the way Rihya looked at Aldashir banished any doubts he had. She looked at the Departed the way he'd looked at Miri when they had first met, far to the north in Little Vale. He wanted to say something, wanted to scold her, tell her she was crazy for feeling that way, but he knew she wouldn't listen. It would only make her angry, and he'd just gotten her back. *Besides*, that small voice said, *didn't Aldashir and his warriors just save you?*

"Very well, Rihya. Come, join our fires, Aldashir." Ell indicated for them to follow. The prince issued a few commands to his warriors and then followed Ell through the fire-lit night toward the camp.

As they reached the first campfire, Miri limped up to Ell and slipped her hand into his. She cast a worried look at him, but he gave a slight shake of the head, hoping she would ask whatever questions or voice whatever worries she had later when they were in private.

The next few hours were a series of careful, prodding questions—cautious conversations between Aldashir and his high-ranking warriors and Ell, Arendahl, Adan, Dacunda and the rest of the group. Rihya acted as a buffer, setting herself up between the two leaders. The pirates in the nearby camp were also a useful resource to draw upon. After all, Ell and his company had been working successfully with those rogue Departed for more than a month now, and no issues had arisen. Who was to say the same could not be true of Aldashir and his warriors?

Ell focused on the conversation that was currently taking place. "We call ourselves The Thousand," Aldashir was saying to Adan.

"I have heard of you," he replied.

"Really, where?" Aldashir asked, seeming genuinely surprised.

Adan paused before answering, "I spent some time in Dark Harbor. You would be surprised what you can pick up listening to the conversations around you as a...slave." The statement hung poignantly in the air.

Finally, Aldashir spoke. "I am sorry that you were enslaved. My soldiers and I do not support the unsavory treatment of your people. But my brother and father do what they please." Adan nodded his head to accept the response.

"Tell us more about The Thousand," Ell prompted.

Aldashir turned his head to face him. "Well, we recruit very specifically. The first thing we look for is appearance. You'll notice that none of my warriors have modified their aspect."

It was true: Aldashir and his soldiers had normal teeth, not filed to points like the rest of the Departed warrior class. It gave Ell pause. Strangely, that simple fact made him feel much more inclined to trust the prince and his company of a thousand warriors. There was something about the Departed warriors' filed teeth that gave them a grisly, evil aspect, and the absence of those modifications went a long way toward dispelling such presumptions.

"We defend the sea around The Point," Aldashir was saying, "and we keep the humans away from the waters around Dark Harbor. You could say we enforce the alliance—or, we did before it collapsed, after Half-Mask decided the humans were growing weak, allowing revolts in their homeland."

"That is an...*honorable* duty, fighting the humans," Dacunda responded. Everyone was straining to be polite, trying to find just the right words to say to each other.

"I am glad you understand and see it that way," Aldashir said. And he really did sound grateful; there was a note of relief in his voice that was almost palpable.

"Honor only accounts for some of what goes into deciding what is right and what is wrong. Don't let duty and honor fool you," Arendahl grunted, never one to comply with courtesies.

Aldashir's face clouded, and Ell wasn't sure if it was anger or shame. But something in what Arendahl said had struck a chord. Rihya interjected, having seen something in Aldashir's face also, and steered the conversation toward easier topics.

The rest of the night passed in relative ease. Miri was practically connected to Ell's hip, and he wouldn't have had it any other way. They ate, drank, and replenished their energy after the earlier battle. People danced and sang to tunes, celebrating the fact that they were alive. Iyonei's troop were particularly boisterous, and Ell was surprised to note that at one point she even managed to convince Dacunda to join her for a dance. Ryder fit right in with their group and danced and drank the night away with them.

As the night grew deeper and darker, Ell felt the call of sleep tugging on his consciousness. He was nearly at the point of retiring when Aldashir returned from seeing to his men and seated himself cautiously next to Ell.

Ell stiffened ever so slightly but tried to make himself relax. This wasn't an enemy—he didn't think.

"About our fight," Aldashir began, "at the end of the battle, I mean—"

Ell interjected, forcing himself to be polite. This was the last thing he wanted to discuss right now with Miri by his side. "Look, I apologize for my actions. I did not mean to lose my head that way." He could practically feel Miri's eyes slide open from the half-sleep she'd been in and notice her ears perk up. He knew it was his imagination, but it still bothered him. He didn't want to speak of his issues now, not when he'd just been reunited with her.

"I know," Aldashir continued. "I know well that you were not in control." The prince paused then, and the silence that stretched was latent with meaning. At last, he spoke again. "There is a reason you were not in control."

"And that is?" Ell tried his best to make himself speak politely, but his voice sounded hard and angry in his own ears.

Aldashir sensed the antagonism and lifted his hands. "I mean no offense, but you lead your people. You should know what is happening to you."

"'What' is happening to me?" Ell repeated almost dully.

"Yes. It is the Blackness. You said you met my brother, Half-Mask, did you not? When you met him, did he...do something to you?"

Ell swallowed, fear worming its way into his heart. As much as he wanted to ignore this, he couldn't, especially if Aldashir knew something useful.

"Yes," Ell finally muttered to the prince.

"I thought so. He had a dark liquid with him, I am guessing."

Again Ell confirmed his suspicions. "He did. The Prince of Darkness poured it in my wounds."

"This one?" Aldashir indicated his scarred cheek. Ell nodded.

"What else do you know?" Ell asked, his interest piqued now.

"You have been feeling dazed at times—cloudy thinking—and experience a battle lust that is hard to control. There is an unpredictability in your emotions now, as well." Aldashir sounded as though he were listing the symptoms of a disease. Maybe he was.

"What of it?" Ell prodded again. He wanted answers.

"As I said, it is the Blackness. My brother began the transformation in you, a transformation into what your sister tells me you call 'the Unsired'."

White hot rage shot through Ell as he realized the truth. On some level, he'd already known—Half-Mask had basically said it to his face after their duel in Dark Harbor—but hearing it now, from Aldashir, confirmed all of his fears and forced him to confront them. Half-Mask was making him into an Unsired! It was almost more than he could bear.

"How?" Ell asked through gritted teeth. He was sitting up straight now, and Miri was fully awake at his side after his body had shifted.

"The dark liquid he poured into your wounds is from a special location, a special...source," Aldashir murmured, a string of fear almost creeping into his voice. Almost, but when he spoke again it was the regal, haughty tone he normally used. "The liquid is his tool for inciting the Blackness. We do not allow those who the Blackness has touched to enter The Thousand," Aldashir finished, steel in his voice.

Suddenly, Ell felt self-conscious. According to the prince, he had the Blackness. Shame winnowed its way into his heart. Miri's hand grasped his tightly, as if reading his thoughts. He held her palm to his just as hard. Ell pulled on the anger he'd felt since he was just a boy, the hate he felt for Half-Mask and all of his enemies. He stoked that fury, willing it to banish his shame. He didn't have time for that now; he had to focus his strength and energy on useful things.

"Where is it? What is this source called?" he demanded, not even fully realizing that his voice was just as regal and commanding as the prince's. He was angry, but he also felt an inexplicable pull to this liquid, some desire buried so deeply that he could not explain it.

Aldashir paused as if realizing that answering would well and truly make him a traitor to his family. The pause was not long. "It's located in the Midnight Cove. The source you ask of, they call it Black Water Well."

CHAPTER SEVEN

"I'll destroy it Arendahl. I know I can do it!" Rihya watched Ell seethe as he spoke with his old mentor, pacing around as if he couldn't make himself stand still.

"We don't even know what exactly it is yet," Arendahl cautioned while the rest listened, waiting for an opportune moment to speak. Ell had called the heads together at first light, and most were groggy after a night spent carousing, unlike him who had clearly spent most of the night in a fitful state of hyper-focus.

Ell scoffed, "Don't be ridiculous. That black liquid Aldashir speaks of, what I saw with my own eyes after dueling Half-Mask—it can only mean one thing. An *opposite source*."

There was a stunned intake of breath around the morning campfire, and Rihya realized hers was one of the many. "That's not possible, brother. There is only one source, *the* Source, and it is in Andalaya," she said without thinking.

Her brother shot her a withering look. "Don't be naïve, Rihya. There are worse things in the world than we think. Nightmares do exist." Ell had a haunted look, and Rihya's heart wrenched in her chest. She knew what Aldashir had said to him last night, knew the fear and worry that must be gnawing at her little brother.

"So, you want to destroy it?" Adan said with Dacunda nodding along beside him.

"I do, and I will!" Ell spat, almost like an oath.

"How?" Arendahl cut in again, the voice of reason.

Ell sighed in exasperation. "I don't yet know the details, but I've managed to figure things out on the fly before. I crossed the Fracture, didn't I?" Rihya could see that he was getting agitated. She was glad Miri was standing right beside him to place a calming hand on his arm.

"That may be, boy, but this is different. You're speaking of a direct strike against the heart of the Southern Kingdom. You'll need bodies, warriors, more than we have," Arendahl said.

"Maybe not more than *we* have," a voice put in quietly. Rihya turned to see Aldashir striding over from his side of camp, morning fog clinging to his black breeches, tunic, and cloak. Involuntarily, her heart leaped in her chest. She forced herself not to smile; this was a time for serious talk.

"'We'?" Ell asked. "I mean no offense, Aldashir, to you and all you did for us yesterday, but you were not invited to this conference." Some of the stiffness had gone out of her brother's voice when he addressed the southern prince, but not all of it. There was still a wariness about him. However, Rihya couldn't blame Ell. He didn't have the benefit of over a month of sharing Aldashir's company to get to know his character.

"Yes, we. And since you are discussing what to do with information I gave you, I feel I am entitled to attend this meeting," Aldashir said firmly. If only he could lose that regal tone, he might win them over more quickly. Maybe a nick from one of her blades would take him down a notch. Her hands twitched, but she restrained herself.

Ell and Aldashir shared a long stare before the former conceded. "Very well, you may stay. But if you are one of us, then you are one of us. There is no turning back," the iron in her brother's voice chilled her. Aldashir, however, did not wilt under Ell's gaze.

"The moment I saved you and your people last night there was already no turning back. My brother and father are not known for their understanding or their mercy."

"And why *did* you help us?" Arendahl asked the prince.

Aldashir hesitated. His eyes flicked toward Rihya for just a moment, and her heart fluttered, but then he was staring at the old elf again. "Honor. I am honor bound to defend my people, and someone once told me that means to not only protect them from the dangers from without but from within. You and yours are fighting those very dangers." Rihya's heart swelled as she realized he was quoting an earlier conversation with her. She forced the feeling down ruthlessly. Who was she, some whimsical, love-struck girl? *Love?* The thought came crashing into her consciousness and threatened to erase every thought from her mind. It couldn't be love, not yet. She forced herself to pay attention.

Ell was all focus and he cut through Arendahl's questioning. "So, with The Thousand, we would have enough?"

The prince nodded. "And under my ship's banners, we'd find it easier to reach the Midnight Cove. There will be questions as we pass with such numbers, but my standard—the standard of my family—should be enough to secure us passage to the Black Water Well."

"It's settled, then," Ell declared decisively. "We strike a blow directly at Half-Mask's heart!"

"Is it settled?" Iyonei interjected. "Who made you absolute commander of these forces? Whatever propaganda Arendahl has been spouting on your behalf, I see only a boy with no control over his emotions or actions, not to mention other potential...issues." Her gaze flicked to the blackened scar on his cheek.

Rihya's brother opened his mouth to object, red spots darkening his fair cheeks in what was either embarrassment or anger, but Dacunda cut him off. "I know what my nephew is capable of, Iyonei. If he thinks he can do this—destroy this opposite source—then I believe him and will follow."

Dacunda's words gave her pause. "You really believe that much in this wild youth? You're the most cautious fighter I know." Somehow, when she called him cautious, this time it didn't sound like the jibe it normally was but more of a compliment.

"I do," Dacunda said firmly in response.

"Very well," Iyonei said. "Don't lead us astray, boy."

Ell smiled grimly. "I won't. First light tomorrow, we sail for the Midnight Cove. I promise you all, I'm going to destroy the Black Water Well."

———

RIHYA SAT next to Aldashir near the fire while a pot of hot oats bubbled over the flames. The meeting had broken up, and people had dispersed to their separate corners of the camp to eat, go back to sleep, or attend to whatever else their morning rituals necessitated. She looked over at Aldashir beside her. They had not kissed again since they'd been aboard his ship but, looking at him, she ached to do it again. He caught her staring, and a quizzical smile graced his lips.

"What?"

"Nothing. I mean, are you sure you want to join with us?" she covered, not wanting him to know what she'd really been thinking.

He blinked, a cautious note entering his voice as he said, "I thought you'd be pleased."

"Oh, I am," she said more quickly than she would have liked, and she felt her face flame up. If she were looking in a pond right now, she was certain her green hair would have been set atop a brilliantly red face. She cursed silently in embarrassment. "I just wanted to make sure..." she finished lamely.

"Well, I am certain," the prince confirmed with a smile, and he really sounded sure of himself. She answered his smile with one of her own. "Besides," he continued, "I meant what I said earlier. You made a good argument for joining you back when we were at The Point. If I do nothing to stop the Blackness—to at least *try* and stop it—what kind of elf am I?"

Tentatively, Rihya reached out and grasped his hand. "You're a good elf. This is only further proof." He held her hand for a long moment before she again grew slightly self-conscious and disentangled their fingers. There could be people watching. He smirked knowingly and wrapped his strong, dark fingers around the spoon he had been using to eat from a bowl of grain.

Again, a cautious look appeared on his face. "I mean no offense, Valerihya, so please do not take it so—"

"Just spit it out, whatever you have to say," Rihya prompted.

"I am worried for your brother."

"Why? He'll be fine, he always is."

"Are you sure? The Blackness is...powerful. I've never seen someone resist it once the process has begun." Aldashir had a sad look on his face, as if thinking of old friends and comrades lost to the darkness, a fate worse than death in his eyes.

A chill ran through Rihya. "You don't know him. You don't know what he's capable of," she muttered stubbornly. "Ell will pull through."

"I have no doubt that Elliyar is strong. I experienced it firsthand last night when he defeated me like one would a child." The prince grimaced sourly at the memory. "But the powers of the Black Water Well are equally strong, if not stronger. I am worried it will cloud his judgment, especially because he appears to be becoming something more than an Unsired. You know, when we were fighting last night, I swear I saw smoky tendrils wafting from his fingertips. I have only seen two other people manifest that power." His solemn voice told her exactly who those two people were.

"I believe in him," Rihya said simply, clinging to the hope that all would somehow right itself. "You should, too, if you're going to join our group."

"Very well. I believe in you, in your faith. Is that enough?"

"It's enough for now," she teased.

A rustle of movement sounded to her left, and she saw Miri melting away into the camp, her distinctive limp marking her. How much had she heard of their conversation? It was nothing she wouldn't be aware of by now, at least not if Ell was in any sort of sharing mood. Although, knowing her brother, he wasn't. Rihya hoped that wasn't the first Miri had heard of Ell being infected with the Blackness.

She was snapped out of her worry by an unfamiliar voice. "So, I hear you are good with blades. Just how good?"

She turned to look at a pixie blonde elf of about the same height as herself, maybe even somewhat shorter.

"Good enough," Rihya answered.

"Care to test that?" the elf challenged.

Rihya grinned. A little friendly competition might be just what she needed to take her mind off of worrisome matters. "Lead the way."

The pixie blonde extended her hand and they clasped forearms. "I'm called Briesom, and I'm the best knife fighter in Andalaya."

"Well, we aren't in Andalaya, are we?" Rihya smirked.

CHAPTER EIGHT

After Miri had heard enough of the prince and Rihya's conversation about Ell—she felt guilty for eavesdropping yet couldn't help but be relieved to get more information on his condition—she limped back to her private portion of the camp that she shared with Ell. She'd seen the way Rihya had looked at the prince and was happy for her, but her worry for her mate preoccupied her at the moment.

Most of the elves from both north and south slept under the stars, but Ell and Miri hadn't seen each other in months and wanted their own space, or as much of it as was possible. He had commandeered an unused sail from Captain Piripeos' ship, The Water Wasp, and had fastened it to one of the walls in the ruins, creating a half-tent with enough room for a modicum of privacy.

She ducked her head and entered their makeshift tent, Ell's name already on her lips, but her voice died in her throat. Ell was bare-chested which, at face value, should be nothing new to her. However, the strange, black scar that marred his cheek—courtesy of a duel with the Prince of Darkness—was not the only new scar on his body. A hideous, black welt had formed on the upper part of his chest, and another raised scar roped along his ribs.

Ell saw her enter and swore under his breath, hurriedly attempting to put on his tunic. What with his late arrival, meetings, the battle, and plans for what might happen next, Miri had hardly had a moment alone with him, certainly not enough time to be properly intimate. As such, seeing him sans tunic was a shock.

She rushed to his side. "No, love, don't hide them. Never hide anything from me," she told him mournfully. The scars looked like they must have been horribly painful to acquire.

Her mate shrugged uncomfortably. He never wished to speak of such matters, but she wouldn't let him shrug her off this time. He needed to open up. "Talk to me, Ell."

After staring at her for a long moment with a pained grimace on his face, he finally spoke. "Nobody knows about them. I don't know how they'd react. These are more concerning than the one on my cheek." His whisper was almost conspiratorial.

"Nobody?" Her eyes widened in surprise. Why had he been keeping this a secret? Then she saw the look in his eyes, that half-ashamed look that spoke volumes, and she knew exactly why he hadn't mentioned it to the others. He was embarrassed.

Miri began tracing his scars lightly with one forefinger. If she could get him to see that he had nothing to be ashamed about, then maybe he could relax, loosen up and just be with her for a moment. Talk to her, let her in to what must be swirling in his head. The conversation she'd overheard between Rihya and Aldashir surged back into her mind, the blackened scars on Ell's chest confirmation of the prince's words. What had happened to her mate? What *was* happening to him?

Ell's hands came up to hers, clasping them gently but firmly, stopping her from tracing his old wounds. "Stop."

"Sorry. Do they hurt?" she asked, at once concerned that her idle touching might have aggravated them.

"No! Yes. I don't know, I guess a bit," he mumbled raggedly. "I just—I just don't want you touching them. I don't want you to have to be a part of that...a part of that bad part of me."

She reached her hands up—cupping his cheeks—pulled his face down and kissed him. "We are Joined. There is no separation between those who are Joined, even less so between us." She smiled warmly and then tapped her head and his to signify the Graft.

He almost shuddered as she spoke. "So you saw it all?" The resignation and defeat in his voice pained her. This was the side he only showed to her. Ell pulled on his fury and passion when it came time to fight and to lead, but with her he showed a different, more vulnerable side.

"Yes." Simple was best for now; let him proceed how he wished.

"Then you know how I got these." He touched his scars. "You know who gave them to me and what he did to me."

"I've gleaned or guessed the necessary information," she confirmed.

"Well, it's happening." Ell flopped down onto their bedroll in defeat.

Miri lay down beside him, her leg twinging slightly as she put her weight on it. "It's never over. If there's one thing I've learned from being with you, Ell, it's that you never, ever give up. You'll find a way through this." She said the words with perhaps more force and belief than even she really had, needing to convince herself just as much as him.

"Maybe," Ell said doubtfully. He grabbed her hand and Miri flashed back to when she'd accessed the Graft during his duel with Half-Mask, remembering how terrified he'd been when the Prince of Darkness had done...whatever it was he'd done to him. Ell must still be terrified now.

As if echoing her thoughts, he said in a small voice, "I'm scared. I can feel it."

"Feel what?"

"You know...*it*. Lurking just beneath the surface. That terrible urge to do things. Things I shouldn't do. Acts no good person should ever do or even *desire* to do."

She gripped his hand tightly before letting it go. All of a sudden, talking didn't seem so important—not compared to everything they were facing. She hadn't seen him in months, and here they were speaking of horrible things. They were things she wanted to speak of, wanted him to open up to her about, but not now. Not right now.

She rolled over, and her hands started roving his body, softly touching his stomach, his chest, and then she felt an urgency pull her up toward his face. Who knew where they would be tomorrow or the day after, but they were here now. Together. Their lips met, and Miri could feel that Ell's fire for her was just as strong as hers. They melded together, and then he was pulling her tunic over her head and crushing her to him. He rolled over and pinned her, and she wrapped her arms around his neck and pulled him close, pressing her lips as fiercely to his as she ever had. Their tongues met, and then she rolled as well, now pinning him against the bedroll with her hips. She could fell Ell smile as they kissed, surprised by the strength she'd gained since they parted ways; all her training with Brie had paid off in an unexpected way. A small giggle bubbled from her lips and Ell echoed it as the urgency slowed and they began to explore each other again after so long apart. They moved together slowly, surely, here moving faster, there slowing again until everything in the world faded away from them and theirs were the only two bodies left. Creation blurred and became unimportant. All that mattered was that they were together. Miri was finally reunited with her mate, and she never planned on letting him go again.

———

SOMETIME LATER—MIRI didn't care to venture a guess as to just how long—shouts of excitement startled the two of them out of their blissful coupling.

"What do you think it is?" she asked Ell, a tiny worm of worry gnawing at her stomach. Enemies couldn't have found them again yet, could they?

"Don't worry, love. That's Rihya's voice, if I'm not mistaken, and it sounds like she's laughing." He cocked his ear toward the tent opening to better hear. More shouts erupted from around them.

"Should we go see what the fuss is about?"

He pulled her back to his side reluctantly. "Let's just stay here. Forever."

She smiled. "If only that were possible. Come on, you are a leader here. We should see what's happening." She stood up and pulled her tunic back over her head. Elliyar let out an exaggerated groan, making her giggle. "Don't worry, there's always later."

"Tonight?" His youthful eagerness reminded her of a forest animal with its ears perked up in excitement.

"Who said anything about waiting that long?" she murmured, leaning down to kiss him thoroughly then straightening back up. "Come on."

He sighed, but this time there was a certain level of contentment to it, a satisfaction she'd not seen in him since they'd come back together. She admired his lean, toned body as he dressed. He wore a dark-green hooded tunic and tight, brown breeches. The clothes were better suited to a forest than this arid southern land.

"Shall we?" Ell extended his hand to her as they ducked through the entrance of the tent. They walked toward the noise and pushed their way through a crowd of people encircling two elves engaged in a contest.

"Best of five!" Rihya cried, her earlier laughter turned to frustration.

"If you wish," Brie answered mockingly and then shot a wink at Ryder who let out a loud guffaw when he caught a glimpse of Rihya's vexed face.

The two paced the distance away from a target and set themselves to throw. Ell and Miri walked up to stand beside Ryder.

"The blonde lost the first match but won the next two. Rihya doesn't know what's happening." His smirk spread to Ell as he watched his sister fondly, but he showed his solidarity nonetheless with a shout of encouragement for his sister.

The two elves eyed each other up and down before Rihya inclined that Brie should throw first. The blonde pixie tossed her hair in an unconcerned fashion and, in a matter of moments, sent three blades whistling through the air, one after another, to strike in and around the middle of the wooden target they had erected.

Rihya eyed the target herself and then threw her three knives. This time, her face lit with satisfaction as they clustered in the very center. "Looks like we're even, Briesom."

Brie made a sour face and Miri was torn as to whom to route for. She loved them both dearly, about as much as she loved anybody after Ell. They marched up and pulled their blades from the wood, Brie tearing hers out a little more forcefully after her loss.

"Last match," Rihya stated.

"Last match," Brie echoed, gazing with renewed focus at the target.

Rihya cast her knives in quick succession and they found their way close to the middle. She shot a worried look at the blonde elf, unsure if her turn was good enough.

Brie stepped up and took her time this round. She threw one knife and it sailed gracefully through the air to stick quivering in the very center of the target. She threw another and it struck close. Rihya's face fell as she saw her imminent loss. A look of surprise was there, as well. She was not used to being outshone when it came to short-blade work.

Ryder laughed again. "Look at her face. Back from the dead, but she can't win this. This will be teasing fodder for days!" The gleeful look on his face made Miri giggle. Ryder and Rihya ribbed each other at every chance they got.

In his exuberance, Ell's cousin let out a loud, "Come on, Brie!" But his shout was right in the midst of Brie's throwing motion. Her eyes jerked to the side as if to see who'd yelled so forcefully on her behalf, but then she tried to refocus all in the fraction of a moment that it took to throw a knife. She couldn't quite manage it. Her cast was off, and the knife spun awkwardly through the air, clattering off the target without even embedding itself in the wood. Rihya shot a satisfied glance at a now-glum Ryder as Brie shot him a disgusted look and shook her blonde head.

"Whoops," Ryder muttered and then shook it off with a laugh. "Oh well, at least we know that someone other than you, Ell, can give Rihya a run when it comes to knife work."

Brie still looked frustrated as she pulled her two blades from the wood and grudgingly congratulated Rihya for the victory, but Miri noticed she sent a covert, less-than-angry glance at Ryder, appraising Ell's tall cousin. Miri covered a smile with the hand that wasn't holding Ell's.

"What is it?" Ell asked.

She laughed. "Nothing." She would keep her observations to herself for now.

"Care for a bout?" A smooth, regal voice asked from behind them.

Ell turned with Miri, and they dropped each other's hands. Aldashir stood close and offered a sword to Ell, hilt first. Miri could just see his standard flapping in the breeze from the very top of the main mast of his warship in the harbor below. The flag was a black rose set against a red river framed by more black.

Ell paused before taking it, and Miri could practically see him weighing up the costs and benefits of saying yes or no to the prince. In the end, he seemed to decide it might be a good idea to foster good will between the two factions of elves.

"Are you so eager to fight me again?" Ell asked Aldashir, his mouth twitching into a half-smile.

"I yearn for a fair fight," he responded.

"And last time was not fair?" Miri asked, leaping unnecessarily to Ell's defense. She had watched the fight from above the fray with the archers. She knew Ell had not cheated in any way—lost control, yes, but not cheated.

"I meant no offense, Miriyah. I simply am referring to the fact that your mate possesses abilities the likes of which I do not and never will. One-on-one we can never be even. I was hoping for a mock duel between us, one in which he doesn't make use of any powers beyond the normal for any elf such as I." The prince finished with a half-apologetic smile upon his face, and it was more than enough to smooth over any ruffling Miri had felt at the insinuation that Ell was less than honorable. She decided she liked Aldashir, and it was nothing to do with the fact that Rihya was quite obviously smitten with him. Well, maybe it had everything to do with that, but after all, sisters had to stick together.

Ell hefted the long blade in his hand and swung it lazily a few times. "I prefer daggers," he said simply.

"Ah yes, much like your sister. I noticed. But perhaps for the sake of entertainment we can give our two groups a sword-on-sword show?"

Ell nodded in agreement and stepped into the circle that had readily been forming once onlookers realized what was about to occur. Aldashir stepped in to the circle, as well, and the two warriors began limbering up with stretches and swipes of the swords through the air. Miri was relieved to see that Ell looked calm rather than the twisted mask of fury he'd worn during the battle. That side of him had actually frightened her, although she would never show that or admit it to him. It would break him if she did.

A few shouts of encouragement from both factions echoed into the odd stillness that preceded the duel, but before long chatter began to ring out again and certain elves began taking bets on who would win in what was already being tipped to be a 'fair' fight. Miri wished they were using practice blades instead of freshly sharpened weapons, but she knew there was enough Source Water—the healing water that could be found at the Source far to the north in Verdantihya, the ruined capital of Andalaya—in the camp to heal just about any wound Ell might sustain in a practice fight.

Arendahl stepped into the circle, nominating himself to officiate, and no one dared dispute. The oldest elf by far between both factions, there were many things in which he got his way, most people not having the heart or the courage to contest with his iron will.

"How will you measure? First to disarm? First to draw blood?" The old, greying elf directed his question at the air between Aldashir and Ell.

The two warriors looked at each other and, in unison, they both shrugged. "First to...win?" Aldashir proposed rather nebulously. Ell grinned the first genuine smile that Miri had seen him send the Departed's way and agreed. They touched swords, crossing them before waiting for Arendahl's mark.

"Ready, begin!" Arendahl shouted, and they both leaped away from one another into a dueling stance, legs bent and ready to move, swords at the ready.

They circled one another cautiously and parried a few almost lazy strokes of the sword, testing one another, each feeling his opponent out. Miri saw a look of enjoyment upon Ell's face, and it was mirrored by Aldashir's. They were warriors, born for the fight whether it was a real battle or a mock duel.

Still they circled and tested, but their feints and thrusts grew quicker and their transitions more rapid. One would lunge forward and press the other only for the second to recover and return the same. They were more evenly matched than Miri would have guessed. Ell didn't tap his powers, but he had always been a great fighter. His quickness gave him the edge over most opponents, but Aldashir seemed to be his match. They danced together, their duel eliciting *oohs* and *ahhs* from the bystanders as sparks flashed from where their weapons clashed. Miri glanced over and saw an excited look in Rihya's eyes.

The duel went on and on until Aldashir inflicted a shallow cut to Ell's shoulder. Ell stepped away and held up a hand for a pause. They both stopped, breaths heaving in great, gasping pants.

"Can't have a good tunic ruined by a duel," Ell chuckled with another genuine smile, and Aldashir grinned an understanding response. Ell quickly pulled the hooded tunic up and over his head and tossed it aside just as Aldashir did at the same time. There was an audible gasp from the crowd. Ell looked around in confusion for a moment before realizing what he'd done. The very thing he'd been hiding from his family he'd just exposed to the entire army in a moment of forgetfulness. It was as though letting go and enjoying the duel had caused him to forget what he'd been focusing on for so long.

Miri had seen Ell's lean, muscled torso only minutes ago in their tent, but Ell's face darkened as he saw Aldashir along with both the northern and southern factions staring in horror at his wounds. The ugly, black covered-hole in his chest left behind from a hideous puncture wound, and the thick, raised scar along his ribs glared out at the crowd. The dark prince muttered a few choice curses and nervously watched Ell the way one would watch something extremely dangerous. He muttered a few things under his breath, and Miri could swear she heard him say something that sounded like 'Spectralist', but she did not know what that meant.

"Courtesy of your brother," Ell muttered, all light and enjoyment gone from his face as he reluctantly squared off again with Aldashir. There was no hiding now. He made no move to pick up his tunic and dress again.

"Well, shall we continue?" he prompted as if impatient to be done with what he had only moments before been enjoying. A trickle of red ran down his arm from the shallow gash on his shoulder. *But wait, is that a hint of black mixed into the red of his blood?* Miri felt chilled.

Aldashir resumed the ready stance and they recommenced their duel, but the tone was different now. The good humor was gone, and they refocused their efforts in a different way, both striving to best the other, all while the crowd's mutters increased—coming from both northern and southern factions. Perhaps Ell had been right to hide his blackened scars for so long if the elves he led were to grow so unsettled by seeing them.

Miri chanced a glance at Ell's family and saw worry in the weathered creases of his parents and sister's faces. Surprisingly, or perhaps not, only Rihya looked unfazed, staring at Ell with a strong look of faith on her face. Miri could have kissed her for the belief she had in her brother. He would need to lean on that confidence.

Ell and Aldashir circled around one another again, the duel growing fiercer, both fighting in earnest to win. What had been a dance, a musical clash of blades in the sunlight, was now more reminiscent of two snakes fighting to stay alive, fighting to vanquish one another. Both inflicted shallow cuts—nothing serious—until finally in one long, drawn-out rally of swords and strokes, moves and countermoves, they both swept in at each other and ended with their sword tips pressed to each other's throat.

"So, a tie," Arendahl declared quickly, seeming almost eager to end the match and get Ell back into his tunic and away from the eyes resting upon his scarred torso.

"Well fought," Ell murmured.

"And you," Aldashir responded.

Miri limped forward and pressed a waterskin of Source Water that she had procured when the duel began into Ell's hands, and he drank deeply of the mystical liquid. Miri saw a few of his smallest cuts vanish and the larger cuts begin to grow back together. *Am I imagining it, or is it happening more slowly than it usually does?* A murmur of unease from some of the nearest onlookers confirmed her worries. Eventually, however, the small cuts closed completely. Ell bent over to grab his tunic and put it back on, eager to get out from under the scrutiny of the watching elves.

He thrust the waterskin toward Aldashir as an afterthought, Miri guessed, since he barely seemed to be paying attention, preoccupied as he was with new worries. Aldashir grasped the waterskin thankfully and poured a long drink down his throat.

Silence so deafening it could have been loud pierced the air. Every eye turned to watch the dark prince. Ell stared, and Miri gazed incredulously as Aldashir drank. His wounds were closing! How could that be? The Departed had severed their link with the land—with Creation—long ago, so the Source Water shouldn't heal him. Slake his thirst like normal water, maybe, but not heal him.

And yet it did.

Rihya stepped numbly to Aldashir's side as the prince stared in wonderment at the small cuts and wounds closing all across his arms and chest.

"What are you now?" Rihya asked, clearly thinking out loud.

"What do you mean?" he asked, still marveling at his healing flesh.

Rihya took the waterskin and swallowed a big gulp of the substance, as if pausing to drink allowed her to think. Whether she needed to do so due to nerves or excitement Miri was not sure.

"I mean, if you're healing—if the Source is healing you—then can you even be called 'Departed' anymore?"

Her statement echoed out across the courtyard louder than she'd anticipated. The question rang unanswered into the sunlit sky. Nobody had the courage to venture a guess as to the answer.

CHAPTER NINE

Ell was stunned. Aldashir was healing. But did that mean all Departed could be healed by Creation. Lore said that when the great schism happened, and the southern elves had broken away from the north centuries ago, they had forsworn their connection to the land, to Creation. They had *departed* from the land. Perhaps that lost connection to their world was not as lost as everyone had thought.

He started to walk toward Aldashir to talk with him about what had just happened, but the prince was glancing nervously his way and whispering furiously to Rihya. It seemed he was much more concerned with Ell's condition than his own.

He heard a few urgent whispers of the conversation between his sister and the dark prince. "He's fine, really," Rihya was arguing half-heartedly.

"He's not. I promise you. Those scars! I've only seen their like on my father and younger brother. The Black Water Well does not work to heal just anyone with the Blackness in such a manner. And did you see during the battle there were wisps of smoke coming from his fingertips? I spoke with some of the pirates who claim his touch can cause disease, now—that they witnessed it with their very eyes during the revolt on the human continent."

Rihya shot the prince a dark look. "Well, what are you suggesting?"

Aldashir sighed. "I don't know, Valerihya. I want your brother to be well, for your sake and for everyone who counts upon him. But I have a strict code within The Thousand. We do not allow anyone who has been touched by the Blackness to work side by side with us. And Ell is clearly more...he may even be like my brother and father by now. A Spectralist."

"You can't leave! You just joined us." Rihya's voice sounded particularly small in Ell's ears. Miri stepped up beside him, listening alongside him to their whispered conversation.

"I—I do not want to, Valerihya."

"Promise me you won't leave. We'll figure this out. We always manage to do so." Rihya had adopted her bullying voice; it was the tone she used when asking and being polite was not going her way.

The prince stared at her for a long moment before leaning in close and saying, "Fine. I give you my word. I'll not take my support away."

"Good." Rihya nodded in satisfaction.

Ell had heard enough. Rihya might have just saved one ally, but he had enough to contend with even within his own faction.

"Let's go," Miri urged, tugging on his arm, seemingly as eager as he was to get out from under the watchful eyes of the other elves.

And both sides were indeed watching him. Dark elves peered over nervously while the Highest—Ell's own kin—looked at him as if he were something they'd never seen before, and not in the good way like when he'd first manifested his powers as a Water Caller.

They were making their way out of the crowd and back toward their private tent when Arendahl, Adan, and Dacunda waylaid them.

"We need to speak, son," Ell's father said.

He nodded. "All right." He then paused so that they could start.

"We are concerned the extent of your...condition is worse than we first realized," Adan told him. "Is it wise to go directly to the source of that condition?"

"You don't think we should move on Black Water Well," Ell stated, reading their direction of thought.

"Don't get defensive, boy, we're on your side," Arendahl barked.

Ell gritted his teeth. The last thing he wanted was to argue with these three right now. "I get that you're concerned, but I feel it—this is the right decision. We should destroy the Black Water Well."

"And how do you even propose to do such a thing?" Arendahl cocked his head in question.

Ell floundered. "I don't know, I'll..." Finally, he clamped his mouth shut, as no answer was readily arriving.

"There is no shame in not knowing, Elliyar, but there is shame in needlessly risking the lives of your warriors," Dacunda cautioned.

That did it. Ell felt the rage he'd bottled up about what Aldashir had told him concerning Half-Mask and the opposite source threatening to burst forth. "It's not needless! How many times have I done the right thing by trusting my instincts? You said we would never rescue my father," he shot this sentence at Dacunda and Arendahl. Then he turned to Adan. "And you, Father, even after we rescued you from Dark Harbor, you fought against my decision to attempt to cross the Fracture, saying it was pointless and would end in failure—in suicide! But look, Mother and Delle are here today." Ell's father and uncle grimaced slightly as if shamed by his rightful accusations.

Arendahl, however, was not so easily cowed. "Luck runs out eventually, boy." His steel-grey eyes bored into Ell's.

"I can do this." He said each word slowly and forcefully. And he could; something deep inside him knew it. Ell ignored the teeny-tiny little voice that was buried even deeper than instinct, the one that whispered from the dark part of him, the part that had felt an inexplicable call to the opposite source ever since Aldashir had mentioned it.

"You've been blowing the horn for Ell all over Andalaya for months now, Arendahl. You can't thrust leadership upon Ell and then expect him not to make decisions," Miri piped up to his side. Ell looked at her, glad of her support. Arendahl stared at her keenly but didn't respond. And suddenly, Ell agreed with her, totally and completely. He was done having his actions, his thoughts, and his body scrutinized. They either trusted him or they didn't.

"Look, this is what I'm proposing. We marshal our forces—what we have here combined with what Aldashir can muster—and move on the Midnight Cove. We get in close and attack. I destroy the opposite source, and we'll have struck an astronomical blow against the enemy. The opposite source is how the King of the South and Half-Mask are creating Unsired, after all. That's my plan, so either fall in line or oust me from command. Either way, I'm done answering your questions at every turn."

Adan put a hand on Ell's shoulder, and Dacunda was not far behind in his support. "We are with you, Elliyar. We are just worried. Besides, you're a good leader. I'm proud to follow you." Dacunda echoed his assent.

Arendahl however, stared at Ell with an unsettled look upon his face. Finally he spoke. "I am with you also, boy, but remember," the old elf held up a cautionary finger then continued, "just because you lead does not give you the right to absolute control. If you truly believe that it does, then that is just one more thing about you that worries me." And with that, the grey-haired elf turned on his heel and strode away, leaving Ell to stew on what he'd just said.

Ell shook off his annoyance at Arendahl. "We continue as planned, then. We strike camp at first light tomorrow and sail toward the Enclaves. We should be able to spread our warriors between Piripeos' ship and those that the prince brought with him."

"What of the human ships? Would they not serve?" Dacunda proposed.

Adan shook his head before Ell could respond. "No, brother, the human ships would draw too many eyes in the south seas near the Enclaves. We cannot do with unwanted attention. Our plan hinges on traveling under the prince's known banners to allow our small force to get within striking distance of the Midnight Cove."

Dacunda nodded. "Done, then. I'll make sure that Iyonei and her people are ready."

Then it was just Ell and Miri again. He reached out for her hand; he needed her strength now. They strolled together back to their tent where they collapsed onto the bedroll side by side. Thoughts whirled around Ell's mind. Doubts, fears, desires, beliefs, all warring against one another. He'd spoken strongly to the others, but was he really doing the right thing?

Miri broke his agitated silence. "You know I believe in you, Ell. I am with you all the way to whatever comes."

That sounded ominously like the way she talked before she chastised him for something. "All right," he murmured, waiting for the hammer to drop.

"I stuck up for you when they were questioning you, but that doesn't mean I think you should ignore their counsel. Maybe Arendahl was right. A leader shouldn't grasp too hard to keep absolute control of things."

Ell sighed. "I heed counsel." The last thing he wanted was Miri against him. He told himself that his voice didn't sound petulant.

"Relax, Ell, I know you do. Sometimes. But at other times you don't. Tell me, why do you really want to march on the Midnight Cove?"

"I already told you and everyone else, I want to destroy it." He rolled over onto his side so he could see her as they spoke. She lay on her back, golden hair braided at the wings of her head and wrapped back like a crown, the rest of her hair cascading down her back and spread out around her head. Her features were beautiful, but just slightly less refined than most elves—her nose just wide enough that it would never be called 'elegant'. But she was still stunning, perfectly imperfect. Perfect to him.

She shook her head and reached a hand up to lovingly touch his face. "I know when you're lying, or at least telling only part of the truth."

Ell swallowed. So she wanted to know, did she? Fine, he would tell her. "I do want to destroy it because it will hurt our foes. But you're right, there's more." She waited expectantly as Ell struggled to find the words for what he only barely understood himself. "I also want to destroy it...for me."

"What do you mean, love?"

He sighed. Voicing this was hard, but the secret was well and truly out now. No point in hiding it anymore. "There's something wrong inside me, something...off. Don't disagree," he cut her off before she could speak, having already opened her mouth to object. "I know you've noticed it, whether through the Graft or like everyone else by simply watching me."

"Fine. Yes. It's the reason I convinced Arendahl to meet you down here. I Grafted into your head during the revolt and noticed some worrying differences," she admitted. Ell loved her for putting it so delicately. *Worrying differences*. Not the Blackness, not that he was possibly transforming into an Unsired, or worse, a Spectralist—whatever that was exactly.

She seemed to sense his vulnerability and pulled him close into an embrace. "I'll never leave you. I made up my mind this autumn when we were apart that I'd never let us be separated again. Crippled or not, you're stuck with me," she teased.

He tried to laugh, but a half-sob tore from his chest instead. He stifled the fear and pain and anxiety. He didn't want to cry in front of her again, not so soon after the last time. "Well, I need you," he mumbled, his face pressed into her neck as she held him close. "I need you more than ever."

"I know, and I'm not going anywhere."

Ell pulled out of the embrace and braced himself on an elbow and stared down at her. Hope tugged and fought at the worry in his chest. "What I was trying to tell you a moment ago is that I want to destroy the opposite source for *me*. I can't help but hope that if I can manage to destroy Black Water Well somehow, then maybe I'll—I don't know, cure myself or something? Almost like if I can destroy it, it will somehow be enough to fix me."

"Do you really believe that?" Miri breathed.

Ell shrugged self-consciously. It was hard to even speak of this. The darkness in his soul implanted by Half-Mask felt shameful, like something to hide. But he had to stop hiding from Miri. He couldn't hide his vulnerabilities from her anymore. Besides, he wasn't sure if it was even possible now. Her ability with the Graft seemed to be improving, and that gave her access to his mind in a way that he had no control over.

"We can only hope," he said, the disquiet in his head an equal balance to the hope.

———

THE NEXT MORNING, the camp packed up. Tensions were high between the two factions of elves. It was as if the revelation of the extent of Ell's condition during the duel yesterday had caused some of the goodwill between them to revert back to suspicion. The Departed reluctantly followed Aldashir who had been convinced by Rihya that Ell was still worth siding with, but their eyes were clouded with doubts and mistrust. Likewise, the Highest who looked at Ell didn't seem to appraise him much differently, but they all looked at each other the same way. It was a mess, but it hadn't completely fallen apart yet. There would be time to fix it as they sailed. He hoped there would be, anyway.

Ell boarded the prince's warship instead of Piripeos' smaller smuggler's vessel. His family boarded along with him. The leaders needed to be on the ship together to be able to formulate plans for what lay ahead. They set sail with the morning sun lighting up the walls of Akan Deraiya. The Shining City, illuminated their backs as they started the journey toward The Point first to enlist the rest of Aldashir's men, and then on toward the Midnight Cove and the Black Water Well that lay within it.

Ell stood at the prow of the ship, staring ahead as their course swung slowly to the south.

"Your sister likes the prow, as well. I've always preferred the captain's deck myself." Aldashir had walked up silently next to Ell and spoke over the sound of waves lapping against the hull of the ship.

Ell nodded. "It's something about being in the vanguard, I think. She never liked waiting for anything, always wanted to be first—in arguments, in contests, and especially into battle."

"She is fierce, Valerihya." Aldashir spoke with a half-smile upon his face.

Ell turned his head to look at the prince. "Are we good?"

"How do you mean?"

"I mean, you sounded pretty opposed to our recent alliance after yesterday's duel."

"Ah, you overheard my discussion with your sister." The prince was courteous enough not to call it eavesdropping. Ell nodded. "It was a knee-jerk reaction born out of years of habit, but your sister convinced me otherwise. I am still with you."

"Good," he said, relieved, "because we cannot hope to do this without you."

"I know. But you must promise me something." Aldashir put a hand on Ell's shoulder, the touch friendly and a reassurance of strength while at the same time the iron grip hinted at a warning.

"What?" Ell asked.

"You must swear to fight it."

"'It'?"

"You know what I speak of: the Blackness. You must fight it with every ounce of your being. I do not want to fasten my ship to an already sinking vessel." The prince's allegory was made all the more poignant as their small fleet struck toward the southern seas.

"I *am* fighting. I've been fighting for months now," Ell told him, again self-conscious.

"Months!" the prince exclaimed in astonishment.

"What?"

"Nothing, it's just that the Blackness usually takes much less time to secure its hold on a person." Aldashir gazed at him uncertainly, and Ell wasn't sure if it was a good or bad look this time. He chose to think that it was good.

Ell turned his gaze back to the ocean before them. The ship rose and fell on the light swells of a calm, late-autumn sea. So, he'd already resisted longer than most. That boded well, didn't it? It was just about the best news he'd heard regarding his condition in a long time. He allowed himself to smile. Perhaps he'd beat it yet.

CHAPTER TEN

The-elf-who-had-once-been-Silverfist slunk through the Lower Forest. That was how he thought of himself now: *once* Silverfist and *once* an elf. He was no longer completely either, now. Instead, he was some kind of hybrid between living and dead. When his re-creators—that was how he thought of them—had supernaturally exhumed his body from the shallow grave in which he'd been left to lie, the-elf-who-had-once-been-Silverfist had clawed his way to the surface. He'd scrabbled and panted for breath, and he had found it. Now, moving rapidly from tree to tree, he had covered as much ground or more than he could have when he had been fully alive. He attributed the endurance he now possessed to the purpose he felt buried inside of him, the purpose that had already been there calling him to wakefulness, beckoning him to leave behind oblivion.

That purpose was hatred.

He hated the name Wintermoon, and yet he sought it. It was his sole purpose in this new existence. Half-Mask and the King of the South—the Spectralists who commanded him—had assured themselves of that. They had ensured that the-elf-who-had-once-been-Silverfist would awaken and feel the pull for revenge that they had reinforced in his new consciousness. As if he had needed reinforcement. He hated the old Wintermoon, but he hated the new Wintermoon even more—the new one had killed him, after all. He had plenty of hate to pull on, more than enough to seek retribution, even without the purpose they had implanted. But the purpose was still there, needed or not, and it called him onward.

Another Spectralist, or something of that kind, flirted with completion to the south, far to the south. And so a hybrid sought another hybrid. There was a certain aptness to it. It was fitting.

The-elf-who-had-once-been-Silverfist passed a small pond and paused for a moment to drink. But before drinking, he knelt and grasped a handful of soil and pressed it to what was left of his nose, remembering the smell of the grave, just to remind himself of who and what he was now. Having done that, he released the soil and cupped a handful of water to his mouth and drank. Some of the water fell through his less-than-fully-fleshed hand, but he managed to get enough. Much of his body was like that—not fully fleshed. Ropey, vine-like skin had grown back during his awakening, but not fully. He gazed into the pond. Some places were without skin, others lacked meat altogether. His cheekbone and jaw protruded from the side of his face, completely uncovered. Well, he supposed it was asking too much for his new existence to be a pretty one.

The-elf-who-had-once-been-Silverfist laughed, and his throat made a ghastly rattling sound as he did so. He stared into the water, appraising himself. He might be unsightly, but vanity had left him for good once he'd awakened with his new purpose. Find Elliyar Wintermoon and destroy him. Kill the boy from the north, despite what kind of sickening hybrid of dark and light he might have become. The-elf-who-had-once-been-Silverfist could feel him from afar, courtesy of the purpose he'd been given, could sense the differences in him, the darkness that swirled and bubbled just beneath Wintermoon's surface.

It would be a pleasure to kill him. The-elf-who-had-once-been-Silverfist cast one last glance at his reflection in the pond before moving on. Ragged, partially decomposed tunic and breeches clung to his diseased-looking body. Yet the strangest thing of all—the oddest thing about his entire appearance, about the body he had awakened to find with his new existence—was the fact that he could see at all. How did one see without eyes? Hollow sockets glared back from his reflection and, despite not being able to explain it, the-elf-who-had-once-been-Silverfist felt satisfaction that, in fact, he *could* see.

Killing the boy would have been ever so much more difficult if he could not see. And so he moved south, picking his pace up to a run. He could feel Wintermoon to the south, and his purpose burned within him, urging him on to catch the boy and kill him.

And so he ran south, toward his new fate, toward his new purpose. A dead elf was going to add to the ranks of the dead. And the name he would add belonged to Wintermoon.

CHAPTER ELEVEN

Miri threw back her head and laughed at something Lliaria had said, obviously enjoying the comment immensely. Delle, Ell's oldest sister—it still felt strange to realize that he had another sister—laughed, as well. Ell leaned against the main mast, watching his new family bond with his old family. Or was it the other way around? Either way, the sight warmed him. He liked seeing Miri put her hand familiarly on his mother's shoulder as they spoke, watching her eyes light up as she listened to Lliaria speak. Ell new she was trying on his behalf. It was important to get to know his parents, after all. But he knew that it was something deeper, too. Miri's parents had died long ago, in the raid that had left her with a crippled leg, the injury too bad to heal properly without a sufficient supply of Source Water to mystically enhance the process. As he watched Miri with his mother, he suspected that she was making up for what she considered a lost opportunity: the majority of her life spent without parents.

"A sight for sore eyes." Adan walked up and nodded toward his wife and Miri.

"Yes," Ell agreed, smiling. "I never would have imagined such a thing would be possible. Just a matter of months ago I believed you all were dead. And now look." He indicated the three women talking across from them.

"You made this happen, son. You should be proud. *I* am proud of you."

He nodded. "We all did, really. I couldn't have done it alone."

"A good leader knows when to accept praise." Adan smiled lightly, and it was almost a strange look on his harsh, weathered face. Years of slavery had hardened him, but slowly he was softening a bit around the edges.

Ell sighed. "I can't shake what Arendahl said before we left Akan Deraiya. Am I holding too tightly to command? Am I even fit to command? What with all the...issues I'm experiencing." Ell tapped his temple self-consciously. It was still hard to speak to anyone other than Miri about what Half-Mask had done. Truthfully, he wasn't sure the others really knew the extent of the battle that was taking place inside of him. He wasn't even sure if he *wanted* them to know.

Adan put both hands on his son's shoulders and turned Ell to face him directly, serious eyes boring into his. "You've taken what an elder said to heart. That's a good thing, Ell. You're young and still learning, but I promise you that you're a good leader."

"I am?"

"Yes. Some leaders work. They make themselves good leaders through the everyday act of giving confidence to their warriors, by holding discipline, and by learning to be better. But some leaders are different. Some leaders have command thrust upon them whether they are ready for it or not. They may not seem to have the experience necessary, yet time and again they manage to do the impossible and inspire those they lead. Neither type of leader is better, but the second kind must make absolutely sure that they surround themselves with wise voices to consult." Adan paused and stared searchingly at Ell as if to see if he was really listening. "Look, son, you might have claimed command —might have fought for it—but it was also thrust upon you when you discovered your powers as a Water Caller. Arendahl has been raising forces for you for months in Andalaya through no request of your own. You've had leadership forced on you because of what you possess, because of your ability to inspire. You are the second type of leader, and you will need to listen to those around you. I'm glad you think so hard about what Arendahl said; it is important to do so, but don't let it shake your belief in yourself." Once finished, he patted Ell's shoulder a bit forcefully.

"All right, Father." Ell paused then said, "Thanks." It came out almost shyly. So, this was what it was like to have a father—someone who unswervingly saw the best in his children, someone who believed in them and told them so when they needed it most. Impulsively, he pulled Adan into a rough embrace.

"What's this?" the older man asked when they broke apart.

"I'm just glad you're back," Ell mumbled.

Adan smiled knowingly and clapped him on the shoulder again. "Come, we should find Arendahl. We have much to consider about what lies ahead."

Ell nodded his agreement. He peered around the deck looking for the old elf. Ell saw Brie and Ryder sharing company, engaged in what looked to be some sort of eating contest. Somehow, against all expectations, the pixie blonde was holding her own against Ell's large cousin. Rihya was standing next to Aldashir, so close they were almost touching, watching the event with a small crowd of Departed. They laughed, and Ell was surprised to see that the normally haughty prince seemed to relax around his sister. Something was happening there.

Adan noticed his gaze. "She is taken with him."

"I do not know if it is wise," Ell said reluctantly.

"And why not?"

"We have been enemies for so long, it just doesn't feel quite...right," he finished lamely.

Adan looked at Ell, then back to Rihya, and then back to Ell. "Your sister, Valerihya, is impetuous, brash, and quick to anger. But she is a good judge of character. You must trust her, I think. Besides, the whispers in Dark Harbor about Half-Mask's elder brother were always surprisingly positive. Most people loved him, much more than they did the King or Half-Mask. Well, those who weren't firmly in Half-Mask's pocket, anyway. Word said he was noble, honest, and fought well to protect the southern seas from the humans. He was a large part of what preserved that tentative alliance between south and east."

"An alliance that harmed *us*," Ell remarked pointedly. "Don't forget that."

"I have not, and will never forget," Adan said strongly. "It cost me twenty years!" He stared at the prince across the deck and spoke without looking at Ell. "However, put yourself in his shoes, Elliyar. He had a duty to his people, to those not corrupted by the taint of the Unsired and the Black Water Well. He protected the southern seas as a show of force to ensure the alliance was necessary for the humans to accept. In the end, it may prove folly not to have opposed his family sooner, but at the time he must have done it out of love for his own kind."

Ell thought, not speaking. If his father could forgive the prince after everything he'd been through these past decades as a slave, then who was Ell to hold a grudge against him? The discussion passed when Ell saw

Arendahl flanked by Dacunda and Iyonei leave his cabin and enter the deck. He pointed them out to his father. Adan and Ell strode across the deck to speak with them.

"Well, boy, any bright ideas on how you plan to destroy this opposite source?" Arendahl was ever-blunt and to the point.

Ell flushed. "Not yet," he said quietly.

"Not yet," the old elf mimicked. "Heh, you'll have to do better than that unless you plan to lead us all to a pointless death in the heart of the southern Enclaves."

Dacunda put a staying arm on the elder's shoulder. "Peace, Arendahl. Elliyar will come up with something. He always does. The plan for how to cross the Fracture came at the last moment." Ell felt a rush of warmth for his uncle almost as strong as the one he'd felt earlier for his father.

"Well, have you even thought about it, boy?" Arendahl ignored Dacunda in typical fashion.

"Honestly, not much. I'm sort of...frightened," Ell confessed, surprised by his own truthfulness.

The old elf's iron gaze softened just slightly. "Scared of what?"

"I know I can destroy the Black Water Well—I can just feel it, that knowing, even if I can't explain it. But I also feel a...a pull, an attraction toward it that comes from the other side of me." Ell danced around verbalizing just exactly what that 'other side' of him was. They knew enough to surmise what he meant without him having to shamefully vocalize it. Iyonei's expression took on one of distaste while Dacunda and Adan exchanged worried looks.

Arendahl just stared at him stoically before responding, "Everyone's got a bit of darkness in them, boy. The trick is just to not let it swallow you whole."

"Yes, but not everyone has *this*," Ell muttered, half-beseeching and half-annoyed that the old elf seemed to be trivializing what he was fighting within himself.

"Being afraid is no excuse not to try and plan for the future. Deal with the fear and press on." Arendahl's slate-grey eyes bored into his. Ell swallowed and then nodded. Arendahl was as good as could be when it came to making a person confront a hard truth.

"I will."

"Good, then," Arendahl barked. "Now I'm going to get a breath of fresh air—alone. I'm sick of Iyonei nattering my ear off about strategies and tactics for when we reach the Midnight Cove as if I've never been in a battle." The old elf snorted as he shot a glance at the one-eyed warrior.

Iyonei flushed but maintained a solid gaze even as Dacunda smiled at Arendahl's ribbing.

Iyonei shook her head as Arendahl walked away to lean over the rail and gaze at the southern shore sliding by in the far distance. "He acts like I am an annoyance," she sputtered angrily.

"He acts like that with everyone," Dacunda tempered her with an allaying hand on her arm. "Don't take it personally."

Iyonei turned her gaze to him and sized him up. "And who are you to tell me what to take personally and what not to?"

Dacunda threw up his hands in vexation. "I don't know why I try!"

Adan chuckled, and a knowing look fleetingly crossed his face. "She does that with everyone, Dac. Don't take it personally," he echoed his exact advice.

Dacunda grimaced sourly and walked away, but Iyonei guffawed, "I like you Adan, more than I like your little brother." She made to stride off, as well, only in a different direction than Dacunda's, but Adan spoke under his breath and stopped her in her tracks.

"Somehow I doubt that," he said softly, almost to himself.

Iyonei turned back to look at him, suspicious, but when he didn't repeat himself or say anything more she strode away to join some of her followers that were onboard. She struck up a conversation with Satiri and Yendil across the deck.

"Father, I want to speak some more with Arendahl. I'll find you later." Ell turned toward the old elf after Adan smiled graciously and offered a quick goodbye.

Ell cautiously walked over to the grey-haired elf. His careful approach didn't yield its desired result, however.

"I thought I made it clear I wanted a moment to myself," Arendahl barked waspishly.

Ell didn't answer, just leaned over the rail and stared at the far coastline along with Arendahl. A few minutes of silence might smooth the old elf out a bit. Ell looked at the mouth of a river on the shore. A muddy, red-brown color spilled out of the mouth and into the ocean, the water acquiring the color of old blood after washing away and eroding the walls of the dirt and clay canyon through which it flowed. Most of the southern coastline was made up of either yellowish or reddish earth and stone. Ell gained a bit more understanding of Aldashir's standard; the red river behind the black rose made more sense, or at least the river part did.

"It's got a strange beauty," Arendahl said finally after Ell had given him a few minutes of quiet. "But I still miss the black bark and grey needles of the Dreampine trees in the north." A longing entered Arendahl's voice as he spoke of their surroundings and the river spilling bloodily out into the southern sea like a wound.

"I miss it, too," Ell murmured. Arendahl grunted in a typically stilted response. They stayed silent for a few more minutes before Arendahl finally seemed ready to break the silence for good.

"All right, boy, out with it. What did you want to speak of?"

"Well, I've been wanting to talk with you for a while now about something that happened during my duel with Half-Mask."

"More about this? I thought we settled your fears earlier," Arendahl said.

Ell shook his head and angled his body to look at the old elf. "No, we did—or as good as can be for now. What I wanted to speak to you about has to do with my abilities as a Water Caller. When the Prince of Darkness touched me, he put a disease on my skin that threatened to destroy me." Ell shuddered as he thought of that moment.

"Same thing you've been doing in battle lately, eh?" Arendahl commented, tactless as ever.

Ell gritted his teeth. "Yes," he forced out.

"No need to get bashful about things now, boy. I know what's going on in you, it's no secret. Just get on with your question."

He nodded and focused on the topic he wished to discuss. "When Half-Mask infected me, I was able to heal myself. I had kind of assumed that wasn't possible, that we could only heal others and had to rely on Source Water to fix our own wounds. I figured that because when you first taught me about healing you wouldn't cut your own hand like you did mine because you said I wasn't able to heal you yet." Ell thought back to months ago before he'd even reached Dark Harbor and freed his father. "I assumed that you'd have let me try if you could heal yourself, even if I wasn't able to."

Arendahl considered him thoughtfully before speaking. "Intuitive guess, boy. And you're right, I couldn't. I've never been able to heal myself with my power. But it could be you're stronger than me—well, actually, we know that's true. I guess I'll have to adjust what I know to be possible and impossible."

Ell felt blood rush to his cheeks, this time from pride rather than embarrassment. The old elf barreled onward: "But this brings up a good point. How long has it been since you trained, boy? Too long, I imagine. We'll start your lessons up again."

"Starting when?" Ell asked.

"Starting now."

————

ELL STARED up at Aldashir's fortress at The Point as it slowly drifted away from them. They had been a few days reaching it from the time he'd started training with Arendahl again, and they'd spent one full day and two nights within its strong walls. The Point's fortress was circular with strong, rounded walls that carried an elegant simplicity. There was a single tall tower standing in its center from which the prince's standard flew, just as it did from his ship. The black rose against the red river framed by black. If Ell was being honest, it was a good standard. There was more beauty in it than those of many of the nobles he'd seen during his days in Dark Harbor.

They had spent the day gazing out over the sea from the walls of the fortress, discussing strategy or, at times, discussing anything other than strategy to give themselves a reprieve from what everyone knew would be dark times ahead. All that day, Aldashir marshaled his soldiers and spoke to them, galvanizing his ranks and assuring that they supported his cause—rebellious as it might seem. Ell was astounded to see that his warriors trusted the prince's word and obeyed him more closely than just about any military force Ell had ever seen.

Rihya stood beside Ell, looking at the fortress as The Point slid away. "It wasn't bad, as far as imprisonment goes," she said, her flippant tone belying the thoughtful expression on her face as she gazed at the harbor.

"No cage can be good, Rihya," Ell murmured, "regardless of how softly you sleep and how well you eat."

"Don't you think I know that?" Rihya's eyes flashed dangerously, a warning sign that he'd come to recognize over the years.

Ell held up his hands defensively. "I meant no offense."

She sniffed. "Did you not? I know you don't like him. I see the wariness with which you stare at him. What must you think of me, over a month spent in his company?"

He put his hand on his sister's shoulder. "Rihya, I could never think of you with anything less than pride. You are the fiercest person I know." He grinned at her, hoping to diffuse whatever situation was threating to boil over between them. He'd just gotten her back, and he didn't think he could bear arguing.

"Why don't you like him?" Rihya pressed, one lip caught pensively between her teeth. He saw her sneak a glance toward the captain's deck where Aldashir was issuing orders.

Ell's eyes narrowed, "Why does it matter so much?"

Rihya shrugged. "You know, I really think he wants you to like him."

Ell laughed a short laugh. "I wonder why." It was not a question.

"Because you lead us in this venture, Ell. Is it so strange that he would want you to like him?"

"Is that the only reason you can think of?"

Rihya had the good grace to at least blush. "It's the most *important* reason," she said a bit more forcefully than was necessary.

"I guess I do like him," Ell admitted. "It just doesn't come naturally, trusting the Departed."

"You cast in your lot with the pirates with relatively little hesitancy," Rihya fired back.

It was Ell's turn to shrug. "It just feels different. The pirates are subversives, actively disobeying our enemies; they hold no love for Half-Mask or the King."

"Neither does Aldashir. Besides, he has convinced a thousand southern warriors to strike out against his father and brother. He's on our side. That cannot have been an easy decision to make. It has to count for something. Could you have made the same choice were your roles reversed?" Rihya was fighting awfully hard on Aldashir's behalf. Ell had a good idea why, too, even if she wasn't ready to admit it to him yet.

"None of my family are Spectralists," Ell said calmly.

"Well, my brother is half of one." He saw the regret on her face as soon as the words had left her mouth.

Ell stiffened and turned to leave. He really didn't want to fight with her now, but that had stung too much. If he stayed, they would have harsh words.

"Wait, Ell, I didn't mean it..."

He turned back. "Are you sure?"

"I promise, I didn't mean it. I don't know why I said that." Rihya reached up to touch his face, but he leaned back slightly. It was still too fresh a wound.

He sighed. "I'll give him a chance, Rihya—in more ways than just being an ally. For you. I just hope you won't feel the need to insult me next time to get me to do so." He turned and walked away, subconsciously searching for Miri. He always looked for her when something went awry.

Ell looked behind the ship and saw double the fleet sailing than that with which they had arrived. Aldashir had left only a small force to defend The Point. He was placing his complete trust in Ell, trusted that Ell could indeed destroy the Black Water Well. Aldashir was holding more than true to his word and his faith in his northern cousins. Ell had to give him respect for those choices.

Ell avoided Rihya for the rest of that day, choosing instead to spend his time with others in his family. He sat and talked with his mother and Miri for an hour or so, traded jokes with Delle who, it turned out, despite her seemingly quiet nature was almost as accomplished a storyteller and jester as Ryder. Ell went a few bouts with his father, matching his own dueling daggers to his father's sword. Finally, he rounded out the afternoon leaning against one rail and speaking with his uncle and Iyonei.

"The humans have numbers still—vastly superior numbers—even on this continent, but I think the revolt in Etheros will draw some of their attention away from us," Dacunda was saying.

Iyonei nodded, as did Ell. "My fingers are itching to take the fight back to them," Iyonei muttered, her fingers actually twitching.

"You'll have your chance to fight soon enough," Ell told her. He knew relatively little about this warrior elf other than the fact that her one good eye was nearly as granite-hard as Arendahl's. She grunted.

"It is good that the revolt occurred, in more than just principle," Dacunda continued. "It is also good that my son leads them. He and Kalabi and those with military experience from before their captivity will allow them to have a better chance of successfully winning their full freedom." There was a note of pride balanced with regret in his voice. "If only there had been more of you, nephew, to render their fight unnecessary and guide us all back across the Fracture."

Ell knew his uncle didn't mean to make him feel guilty, but he did all the same. Dahranian, Kalabi, and countless others he didn't even know fought a war on his behalf—one of his making—and he was a thousand miles away. He tried to shrug away the guilty feeling and focus on the fight ahead.

"You miss him." Iyonei's voice was surprisingly gentle as she turned her eye to Dacunda. He nodded soberly.

"I do. He is like my shadow, always there, always beside me—he even looks like me." Dacunda laughed, though it was still with a note of bitterness.

"If he is anything like his father, he is strong. He can win his way back to your side. And if not, well, if not you will meet him in the next Reality." Again, Ell was surprised by Iyonei's tone.

The warriors' way of looking at life. Ell had been raised by Dacunda to think the same way. This world was the First Reality, where life took place. The Second Reality was a realm of ideas of primal forces: chaos and order, love and hate, good and evil. It was a nebulous reality not easily defined. The Third Reality, what warriors commonly referred to as the next reality, was the life that awaited them all after this one.

Dacunda nodded gratefully and, even more surprisingly, grasped Iyonei's hand in gratitude. It was a quick but unexpected show of emotion, and Ell averted his gaze, not wishing to intrude. Footsteps sounded, and he turned his head to see who was approaching. Aldashir strode confidently toward the three of them, his long, black locks flowing on the sea breeze.

"Elliyar, Dacunda, Iyonei," he said in greeting.

"Aldashir," they greeted in return, voices echoing each other.

"I cannot help but feel uneasy leaving The Point and the southern seas so unguarded," Aldashir said.

"There is no other recourse. The opposite source must be destroyed," Dacunda said firmly, one hand gripping the hilt of his belt knife as if he wished he were already in battle and striving to do so.

Aldashir nodded reluctantly. "But the humans are sending more numbers south. The alliance is all but broken. It won't be long before they invade by sea."

"A problem for another day, Prince. One battle at a time. Besides, they will be busy trying to quell the rebellion led by Dacunda's son," Iyonei added.

And with that, Dacunda and Iyonei bid Ell and the prince farewell before making their way along to speak with Adan and Lliaria. Left alone with just Aldashir, Ell couldn't help but feel uncomfortable.

"So, you know there's no going back, right?" he finally said.

"As you've said before," the prince responded calmly.

"But this time you've emptied your nest, left your border unprotected." Again the unease returned to Aldashir's face, marring the cool confidence bordering on arrogance that was usually there. "What finally convinced you to do so?"

The dark prince thought for a moment, and Ell wondered if perhaps he wouldn't answer. Then, at last, "Apart from your sister?"

Ell was forced to laugh. At least the prince seemed to be more forthright about his emotions and intentions than Rihya. "Yes, apart from my sister—which, by the way, walk carefully there. One wrong step and I'll make sure you regret it."

"I hardly think she needs protecting," the prince responded wryly.

Surprisingly, Ell found himself laughing once more. "True. Well, will you answer my question?" he probed again.

Aldashir inclined his head. "Very well. I suppose all of your words—yours and the rest of your people's, really—convinced me. Especially Valerihya. She helped me see that this fight to destroy the Black Water Well is a blow against the Blackness. That plague is tearing my people apart, turning them into something they are not. If we don't arrest that curse in its tracks, I won't even have a people to rebel against—not in any real sense of the word."

"So you have no choice but to fight with us. I know how that feels." Ell ran one hand back through his wavy blond hair, suddenly bone-weary after all of his years of fighting.

"I guess you do at that," Aldashir agreed, dark eyes showing regret and understanding. "But do you have any idea what it's like having a curse sweep through your people, not knowing how to fight it, not daring to fight it openly, knowing that your very kin will kill you if you do?"

"Not exactly. But I do know what it's like to fight a curse."

Aldashir rolled his shoulders uncomfortably at Ell's mention of the Spectralist powers within him that threatened to break forth at every turn. Yet the prince's discomfort at his comment seemed mixed with a sense of relief in hearing that Ell did understand. Suddenly, Ell realized he really did get it: he understood the difficult situation the prince had been in these last years, what Rihya had been trying to get Ell to see earlier that day.

"You handled it as best you could," Ell volunteered.

"Then why do I still feel shame?" Aldashir practically whispered. "Your land is broken because of mine."

"Sometimes we find ourselves in circumstances where all we can do is fight to survive, strive to make the best choice we can out of a horrible set of options."

Again Aldashir looked at him gratefully. The prince allowed a smile to breach his face. "Are we becoming friends?" he asked half-jokingly.

"Not so fast," Ell responded in pretend shock. "I don't think history is on our side."

"Perhaps not more recent history, but long ago we were one people. In the First Days, we fought the same battle." Aldashir had switched back to a serious tone.

Ell simply nodded and sighed. Those days were long gone, and yet the war of the First Days had returned. The Unsired, Spectralists, and dark creatures sought domination. Who said that the free elves couldn't band together as one once again?

The two of them stared over the rail of the prince's warship, sails cracking in a stiff breeze. Despite everything they faced—despite his condition—Ell couldn't help but feel that perhaps there was a greater cause for hope than he'd previously thought.

And so he stood shoulder to shoulder with Half-Mask's brother and sailed into the setting sun.

CHAPTER TWELVE

She tossed her green hair in the midday sun. It was longer than it usually was, having been months since she'd had the opportunity or the time to cut it to the shorter length that she preferred. Rihya's hair was creeping down past her shoulders—almost. Many warriors of the Highest kept their hair in braids or tails to avoid entanglements while fighting, but Rihya simply kept the length right below her jaw and it seemed to do the trick. For a moment, she paused. What would it be like to have longer hair? Would it soften her features somehow? It seemed like the mindless meanderings of a little girl, not a warrior blooded in more skirmishes and raids than she could count. Her sudden fascination with the length of her hair had absolutely nothing to do with her simultaneous fascination with a certain dark-haired Departed. At least, that was what she told herself.

Aldashir was across the way, all perfect posture and haughty stare, surveying his sailors and soldiers and issuing orders even though hardly an order was necessary since their course was a straight shot toward the Enclaves. It was a voyage any novice sailor could chart. He was tall and, like most Departed, he was thicker in the shoulders and chest than his northern cousins. He had piercing, dark eyes that were insufferably arrogant most of the time. *Most* of the time. Arrogant except for those moments where his noble façade dropped, and he stopped trying to command and control. His lips were full and...*why am I thinking about his lips?* Rihya shook her head to clear it. Unfortunately, Aldashir must have had some type of extra sense, because he glanced across the deck and smirked slightly when he noticed her staring at him. Rihya felt her cheeks color, and a glare replaced the thoughtful look that had been in its place a moment earlier.

She wanted to slap that smirk off his face. And she wanted to grab a handful of his raven-black hair and yank his head in close for a kiss. She glared even harder at the prince, causing his smug look to fade and a quizzical expression to arrive on his face instead. Rihya let out a little sound of vexation. She was annoyed with herself for getting so distracted. It wasn't as if there were a lot of important things to do right now, but still, a seasoned warrior didn't lapse into daydreams. But she was also annoyed with Aldashir—for *lots* of things. She was frustrated with his arrogance, with those knowing smirks of his and the way his hair fell so beautifully around his shoulders and down his back. She was annoyed with his haughty attitude and with the insufferable way he hadn't tried to kiss her since that first time on the ship while sailing to Akan Deraiya. No matter that there hadn't really been a good time to find a moment alone since. Most of all she was angry with Aldashir for making her think these thoughts, for making her feel like a love-struck little girl rather than the warrior she was.

"Staring will not accomplish anything. Or should I say *glaring?*" Her father stepped up silently beside her, and his voice startled her from her thoughts. She turned her glare on Adan.

"I can't imagine what you are talking about," she said loftily after noticing that her firm gaze had no effect on him.

Adan chuckled. "I think we both know that isn't true."

"What isn't true?" Lliaria stepped up beside them, as well. Her mother's footsteps were nearly as quiet as Adan's.

"Nothing!" Rihya said grumpily. Her gaze involuntarily flicked across the deck to the prince. She hurriedly looked away and back at her parents.

Lliaria noticed her glance and made a little knowing sound from the back of her throat. "Ah. I see."

"What?" Rihya asked crossly. Her frustration was rising. This damn ship in the middle of the ocean meant that there were no enemies to fight, no raids or ambushes in which to partake. Adan and Lliaria seemed to think they knew something she didn't. Or, at least, they knew something she didn't want to talk about. Worst of all, that idiot Aldashir hadn't tried to get a moment alone with her in days. Regardless of whether or not he was busy, it was unacceptable.

Lliaria and Adan shared a glance and idly clasped hands as they laughed knowingly together.

"What?" Rihya asked again a bit more loudly.

"Nothing, dear. If you don't want to talk about it or aren't yet ready, then we can save it for another time," her mother murmured comfortingly, cupping one work-callused hand to Rihya's cheek.

It was as if that simple deference to Rihya's wishes, the concern for what she did or didn't want to speak of, broke the dam. These were her parents, after all. She wanted to talk to them, wanted to make up for all the lost time. If she couldn't speak her mind with them, then with whom could she do so?

"It's just, I have no idea what he's thinking, where he stands with us... what he's feeling."

Rihya hated the way her words came out sounding almost like a whine—like a little girl's plaintive statement. Well, it was one more annoyance to chalk up to Aldashir's account. She'd make sure to nick him with a blade at a later date. A little cut here or there went a long way toward reminding people where they stood. She'd been doing it to Ell and her extended family for years. Nothing a sip of Source Water couldn't heal.

"Well, have you asked him?" Lliaria asked, making it sound like the simplest thing in the world.

Rihya looked out over the water and bit her lip. "No, I guess I haven't." She scuffed one foot along the deck.

"You will never know anything unless you speak of it," Adan echoed his mate's sentiments.

Rihya kept biting her lip, thinking. They seemed remarkably all right with this discussion, better than she'd expected. She'd thought that, given their recent history, she might face more opposition from them. More like she had with Ell.

"So, you're all right with..." she trailed off, unable to think of an adult-sounding description of what they were really talking about.

"With what, dear?" Lliaria asked, a look of feigned innocence on her face.

So they were going to make her say it. Rihya exhaled in a long sigh. "With my having...*feelings* for Aldashir."

Adan smiled warmly, eyes twinkling with repressed mirth. "Was that so hard to say?"

"Yes. No. I don't know," Rihya said, her gaze again involuntarily turning back across the deck toward the prince.

"The first step is always admitting to yourself what you feel," Lliaria said. "And no, we do not have a problem with it."

"But you were both held captive for so long that I just thought maybe you *wouldn't* be all right with it."

"There is nothing inherently wrong with the Departed, my daughter. Many have been warped by Half-Mask and his vile opposite source, but at base level they are mostly just ordinary folk trying to scrape by in Dark Harbor or the Enclaves beyond." Adan spoke solemnly and with more compassion than Rihya would have expected from an elf who'd been enslaved by those very people for two long decades.

"Your father is right, Valerihya. Go slowly, get to know this Aldashir better, but for now he is one of us—or we are one of his company. What I mean is, it appears as though we are on the same side."

"I suppose I just thought you'd hate him and be disappointed in me, given that he's family with Half-Mask and the King of the South," Rihya said in a small voice.

"Hate is a big commitment," Adan said, "too big most of the time. Little things we can hold on to because the hate they develop is small. It is always better to let it go, as that's more freeing for your mind and heart, but those little things are manageable. Not so with big offenses. With a large offense, we must either settle the score or let it go completely, otherwise the hate it generates will swallow us whole."

"So you're just letting it go, your enslavement?" Rihya asked incredulously.

But it was Lliaria who answered. "Truthfully, we are probably doing both. We are actively fighting back, striving to strike a blow against those responsible for what was done to us—Half-Mask and the humans."

Adan nodded in agreement. "And we are letting go of the fact that others of the Departed might have unwillingly participated in our enslavement. The prince is an ally now, and we must embrace him as such."

Rihya smiled at her parents in relief, but then a thought made her swallow that smile. "What if he doesn't feel the same way?"

Her parents looked at each other and then back at her. "You'll never know unless you speak with him," her mother told her.

Rihya smiled again. "I'm glad you are back." The statement was a drop in the ocean compared to how happy she really was to have them back in her life.

Adan put his arm around her shoulder. "And I am glad to have you back, dear one. The months spent thinking you had died were harrowing. Besides, your brother is not the same without you by his side. He's less himself without you."

"Oh, so my effect on my brother is the only reason you're glad to have me back?" she teased.

"Of course not, Valerihya!" Adan chided. Apparently, he had taken her joke seriously. "Yet I cannot help but feel that your brother is key to all of this. To our survival."

She nodded somberly and followed her parents' gaze to the distant shape of Ell standing at the prow of the ship outlined by the sun.

Rihya spoke with a firm faith. "He'll come through for us. He always does."

CHAPTER THIRTEEN

Miri limped slowly toward the front of the ship. She'd limped for so long that she hardly noticed her lame leg anymore. Besides, her body felt stronger than it ever had before. She didn't feel frail any longer. It seemed all the training and even fighting she'd done these past months had paid off.

Ahead of her, Miri watched as Ell and Aldashir leaned over the rail. They had been spending more time in each other's company of late. The leaders of the two factions would do well to get along in a situation like this, and both of them seemed to realize that. They were making the effort. Although, Miri wondered whether it was strictly business to Ell or if he perceived Rihya's feelings toward the prince and was striving to make an effort. She stopped and leaned against the front-most mast of the giant warship, close enough to overhear the conversation between the two of them.

"What's it like?" Aldashir was asking.

"What's what like?" Ell responded.

The dark prince ran one hand through his raven locks almost wearily. "You know, the power, the ability. What's it like to be so strong? If only I'd had that kind of power, I could have opposed my family sooner."

"You could have opposed them anyway. We always have a choice," Ell said firmly. Miri winced. Sometimes her mate's passion did away with his tact.

Ell put a hand on the prince's shoulder rather quickly after his statement. "Sorry, that was a bit self-righteous, wasn't it?"

Aldashir had the good grace to laugh it off. "Just a bit. But don't worry, I won't tell anyone. Well, anyway, are you going answer my question?"

Ell paused before speaking. Their backs were to Miri, but she imagined he had that soul-searching gaze he always got when pondering hard what to say.

Finally Ell spoke. "Water Calling—that's what I am, a Water Caller—is like nothing I can truly describe. It's a connection to the land, to everything around me. It makes me stronger. I can tap into all the latent energy in the water all around us. It focuses me, as I am able to bend that power to my will and do specific things, like heal or physically manipulate the water, or send my senses out *through* the water."

"It sounds incredible," Aldashir said wistfully, almost jealously. "It must be wondrous to have control over such a power."

"I only have control some of the time. Used to be I hardly ever could control it. I'm much better now, once I accepted it for who I am and quit fighting to earn the power. But my recent condition makes control of my Water Calling abilities challenging. Or, at least, it makes control of everything challenging: emotions, thoughts, body, all of it, and by extension my powers."

Miri leaned forward, surprised that he was being this open with the prince about his inner struggle. She had thought it was only with her that Ell spoke so openly. Part of her knew she should feel jealous, maybe even a tiny part of her *was* jealous, but mostly she was just glad he was speaking of it instead of bottling his emotions away. Speaking could only help.

Involuntarily, she took a step forward, eager to hear what else her mate had to say about his battle with the darkness swirling within him, but yet again her lame leg betrayed her. Her toe caught, just slightly, and she stumbled. Miri didn't fall—she righted herself before the embarrassment of such a clumsy maneuver—but still, correcting her balance made a noise. Warriors that they were, both their heads whipped around in unison, alert and with their hands on their daggers. Both relaxed when they saw it was only Miri and not a threat. Only they would be so on edge while on a friendly ship in the middle of the sea.

They were a study of contrasts. Ell's wavy, dirty-blond hair wafted in the breeze, the complete opposite to Aldashir's silky, straight black hair that hung below his shoulders. His swarthy skin and eyes stood out next to Ell's northern complexion, like the moon against the night sky.

"Miriyah." Aldashir inclined his head politely, practically brimming with noble courtesy.

"Sorry to interrupt," Miri said, her cheeks still red from the embarrassment of nearly falling over her own feet.

"Don't you mean 'eavesdropping'?" Ell asked, his mouth quirking into a sly smile.

She slapped his shoulder in mock outrage. "Me? Never!"

Ell laughed jovially. "If you say so, love."

Aldashir watched them with a funny expression on his face and, for an instant, Miri couldn't help but think he was imagining what it might be like to speak and act this way with Rihya.

"Did you really know I was listening?" she asked, eyes narrowing shrewdly. Sometimes she wondered just how keen Ell's senses were. A warrior's ears were tuned to their surroundings, and Ell seemed to be even a step further, whether from his Water Calling abilities or not she didn't know.

Again Ell smiled with a self-satisfied look. "Would I lie about this?"

Miri made a noncommittal response in her throat and continued to stare at him, trying to ascertain the truth.

Aldashir bowed to Miri and nodded to Ell. "I believe I will leave you two to yourselves to debate the keenness with which your ears hear each other." The prince showed them both a small smile as he looked at them, and again Miri had the feeling he wasn't really seeing them but himself and another in their stead. "It was a pleasure speaking with you," he said to Ell and then turned and strode away.

Miri leaned one side against the rail and pulled Ell close for a lingering kiss, their mouths sharing heat.

"Did you miss me?" she teased with a giggle.

"You know I always do," he replied sincerely.

"I was surprised to hear you speaking of your powers and your...issues so candidly with the prince."

Ell made a puckered face, his lips grimacing slightly while he stared morosely out to sea. "I guess it's because he knows so much about the Blackness, can tell me things and can provide insight. It makes it easier to speak with him than with others. Besides, it's easier to bear the pity, fear, or distaste when that look is on the face of an acquaintance. Ally though he may be, it is nothing compared to the pain I feel when I see it on the faces of my friends and family."

"Or on mine?" Miri pressed quietly.

"Especially on yours."

"And do I look at you like that often?"

Ell shook his head. "No, but I wonder sometimes if you would were I to speak of these things to you more often."

"So you deliberately avoid speaking of them with me?" she asked, a flash of annoyance entering her voice. She had thought they were past Ell's insecurities surrounding matters such as these.

Ell sighed, picking up on her frustration. "I don't know. Maybe? I'm not trying to hide things from you, it's just…I don't know if I could stand to have you pity me, or worse, fear me."

He turned his gaze away from hers as if he couldn't even look at her. Miri cupped his cheeks and turned his face back, forcing his eyes to meet with hers. "That will never happen. I promise."

Suddenly, Miri felt an overwhelming desire—no, not a desire, a *need*—to get rid of this opposite source, this liquid from the Black Water Well that was polluting Ell's body and mind. She wanted to help him, but she just didn't know how. And then it came to her. She had something within her power that no pair of Joined mates had had in Andalaya for many centuries. Miri had the Graft that she had forged into Ell's consciousness, a one-way link into his mind and emotions; a Graft that she was getting better at accessing every day. Perhaps that could help somehow.

Filled with a new determination, Miri spoke again. "I'm going to access the Graft now." It was not a question. Her firmness seemed to startle Ell, so much so that he didn't argue with her the way that he often did. He still felt uncomfortable with the Graft, didn't want Miri accessing it and entering his mind. Ell felt he needed to protect her from himself. If only he knew how little she needed that type of protection. What she needed was to be let in, fully and completely.

Miri faced him and placed her hands against his temples, feeling the blood flicker and pump through the tiny veins on the sides of his head. Ell closed his eyes as Miri accessed the link. She poured her consciousness through the Graft and into her lover's mind.

Ell was a typhoon. A whirling, swirling, Water Calling cloud of emotions. Fear battled with belief and love, grit and resolve collided with an unrelenting tide of confusion. Yes, confusion wormed its way through everything it touched.

Miri sifted through Ell's soul. There was his love for their cause—their fight for the people of Andalaya. It was a flickering torch fighting an encroaching darkness. She turned her gaze further and saw his burning bonfire of love for her, a beacon against a sea of black. She would have been overwhelmed by it—by the realization of the depth of his emotions for her—if she had not seen it before, had not been warmed by its truth whenever she accessed this link to his mind. And now she was focused, too focused to be distracted even by so pleasant a diversion.

Miri sought. If only she could find the root of the issues. She pushed herself, her consciousness, farther into Ell's mind than she'd ever done before. Miri wasn't even sure what she was doing. It felt a lot like the uncertainty she had felt when she first forged the link, acting on instinct and desire.

Nothing. No hint of an answer awaited her. Still, she pushed harder. She strained her consciousness, her *love*, toward his very core. She sought the seed of darkness that was polluting her fierce lover. And through it all, confusion reigned. Confusion reared its monstrous head and fought against her, almost as if there were truths buried deep within Ell, truths he hadn't yet realized, didn't know and couldn't know until he was ready to confront them. Untold truths that were clouding his thoughts, impairing his abilities to heal himself and purge himself of the Black Water Well source that flowed inside him. It was as if the darkness was sowing seeds of turmoil as it fought to stay alive and overtake him.

Miri gathered herself to push yet deeper into him when hands grasped tightly to her wrists, breaking her concentration. Her eyes popped open in annoyance. Couldn't he stand still for just a moment and let her try to fix him? She *would* fix him.

"Enough, Miri!" Ell gasped for breath, and she was surprised to see him on his knees before her, sweat on his forehead and unease in his eyes.

"It's only been a few minutes. Just give me more time. I know I can find a way to fix you."

Ell stared at her even more uncertainly. "A few minutes? Miri, it has been more like half of an hour."

It was Miri's turn to be confused. How had the time passed in such a way? Ell stood, wobbly on his feet. "Enough," he repeated in a softer voice. "I'm going to go see about some food. I feel famished."

"We're going to do this again. Once a day, I'll try to sort you out somehow by using the Graft." Again, she wasn't asking him. Ell opened his mouth to object, but something in her expression must have quelled him. Reluctant, he nodded.

"Fine. I really am going to get some food now, though."

Miri let him turn and go, watched him walk toward the galley with unsteady legs. "I will fix you," she whispered her promise. And, somehow, she knew that she would.

When Ell had gone, a body dropped lithely down from the rigging above the mast just beside her. Arendahl landed in a graceful crouch and stood up slowly.

"Well, that was interesting," the old elf grunted.

"You saw it all?"

"All of it."

Miri swallowed. "What was I doing to him?"

Arendahl shrugged. "No idea. But one thing I've learned is that when you lose track of time the way you did, it means *something* is happening."

"I didn't hurt him, did I?" Miri asked worriedly.

"Heh, don't know if a bit of injury wouldn't be worth it at this point if you could somehow solve his tainted problem," Arendahl said, alluding to what Half-Mask had done to Ell.

"Arendahl, I don't want to hurt him!" Miri responded, shocked.

The greying elf waved a hand at her. "Relax, girl. I doubt you even could. You care too deeply for him. No, I think your role in all this will be quite the opposite."

"What do you mean?"

He peered at her. "He's the center of this. Every hope we have hangs on him, on his being strong enough, bold enough, powerful and advanced enough in his abilities to defeat the enemy."

"And...?" Miri pressed.

"And I'm not sure he is—or even can be—in his current state," Arendahl answered grimly, his face no less than granite.

"You think we'll lose?" Miri asked, fighting back a hopeless feeling. If even the wisest and most determined elf she knew felt that way, then what were their chances?

Arendahl's eyes held hers in an iron gaze before he spoke. "Before, he was always the one who had to protect you, had to save you. The roles have changed. I can't shake the feeling that what that boy accomplishes from here forward will correlate directly with whatever you manage to set right in him. He's used to saving others, but it's you who will now have to save him somehow—and, by extension, us all."

CHAPTER FOURTEEN

H is Water Calling abilities slipped away from him like water through a fist's grasp. Ell could feel it, the swell of power, that deep pool of potential in his chest, and just as often he felt it trickle through him, evading his ability to tap into it. Ell let out an exasperated sigh at yet another failed attempt at training. It felt like a regression, back to the days when his control over his power was inconsistent at best.

"Again, boy! I never trained a quitter," Arendahl barked, a typical glare on his face.

Ell drew a deep breath and sent his consciousness out, stretching it into the land around him, feeling the water in creation, sensing the tiny particles of Source Water that had traveled through rivers and oceans and rains to make their way even here, so far from Verdantihya and Andalaya. This time, as Ell sought to tap his abilities, it felt like plunging a hand into a pool of water only to realize that the pool was murky and oily, not clear and cool as expected. This sensation had also been happening more often lately. Ell had experienced it when his abilities felt tainted like this. Although he could touch them, they often came with something else—another type of power. A power he was terrified of, yet he was unsure of how long he could resist touching it. There was a seduction to the other side.

Ell let his powers go. He wouldn't risk tapping both sides of himself right now. Not right in front of Arendahl.

"Why are you stopping?"

Ell shrugged uncomfortably. "It's there. They both are, I mean. I can feel my abilities, but if I tap into them now they'll come with something else. You know what I mean—*it*."

Distaste soured Arendahl's face. "Push that part away. You can do this, Elliyar."

He just shook his head. "If I tap them now, they'll come with both. There's no way around it."

"Fine, we'll take a break."

"Unless..." Ell paused, not sure if he even wanted to voice his thought.

The old elf harrumphed noisily, waiting impatiently for Ell to speak. When he didn't, Arendahl rolled his eyes. "Spit it out, boy. Just say what's on your mind."

"Well, what if I did just that—tapped both, I mean. What if I really gave in to both, just for a short while. I'd pull myself back, of course, but it might give me the edge, using both sides of my powers to defeat Half-Mask." Ell hated to admit it, but he feared the Prince of Darkness. Any advantage he could acquire before having another meeting with him would be welcome.

"Could you now?" Arendahl mused.

"I could, I know so!" Ell confirmed, surprised by the note of longing that entered his voice. A cold uncertainty and trepidation balanced his strange eagerness. "I could tap both, and it could give me the edge."

"That's not what I meant. Could you really pull yourself back from that precipice once you stopped fighting it with everything you have?" Arendahl's words sent a shiver down Ell's spine. *Could I?* He wasn't sure. And that uncertainty made him certain the old elf was wise to caution him. *But if that is so, why do I long to try it so badly?*

"You're right, of course. I'll keep it at bay, keep the darkness at arm's length as long as I can," Ell agreed. "Couldn't you just heal me?" A plaintive note entered his tone. That would solve everything.

Arendahl shook his head. "It isn't so easy, boy. You're not sick or injured."

"I'm not? Then what am I?"

"Transforming."

Again, Arendahl's blunt statement sent a chill through Ell. He shrugged it away as best he could. What would become of him?

Arendahl spoke again. "If it were just the change to Unsired—the Blackness, as Aldashir calls it—perhaps I could heal you. Your own experience touching the dead Unsired you killed before you knew of your powers indicates that healing might be possible. Alas, you are something more. You are a Water Caller, and so that change evoked a Spectralist side of you instead, something I have no doubt a simple dose of Source Water or the healing touch of my powers cannot change. No boy, the fix will have to come from within you, I fear. Or within something else that is inside of you." The old elf's eyes flickered quickly toward Miri who was standing a distance away, speaking happily with Lliaria. Those two had taken to each other nearly as quickly as Ell's mother had reconnected with her daughter by blood.

Arendahl's gaze firmly held Ell's eyes again and interrupted his thoughts. "Again. Try again, boy. Maybe this time will be different. Maybe this time your abilities will come without that parasitic power clinging to it." Even Ell could hear the false hope in his voice.

He tried again to no avail. Right now, the two powers dueling within him seemed to be a package deal or none at all. He sighed again, readying himself for another attempt. There was nothing to do but keep trying.

———

Days passed, and their ships made steady progress north and west. Miri was as good as her word and accessed the Graft every day, trying to fix Ell to no avail. Her failures, as she perceived them, left her moodier than normal. Even so, she was still often there with a ready smile or a quick laugh when Ell needed it most. He counted on her more than ever. Sometimes just her presence was enough to offset his own inner struggles.

Ell sat with his family around a few overturned barrels. They had decided to take their meal on deck in the open air rather than in the galley. He spooned a mouthful of spicy stew containing all types of unknown sea creatures into his mouth. If there was one thing these southerners knew it was how to cook. He said as much to Aldashir who had joined them in their meal and now sat between him and Rihya.

"Do you have nothing like this in the north?" the prince asked curiously.

"We do," Rihya said, answering the question instead of Ell, "but the north is all freshness and sweetness. Honey mead instead of fire ale, fruit and nuts and hunted game roasted over an open flame instead of spicy bowls full to the brim with an assortment of sea creatures."

"Perhaps you'll show it to me," Aldashir murmured.

"Yes, I think you would like the north." Lliaria smiled on Rihya's behalf.

Ell didn't think he'd ever seen his sister blush, but she did then. Unfortunately, grimness clouded his thinking. "If we survive this," he interjected.

Aldashir grimaced. "Yes. It will be challenging to complete what we wish to accomplish. Have you plans yet on how you will destroy the Black Water Well?"

Ell swallowed his food. He didn't have any idea how to rid himself of the opposite source in his own veins let alone destroy the place from whence it came. He decided to feign ignorance rather than engage the discussion in that way.

He turned his attention to his father. "Will there be many slaves in the Enclaves? Any upon whom we can count to bolster our numbers?"

Adan also swallowed his bite before speaking. "It is doubtful. There are, of course, slaves all throughout the south—except at The Point," he clarified quickly for Aldashir's benefit, to which the prince inclined his head gratefully. "But they will be in smaller pockets with few of each other to count upon for support and hope. They will likely be as much or more downtrodden than those we encountered in Lu Fang."

Ell nodded somberly, as did Dacunda and Ryder. Iyonei peered at them, confusion darkening her features. "What, did the slaves not wish to revolt in the human city? I thought they fought well? Dahranian even stayed to lead them." She turned her question toward Dacunda who sat next to her. They could often be found in surprisingly close proximity these days. Ell wasn't sure what to make of it.

"He did. They fought well in the end, both the human and elf slaves. But at first they were terrified. Too scared, too subdued to fight. It took the death of a dear elder for them to be sparked into action."

Lliaria joined in. "You cannot understand the hopelessness of bondage, Iyonei. A warrior like you knows only the battle. What would you do if those weapons you cherish so dearly were taken from you?"

"I would never be without weapons," Iyonei said proudly, holding up two clenched fists. "I would fight. Always."

"So you say," Adan said. "But one day, without even realizing it, the enemy you are fighting changes. At first you are filled with zeal to fight the foe that has captured you, but sooner or later you wake up and realize the formidable foe you face is despair and that survival is all you can strive for any longer."

"You were always the bravest of us all, Adan. If you say it is so, then I will take your word for it," Iyonei said, yet the look on her face was still uncertain, as if she couldn't imagine a world in which she gave up her endless battle with the humans and Departed. Ell sometimes forgot that Iyonei, Dacunda, Adan, and Lliaria had all known each other long ago. It was odd to hear them speak of the past in such a way.

The conversation then turned to more mundane things. Ryder and Brie—Ell had learned that the little, blonde elf rarely left Miri's side, so close had they grown these past months—were engaged in a spirited debate about the best weapon to wield. Ryder obviously favored the long-axe that was never far from his grasp, bits of moss clinging along the haft just like many of the northern weapons, reflecting the Highest's connection to the land. Brie, on the other hand, was passionately defending hand axes.

"I could swing twice, three times with mine before you get one away with yours," she said confidently.

"Yes, I agree. My knives make quick work of most foes," Rihya sided with the blonde, and the two shared a grin.

Aldashir sided with Ryder. "When wielded correctly, the reach of a sword or long-axe balances the speed of smaller weapons."

"Hear, hear," Ryder agreed with the prince.

Ell tuned the rest of the conversation out as he stared around the fire. His parents were discussing trivial matters with each other, light and content smiles upon their faces. Miri was leaning against his shoulder, silent as he was, and Iyonei and Dacunda were speaking of Dahranian and what strategies he might be employing in his bid to win true freedom for the slave army. He looked around and couldn't remember a time when he had seen more family or people as good as family all together at once. Arendahl stood nearby and to the side, observing the group, and even his usual stone gaze was softened as he watched. Miri snuggled closer in to Ell, and he enveloped her shoulders in a one-armed grasp.

"Land ho!" a sentry called from the crow's nest above. All conversation ceased, and Ell and his friends and family gazed out across the sunset waters as they approached the southern-most Enclaves. The tides and winds were with them and, as twilight neared, Aldashir's ship and those in the rest of the fleet were carried swiftly toward the land ahead. One bigger island rose up on the right while smaller ones speckled the horizon around it. The fleet would have to disperse slightly to navigate its way through the islands, as many of the channels were too narrow for more than one or two ships to pass through at once.

"Will we be stopped?" Adan asked the prince.

Aldashir shook his head. "My royal standard should be enough to carry us through. For now."

Silence greeted that final statement and all it implied.

They were well and truly in the heart of the southern kingdom now. Their course was set toward the lifeblood of this southern depravity—the Midnight Cove in which the Black Water Well resided—and Ell couldn't help but feel the swelling sensation of destiny as his course carried him toward the fight of his life.

Yet a small part of him—a tiny, insignificant part, one that he shoved away and buried deep down as soon as he felt it—couldn't help but feel much like he did when returning to Andalaya and Verdantihya.

Some small part of Ell's consciousness cried out for the Black Water Well, and he worried that it might grow stronger with each passing league.

CHAPTER FIFTEEN

Dark Harbor was a bustling mass of elves selling wares, picking pockets, and fighting in the muddy streets. Half-Mask loved it. He regretted having to leave the Midnight Cove and Black Water Well behind him, but it was necessary for now. And, for now, he could at least enjoy where he was. As he walked through the teeming streets, he casually backhanded one of a pair of brawlers and sent the elf flying with his additional strength as a Spectralist. Why enjoy something simply by observation when joining in was so much more pleasurable? He turned his gaze to the other street brawler and stalked closer, the elf petrified in fright. Half-Mask wasn't angry at the elf, he simply wanted to feel bone crunching beneath his fist.

The elf moved his lips as if trying speak, but no words came out. The street fell silent as the people of Dark Harbor watched Half-Mask strike him with a vicious blow, leaving a caved-in cavity of skull for his efforts. The elf sank to the ground in a muddled heap. Dead.

Death was a nice, pretty thing, a plaything for one so powerful as he. And he *was* powerful. Half-Mask stepped over the body, his black cloak flowing behind him, his form-fitting black mask covering the left side of his face. The Prince of Darkness swept through the streets, an entourage of soldiers in his wake. Murmurs and whispered warnings preceded him through the capital's crowded thoroughfares. Now that people knew of his arrival, silence greeted him at every corner. No matter; a taste of blood had given him his fill. For now.

His father, the king, was not with him on this venture, having stayed behind in the Midnight Cove. The king rarely left Black Water Well, so addicted was he to the noxiously seductive liquid. Its fumes and droplets were death to many, but they could also change those they wished into their servile brethren, the Unsired.

But no, duties required that Half-Mask pull himself away from the source of such lovely delights. The kingdom required its prince—its true prince, the Prince of Darkness—to attend to matters of war and expansion. The alliance was gone. Half-Mask and the king had both agreed when word arrived of the slave rebellion in Etheros that the humans were weakening. The time was ripe to end the alliance and cement their hold over this continent once and for all. The Highest were scattered, a shattered people just as their kingdom was broken. The humans were the danger now. Even distracted as they were by matters at home, their numbers were still swelling here.

Half-Mask passed guards as he entered his palace grounds. Elves bowed and cowered before him in such a way that they did not even do for his father. He smiled at that thought.

"Prince of Darkness," one particularly brave elf ventured the greeting as Half-Mask walked through the palace doors.

He hardly paid the lowly creature mind as he swept through the entryway and into his throne room.

"My Prince." A soldier approached with a parchment clasped nervously in his hands.

"What is it?" Half-Mask asked.

The soldier proffered the tiny scroll and then quickly took a step back, as if worried of being struck, as if Half-Mask was a snake coiled and ready to strike. The prince unrolled the scroll and read.

"Damn the humans!" he swore in annoyance, crumpling the parchment in his fist. "Never fear, though, a few extra units reinforcing their camps on the eastern shore will make no difference once I awaken our true allies from their slumber."

A dark light gleamed in the warrior's eyes as he eagerly anticipated the same occurrence. "We will crush them behind your leadership, Prince of Darkness."

"Yes, we shall. Although, it is surprising that with the rebellion taking place across the sea they still have men to spare to send west." Half-Mask thumbed one lip as he pondered the news of human reinforcements.

"It is as you said, of no consequence." The warrior bared his filed teeth, emboldened, it seemed, to speak, seeing that Half-Mask had responded to him. "With your guidance, we will be unstoppable."

Half-Mask flicked one hand at the warrior, shooing him away. He had no time for flattery or petty annoyances. He'd come back to strategize on how to oust the humans from the continent, and he meant to begin planning in earnest to see it done, and done by the end of the winter that was fast approaching. Even now, thunder from a winter storm rumbled overhead, shaking the very stones of the palace with its terrific rumbling.

And yet the soldier had not left. Unease entered the warrior's expression. "My Prince, there is more."

"Well, out with it."

He pulled another parchment from a pocket and handed it to the Prince of Darkness. Half-Mask took it and opened it. Reading quietly to himself, he mumbled the words out loud. "My royal brother has deserted The Point and has been seen sailing into the Enclaves with a full fleet not a few days journey from the Midnight Cove!" Half-Mask swore in annoyance more than worry. His brother had always done his duty, keeping their southern border secure, guarding The Point by day and by night, by sea and by land, by sun or by storm. "But why?" Half-Mask mused. "Why would he abandon his post now, when our alliance is finally gone?"

"There is yet one more missive, my Prince." The warrior handed one more parchment over to Half-Mask.

He snatched it viciously from the elf's hand. What could there be to report now? Again, he read aloud, more for his own thinking than for any need to share it with a lowly errand warrior. "What!" he exclaimed. "Another fleet has been gathered in the northern Enclaves and sails south toward the Midnight Cove, as well. Led by whom?" Half-Mask demanded.

"I can only report rumors, my Prince. They say a half-dead elf and a young traitor are at the prow of the lead ship. They say the half-dead elf has gathered a small army on your behalf. He proclaims to be operating under your direction, and none have dared oppose him," the warrior bit out nervously, and Half-Mask had no doubt that reports of Silverfist's current state could not possibly be more gruesome than the reality. The warrior was right to be nervous. The dead had risen and had done so at Half-Mask and his father's command.

Then it hit him.

His brother sailed on Black Water Well. His brother, who never ever abandoned his duty. Yet so did Silverfist and Borian, the traitor, and there was only one reason Silverfist would sail for the Midnight Cove.

"Wintermoon means to take the fight to us," Half-Mask whispered the revelation aloud with a grimace and tore the parchment in half in the process. "And he's turned my own blood against me." It was the only possible solution as to why these two occurrences could happen.

"Prepare me a ship to set sail for the Midnight Cove. I must return at once."

The soldier bowed and then scampered away to do Half-Mask's bidding. It would take Half-Mask longer to reach the Midnight Cove than either of those two fleets. Much longer, since he was farther away than either one, in Dark Harbor. But at least his father was still there. Yet Half-Mask had to try and intercept his foe. Planning against the humans could wait a few weeks longer yet. Now he had to figure out what the boy was planning. The Prince of Darkness felt more nervous than he had in a long time. What could the boy be brewing up this time?

CHAPTER SIXTEEN

The-elf-who-had-once-been-Silverfist felt the salt spray against his face. Or at least what was left of his face. Borian, the young traitor, stood uncomfortably beside him. The youth had met him at a Pillar in the Lower Forest, sent there to work alongside him by their common master.

Silverfist turned his gruesome head to look at the youth. The sea air was tickling the exposed flesh and bone on one cheek uncovered by skin. "Just think, Borian, one day you too could possess all the rewards that I experience for your service to the crown. You, too, could cheat the grave." Silverfist raised a diseased hand and touched the red Traitor's Tears tattooed on Borian's cheek. The boy recoiled in revulsion, and Silverfist rasped a laugh, the sound of death's humor.

"You are certain he is to the south?" Borian dodged responding to Silverfist's statement.

"I feel him ahead of us. Our courses will intersect soon. It is only a matter of days before we meet. And meet we shall, once again, although this time at the well of my deathly rejuvenation." Silverfist touched his own gory cheek as he spoke.

"Good," Borian said through gritted teeth, "we have a score to settle."

"And what did Wintermoon do to earn your wrath? What did he take from you?" Silverfist asked, only managing to summon the most idle form of curiosity. In truth, he could hardly keep his thoughts from the burning purpose within him, the desire, the *need* to end Wintermoon once and for all.

"It's not what, but who," Borian muttered.

The-elf-who-had-once-been Silverfist laughed again, a shuddering, dry sound. "Scorn turned you traitor. At least I had the decency to earn my brand as betrayer for a good reason: victory. Not the childish remonstrations of spurned love."

"I am who I am, and I did what I did. I will not be mocked!" Borian burst out at Silverfist's jabs. The two traitors shared a glare for a moment until Borian seemed to realize just who—or, more accurately, what—he had yelled at. Silverfist's deathly stare was enough to unnerve any elf, even a hardened traitor.

Borian cleared his throat and looked away nervously. "Will we have enough warriors?" He turned to indicate the ships that Silverfist had bullied his way into commandeering in the name of Half-Mask. At least his current physique had some perks in that it terrified most into complying with his wishes even more quickly than they had in his first life.

"I feel him leading even from afar. He has people of his own to command. I know not whether our fleet is enough. But I will kill him, I promise you." Silverfist glared at the young traitor as if he were Wintermoon himself.

Borian's eyes glittered with hatred, as well. "Then on one thing we are in complete agreement. The cursed line of Wintermoon ends at the end of our blades."

"My blade, not yours," Silverfist growled as he clenched his fists. "I'll extinguish his life with my very hands if I have to in order to see it done. Is that clear?"

Borian nodded again, still nervous, and edged farther away from the half-dead elf beside him. South toward the Midnight Cove they raced across the waves, a winter storm at their back.

CHAPTER SEVENTEEN

Rihya and Briesom danced back and forth in a whirling bout of blades and hand axes. Rihya had to admit that whether the little blonde fought with knives or with her hand axes she was difficult to defeat. Each held back just enough to make sure that neither inflicted grave wounds, and in that regard, it was unlike real combat. But for a practice bout, they were remarkably ruthless. A number of small scores and cuts marked their arms and bodies, and there were even one or two cuts to the face.

Rihya ducked into a roll to avoid one slash of a hand axe and came to her feet in a crouch only to find that Brie had anticipated her maneuver, meeting the side of her head with a sharp blow from the haft of her axe. The hit sent Rihya woozily to one knee. She breathed heavily, fighting to regain clarity of mind.

"Are you all right?" Brie asked with concern. They both had reputations for feistiness, and a friendly rivalry had struck up between them in the weeks since they had first met, but they genuinely liked each other. They might treat a practice bout as near combat, but neither wanted the other injured.

Rihya grasped the forearm that Brie extended down to her and let the other elf hoist her to her feet. "I'm fine," she gasped, still out of breath. "Nothing a few sips of Source Water won't cure. Looks like you got me this time." Rihya's mouth twisted ruefully.

"It's only fair, I guess, since you won the last two."

"War's not fair, though," Rihya replied.

Brie shook her head in agreement. "True, it never is. Good thing we aren't at war. I'd not like you as a real foe." The blonde's grin was infectious, and Rihya responded with one of her own while accepting a flask of Source Water from Ryder.

"Not too much; we want to conserve as much as we can. Who knows when we'll be able to replenish our supply again?" Ryder cautioned. "If you hadn't clumsily gotten yourself brained a moment ago, we wouldn't even have to waste any," he teased.

"Oaf!" Rihya shoved him, half-playfully, half in real annoyance. "Don't test me. I'll duel you next, and not for mock if you aren't more careful with your words."

Ryder raised his hands in pretend fright. "I'm terrified."

"She might just have a second set of hands to join her. Two on one would surely tilt the scale so far in our favor that the outcome would be a foregone conclusion." Brie stepped up next to Rihya and faced Ryder with narrowed eyes. An ominous finger tested the edge of her hand axe.

"You females, always sticking together," Ryder muttered. "Oh look, it seems our dear Prince has returned." Ryder was always among the best at seamlessly transitioning away from dangerous topics of conversation.

"Where?" Rihya wanted to curse the eagerness she heard in her own voice at Aldashir's mention. Ryder seemed to notice and barely managed to stifle a snicker.

"There." Brie pointed, one hand extended toward the dock at which they were moored.

They had been anchored in the harbor of the small port for a few hours now. Aldashir had been adamant that it was time to replenish supplies, and he'd also said he wished to glean whatever information he could about the current political climate and what might lay ahead of them. As a royal, he placed much stock in what he called 'the people's climate'. Others in their group had argued against stopping, fearing that to slow down their course toward the Midnight Cove might illicit preemptive resistance to their progress, but Aldashir had assured them that his banners had carried them this far and would continue to do so, at least until they reached the cove that held the Black Water Well. Once there, all bets were off, as it was defended primarily by Unsired— the Blackness, as he called it.

Rihya watched the prince stride forcefully toward his ship, merchants and dockhands and warriors all bowing as he passed. Some even looked as if they bore genuine respect for him, not fear. It was one of the many things that appealed to her about him. This small backwater bay was full of brackish water, and the stink of refuse mixed with the humidity in the air—even in the winter time—and rain-sodden air did little to dampen the stench. Aldashir, however, paid no mind to it, his expression free of any distaste. A ship's captain most of his life, more at home on a deck than on dry land, he was likely used to such smells coming from ports like this. Rihya, on the other hand, was not.

"Try to contain your excitement, cousin," Ryder said as he observed Rihya staring.

She turned dagger eyes on him, and then all in one flash of motion she pulled a knife and nicked him on the arm. It barely drew blood, at least by her standards, but Ryder grimaced in annoyance.

"You are too free with your blades!"

"You should know better than to annoy me," she responded, her voice sweet as honey.

Ryder stuck his hand out toward Brie who still held the flask of Source Water. "A sip, please?"

Brie shook her head in mock concern. "Tsk, tsk. However will you learn your lesson if you are simply allowed to heal yourself? Besides, like you just said, we don't want to 'waste' our supply, do we?"

Ryder growled something unintelligible and stalked off. "For someone so big, he manages to let two small females bully him quite a lot," Rihya laughed.

Brie smiled, but her eyes changed as she stared after him. "Still, he is quite physically impressive, isn't he? I imagine he's quite formidable in a fight."

"You'll have a chance to see for yourself soon, no doubt. I cannot believe we'll be able to travel much farther into the heart of enemy territory without something going wrong. Then it'll be our steel that protects us, not Aldashir's black rose."

"Too true," Brie agreed, "but until then, his rose we have." The pixie elf winked at Rihya and ducked away as she nodded her head toward the approaching Aldashir who had boarded the ship.

Rihya felt her stomach flutter, and she ground her teeth at the sensation. "Prince," she greeted overly formally to try and quell the flutters.

He tilted his head and looked at her quizzically. "You haven't called me that in weeks. Have you forgotten my name?"

"Well, it seems you have forgotten me, so can you truly be surprised?"

The words were out of Rihya's mouth before she had time to think. She felt red flush her cheeks. *Did I really just say that aloud?*

Aldashir's dark face clouded. He looked hurt, then worried, and then simply uncertain. "I meant no offense. I have been busy sending pigeons to the other ships. Corresponding with my captains is a necessity, as is planning strategy."

"I know," Rihya said stiffly. And she *did* know that. She knew all of it, and it made complete sense. But how was someone supposed to tell another that they wanted intimate privacy, that they wanted to share a kiss in the shadows, wanted to be made of equal importance to all other things? She couldn't just come out and say that, could she? Not when she didn't even know where Aldashir stood. Rihya thought back to her parents' advice about simply speaking her mind.

"What is it that you want, then?" he asked softly, taking a step closer, making her breath quicken. His eyes were so dark, and his hair gleamed black like the petals of the real roses that soaked up sunshine in his gardens and inspired the standard that flew from his mast.

Rihya glanced away, seeking something—anything—to anchor her nerves. She'd found herself more nervous around Aldashir lately than she had ever been before. Across the deck, Rihya saw Miri limp quickly toward Ell as he exited the cabin and entered the deck. Miri wrapped her arms around her mate and kissed him soundly.

She might as well just say it. "I want that." The words came out more mumbled than she intended. She could face certain death without flinching, yet somehow speaking her mind to Aldashir had become difficult beyond belief.

"What? A lame leg? Here in the south it's viewed as quite a weakness to be crippled," Aldashir responded densely. Much more densely than she would have expected of him. He was usually quite bright.

"No, you idiot. I want what *they* have, that connection. And besides, I'd be careful of what you say about Miri. I'll not stand to hear ill words spoken of her. Until a few weeks ago, she was the only sister I had. Don't forget there's more to her than meets the eye! Just ask my brother."

"Of course, I meant no disrespect. It was simply an observation," Aldashir placated while reaching for her hands. "So, you really want such a connection? With me?"

"Who else? Have you seen me kissing another?" Rihya shot back, all the fire she usually felt rushing back instead of the nerves she'd known lately.

"No. I just—I wasn't sure you'd want to...kiss me, that is, now that your family is with us. I wasn't sure what they thought of the idea of us being...together." The way Aldashir said that final word almost reverently made Rihya's annoyance melt somewhat. Just a little bit, though.

"Those of them I've spoken to are fine with it. And besides, even if they weren't, I make my own choices. As do you." She slipped her arms around his waist. He really was quite tall.

Aldashir loomed over her. "Are you certain?" he asked quietly.

"Yes. I haven't been this sure of anything in a long time. Besides, I don't think anyone has ever waited so long for a second kiss in the history of this entire world."

The prince laughed and pulled her close, waiting no longer. Their lips met again and again, and before Rihya knew it, he'd managed to shuffle them to a mast she could have sworn was nowhere near where they had been standing and pin her against it. They kissed breathlessly for a time before breaking apart, their faces gaining only a slight separation while their bodies stayed crushed together.

"What does this mean?" Aldashir asked.

"Whatever we want it to," she answered.

He smiled. "Sounds good to me."

They kissed again until they'd spent their fever for the moment. Together, they leaned over a nearby rail, watching the small port bustle with activity. Elves were carrying barrels to and fro, many of them entering the hold of the ship upon which they stood.

"What did you mean by your comment about Miriyah, that there is more to her than I know?"

Rihya sucked in a deep breath, not sure how to answer. It wasn't a secret or anything, but she hardly understood the Graft herself. She had brought it up, though, so she might as well try and explain. "Last summer, not long after she and Ell were Joined, Miri did something no elf had done in centuries—for nearly as long as we'd been waiting for Water Callers to return before Arendahl arrived."

"Go on," Aldashir urged.

"She forged a Graft. It's something generated by her compassion or depth of emotion or something like that. Her love for my brother was strong enough to force a sliver of her consciousness inside of his own and forge it with his. She can access that link to his mind at will now, see through his eyes, feel his emotions and thoughts."

"And will you do the same to me?" The prince nudged her playfully with a teasing look.

"Who said anything about my loving you?" she fired back.

"Do you not?" Aldashir asked, disarmingly sincere. He had a way of jumping from jest to seriousness that left Rihya shocked and breathless at times.

She swallowed. Maybe she did love him, but it felt so big to come right out and say it. Aldashir waved a lazy hand in front of her. "Forget it. It was merely a playful thought." He switched the conversation back to Miri. "That must be a powerful tool, her access to his mind."

"Arendahl thinks so. And I think she's beginning to agree," Rihya said, glad of the change in topic. She might have spoken her mind earlier, but that was a far cry from what the prince was hinting at.

"There are many in your party who possess such mystical signs. They are attributes of an age long gone," Aldashir murmured almost wistfully. "It is enough to make me wonder whether my people were wrong to depart from yours all those years ago. All we have achieved is the Blackness."

Rihya put her hand on his. "What has become of your people makes me hurt for you. But you're with us now, fighting to rectify that."

"Indeed," the prince said.

"Besides, Source Water healed you, so maybe you didn't depart from us as far as you think." She smiled at him, hoping to cheer him up. It seemed to work.

"Perhaps there is hope for us yet. The Thousand are good elves, not like so many in Dark Harbor."

"I *know* there is hope," Rihya said, entwining her fingers with his. "You are proof of the good."

CHAPTER EIGHTEEN

Ell stared overboard as the warship passed through a particularly narrow stretch of channels between smallish islands in the heart of the Enclaves. They'd sailed next to bigger isles with tiny port cities and harbors full of dirty, refuse-filled water, the stench wafting out of the sea and reaching Ell's nose even though they did not drop anchor there. Small keeps and fortresses adorned cliff sides above the ports, refuges for the nobles who ruled their territory on behalf of Half-Mask and the King of the South. Those keeps and fortresses punctuated the incessant, tropical greenery of the Enclaves. These narrow, brackish channels felt like nothing so much as backwater passages. Giant, swimming lizards with teeth protruding from the sides of their mouths slid lazily from the shore into the sea. Rain came down in sheets, pelting the water, dimpling it, and then, as the rain gained force, churning it into a murky, dark blue-green. It wasn't warm any longer, but the rain wasn't freezing cold the way it was in the north during the winter.

Sopping wet, Ell thumbed his dagger hilts, the forearm-length weapons curved slightly at the tip and strapped to his outer thighs. They were steadily moving closer to the Midnight Cove, and Ell still wasn't sure what to do. How was he going to destroy the opposite source—the Black Water Well?

He'd operated like this before, flying into battles without strategy. He'd rescued Miri from the Pillar on nothing more than sheer grit. Ell had guided his people safely across the Fracture not once but twice, and done so on instinct, the knowledge of how to do so coming to him at the final possible moment. But this felt different. This time, he knew that he needed a plan. The Black Water Well wasn't just an obstacle to overcome, it was also inside of him. He needed a plan for how to deal with it. But no plan came. And his anxiety grew.

"We will arrive by this time tomorrow." Aldashir stepped up next to Ell, his dark, hooded cloak pulled up over his head, doing very little to prevent him from getting soaked in the deluge of water falling from the sky.

"At the Midnight Cove?"

"Where else?" the prince responded.

"You are sure we have enough warriors to take the fortress?" Ell asked not for the first time.

Aldashir breathed in deeply. "One never knows for certain in battle, but I like our odds. Especially with you and your greying mentor. You two tip the scales. Even if my father is there, it will still be two on one, and he never liked a fight where the odds aren't in his favor. Without either of you, I'd not likely be so confident."

Ell nodded. He and Arendahl really could determine the outcome of a battle. They had done it before at the battle for Little Vale. "Truly spoken, Aldashir."

"Besides," the prince continued, "we have surprise on our side. My standard flies above the ship. They'll not realize we mean to attack until we draw steel. It'll give us another edge."

"Still, they have the walls on their side," Ell countered grimly.

"I am hoping they'll let a company of my men in the gate when they see me. I'll bring enough to hold it open. It won't be enough to tip them off to our plan, but enough to hold the gate for the rest of you. The battle could be over before it starts if we take the gate from the outset." He spoke with the confidence of an elf who had commanded in many a combat encounter.

"Hope is a dangerous luxury in battle," was all Ell said in response.

"It is." The prince stared out grimly over the water, droplets of rain running down his face, his raven-black hair clinging to his forehead and neck. "But I did not have even a glimmer of it before I met you and your sister. Hope is what got us here, so now it will have to carry us through."

"And what will my sister think of your plan to martyr yourself holding the gates open for the rest of us?"

Aldashir glanced at Ell uncomfortably. "I have not told her."

Ell snorted a laugh. "If I know her, she's probably already figured it out. We'll just have to reach you quickly, I guess, otherwise she'll never forgive me."

The prince chanced a sidelong glance at him. Ell tilted his head up and let the rain pelt his face so hard it hurt before speaking again. "Stop staring at me, Aldashir."

"Forgive me. I just..."

"You just what? Spit it out," Ell interjected and almost laughed at suddenly finding himself sounding so similar to Arendahl.

"You seem all right with it, that's all," Aldashir ventured softly, quietly enough that Ell could barely hear him over the pattering rain.

"With what?" Ell asked.

"You know, with Valerihya and me being together."

Ell sighed. "Not that it would matter to her if I wasn't, but yes, I'm fine with it. I'll admit I've had my reservations about you; your family has been no friend to me. But you're here with us. You've chosen the right side of this conflict. Besides, if I can make friends with a bunch of smugglers and pirates, I'm sure that us being friends falls a long second to that. Anyway, I kind of like you."

"And are we? Friends, I mean."

Ell stared at him before finally nodding. "I think so. Don't you?"

The prince smiled. "I do."

They gazed in silence over the water, staring at a half-sunken ship that protruded from the water near the shoreline. It must have been there a long time, for trees had grown around its wreckage. They were skeletal, barren of leaves in the winter, sticking up out of the water like the fingers of a dead behemoth. The swimming lizards drifted lazily in the water around the shipwreck. *It is not the first we've seen, nor will it be the last*, Ell thought. The heart of the Enclaves was speckled with wrecks old and new. As good of seafarers as the Departed were, the sea and its storms were still a cruel mistress.

Aldashir broke the silence. "We'll only have one chance at this."

"At destroying the opposite source?"

He nodded. "You'll be able to do it, right?"

"I will." The promise echoed hollowly across Ell's tongue. *Will I?* He had no idea of how to do it yet, and he was running out of time to solve the riddle. A darkness flickered in him as he thought about the Black Water Well. Ell wished he could say it wasn't thrill, wasn't excitement about the prospect of seeing the other source, but he couldn't. That would be a lie.

Grimly, he shoved his subconscious down and tried to focus on figuring out a way to destroy the opposite source, the very thing he felt excitement over finding.

————

THE RAIN WAS STILL DESCENDING in waves; it had been since yesterday. Only, today, thunder and lightning had joined it. The swells of the ocean snarled and raised their choppy heads, even in the narrow channels between the Enclaves and islands. Wind whipped through the palms that lined the shores. Vine-covered cliffs on the isles around the channels formed tunnels for the wind to scream through.

"Is this normal for this time of year?" Ell asked.

Aldashir nodded. "Winter storms are common, and this is no different. You simply get used to it in this part of the world."

"Does it ever snow?" Rihya asked as she stood alongside them on the captain's deck.

Aldashir held the tiller in his hands, taking a turn at steering his great warship. Often he left that duty to others, but he claimed to enjoy the feel of the smooth wood beneath his hands from time to time. "Snow?" He cocked his head in confusion, and then a light seemed to flicker in his eyes. "Oh, you mean the frozen water that falls from the sky in the north. No, it's never been cold enough for that this far south. Just gales, thunder and lightning, typhoons, and the endless rain."

"A land without snow sounds sorrowful," Rihya murmured contemplatively.

"I wouldn't know," Aldashir said. "It's not like I have anything for comparison."

Rihya reached over and took his hand. "I'll show you snow someday."

Ell glanced sidelong at the two of them. He'd witnessed them growing significantly closer the past day or so. He supposed he was comfortable with it. He had to be, really. It wasn't like Rihya would ever listen to his counsel on a matter like this. Besides, if he was being honest, he was starting to actually like the prince as more than just an ally. Aldashir was calm and insightful yet ready with a smile or a laugh. And he was good with a blade—there was no questioning his skill. One just had to be able to get beyond his noble haughtiness. Ell figured it was so ingrained that he probably didn't mean to speak with such a formal, arrogant tone at times. Well, Rihya seemed to have found a way past it, so Ell could, too, for her sake. Plus, when it came to it, he trusted Rihya's judgment.

Aldashir had decided to take more personal control of the ship's course today, and his steady hand on the tiller guided the vessel gradually around a bend along the coastline. A cove opened up ahead of them. Ell could see dark, inky-black water seeping out toward the rest of the sea, emanating from the fortress that stood at the cove's heart.

"The contrast is greater in better weather, when the sea around the isle is not so dark, but you can still see the change in color. It's liquid from the Black Water Well seeping out through the very earth and rocks of the isle. We've reached the Midnight Cove," Aldashir said grimly and then called for his second to take over the tiller.

Thunder thrashed in the darkened sky overhead as Aldashir handed the tiller to a capable elf and the three of them descended the stepladder to the main deck. Ell looked behind and saw the fleet gathering behind the head ship. It would be enough to take the fortress. It had to be.

Ell and Aldashir walked with Rihya toward where Arendahl and the rest of Ell's family were gathered. Ell nodded grim greetings to the rest of them. They'd all seen enough battles to know what lay ahead. Of all the group, only Iyonei seemed unconcerned. In fact, she looked positively thrilled at the prospect of a fight, a wild grin plastered to her face as if put there by the sheeting rain that soaked her hair and made the sodden eye patch she bore stick to her socket.

"I've been waiting days for this," Iyonei said with a laugh, one hand gripping the hilt of her sword.

"Well, the wait is over," Aldashir said, and waited to speak further until a few of his commanding Departed officers joined their final meeting before the battle. When the officers arrived, and assumed stoic stances beside and behind him, the prince continued, "It'll be only a matter of minutes before we enter the cove and make port. My ships will follow us but, to avoid suspicion, a bulk of the initial fighting will need to be carried out by us. If too many ships make port at once, it will raise suspicions."

"How do you plan to scale the walls?" Dacunda asked, staring up at the blocky fortress on the rocky shore of the Midnight Cove.

"I don't. If only this ship makes port and I descend with just a small company of my warriors as an honor guard, then the gates will open for me. It is my family, after all, who rule." Aldashir's mouth twisted bitterly. "When we reach the open gate, we'll hold it open. At that point, it becomes a race to see whether the rest of you and my other ships can reach the docks and then the gate in time to take advantage."

Rihya's eyes narrowed. "That will be dangerous. You'll be outnumbered."

Ell put a calming hand on his sister's shoulder, imagining how he'd feel if Miri were the one leading a dangerous mission like that. "Arendahl and I can accompany Aldashir. We can tip the scales our way."

The dark prince shook his head, rain flecking off his hair and face as he did so. "No, you'll stand out. Your fair complexion cannot be hidden."

"We'll wear hoods," Arendahl grunted.

Aldashir again shook his head. "I said no. The entire operation hinges on not having to storm the fortress. The walls are high, and the Midnight Cove is defended more heavily than anywhere except for perhaps Dark Harbor itself. If we fail to gain entrance through the gate, we'll be forced to go over the walls. The loss of life would be unacceptable. It isn't like we have warriors to waste."

Arendahl glanced at Ell who nodded reluctantly. "I suppose that makes sense."

"What? Ell, no! That's too dangerous." Rihya was practically spluttering with worry.

He turned to his sister. "Rihya, the instant Aldashir draws steel, Arendahl and I will be over the side of the ship and onto the dock in a flash. With our enhanced speed, we'll reach his side before you even know it. It'll be enough to keep him safe until the rest of our numbers arrive."

"It had better be." She glared at both Ell and Aldashir as if they were equally at fault. Surprisingly, Aldashir smirked a bit at her and then winked at Ell, actions which annoyed Rihya even further but seemed to somehow dissipate the argument, especially as the prince slipped an arm around her shoulders. Rihya half made to shrug him off as if self-conscious, but in the end, she let his arm linger and even leaned into him. Ell pondered the prince for a moment. He'd diffused Rihya's temper with a smile, an arm, and a wink. Perhaps they were a better match than Ell had given them credit for.

"Very well," Adan summarized, "we wait for Aldashir and his honor guard to hold open the gate, Arendahl and Elliyar jump to their aid, and the rest of us follow as quickly as we can. Then the fighting starts in earnest."

"No, then the *fun* starts," Iyonei corrected him fiercely, still grinning. She turned to Dacunda. "Stick near me, Dac, and I'll show you how to actually have a good time in a fight."

Dacunda stared at her a moment before a slow, small smile crept onto his face. "That doesn't sound half bad, Iyonei." The one-eyed warrior started to smile at him in return until Dacunda continued with a straight face, "Besides, with Dahranian away in Etheros, I'll need a second to watch my back. He usually fills the roll, but you will do."

"Second! I'm not anybody's *second*!" Iyonei spluttered until she noticed the twinkle in his eye. She closed her mouth with a vexed look while Dacunda chuckled.

Ell looked ahead and watched the ship slide closer to port. Black water lapped around the sides of the ship, staining the wood of the hull. Ell saw no fish, no sign of life in the Midnight Cove, and the smell was not like that of a normal dock. No scent of dead sea animals or refuse wafted into the air, only a pungent, smoky, pitchy smell and a hint of the Bonewinds in the air.

Ell and Arendahl shared a glance. Bonewinds meant that the fortress was likely guarded by mostly Unsired—no surprise, really, when Ell considered what Half-Mask wanted to protect within its walls.

The ship docked, and Ell and his northern companions kept hoods up to hide their lighter hair and fair complexion. Aldashir strode purposefully down the gangplank followed by about ten of his most trusted and hardy warriors. No shouts of greeting hailed from the wall above the gate as he approached. An eerie silence hung in the air. Ell tapped his abilities in order to be ready for what was coming. He stretched his consciousness out into the ocean around him and pulled deeply on its vast power. He felt a thousand droplets of rain in the air and drank from their strength, feeling his abilities swell like a reservoir within his chest. And then a thousand more, and a thousand more droplets. Water was all around, and as a Water Caller he tapped into the limitless power of creation at his fingertips. Ell saw Arendahl close his eyes and kneel down, placing his hands against the deck of the ship in the necessary way for him to tap his abilities—an old crutch he'd made sure Ell had avoided when training.

Aldashir and his party came to a stop before the ironbound oak gate. Stillness hung in the air except for the thrashing of the stormy rain, but then the gate creaked and opened. Aldashir stepped swiftly into the grim fortress' open maw. Ell saw steel flash from the prince's sheath in a lightning burst, and he turned to Arendahl and yelled, "Now!"

They leaped over the rail and, with their ability-infused bodies, they took the distance between the ship and the fortress in mere bounds. A ruckus was already rising, vying with the storm for supremacy of noise. The clash of steel and grunts of pain and anger echoed toward Ell from ahead as the prince clashed with his one-time allies. The shouts and war cries of the rest of Aldashir's company of The Thousand as well as Ell's northern brethren followed behind.

Ell reached the gate first and, in a swift motion even as he ran, he freed both his dueling daggers from their sheaths. One tip up and the other gripped with the tip down, he dealt death as he entered the fortress, whirling his body and the forearm-long daggers as he went. Arendahl followed with his sword, and they rushed to the support of the already beleaguered Aldashir. All but three of the prince's companions had already fallen under the onslaught of the defenders, so outnumbered were they. Ell saw him fighting on determinedly, a gash on his thigh already marking his contribution to the battle effort. Aldashir caught sight of Ell and smiled grimly as he and Arendahl swept through the fray. They were faster, stronger, and more dangerous than the rest, and they made the difference for now. Aldashir fell back and caught his breath while Ell and Arendahl wreaked havoc on the attacking Unsired.

Sickly splotches of disease marked the Unsired's bodies. They had a blankness to their eyes and an unpredictable way of moving, a jerkiness of motion that identified them as what they were. They were strong—more powerful than a normal Departed—but they were no match for two Water Callers in full force. Ell screamed defiance at his ancient enemies as he separated hands from limbs, hamstringing and crippling opponents as he spun through the throng of elven bodies. He chanced a glance behind and saw that the rest of their reinforcements had arrived. The Thousand belonging to the prince and Ell's northern companions were mostly disembarked from the ships, and the front line of them had already reached the gate. Rihya was at the fore, her dyed-green hair whipping wildly in the wind. She stood back-to-back with Aldashir and fought the Unsired as they came on.

"Come, boy, they have this handled." Arendahl gripped Ell's shoulder with a strong fist. "Let them attend to the battle, for we have another fight ahead of us. The real fight, the reason we came here."

The Black Water Well.

Ell could smell bitterness in the air. It was a tainted, unfamiliar smell and could only be the opposite source wafting through the cove as it permeated all aspects of the land and water surrounding the isle. Ell nodded to his old mentor and they fought their way forward, cutting a swathe through the once-Departed and now-Unsired who attempted to meet them.

Their opponents fought viciously, methodically, and without fear, but they didn't have the numbers. The Midnight Cove was heavily protected, but it was not large. The fortress did not house more warriors than Ell and Aldashir had brought. Add the two Water Callers to the mix, and the numbers were in favor of Ell's group. And so they killed. Ell and Arendahl sliced their way through the crowd of enemies until a darkened passage appeared beside them.

Ell felt an instinctual pull, and he ducked away from the fighting into the passage without even thinking. Excitement stirred in his breast.

"What is it, boy?" Arendahl asked.

"I—I don't know," Ell stammered, unsure of the sensation.

"I do. You feel it, don't you?"

Ell swallowed almost fearfully. A battle raged around him, screams and the sound of steel clashing with steel tore through the air, and it held no fear for him. Yet the battle within, that darkness Half-Mask had seeded in his soul, terrified him absolutely.

He nodded. "Yes, Arendahl. That must be it. I can feel it. Follow me."

There was no time to waste. Ell wanted to be free of the taint inside him as soon as possible. At least, that was what he told himself. It couldn't be the strange, lust-like sensation he felt at the prospect of actually seeing the Black Water Well.

Ell led Arendahl down the side passage, guided by instinct, guided by whatever dark pull the opposite source was exerting on his body and mind. It might be terrifying, but there was no denying that the pull he felt guiding him was useful; it was like a map through the innermost bowels of the stone fortress. Ell took turns and corridors. He led them down a flight of stairs. They fought their way through three different groups of warriors who were making their way to the main battle near the gate, but a few Unsired couldn't slow them down.

And all the while, the strange pull inside of him grew stronger. He could sense they were growing close. The terror grew too much for him. He stopped, panting.

"What is it?" Arendahl whispered.

"It's too much. I can feel it growing in me. It's like the closer I get the harder it is to contain that side of me," Ell responded.

Arendahl reached to his hip and took out a tiny, emergency flask of Source Water. "Drink this. Perhaps it will help strengthen you and stave off that which you fear."

Ell did as he was told. He downed the small flask's contents with a giant gulp. He noticed no immediate effects but forced himself to slow his breathing. "What if I lose control?" he asked Arendahl.

The old elf stared at him grimly. "Don't."

"But what if I do? What if I can't keep the darkness at bay any longer?"

Arendahl just stared without answering. He jutted his chin forward, indicating that Ell should continue to lead them. Ell took a deep breath and silenced his fears as much as he could. Still, there was no denying that the closer he got to the Black Water Well the more he felt like he was going to lose control. He imagined himself a cauldron of pitch, bubbling and boiling until eventually the darkness—the dark liquid inside him put there by Half-Mask—would eventually boil over and consume him. He shuddered. For a moment, he felt the strange impulse to turn to Arendahl and stick a dagger in his heart. Ell fought the manic feeling down and forced himself to lead them onward to the fortress. Torch-lit walls surrounded them, rough-hewn as if carved from the rock of the island itself. On they went.

He stopped in front of an oaken door. "Here. I can feel it."

Arendahl looked at him and then back to the door. "Well, what are we waiting for?"

Ell put one hand gingerly on the door and pushed. It swung inward, creaking on old hinges. A room opened up before them. It was empty of all except a small, stone well in the middle of the floor, its frame coming up to about mid-thigh. A dark, cloaked shape slumped over the edge of the well as if drunk on its contents. One diseased hand dangled into the liquid, but the hood was pulled up, concealing whoever it was. Ell and Arendahl stepped inside, and their footsteps echoed oddly in a strange stillness. The sounds of battle were long behind them, and quiet pervaded as if they'd reached the eye of a storm.

The figure bolted upright at the noise made by their footsteps, like a sleeper wakened from slumber. The hood fell off the elf's head and revealed a horrifying sight. It was a Departed, but the face was so covered in sores and disease it looked a wonder that there was any skin at all. The disease must have covered his entire body, because the hands that could also be seen were sickly and diseased, protruding from the sleeves of the cloak.

The stupor left the elf's face, and a cunning look of pure evil and arrogance replaced it. "So, two of you," he sneered. "Well, two and a half, right? You're a bit of both now, aren't you?" He directed his comment toward Ell with a ghastly smile upon his pocked face, his eyes looking like nothing so much as two wells of darkness.

"And who are you?" Arendahl murmured, eyeing up his opponent. The old elf took a step away from Ell. When the fight came, it would be best to be able to attack from different angles. Ell sidled the opposite way.

"I am the first. I am the ruler of this land. I am the King of the South," the creature rasped in a deathly voice.

"So, we finally meet," Arendahl said. "This has long been coming."

The king sneered scornfully. "And who would you be that we should meet?"

"I suppose it's of no matter now. You'll be dead soon," Arendahl answered, gripping his hilt tightly and shrugging off the king's disregard.

The king turned his black eyes on Ell. "You're one of us. Mostly. I know you can feel it, can't you? You can feel the Spectralist in you wanting to get out. Let it loose, unleash it! Join us! We could be all-powerful."

Ell gritted his teeth and fought off a wave of darkness that threatened to wash over him from the inside out. He forced it down.

"No, no, no. Don't do that. You must embrace it. At first I thought my son ill-advised to change you, but now I see what a powerful ally you will be. Come, join us." The king reached out a sickly hand toward Ell, beckoning him. His nails were uncut, and blood of some kind speckled the skin.

Ell shook his head, involuntarily taking a step back. "No, I won't."

"Yes," the King of the South purred. "Let go."

"No!" Ell screamed, clenching the hilts of his daggers so tightly that he felt they might never come unstuck from his fists. "Never!"

"Then die!" the king shrieked, and suddenly he pulled a sword loose from a sheath hidden inside his open cloak. He moved smoothly, quickly, serpent-like, switching from his voice full of power and promises to attack in an instant. Just like Half-Mask had when Ell dueled him in the nighttime streets of Dark Harbor.

The king lunged toward Ell, his sword a steel blur as it descended in a killing arch. Ell managed to raise both his blades up and cross them to absorb and then deflect the blow. Steel grinded and sparks flashed. Arendahl darted in from behind the king, seeking a swift end to the fight, but the King of the South spun away too quickly. He moved like a Water Caller, too fast for a normal elf. His black hair hung down his back, the sides of his head shaved. His filed teeth showed through his snarl. Ell and Arendahl advanced together, coordinating a series of attacks, and the three of them dueled their way around the strange chamber in the bowels of the fortress.

Ell ducked a slash and whipped in close to deal a gash to the king's forearm. The king grimaced but delivered a counterstroke and inflicted a gash on Ell's cheek, all the while beating back Arendahl's advances.

"Another scar for you pretty face," the King of the South mocked Ell and the blackened scar Half-Mask had inflicted upon him months ago.

Ell and Arendahl fought on grimly. It was a short but vicious duel. Strikes, blows, and injuries were dealt to all. Ell took another wound to his shoulder while Arendahl was nearly skewered by a particularly quick lunge, barely managing to avoid it and instead taking a graze to his ribs. Despite the king's ability to hold his own against two full-blown Water Callers, inevitably they wore him down. The King of the South took a cut to his leg, Ell nearly able to hamstring him as he so often did his opponents. Arendahl paid his enemy back and delivered a cut to the king's chest.

He screamed in fury, swearing curses at them and their ancestors. Laughing and then screaming. If ever there was a cunning and yet unbalanced elf, it was the King of the South. Every time they grew close to defeating him, the king activated some Spectralist ability. Arendahl delivered a stroke that should have lopped off his arm but, just before contact, a look of concentration crossed the king's face and the arm turned smoky and insubstantial while Arendahl's blade passed through without harm. Again and again, the king avoided their killing strokes by utilizing his smoky power.

But it wasn't without cost. Ell could see him slowing. The king weakened with each use of his powers of insubstantiality. He lost energy. It was only a matter of time. Ell and Arendahl worked in unison, they wore him down and pressed him into a corner of the chamber. A vicious sneer creased the king's face.

"No," he muttered hoarsely, almost to himself. Then he screamed, "I'll not die today!" He snarled at them then threw back his head and laughed maniacally, alternating between cornered beast and mad elf.

"It's over," Ell said, nearly out of breath.

"It's never over!" the king shrieked, and then he summoned a look of even greater concentration. The King of the South dropped his sword as if it meant nothing, as if it was hardly more than a simple tool. He clenched his fists, and a look of immeasurable effort clouded his features. Ell and Arendahl plunged toward his unguarded chest, but as they reached him his entire body flickered into vapor, a smoky version of an elf. He cackled again before wafting through the chamber wall.

"We'll meet again," the king's voice echoed back to them even as he disappeared.

Arendahl swore and banged his fists on the stone wall in rage, but suddenly Ell could hardly think of anything other than the well in the room. The king was gone, fled to survive and fight another day. The battle near the main gate was likely in their favor. And now here he was, finally face to face with it: the Black Water Well.

Ell approached it eagerly, yet almost gingerly, alternating between dark thrill and wary caution.

"Careful, boy. Careful."

Ell ignored the old elf's words and walked all the way up to the stone well as though in a trance. He stared down into its inky depths. Mesmerized by its sickness, its beauty, he reached a hand down to cup the water to his lips. An iron grip stopped him. "What are you doing, Elliyar?"

Ell didn't answer, he just struggled like a child to free himself. He wanted a sip, just a taste. Whatever dark part of him had been buried now reared its ugly head and fought ferociously to break loose. "Let me go, Arendahl!"

"No." Arendahl wrapped him up in a vice grip and held him—a thrashing, fighting Elliyar—until the bout of darkness passed and sanity returned.

Ell shook his head to clear it. What had happened? Was he even in control of himself any longer? "I...I don't know if I can do this," he whispered.

"Tap into your instincts, boy. You always manage to find a solution," Arendahl said, voice full of belief.

"No, it's not that, it's..." but Ell couldn't finish.

The typically impatient Arendahl interjected, "It's what? What is it?"

Anguish forced its way onto Ell's face. "I don't know, it's like I'm not sure I want it to be destroyed now." Again he stared, mesmerized by the liquid. Dark rainbows of half-colors and shades of black swirled together. Again, he reached a hand down.

Arendahl grabbed Ell by the shoulders and shook him. "Get it together, Elliyar! We came here for you to destroy it. Now do it already!"

Ell again pulled back and cleared his head. "I need some air. I can't do this, not right now," he muttered and stumbled away, out of the room and back along the corridor through the heart of the fortress at the Midnight Cove.

"Come back, Elliyar. Come back!" Arendahl's voice echoed as he ran. But all Ell could do was run even harder. All he knew was that he needed air, needed clean air and time to clear his head. Time to think. But think of what? He had wanted this, hadn't he? Wanted the well destroyed and gone.

But did he really? He wasn't sure any more. It was so darkly sweet and seductive. All of a sudden, the darkness that had been buried deep inside Ell didn't feel like it was buried at all. Suddenly, it felt as though there were two of him, two Elliyars fighting for control. And something told him that only one could survive.

CHAPTER NINETEEN

The-elf-who-had-once-been-Silverfist gripped the rail on the captain's deck of the warship he commanded. Some of the skin on his fingers had sloughed off in places, and he could feel bone grinding on wood as he grasped it. Silverfist stared eagerly ahead in anticipation. It would not be long now. He could feel the closeness. Wintermoon was nearby, and Silverfist had a small army at his disposal. This time it would be done, finished. This time, *he* would kill the boy and not the other way around. Let Wintermoon taste the grave this time. Let Wintermoon embrace the void.

"How long before we arrive?" he asked the Departed sailor who held the tiller, guiding the warship between Enclaves.

"I've sailed this route before," the elf answered nervously, "it shouldn't be much farther. You can just see the Midnight Cove on the horizon. With the wind at our back and the gale in full force, it shouldn't be much more than an hour." The elf swallowed. People were always nervous around Silverfist now. He figured it must be his physical appearance. Most found a half-dead elf discomfiting.

Silverfist grabbed the elf by the throat, relishing in the gurgling sounds he made as he tried to breathe. "Do I frighten you?" he whispered, moving his skeletal face in close to the elf's own.

The Departed didn't even answer, he just nodded vigorously, unable to speak through the tight grasp.

Silverfist tightened his grip for a moment longer, then released. The sailor slumped to the deck, one hand flailing for the tiller as he tried to regain his balance.

"Why?" Silverfist asked.

"What...what do you mean?" the Departed stammered.

"Why do you fear me? Is it...all of this?" Silverfist motioned with one boney hand toward the rest of his half-decayed body.

The elf rolled his shoulders uncomfortably. "I—I don't know."

Silverfist leaned in and spoke calmly and quietly again, his voice rasping over vocal chords that had been savaged by the grave. "I want to know. You had better give me a truthful answer now. Indulge my curiosity, or I'll indulge it myself in other ways." He fingered the tip of his belt knife that he'd drawn whilst talking.

The elf swallowed again and tried to collect himself. "I guess it's your eyes more than anything."

"My eyes?" The-elf-who-had-once-been-Silverfist asked, cocking his head to the side in thought. "I don't have eyes."

"Yes. I mean the sockets. They look like..." he stammered and then trailed off.

"Like what?" Silverfist prodded.

"Like they belong to a dead person." The elf cowered away as he finished speaking, as if worried that his honesty would earn him more pain.

Silverfist laughed hideously. "That's because I'm not alive. Not completely. No one really can be when they've been snatched out of the long sleep. I'm half-dead, and I am here to kill, to add to my number." He grinned at the Departed, his teeth no longer the white they had been in life.

"Yes, master, I see that. And this—this is all at the Prince of Darkness' bidding?" The sailor motioned behind them to the small fleet of ships that Silverfist had gathered in the name of the prince.

"Yes, of course! We all serve Half-Mask, don't we?" Silverfist snarled. He wanted Wintermoon dead more than anything, but he wished he wasn't forced into the task by the prince and king.

The sailor cowered away again, realizing now that he'd truly overstepped. "Apologies, master."

"Yes, cower, dog. I am your master, you do what I say when I say it." He turned away and stared grimly out over the stormy, windswept seas. "Just as I do what my masters say," he whispered bitterly, hating the purpose inside him for which he had risen, hating the way it commanded and controlled his will, all the while realizing he would be doing the same thing even if it hadn't been thrust upon him.

He would see Wintermoon dead or die again himself.

"Midnight Cove, ahead!" the lookout called down the sighting.

Silverfist slammed his rusty, silver fist onto the rail in excitement, splintering bits of the wood as he did so. "Yes, soon it will be time. The boy can't face down an army all by himself, now can he? Not one of this size." He practically purred the words to himself as he stared forward through the sheeting rain. Soon. In a matter of hours, he would have unburdened himself from his purpose. Soon, the boy would be dead and Silverfist would have his revenge.

The next minutes passed slowly, *so* slowly as he waited for their arrival. Anticipation weighed upon him, but pass they did. The ship drew closer, and vision through the storm cleared. As they approached the Midnight Cove, its inky waters mixing with the midnight blue of the stormy sea, Silverfist saw what lay before them.

He howled with fury, screaming curses at the winter air. His metal fist crushed the rail to smithereens and then, for good measure, he crushed the skull of the elf next to him. Blood and pulp flecked the deck.

Another warrior rushed up the stepladder to the captain's deck. "Sir, they have a fleet of their own—an army!"

"I can see that," Silverfist said through gritted teeth. He cursed again. It was just his luck that the boy had an army of his own.

"What are your orders?"

"Attack!" Silverfist commanded furiously. "We'll take them unawares."

"Very good, master." The elf rushed away to issue commands.

With lifeless holes for eyes, Silverfist gazed bleakly out over the inky waters of the Midnight Cove. Sailors on his ship shouted, steel was loosened in sheaths all around him and echoed beyond on the ships following. Elves raced to and fro on the docks, just now seeing that they were about to be set upon by a foe.

Silverfist grinned as rain spattered the exposed bones of his left cheek and jaw. If a battle was what Wintermoon wanted, then a battle he would get.

CHAPTER TWENTY

Miri hung back like she usually did during full-scale confrontations. Flanked by Delle and Lliaria, she loosed arrow after arrow into the ranks of the Unsired who were defending the Black Water Well. They might be stronger than the normal Departed, able to withstand more pain, stay upright, and keep fighting with more injuries, but if they were feathered with enough arrows, they would go down. Miri had let Brie join the combat instead of staying by her side as she had done in recent battles. With Lliaria and Delle right by her, Miri felt safe—well, as safe as was possible during a fight. Besides, the look of eager anticipation in Brie's eyes as she leaped forward into battle next to Ryder was enough to confirm that Miri was right to let her go. Brie had looked after her for months now, but at some point Miri had to be able to look after herself.

"Just stay beside me," Lliaria said with a calm smile. Ell's mother was the embodiment of tranquility. She wasn't he most battle-hungry of any of the elves by far, but even she could placidly face down charging Unsired as if she hadn't just spent two decades without having held a weapon.

"All right," Miri answered.

Delle nodded and smiled at her. "We'll stick together. Strength in numbers, right?"

Miri nodded back. And so it was that, as Ell and Arendahl raced ahead, fighting their way forward into who knew what part of the fortress, Miri spent the next hour sending shaft after shaft toward her enemies.

The mass of allied Highest and Departed met the Unsired defending the gate in a terrific clash and, with the aid of Ell and Arendahl at the fore, they forced their way inside. Miri and Ell's mother and sister followed behind the others, picking off targets as they went.

Understandably, Lliaria led them to follow not far behind Adan. It seemed that two decades apart meant she didn't want to let Adan out of her sight. Ell's father fought beside Dacunda and Iyonei, and arrows from Delle, Lliaria, and Miri's bows sailed beyond them, thinning the crowd of Unsired pressing forward to fight.

The battle was brutal. Blood stained the flagstones that lined the ground at the gate. Miri saw rivulets of red running toward the water of the cove to disappear into the blackness of the liquid beyond. As the attackers forced their way inside, their vision strained. Outside, the storm raged on, but lightning strikes and the overall gleam from outside kept it light enough to pick targets. Once Miri and the rest of the attackers had forced their way inside, taking down enemy targets was much more difficult. She fought behind a wall of her allies, protected from needing to defend herself with hand-to-hand combat. As she limped forward, she squinted through the torch-lit interior of the fortress, straining to tell the difference between her Departed allies and the Unsired they faced. Anybody carrying sickness or diseased parts became the target of her arrows.

Her shafts buried themselves in eyes and necks, pierced the leather vests many of the Unsired wore on their torsos. Shouts, screams, and grunts of pain echoed through the fortress, and chaos reigned. Offshoots of the battle spread into hallways and corridors, into empty chambers. Pockets of enemies clustered together, surrounded by Miri's allies and vice versa. Hard-pressed northern and southern compatriots often found their backs pressed to the rough stone walls, defending themselves desperately against the unnervingly fearless and almost stilted attacks of the Unsired. It was as if the Unsired had no will of their own other than to do the bidding of their masters which, in this case, was to defend the Black Water Well to the death.

Inevitably, elves fell—on both sides—but eventually Miri and her allies pressed forward and gained the advantage. Ell and Arendahl had left a swath of bodies in their wake, tipping numbers slightly in the attackers' favor. Led by Aldashir and Rihya at the fore, flanked by Aldashir's officers on one side and Ell's family and friends on the other, they gradually subdued the opposition. Surrender wasn't in the Unsired vocabulary, though, and so they fought to the death. Ryder and Briesom fought side by side, tallest and shortest of the companions next to one another as if it were the most natural thing in the world.

An enemy elf charged toward Brie's unprotected back. Miri's bow was up in a flash, and she dropped the Unsired with an arrow to his stomach. He fell but didn't die. Brie heard the noise and wised up to the danger, flashing a grateful grin toward Miri as she finished off the injured elf with her hand axes. Ryder wielded his long-axe with precision to decapitate heads and lop off limbs. Miri loosed another shaft, this time over Adan's shoulder at an Unsired moving toward him from the side. Ell's father didn't flinch as Miri's arrow breezed past his cheek, he simply stepped forward in one motion and ran the Unsired through, finishing the job she had begun. Lliaria put a hand on Miri's shoulder and squeezed it in thanks before nocking another arrow of her own and continuing the fight.

And so it went on. The battle raged in the darkness and faint light of the fortress at Black Water Well. Lives were lost, many on both sides, until finally the enemy was subdued. Miri was breathless and exhausted. Her hands ached from straining against the bow and from wrenching arrows from the bodies of the dead as she passed them in order to replenish her supply.

Panting, she approached Rihya and, without thinking, gave Ell's sister —*her* sister—a hug.

"What's this for?" Rihya tossed her green hair as she spoke.

"I—I'm not sure. I guess I thought you were dead before, so I'm just glad that still isn't the case," Miri explained.

Rihya smiled. "You're still not used to war."

"I don't think I ever will be."

"You could have fooled me. You fired your arrows like an archer who was born for it." Rihya's compliment warmed Miri. She had spent a lot of time practicing these past months, working on how to offset her old injury—her lame leg.

"Thanks, Rihya, but still, I do not think I will ever grow accustomed to killing."

Rihya put a hand to her cheek and stared at her seriously. "Good. Not all of us are supposed to. I've lived and breathed this life for so long I know nothing else. For you, it's more a circumstantial necessity. Let's hope it won't always be the case."

Miri smiled and hugged her again. "Thank you."

"Where's my brother?"

Miri shrugged. "You know as well as I. Last I saw, he had led the attack in to support Aldashir and then forged onward. Do you think he's all right?" Worry clouded her thoughts.

"He's fine. Two Water Callers together is more than just about any of our enemies could handle." Rihya put a comforting hand on Miri's shoulder. Her words were sound, but they didn't placate Miri's concerns. Rihya hadn't been Grafted into Ell's mind when he'd dueled Half-Mask, hadn't seen how dangerous a Spectralist was. They were equal to Water Callers in power. Miri wasn't so assured of Ell's safety.

They walked together, picking their way through the dead, helping the wounded. Miri could only take it so long before she had to get away from the stench of death.

"I need some air." She turned to leave behind Rihya and Aldashir, who had joined them.

"I'll come with you," Rihya offered. "Or rather, we will." She cast a shy glance at Aldashir, and Miri realized it was the first time she'd seen the two of them walking with their hands linked.

Miri nodded. "Very well."

"Follow me," Aldashir said and led them to a side corridor which quickly turned into a staircase. The prince knew this fortress; he was part of the royal family, after all, and he led them up to a parapet overlooking the bay.

Rain lashed down on them, and thunder still rumbled in the sky overhead. But the rain felt good as it plastered Miri's hair to her face. Aldashir narrowed his eyes as he looked out over the parapet at the sea beyond. Black water swept outward from the cove and met the advance of another fleet of ships.

Aldashir swore. "We have company. In our condition, having just fought, we'll have our work cut out for us if they are enemies. And they almost certainly will be."

At that moment, a ragged and disheveled Ell burst through the doorway leading from the stairs onto the parapet next to them. He was gasping for air, and there was a stricken, almost frightened look on his face. He gazed without seeming to see, without seeming to recognize that they were there. He panted a moment longer before he realized he wasn't alone.

"Is it done?" Aldashir asked tensely. "Did you destroy it?"

Ell swallowed and then reluctantly shook his head. Aldashir and Rihya exchanged a long look.

"Why not?" Rihya asked her brother cautiously. Ell ignored the question, still seemingly unable to see what was around him. He was breathing heavily, whether from running or something else Miri wasn't sure.

"Your sister, Valerihya, asked you a question." Aldashir's voice had hardened slightly.

Ell turned his sightless gaze away from the harbor even as the ships drew closer and closer. They were clearly enemies, since Miri could see Departed warriors and sailors aboard each deck.

"I...couldn't do it," Ell finally answered. He sounded so weak, so disappointed, and yes, frightened, that Miri went to him and enveloped him in her arms. He returned the gesture woodenly.

"You couldn't," Aldashir repeated flatly.

"I couldn't do it."

"If you cannot destroy the Black Water Well, then I have rebelled and doomed my warriors to death for nothing!" Aldashir's voice rose close to a shout.

"Wait, Aldashir, slow down. That can't be fully what Ell means." Rihya tried her best to temper the prince, but even she cast a few worried looks at her brother. Ell looked more defeated than Miri had ever seen him.

"Ell, are you all right?" Miri took her mate's face in her hands and forced him to see her.

And then it seemed like he really *did* see her for the first time since reaching the parapet. His gaze trailed over her bloodstained hands, dirty from plucking arrows from bodies. They were partially washed clean from the sleeting rain, but not quite. He looked at her haunted, weary face and her worried gaze as she stared back at him.

"I didn't want this for you," he whispered.

"Didn't want what for me?"

Ell motioned numbly all around them and then out to the harbor at the enemy who was almost near enough to attack. "All of this. War, battle, blood. You had none of this before you met me."

"If you even try and take the blame for a ruined world right now, I will slap you," Miri cautioned him sardonically. Unfortunately, her jest didn't garner the smile she'd hoped it would.

Ell changed the subject again. "I may not be at fault, but I'm broken, Miriyah, and that's just as bad. I promised them I could do it. I promised them I could destroy the well. I had no plan again, and this time it finally caught up to me. I got down there, we fought the King of the South, and as soon as he fled, and I looked at the Black Water Well —I mean, *truly* saw it and was in close proximity to it for the first time— it was all I could do to hold onto myself, to hold onto my sanity, my agency as an elf. It was as though I was on the verge of losing all control and becoming one of *them*. And I wanted to, Miri. Some part of me wanted to become a Spectralist." Ell's agonized stammering was like a flood of insight into the struggle he'd been subjected to at the hands of Half-Mask.

"You saw my father?" Aldashir asked with a quick intake of breath.

"We did," Ell answered numbly, "but he's gone now. He fled. Disappeared through a wall as if by smoke."

"I'll help you, love," Miri said, ignoring the talk of the prince's father. The king could wait for now. Enemies were approaching again, and Ell needed his confidence back, needed to believe in himself again, needed to know that he could do what he'd promised. "Let me access the Graft again and see what's going on inside you."

Ell recoiled slightly from her pleading request. "I don't want you to see that part of me," he said vehemently. "It's shameful. It's black and ugly."

She cupped his face. "I've already sensed it before. It's nothing new."

Miri sent her consciousness into his, felt his hurt, pain, and shame. With her back to the harbor, she pushed herself into his thoughts. She felt his energy still pumping through his veins from the battle, but it was dulled by an ache—a desire for what lay below. She felt his second self, the Spectralist side of his consciousness that had been forced upon him. She felt his lust for the liquid that lay in the well. She felt his desire to kill, maim, and spread disease through his very touch. And the worst part of it was, it really *was* Ell who felt all of those things. It was him, yet it also wasn't. It was an alternate version of him that inhabited the same body as the original owner, and it was up for debate which of the two Ells was going to prevail.

Miri sent her consciousness further into him through the Graft, felt her eyes slide into his, felt his sight become hers, and she lost herself for a moment. She was part of him, deeper inside than she'd ever been before. She felt his burning urges to kill, the urges he'd been fighting against so valiantly for months. She wept for him. She wept for herself, for she *was* him. They were one. She felt the reservoir of strength, his ability as a Water Caller pooling in her chest. But she felt a darker reservoir, as well, deep down in her belly, a cesspool of ability that could only be the Spectralist part of her.

Miri reached down into it, into the darkness within. She could touch it. Did that mean she could force it out?

Miri was snapped out of the Graft by a startled Ell as he shoved past her physical body and stepped up to the crenellated wall overlooking the cove. The sudden movement pulled Miri from the Graft, and she lost whatever thought she'd been clinging to.

"It can't be!" Ell muttered hoarsely, staring at the lead ship of the enemy fleet as it finally drew close enough to see onto its deck from the fortresses' high wall.

"What?" Rihya and Aldashir asked simultaneously as they stepped near to the wall to see for themselves.

"He's dead," Ell whispered.

"Who?" Miri asked.

"The Traitor. Silverfist. I killed him last spring. He's dead and buried in a shallow grave." Ell's hand gripped the wall so tightly that cracks appeared in its stone surface. As a Water Caller, the strength at his disposal was enough to crumble stone, especially when he was angry and surprised.

Ell's voice hardened. "I killed you, Silverfist!" he shouted out over the bay. And surprisingly, even through the rain and the noise, the faint sound of echoing, answering, cackling laughter sounded in return. Scorn laced the laughter and derision at Ell's angry shout.

"I killed you," he whispered hoarsely.

"He still looks half-dead," Aldashir observed, finally seeing and then pointing out the form on the deck of the lead enemy ship, the one Ell had already picked out with his keen eyesight.

Rihya shuddered. "What is he?"

Miri followed their gaze and saw an elf. Or, rather, what had once been an elf. It looked as much like a corpse as a living being. Decayed skin covered its body in places, but bone showed through in other parts. The figure of Silverfist was gaunt from the grave, but there was yet a vitality to his movements, a certain strength to them—the strength of death as it clung to an unwilling host. It was her turn to shudder.

"This is my brother and father's doing," Aldashir muttered angrily, in horror of the grotesque mockery of an elf that led the approaching enemy.

"Without a doubt," Ell responded, a certain clarity returning to his voice. It was a clarity Miri hadn't expected from him there on the parapet following his outburst.

Impulsively, she sent her consciousness back into his. She felt his struggle within. Suddenly, though, where defeat and despair had reigned mere moments ago there was now a hardened resolve. Ell stared out over the harbor at his old foe—his *new* foe.

He looked at Miri as if he knew she was in his mind again. "This is evil. Silverfist returning to life, or whatever semblance of existence he possesses, is the embodiment of wrong. I must fix this—fix myself. I'm going to fight again, and fight harder this time." Miri felt his resolve break through stronger than it had in days. She felt his desire to be free overcome his chains to the darker side of himself.

"I'll help you. I promised I'd fix you," she said and grabbed his hand. He squeezed it back.

Ell turned to lead her down the stairs. "Where are you going?" Aldashir demanded.

"Ready the troops. They'll no doubt be attacking us in a matter of minutes. Buy me some time. Don't falter and don't fail. Death is leading them," Ell answered.

"And where will you be, brother?" Rihya asked.

"I'm going to do what I said I would." Ell glanced at Miri and then spoke again, his voice hardening into iron. "We. *We* are going to do what I said I would. We're going back down into the depths of the fortress, and we're going to destroy the Black Water Well once and for all."

CHAPTER TWENTY-ONE

"You seem in better spirits already," Miri panted breathlessly as she did her best to keep up with Ell's quick pace. She limped after him, but it was at moments like this when her lame leg became her biggest hindrance. Ell slowed his pace to accommodate her, and Miri gritted her teeth at the fact that he had to do so. She hated that she slowed him down, especially at a time so crucial as this.

Ell glanced at her as they ran through the narrow corridors of the fortress, passing Departed and Highest alike heading in the opposite direction to deal with the new threat of Silverfist's small army. Ell had a determination back in his eyes that had been missing up on the parapet.

"Seeing Silverfist was a wakeup call. I've been struggling with the part of me that Half-Mask created—fighting it—but if I'm being completely honest, a part of me has been wondering if maybe it wouldn't be better just to give in. To have that extra power and then use it for good somehow," Ell said back, breathing much more easily than she was.

"You know that isn't how it would be. If you gave in, I think that side of you would overtake you completely."

Ell nodded acceptance. "Yes, you're right. And seeing that despicable leech Silverfist was enough to remind me of that simple truth. Only Half-Mask's dark powers would be able to do such a thing: bring a dead elf back to life. Anything that pulls Silverfist from his shallow grave can only be evil. It was a reminder of just why I want this well destroyed and the power and struggle out of my mind and body."

Miri continued to limp after Ell as fast as she could as they took turn after turn. Eventually, they reached a door to a small chamber. Ell pushed the oaken door open and they stepped inside together. Miri felt a shudder go through Ell's body as she held his hand. Whether it was one of fear or ecstasy at the sight of the rough stone well and the dark, pooling liquid inside Miri could not tell.

Ell took a slow step forward and she followed. "So, this is it, the infamous Black Water Well. The source of our people's pain and anguish," Miri murmured almost to herself. Just staring into its depths she could see shadow upon shadow swirling in upon themselves. It was like midnight on a moonless night mixed with how she imagined the sky might look without a single star. A cave with no end in sight, its dark depths hinting at dangers and yet also the possibility of exploration. She could see why it might be seductive. Its enigma was attractive, especially to one as adventurous as Ell. But it was also evil, and she could sense that as clearly as she could feel Ell's hand in hers.

"Are you ready to let it go?" she asked as Ell stared, his gaze transfixed by the murky substance.

"What?" he replied, startled out of his reverie.

"I can see what it's doing to you. You've been fighting it on the one hand, in the sense of an internal battle, fighting it to not take over control of your mind or actions. But you've also got to let it go. I can see there's a real pull for you, one that touches the core of who you actually are. But it's wrong, Ell. It's evil. You *have* to let it go."

"Yes, of course." Ell shook his head as if to clear it. "You're right—you almost always are." He shot a smile in her direction and squeezed her hand.

"Ready?" she asked again.

Ell let out a vexed sigh. "Miri, I have no idea what to do! I told you that."

The clash of battle could be heard echoing toward them through the maze of tunnels and passages leading from the docks. Silverfist's army must have engaged with Aldashir's. They didn't have much time. Ell would be needed soon. At least they still had Arendahl to skew the battle in their favor until he arrived and added another Water Caller to the mix. *If* they finished this—if they destroyed the Black Water Well and managed to fix him.

"That's why I'm here. You might be out of ideas, but I have one or two of my own." Miri grinned at him, trying to project more confidence than she felt. She would do this; she would fix him.

"Oh?" Ell tilted his head in question.

"I'm going to access the link to your mind, all right?"

Ell smiled ruefully. "You've never asked before, so why start now?"

Miri rolled her eyes. "No time for jokes now, Ell." She closed her eyes and sent her consciousness through the link, accessing the Graft into Ell's mind, his heart. She felt his fear and worry. He was much more nervous being in this close proximity to the Black Water Well. In truth, he was barely keeping the darkness at bay. She could feel his desire to reach out and drink it up by the cupful, to use its power to do dark and mysterious things. Miri could feel his mind spinning at the thought of raising the dead and at what questionable deeds he could accomplish. But that wasn't her Ell, and she could also feel him fighting it, forcing away its bludgeons, keeping its more dangerous, seductive appeal at bay. He was strong, her mate, but he needed to be rid of this inner battle. She could feel him weakening and wasn't sure how many more days he could last like this. A person divided could never stand for long.

She pressed herself into his consciousness until they were practically one. "I can feel you—every part of you, every fiber of your being," she breathed.

Ell shifted his shoulders uncomfortably. "I wish you couldn't."

"Don't say that. It isn't your fault what Half-Mask did to you. I know enough to separate your true self from those other impulses floating around in your consciousness. A lesser elf would have lost the battle long ago." She squeezed his hand tightly and he returned the pressure, the grateful look in his eyes enough to break her heart. Ell was wounded, body and mind and spirit, but she was going to right that wrong.

Miri took a deep breath, thinking of what to do next. She had an idea forming: a dangerous, risky idea. It was the sort of plan Ell might usually propose. Could it work? There was only one way to find out.

"Now that we are connected, it's time for the next step. You have to welcome me, Ell."

"What do you mean, Miri? I always welcome you."

She shook her head. "Not when it comes to the Graft. Just a second ago you said you wished I wasn't able to see all of you."

Ell sighed. "Why? Why does it matter? I just want to protect you from the terrible things I experience, or worse, the desires this sickness makes me have."

"I pushed deeply into your mind the other day, so deeply I almost felt like I could touch the Spectralist part of you. That was new. If you welcome me further, maybe it'll give me even more of a foothold to oust it from your consciousness. In a way, I will be ousting it from my consciousness, too."

"Okay, I'll try." Still, he shook his head doubtfully.

"You have to mean it, Ell. Welcome the Graft fully, embrace it like you never have."

Ell visibly steeled himself. "You won't think less of me?"

"I've seen you at your worst, love, and it's changed nothing. I promise this will help. The only way I could think less of you is if you don't do this," Miri told him, trying to allay some of the fear in his eyes.

"How do I do it?"

Miri shrugged. "I don't know. Maybe just relax into the Graft. I'm already in you...I can feel your fear and worry, I can sense your hope that this might work. I can feel it all already, so just add to that, maybe try and—I don't know, stretch your own consciousness out into mine and then pull me even further into yours, sort of the way you do with your Water Calling powers."

"Someone's been listening to my lessons," Ell managed to joke even at a time like this.

Miri stared at him seriously. "I know about as much as there is to know about you. I pay attention to everything concerning you. You're my heart, so how could I not?"

That seemed to somehow be enough to firm Ell's resolve. "All right." He grabbed both of her hands and pulled her around so that they were facing each other. He didn't close his eyes—he didn't need to do that the way Arendahl did while accessing his abilities—but they did take on a faraway look. And then it went even further as his eyes clouded over and a mist of droplets sprung to the air around him. Apparently, he was tapping his abilities even as he was trying to do the same thing with Miri's consciousness. Whatever strength he needed to get this done was fine with her.

Miri pushed. Just as she had when she'd first Grafted Ell, she pushed as hard as she could, instinctively trying to fold a part of herself into him. He pulled and she pushed for what seemed like an endless, indeterminate period of time. It could have been moments or minutes or hours, but finally she felt it. She felt herself sucked up into his consciousness so deeply that she was one with him. She managed to hold a fraction of her consciousness in her own body—her own mind—yet somehow she was further into Ell than she'd ever been.

"There!" Ell gasped. "I think I did it."

Miri swallowed and nodded. She felt the raging battle inside him, stronger and more violent than ever before. She felt his Water Calling abilities and this time, somehow, she knew she could tap them, access them herself if she wanted to. And she also felt the other side, felt the darkness, the Spectralist deep within. Miri knew that if she wanted—just as Ell could—she could touch and hold and use that dark reservoir of power.

"Good, Ell. Good. We've done it." She was in him so deeply that when her voice spoke from her own body it felt strange to hear it from his end, hear it through his ears. It was near, she was only a foot away, but it also felt as if she had heard it from far away.

"What now?" Ell asked.

Miri swallowed nervously. It was time for the risky part of her plan. "Now I help you. Put your hands in the Black Water Well."

"What!" he exclaimed. "That's ludicrous! You've just told me to fight it, and now you want me to do the opposite."

"I told you I'd help you," Miri said calmly, much more calmly than she actually felt.

"How?" Ell demanded. "You don't have powers—not like I do. Besides, if I put my hands in it, in the well, I'll lose control. And with you so connected to me right now, I don't know what will happen—to me, to you, either of us." He was shaking his head. Always he sought to protect her first. Usually it was endearing, but this time it was vexing. There were more important matters afoot than safety. They needed a whole and healthy Ell to win this war, not a whole and healthy Miri.

"You won't lose yourself, love. I'm anchoring you hear, I promise." Miri prayed that was true. "And I do have power. *You're* my power, Ell. My love is my power. No elf has Grafted a mate for hundreds of years, so long that it's been lost in lore almost entirely. I'm special, just like you. I promised I was going to fix you, and I *am* going to do it. And maybe, just maybe, if you're touching the Black Water Well, if you're connected to it as I fix you, then maybe it'll be enough to fix it, also. It might be enough to destroy it." A note of pleading entered her voice. It was crazy, she knew it, but what else could they do? He was losing this battle on his own, slowly but surely.

"That's insane, Miriyah," Ell whispered, voicing her very concerns. "What if it doesn't work?"

"Do you trust me?" she asked, again trying to project more calm into her voice than she possessed.

Ell took a deep breath. "You know I do."

"Then trust me now. I'm letting intuition drive me forward just like you have done so many times before."

Ell nodded solemnly. They turned back toward the well, letting go of each other's hands. They didn't need the physical link now that she was so far into Ell that it felt like they were mentally embracing.

They stood over the well for a moment, staring into its midnight depths. She felt his fear, his worry, and not just for himself. Through the Graft, Miri could sense just how deeply Ell feared for her in that moment. If they failed, he worried she would succumb to the Blackness, too, since she was so entwined with him.

"Ready?" she asked one final time.

Ell nodded jerkily.

"All right, touch it. Stick your hands into the well," Miri instructed him.

This time, Ell did as she said. He reached his hands down slowly, touching his fingertips to the surface of the liquid and, as he did, his face went rigid then slack, and then Miri felt the battle within rage anew, stronger than ever before. The darkness was in ascendancy as he stuck his hands into the water all the way up to the forearms. The only thing keeping him sane, keeping him himself, was the fact that he was already holding onto his abilities as a Water Caller—that and the fact that Miri, a second consciousness, was inside him and anchoring him to himself. She held on tightly, refusing to let go.

"Good," she breathed. She reached down and felt the reservoir of Spectralist powers seething deep inside Ell's soul surging to get out. And this time, she touched it. "Keep it at bay, Ell. Don't give in," she said through gritted teeth.

"I can't hold it off much longer." He grimaced, his face contorted in pain, his features squirming with the ecstasy of touching the dark liquid.

"I'm touching it inside you, love. If you can keep from doing the same, then we have a chance." Miri pushed her touch deeper into Ell's Spectralist side. She fought, she clawed, she scraped to get it out. And as she did, the well itself fought back as if it had a mind of its own. The Black Water Well's liquid reared up. It seethed and became a tall wave threatening to pound down and consume them both. But it never did; Ell held it at bay by refusing to let go of his true self, by holding onto his Water Calling abilities even as his hands remained in the blackness of the water rising up before him.

And Miri fought harder than she'd ever done before. Every bit of training, every arrow she'd loosed, every knife she'd thrown, every raid she'd taken part in over the last months were nothing compared to this. She struggled for a hold against the dark reservoir within Ell. She was touching it through Ell, but she could feel its slimy surface trying to worm its way across their connected consciousness and into her own. She could feel the Blackness trying to make her into an Unsired. But she fought.

Even as fear dulled her senses, she pulled on all of the strength that she possessed—the love that she bore for herself, her mate, her land. She fought the mental battle to hold the darkness at bay on her end. She was special. She reminded herself of that. Arendahl's words echoed back to her: *You will have to protect him now.* And that memory steeled her. This vile substance, this 'power' could not have him. She pushed back, and suddenly she was on the offensive. She bore down on the darkness with the one power she possessed: love. She loved Ell with all her heart and would not let him go.

Miri forced the reservoir up out of the depths of Ell's consciousness toward the surface of his being. As if he could physically feel the darkness leaving him, a scream tore from his throat. It was an agonized wail. It seemed never-ending, but Miri pushed anyway. She gathered her strength for one final push, to finally expel the Spectralist reservoir, and all the while Ell still shrieked in pain. Being inside him, she could feel the agony as one of his consciousnesses split from the other and the darkness was pushed out of him. He was strong, though, her mate. He held his ground even as the agony was almost enough to bear Miri down to her knees. Then she did slump in exhaustion, but even from her knees she pushed. She sent her consciousness so deep inside Ell that they were more than one; they were two in one. She hounded every last shred of the darkness from his being, and as it finally expelled from his mind it also exited his body physically. Tiny droplets of black liquid streaked from his eyes like dark tears. Ell vomited black liquid, and his black scars began to ooze until only normal, lighter scars remained. All the while he was still elbow deep in the Black Water Well which was now practically boiling. If it did have a mind of its own, then it was furious.

Miri gave one final push, and all that remained of the opposite source left Ell's body. She felt his mind clear. She sensed only one of him again and, as she did, the Black Water Well finally exploded, sending the liquid streaking all over the stone walls and floor. It covered them entirely in the dark liquid, but even as it did it began to change color. The black faded to a bluish color and then became clear—the color of most water. Ell still held his Water Calling abilities, and Miri could feel the strength inside of him gaining as the other side—the dark half of his consciousness—left him and the battle within was gone. She let the Graft go now that he was healed, now that the Black Water Well was gone with only an empty fount and a sopping wet chamber in its place.

They knelt before one another, supporting each other even as they were soaking from the liquid that had changed into normal water.

"You were right," Ell marveled. "By expelling it from my body while I was physically connected to it, we destroyed the well itself."

"Lucky guess," Miri mumbled jokingly and slumped her body against his, needing his support to keep from falling over completely. She had never felt so exhausted in her life.

"I can't believe it," Ell continued to mouth his wonderment. "I'm...me again."

"We did it." Miri smiled and reached a hand up to touch his face tenderly as he cradled her.

"*You* did it," Ell said firmly. "Don't even try to share the credit with me. We both know that without you I would have lost the war for my self, my soul."

"I told you I would fix you," she murmured.

Ell stared into her eyes. She could see him drinking in her face. "You did. And you just might have saved the world in doing so."

CHAPTER TWENTY-TWO

Only a few moments had passed since Miri had managed to drive away the opposite source—the Blackness that caused people to become Unsired—from Ell's body and mind. They'd destroyed the Black Water Well in the process.

They were sitting slumped against one another when all of a sudden, an incredible light entered the chamber. Ell recognized the sensation from having experienced it before. He turned his head eagerly, searching for the source. Sure enough, as if personified to enter through the door like a friend, the Wandering Mist streamed in through the chamber doorway. It swirled around them as twinkling, flickering lights of blue and purple and violet. Every spark interchanged in color, shape, and size. It swirled around them like a whirlwind of reprieve, energizing their tired bodies and exhausted minds. The sparks of flickering light winked in and out of existence here and there, some in the shape of tiny stars, or flowers, or butterflies, some like tiny lightning bolts or explosions of bluish-violet color. The mist twirled and danced around them, and they collapsed to the ground not in exhaustion but in sweet relief.

"The Spirit of the Land," Miri giggled giddily.

Ell could do little but stare in awe around him. They had seen this phenomenon before in Little Vale, but it had been only a legend to him before that first sighting, another one of those myths buried so deep in lore that most of the Highest didn't quite know whether or not they believed in its existence. Whispers carried tales of the Wandering Mist and made believers of children and the most full of faith. And Ell had witnessed it more than once now!

"It must be blessing us for what we've done. It's the spirit of Creation, and Creation spun us out to counteract the Unsired millennia ago during the First Days. I suppose the land is happy that you banished the darkness from my consciousness and, by extension, managed to destroy the opposite source," Ell murmured, still staring at it all in amazement.

"Me? We both know it was a joint effort," Miri denied half-heartedly. As if to challenge her modest assertion, the Wandering Mist clustered in on itself and swirled only around Miri for a few moments, the little lights, shapes, and sparks linking in and out, lighting upon her face and arms and in her hair. She giggled again as though pure joy was the only possible reaction to the Spirit of the Land.

"It looks like the Wandering Mist agrees with me," Ell chuckled as he watched in wonder as Creation paid special attention to his mate.

The mist swirled and flickered dizzyingly around Miri for a few moments more before swirling off toward the doorway, its tail end trailing behind it in scattered bits of light. Soon enough, it disappeared into the darkness of the passage beyond.

"How long since this dark place has witnessed a thing like that?" Miri whispered in reverence.

"Probably never. This cove is steeped in evil. I doubt the Wandering Mist has had much occasion to bless it," Ell responded and stood up lithely. He reached down and pulled Miri to her feet. Her lame leg almost caved in on her, and she wobbled slightly until he caught her.

"Thanks. Why do you think it came?" Miri's eyes were still wide with delight.

Ell shook his head and shrugged. "What we just did took a lot out of us. I was on the verge of exhaustion before it showed up. I think it came simply to let us know it approved and to refresh us. Don't you feel better?"

Miri nodded and grinned at him. "I do indeed. And do you?"

Ell knew that she was probing further than just about being refreshed by the mist. "Yes, love, I am well. The Spectralist side of me is gone, never to return," he said, uttering the last part of the statement as an ironclad promise.

"The others must have need of us by now," Miri changed topics, her voice acquiring a worried lilt.

Ell nodded in response and they began making their way quickly through the narrow, darkened corridors of the fortress. "I can make out the sounds of battle far ahead," Ell murmured.

"Then let's hurry. They'll need you!" Miri urged.

Ell gathered her hand in his, and they sprinted as quickly as they could, her leg slowing them only a little. They still made good time and, by the time they reached the entrance, Ell was ready for a fight. The gate had been closed and those who had once been attackers were now defenders. Aldashir held the wall above them against the army that Silverfist had brought.

Ell took the stairs up to the parapet two at a time, anxious to lend his voice or his blade where needed. He reached the top and saw Aldashir shouting orders with Rihya right beside him. The alliance of Departed and Highest were hard-pressed to defend the fortress walls against the new army. Silverfist's legion consisted of average Departed warriors but also a sprinkling of Unsired here and there—Ell could tell by the glazed looks of battle fury on their faces. He and his company had suffered losses to gain the fortress, and now they had to turn around and defend it. The gate was yet closed and the wall still theirs, but they might not be for long.

Ell tapped into his Water Calling abilities. He felt the pool of strength, that reservoir of light and liquid pool in his chest as he pulled on the water, on the creation around him, felt the droplets of water raining from the sky and the surging waves against the wharf—the blackness already dissipating from the Midnight Cove—lend him power. He pulled on it and steeled himself for a fight.

This was what he was built for. And there was a score to settle with an elf who should be dead. Ell grinned and threw himself into the fray.

CHAPTER TWENTY-THREE

Even as he was en route to the Midnight Cove, Half-Mask felt it. He felt it happen, felt it shake the very core of his being. It was like someone had reached down inside of him and yanked out his guts all at once, all those vital pieces of himself missing. It was just *gone*.

The Prince of Darkness shrieked and fell to the deck of his ship. He let out bloodcurdling scream after scream until it felt like he could scream no more. His warriors gathered round him. Those who were Unsired stood blankly, ready to serve. Those who had not yet undergone the transformation to leave behind their designation as Departed carried worried looks on their faces.

Half-Mask staggered to his feet and then immediately fell back to his knees, legs weakened from the shock.

"It's gone," he mumbled as he pushed himself to his feet one more time, limbs tangling in his black cloak, almost sending him plunging to the deck again.

"What was that, my prince?" a Departed sailor asked.

The nerve! To interrupt him at a time like this. Half-Mask felt the familiar fury jolt through his body as he turned and lunged toward the voice. Both hands buried claw-like fingers into the warrior's throat and tore. Blood rained down on his hands, and Half-Mask sagged with the relief of killing as the irksome soldier slumped, dead, to the wooden deck of the warship.

Half-Mask's fingers twitched, and he gazed at the next warrior nearby. It was an Unsired, and it stared at him without fear, only ready to obey, to cast itself from the ship at his very whim. He approached slowly and grabbed the Unsired by the bare shoulders, as it wore its typical, black leather vest. He sank his teeth into the Unsired's neck and tasted blood—black and bitter. It was glorious. Finally, he pulled away and tilted his head back, panting.

It was gone. The thought struck him again. All the blood in the world couldn't replace it. It was gone.

He stared at the Unsired that lay crumpled on the deck at his feet, and something caught his eye. The places where Half-Mask had held the elf's shoulders were shriveled and pocked with disease. It looked normal —the way things always looked when Half-Mask touched his Spectralist powers, so that hadn't changed. But why?

And then the thought struck him, and a smile came to his lips. "Back to Dark Harbor. Now!" he practically yelled the excited command to the rest of his terrified crew.

"What about our course toward the Midnight Cove, my prince?" one sailor asked, braver than his comrades.

"It isn't the Midnight Cove any longer," Half-Mask muttered angrily. "Besides, they've long been there and will likely be gone by the time we leave, their work having been completed." His words tasted bitter. So this was what it felt like to lose. He had lost. The Prince of Darkness let that sink in. He had lost to Wintermoon and his ragtag bunch of companions—companions that included his disloyal, ungrateful brother.

Half-Mask's hands clenched the rail of the captain's deck so hard it creaked, and wisps of black smoke trailed from his fingertips. Another tight smile creased his face. He had lost the battle, but not the war. The smoky haze drifting from his hands was proof of that. And he knew why.

"Hurry! Back to Dark Harbor!" he exhorted his sailors. "Don't make me get the lash!"

———

HALF-MASK PACED ANGRILY in his tower overlooking the city. He sipped from his cup, and the dark liquid burned and cooled his mouth simultaneously. He shuddered with relieved ecstasy. He didn't know what he would have done without it. Still, he took small sips, savoring it, protecting it from overuse.

Steps echoed in the stairway, and he waited tensely to see who had come to seek his presence. The door didn't receive a knock. Instead, the intruder burst in with a frantic flurry. Half-Mask was about to make the person pay, about to devour their very flesh for entering without knocking at such a time as this, until he saw who it was.

"You," he said with as much scorn as he could muster. "You just let them take it. Destroy it. Did you even put up a fight? Or did you just run, tail between your legs?"

"Tell me you have some. Tell me you do!" The figure in the cloak stumbled toward Half-Mask, desperately grasping at the sleeves of the prince's black cloak.

"Control yourself, Father. You are still the king, after all. It wouldn't do to have others see you in such a state."

"Others be damned! Do you have any?"

Half-Masked smirked, dangled the cup of liquid in front of the king's face, and then held it out of reach as his father—the vaunted and feared King of the South—snatched greedily at the air where it had been.

"Give me some," he practically pleaded.

"Very well." Half-Mask sneered. This game was growing wearisome, anyway. They had more important matters to consider.

"Where is it?" the king asked hungrily.

Half-Mask nodded to a lidless cask in a shadowy corner of the room, and the king stumbled over to the barrel frantically, falling to his knees and dipping his hands into the dark water, cupping it to his mouth in large, sloppy gulps.

"Easy! Slow down." Half-Mask's voice cracked like a whip, a strange new authority entering him. "We do not have an unlimited supply anymore. Luckily for us, I had the foresight to stockpile a cache of barrels containing the liquid for a time such as this."

"You anticipated its destruction?" the king mumbled through ink-black lips, stained by the water he was still cupping to his mouth as quickly as he could.

"Not exactly," the Prince of Darkness huffed in annoyance. "But it always seemed prudent to have a large supply on hand in Dark Harbor, distant as we are from the Midnight Cove."

"How much do we have?" the king asked worriedly.

Half-Mask stepped quickly across the room and yanked his father away by the hood of his cloak, sending the elf sprawling across the flagstones of the tower floor. "Not enough for you to spend your time guzzling it in such a fashion!" He put as much derision in his tone as he could, directing a scathing look at his father. "Pull yourself together. We have matters to discuss and a war to win."

Surprisingly, his father did as he was told. Something seemed broken inside him; something had shifted in the nature of their relationship. Half-Mask lamented the destruction of such a precious source as the Black Water Well, but he could not deny that there was a silver lining to be found here. He smirked at his father and pointed to one of the two chairs.

"Sit, father." It was a command.

The King of the South sat, and again Half-Mask felt a thrill of pleasure. This was how it would be from now on. He would consolidate his power here, where it had once been most difficult, against his most dangerous rival. And then he would spread that power far. Yes, very far—as far as possible. This was nowhere near over. Wintermoon would rue the day he had attacked the Midnight Cove.

Half-Mask stayed upright, pacing even as his father sat. The king's pocked face was tilted up at Half-Mask expectantly. "You have a plan?" he surmised, a bit of his old shrewdness entering his voice. Perhaps he wasn't as broken as Half-Mask thought. He would do well to remember that. He could still be wily, the king, and he would need watching. But it was also a good thing. Half-Mask needed the king's power to complete his plans.

"Of course I do," Half-Mask purred. "I always have plans. Plans upon strategies upon contingencies."

"What now?"

"They think they can destroy our source, our Black Water Well, without repercussions!" Half-Mask practically shouted in angry answer. "Their ancestors will wail of the day they made that decision."

"But it's gone," a bit of the brokenness reentered his father's voice as he spoke, and Half-Mask snickered.

"Have some mettle, Father. It isn't near over. We have a strong, steady supply of the well water in my barrels here in the capital. It's enough for us for some time. My powers remain and do not wane—as should yours—so long as the liquid flows in my veins and permeates every part of my body. We are Spectralists, Father. We have power at our fingertips to awaken our allies of old, to awaken them in force. We raised the dead not long ago. What is beyond our grasp?" Half-Mask clenched his fists in determination as a dark excitement overtook him.

He turned to stare out of the north-facing window. He gazed out at the wide view over the cramped, spider-webbed streets of the city, over the dim bay and the ships of the harbor, over the hills and hillforts ringing the bay. He gazed north toward the kingdom of Andalaya—the kingdom he had helped destroy, whose breaking he had orchestrated—over the forests of Legendwood and the mountains beyond. He smiled.

"They think they can do what they did without consequence. I'll show them how wrong they are," he said, his voice sinking to a whispered promise. He swirled the cup of dark liquid in his hand—a refilled cup brimming with contents from the Black Water Well. He dipped a finger in and stirred before drinking deeply. "Arise," he whispered. He felt them shift and rumble, stirring to his awakening. "Arise," he said and felt them untangle themselves from roots and oaken wood. "Arise!" he shouted out the window into the stormy winter air as he watched in his mind's eye as distant boulders loosened on the coast of the continent and trees disengaged from their branches and trunks.

"Arise!" he screamed again, unwisely spilling some of the black liquid in his excitement. The king scrambled over to savor it even from the floor.

Half-Mask watched with a faraway vision as Stone Ogres and Wood Ogres unlimbered themselves from their long-forgotten resting places. Rock of mountain broke free and took form. Boulders in the ocean's surf stood and found arms and legs and shambled onto the shore, red eyes gleaming with deathly promise. The Tree Ogres were trailed by Ghouls, and Half-Mask could feel more mustering together in the far north in the Broken Tree Range. He felt the solitary flapping of Icari wings as he stirred them from their mountaintop perches and aeries.

They were his to control, his by right, by power, and by desire as a Spectralist. He called to them once more: "Awaken, my creatures, my pets, my friends. Arise and do my bidding!" The thunder of the storm rumbled, and lightning crackled as his vision refocused on the space right before him.

The king climbed to his feet, having licked up the spilled liquid like an addict. Half-Mask stared scornfully at his one-time competitor, at his one-time leader, at his father. *He* was in control now, not the other way around.

"You asked what we will do. They think their actions have no consequences, but I will disabuse them of that notion," Half-Mask swore fervently. "They destroyed Black Water Well—fine, we will attack their Source and destroy it once and for all. And maybe more, for after all, our barrels of Black Water Well liquid are not without their tricks."

A light of hope entered the king's eyes. "Yes, yes, yes," he muttered maniacally, and Half-Mask could hear the full-blown madness returning to his father's voice. Fine. The King was always at his most dangerous when fully consumed by the madness.

"Yes, indeed," Half-Mask concurred. "Muster the armies, Father. We march on Verdantihya once again."

CHAPTER TWENTY-FOUR

Even as she stood side by side with Aldashir defending the walls of the Midnight Cove, Rihya saw Ell and Miri race up the stairs from the corner of her eye. She swiftly sawed through the rope of a grappling hook that had been launched up to grasp the wall, and then she did the same with another. Siege ladders had been erected against the fortress wall, and Aldashir and his warriors were hard-pressed to keep the enemy out. They'd taken the Midnight Cove hardly more than an hour ago, losing many elves in the process, and here they were already defending it. The numbers had been in their favor on the attack —especially with two Water Callers—but the numbers were not in their favor now. The enemy army was a little bit bigger and much fresher whereas Aldashir's people and the Highest allied with them were battle weary and bore many wounds large and small, all courtesy of vanquishing the Unsired who had defended the Black Water Well just a short time ago.

Another glance out of the corner of her eye saw Ell throwing himself into the fray. With his strength as a Water Caller, he pushed a ladder laden with tens of elves from the wall. The ladder cascaded to the ground below, shattering bodies and painting the rain-swept ground red. Rihya saw Miri loosen her bow and begin carefully picking targets, striking them at least half of the time she loosed. In a faraway part of her mind, Rihya was impressed with how far her new sister had come in the last months. But events swung her attention back to the fight before her soon enough. Another ladder had latched onto the wall just beyond Aldashir, and the enemy Departed and Unsired had gained a foothold. Aldashir, immediately to Rihya's right, stepped forward quickly to engage as he wielded his long sword in an almost delicate fashion—well, in as delicate a fashion as a person who was butchering flesh could—and hewed through the sudden swarm of enemies who topped the walls to contend with their defense. Shaved sides of heads and teeth filed to points were their common denominator. They were the typical Departed warriors, not like The Thousand that Aldashir commanded. There were also Unsired who fought among them, fiercely albeit blankly swinging axes, swords, and spears as they sought to reclaim the origin of their creation.

Rihya stepped up beside the dark prince—her prince—and swept one of her knives across one opponent's inner elbow joint, severing the artery and rendering the limb limp. She ducked the Unsired's jerky swing of an axe, came up inside its guard, stuck her other knife up into the elf's throat, and twisted. The enemy dropped in a lump, and Rihya dismissed him as quickly as she could pull her knife free. In the mayhem of battle, a moment's hesitation could be the end of her. An Unsired had somehow gotten behind Aldashir, her prince having pressed his attack into the heart of the foray, and the Unsired was about to plant a spear in his unsuspecting back. That is, it was until Rihya lunged in close behind and severed both of the Unsired's hamstrings with two outward cross-strokes. The Unsired collapsed in a heap, and Aldashir heard the noise as it fell. The dark prince flashed a wild grin at her, recognizing her contribution to his staying alive, a grin she responded to fiercely and in fashion before he then unceremoniously plunged his sword into the Unsired's chest as it lay on the ground grimacing and gurgling in its own blood.

Then Arendahl was there beside them, tapping his powers and fighting with the strength, speed, and agility of many trained elves. He pressed into the mass of attackers, killing them outright or forcing them from the wall to their inevitable deaths. He cleared the wall and cast the ladder down while Aldashir and Rihya, among other defenders, caught their breaths.

"My thanks, Elder," Aldashir panted.

Arendahl eyed him with an odd glance. "We are on the same side now, boy. No need to thank me." And then the grey-haired elf was off, away to another part of the wall that was congested with Unsired, much as Rihya could see her brother doing.

"Does he always do that?" Aldashir asked ruefully.

"Do what?"

"Call people 'boy' or 'girl'? It doesn't allow a person much dignity." Aldashir laughed but then grimaced as he felt the sting of a cut sustained on his shoulder.

Rihya stepped close to examine him. "I don't think Arendahl is much worried about what is dignified." She fingered his wound. "This isn't bad. It'll require bandaging later when we have time, but you should be fine for now."

The prince rolled his eyes, of all things. "Thank you for telling me what I already know, Valerihya." He laughed again.

Rihya turned away in a huff. "That will teach me the next time I plan to see to your wounds."

Aldashir caught her hand and pulled her back to him quickly and firmly, ending with their faces close together, him looming over her. He kissed her then, almost roughly and quite passionately. She melted into it. He tasted like sweat and salt, and rain, and there was the iron-like taste of blood from a cut on his lip. She pulled away.

"I like you tending to me," he said with a conciliatory grin.

"There is a battle going on." She pushed away and stared pointedly around them.

The prince shrugged. "Your brother and the elder have it for now."

Rihya looked around and saw that he was right. Two Water Callers on the wall made all the difference, and most of the wall was now clear of attackers, earning the defenders a reprieve. As if echoing the prince's words, a horn from the enemy ships signaled a retreat, and the attackers fell back, away from the wall and to the ships amid a hail of arrows.

She caught Aldashir staring at her out of the corner of her eye. "What?" she asked.

"I'm glad you're unhurt," he said tenderly. Rihya reached out and brushed his hand with hers in response.

But then wit caught up with her and she couldn't help but tease him. "You know, I've survived battles just fine, for many years and without you watching my back," she told him archly.

The prince rolled his eyes but said resolutely, "Either way, I'm glad you have me watching it now." Rihya couldn't help but feel warmed by his response.

A few minutes passed as both defenders and attackers licked their wounds. Then an hour. Rihya sat in weary silence, leaning against Aldashir's body. The rain that pelted them drummed incessantly, almost beating them together the way a smith folded metal and then hammered it into one.

"Does it ever end?" she asked.

"What?" The prince shifted so he could see her as they spoke. Rihya could gaze into his eyes—dark pools of water—forever but, for a moment, she was disappointed that her resting place had moved. She propped herself on one hand as she sat, leaning.

"This rain—does it ever stop?"

Aldashir shook his sodden head. "Not in the winter. It'll be like this for days. Why do you think I chose The Point? It's drier," he answered his own rhetorical question.

"I thought it was all that nonsense about finding honor," Rihya teased.

Aldashir took the ribbing good-naturedly. "Oh, it is, but more about the weather. I wanted to win you over before I divulged my true purpose for staying at The Point."

"All right," Rihya laughed tiredly.

The prince reached a hand over and enfolded her smaller hand in his own. It sent a familiar jolt of excitement through her, but there was also a comfortable feel to it now. Rihya liked that.

Another hour passed. "I would have thought they'd have pressed their advantage and attacked again by now," Rihya murmured, staring out at the fleet in the harbor.

Aldashir shrugged. "When your brother joined the fray, it tilted the scale a bit more evenly. Two Water Callers"—the prince didn't even stumble over saying that anymore—"are significantly better than one, I suppose. No, I think they'll sit back and wait it out. They have the numbers for a siege, and they know we can't afford to wait forever. Eventually, reinforcements will come to their aid."

Rihya nodded. "Makes sense."

"On that note, I supposed we should confer on our strategy with the others." Aldashir got to his feet and held a hand down to help her up. Rihya took it and allowed herself to be hauled up.

"Let's go find my brother."

They walked along the wall until they found Ell sitting with Miri, much as they had been, although he was also flanked by the rest of the company. Adan and Dacunda, their mother and sister, Arendahl, Iyonei, Ryder, and Brie were all in the same area. People were either resting or tending to weapons. Ryder was, of course, eating. He was practically stuffing his face with rations. Rihya shook her head as she passed him and shot him a mocking stare.

"What?" Ryder exclaimed. "I'm starving. Killing makes me hungry, and I definitely killed the most enemies of all of us—well, of all of us *normal* elves," he boasted with a wink. Rihya shook her head and rolled her eyes.

She and Aldashir sat down in the middle of the group. "Is it done?" Aldashir asked her brother tensely.

Ell nodded gravely, but a smile played at his lips. "It is."

"So you made good on your promise," the prince breathed.

"Miri did," Ell corrected, shooting a proud look toward his mate.

Rihya and Aldashir both shot surprised looks her way, as well. They opened their mouths to ask what he meant, but Ell cut them off. "A story for a later time. For now, what's important is that the Black Water Well has been destroyed. We need to be gone from here soon."

"Reinforcements will be coming," Aldashir agreed.

"We'll have to fight our way out, abandon the safety of the walls," Arendahl grunted.

"Fight our way to the ships, board them, then fight our way clear of the harbor. I prefer solid ground under my feet during battle, but either way it sounds a challenge." Iyonei grinned. Sometimes, Rihya wondered if she wasn't crazy. She seemed to enjoy a fight more than anyone Rihya had ever met.

"There will be excitement enough to go around," Arendahl grunted again before hunkering down over a mouthful of dried meat.

Adan leaned forward from the position in which he'd been resting against one of the fortress's wet walls. Thunder shattered the air as he spoke. "I'm not so sure I want to flee. I've seen who leads the enemy. It is from afar, but my eyes are keen enough to recognize him, even misshapen and half-dead as he is. You'll not easily convince me to walk away from a fight with Silverfist. Not after what he did to me, to my family, to us all."

Dacunda nodded in agreement, and Rihya was about to voice her agreement, too. They should deal with the traitor again, once and for all, but, surprisingly, it was Ell who spoke up first.

"I want him dead—again—as much as the rest of you. Believe me, I do," a gritty resolve speckled his voice, and for the first time Rihya really listened, really heard the danger in his tone as she saw him for the fearsome enemy he could be. She was glad he was on her side, was her brother by blood. He continued, "However, I fear we are in a race against time."

Arendahl cocked his head in question. "How so, boy?"

The rest seemed just as confused, but it was Aldashir who shared a look with Ell. A light of understanding seemed to shine in his eyes. "Retribution."

"But the enemy is already here. Where is this race against time that you speak of?" Iyonei demanded.

"He's talking about my family," Aldashir said quietly.

Ell nodded. "Arendahl and I didn't kill the King of the South. He escaped. Half-Mask is clearly not here. We may have destroyed Black Water Well, but *we* also have places of value."

"You think he means to counterstrike?" Arendahl asked, his eyes narrowing.

"My brother is nothing if not vindictive. He'll want like for like. We gouged his heart out, and he'll want yours—ours—as well," Aldashir confirmed.

"Yes," Ell agreed, "I couldn't have said it better."

"Where do you think he'll strike?" Lliaria asked, speaking up for the first time.

"Verdantihya. He'll go for our source, just like we went for his." Rihya was putting the pieces together now, too. "The city is already ruined, sacked two decades ago, but he'll want to take control of it. If he can control Verdantihya and cut us off from the Source, then that would be a blow we might not recover from." Worry darkened her voice as she spoke.

Ell and Arendahl exchanged a long look before the old elf said, "If control is *all* he's after." When pressed, Arendahl wouldn't say more, but both he and Ell seemed concerned, as if some hidden understanding had passed between them.

"We have to fight our way clear, and soon. Rest time is over. We've had a few hours to recuperate, but now we'll have to fight our way clear. Hopefully we can gain open water and outdistance them. Do you think we can?" Ell turned his gaze to Aldashir.

"My ships are better than most. If we fight our way past them, there's a good chance we can leave them behind us," the prince answered.

"Then it's settled," Rihya said, bounding to her feet and feeling a new spring in her step at the prospect of fighting once again. "We take the fight to them. They can sit back all they want, but when we come to them with two Water Callers in our midst, they'll be hard-pressed to keep us back."

"Hopefully," Arendahl cautioned as he fondled his sword handle. "But we all know that battles rest upon the unexpected."

———

WHEN THE GATES of the fortress opened wide and Aldashir and Ell led their allied forces out and toward the ships, Rihya was right beside them. They didn't catch the enemy army unexpected, though. Silverfist knew enough to discern that they would realize staying put wasn't an option. They couldn't sit behind the walls at the Midnight Cove and wait for reinforcements to arrive, so he had placed cohorts of his people on all of their ships. If they wanted them back, they would have to fight to recover them. Aldashir and Ell made straight for the great warship that belonged to the prince. With Ell spearheading the attack, they threw ropes with hooks onto the deck to hoist themselves up. Ell jumped up in one giant bound, and not for the first time Rihya marveled at what her brother could do with the Water Caller abilities that he possessed. He fought like a whirlwind on the deck of the warship, a fearless warrior from the First Days come again. He cleared enough space for Aldashir and Rihya to gain footing on the deck.

They stepped up beside him, shoulder to shoulder, trading blows with the enemy. Unsired populated this ship, almost as if Silverfist had decided to leave a particularly difficult pocket of defense on the warship he knew they wanted to retake at all costs. Yet they were no match for Ell flanked by Rihya and the prince. The rest of the company joined them, and they fought just as the rest of their forces fought to regain their ships and sail away from this place.

An Unsired stepped toward Rihya, and she glided past a sword swipe, effortlessly shifting her body so that the swing missed. She stepped in and opened up the Unsired's belly with one vicious slash of her knife. Aldashir was there beside her, sword flickering in the sodden lightning light of the storm. Rain plastered their hair to their faces as thunder rumbled. The ceaseless storm seemed to echo what was to come. Even should they fight their way free of this isle and make their way back north, the war was coming to a head. They—well, mostly Ell and Miri— had struck a blow at Half-Mask that he would not soon forget. He would want revenge.

Rihya swept through the enemy warriors on deck, dancing lightly as she always did through a fight, using her speed, agility, and diminutive size to avoid blows and sneak in close, eviscerating hamstrings and opening veins. These were the kind of wounds that killed a warrior whether she was technically the one to finish them off or not. Rihya had fought long enough to know that surviving—winning the battle—was what counted, not who received the glory. If someone speared a warrior she had downed, then so much the better. She was a viper amongst her enemies with quick slashes and fast retreats, and she was deadly—oh, so deadly.

It wasn't long before they had cleared the deck of Departed and Unsired under Silverfist's command. They looked around them and saw that Aldashir's company of The Thousand had regained many of the ships. But not all. Some ships didn't fall to retaking. Those warriors who lost the bid to regain their vessel fell back to the docks, regrouped, and then jammed themselves onto those that were retaken already. Time was of the essence. And all the while, the chaos of battle raged. Screams of the dying and wounded pierced the air, grunts of strain, clashes of steel, and of course the perennial winter storm resounded forcefully in the background. The one good thing about the weather was that the endless, pelting rain washed the decks clean of blood and sent rivulets down to the darkened sea to mix with the water of the cove that was already dispersing its fading blackness. Oh, the Midnight Cove was still black in color, but it was seeping outward into the ocean beyond the cove and not being replaced by blackness from the well. In time, it would cease to be dark in color, more akin to the water around it, and the cove's infamous blackness would live on only in memory.

Once they'd regained enough ships and packed their forces onto the ones that had been retaken, they loosened the moorings and set sail out to fight their way clear of the blockade of ships under Silverfist's command. Sea battles were different than Rihya was used to, but they would have plenty of Departed allies with them who were familiar with it.

Still the battle raged, just as the storm did, as Rihya and her companions fought to force their way out of the cove. Hulls of warships grinded against those of their enemies. Some ships became deadlocked, stuck together while the crews fought to defend their decks or attack others. Aldashir's great warship found some space and now fought its way through a mass of ships, archers' arrows picking off combatants on both sides. All in all, the second battle at the Midnight Cove was pure mayhem. Rihya, a seasoned warrior, felt the grip of fear in her heart as she fought through the pandemonium. A lull here as their break from one ship was followed by a clash with another. This time, the enemy fought desperately to board their ship. This was one of the last on their path out of the cove. If they could beat their way past, it was a race to open water and perhaps a clear shot north and homeward.

Rihya engaged a Departed warrior who had swung across the intervening gaps between ships on a rope just as many of his comrades were doing. Aldashir's warship deck was swarmed with enemies; this ship had more than the last to contend with. Rihya ducked the swipe of an axe, but not quickly enough. She felt the tip of it graze her temple, leaving a shallow cut. She darted in close and stuck a knife in her opponent's groin. He groaned in deathly defeat and sank to the deck. She breathed heavily. That had been close. Lose focus now, and she would not be likely to make it out of this battle alive.

Bodies jammed together on the deck, and it became difficult to tell friend from foe. The swarming mass of chaos separated her briefly from Aldashir's large frame, Ell, and the rest of her close companions. Steel rang out and shattered the winter air as sparks flashed from the clashes like tiny mirrors of the lightning above. Rihya fought on, engaging foes, methodically fighting her way through until it happened.

One moment to the next, she dispatched a foe and then the push of bodies shoved her face-to-face with the horrific sight of Silverfist. He looked more than half-dead, his body a mass of ropey, veiny flesh, but in many parts that flesh had sloughed off, leaving gaps of bone along his fingers and arm. His face was the worst, however, with one side of his cheek and jaw simply bone, teeth, and skull. The half-dead Silverfist leered at her and leaped to engage. He had not lost a step; for all the time spent in the grave he'd come out of it stronger, faster, more dangerous, if that were possible. He swung his rusty, silver fist toward her like a club, and she barely avoided the blow, knowing that its impact had nearly killed Ell last spring. She ducked in under his blade and made to open his stomach, but he danced back again, laughing a raspy laugh as he flicked his blade and opened a gash on her shoulder.

Think, Rihya! Don't underestimate him! You won't get off so easy next time. She forced herself to focus. Here he was, the traitor to her people, the reason Verdantihya stood in ruins. Anger boiled beneath the surface. He was responsible for capturing and selling her family into slavery. He had led the attempted sacking of Little Vale. She fought warily but pressed her attack, fighting for her people, for her family, for retribution. The dead should stay dead, and she meant to remind him of that.

Rihya turned away his sword with her blades in a clash of steel and darted in quicker than last time, quick enough that she saw the surprise flicker in his eyes as she moved. But it was too late. One knife found his gut, and the other his chest, scraping bone as it entered. It was a killing blow, and Rihya kept hold of the knife in Silverfist's gut, yanking it out as he staggered back from her. She lost her grip on the knife in his chest, however, and it stuck hilt-deep in his body. He stared at it in shock for a moment but then turned his dead eyes toward her again, grinning a ghastly smile. Silverfist slowly wrapped his sinewy, bone-exposed fingers around the hilt and pulled the blade out like it was nothing. Blood didn't even cover the blade as it exited his body. Instead, the substance was more of a sludge like that found leaking out of a corpse.

"It'll take more than that to put me in the grave again, girl. I'm not going back," Silverfist whispered with a rattling chuckle.

Rihya shuddered and felt the icy fear of the unknown grasp at her heart. *What is he? Is he even alive?*

She pulled another knife from her belt and readied herself for more, but then Aldashir was by her side and a push of bodies surrounded her, pressing the advantage they had gained and forcing Silverfist and his warriors back over the rail and onto their own ship. Aldashir's warriors cut the lines and hooks connecting the ships, and oars pulled hard from the galley to push their ship out to sea. Separation was gained and freedom was in sight, but all Rihya could seem to do was stare in horror and wonder at the receding figure of the ghastly, exhumed Silverfist as he glared after them in anger while they escaped.

Their ship gained open water and sailed into the teeth of the winter wind howling from the north. More and more of their ships—those crewed by The Thousand—did the same. But not all. More elves were lost. It was a battle—it was a *war*, after all. Still, many escaped with them. The race was on, but Aldashir was right. His ships were better crafted and better crewed. As soon as space was given them, they cut north, and his now-diminished fleet began to outdistance Silverfist's.

Rihya slumped against the mast and stared behind them, still unable to shake the horror of what Half-Mask had raised from the grave. Somehow, she knew it wasn't over. Silverfist would keep coming. There had been a light in his eyes, an eagerness that would not likely abate. They would see him again.

The storm continued to rage as the ships sailed into its teeth. They set the course north, The Thousand mixed with their allies from the north and the pirate ship captained by Piripeos. They sailed north toward home.

It felt like ages since Rihya had left Andalaya, but she would see it again soon. They were going home.

CHAPTER TWENTY-FIVE

The trip north felt long, even though by all accounts it was not exceptionally so. Ell drummed his fingers on the rail of the warship as it gradually closed the distance to the shore. Two weeks to navigate the narrow channels and backwaters of the sea and crisscrossing the Enclaves was enough time to clear the majority of them and make for more open waters to the north. The stormy weather had abated slightly but continued off and on to keep their pace steady instead of quick.

"Have you ever seen the north?" Ell asked Aldashir who stood beside him.

"Only in my mind, when stories and tales set free my imagination," he murmured, staring pensively toward the rocky shore.

"Well, it won't be long before you can't say that anymore," Ell responded, amiably slapping his comrade on the shoulder. "We can't be more than an hour or so away from dropping anchor in the shallows."

"True. It will be interesting to see what lines up with the myths our people have created about the north. Are there really trees that are tall as the towers of a fortress?" the prince asked, sounding intrigued yet skeptical.

Rihya stepped up beside them; she was rarely found far from Aldashir these days, or he from her. "Bigger. We call them Evergrow Trees. They tower above the forest canopy, dwarfing all others around them."

"And the beasts, are they real also?"

Rihya and Ell shared a grim look. Ell wasn't sure how much of the northern plight Rihya had told the prince, but he assumed she'd told him most of it. "You'll see soon enough, no doubt."

"Just tell me, is it true?" Aldashir inquired.

"Yes. Ghouls plague the north like flies to a dead carcass. Ogres tread the forest floor looking for meals, and the Icari fly by night, nesting in the high crags. The dark creatures have long since awakened and returned to ravage the land, probably at your brother's bidding," Ell spat sourly. He felt bad when he saw the flash of pain cross the prince's face, but it would do no good to shield Aldashir from the truth of what his family had done.

"I cannot remember a time when I didn't wish to be part of another family, a better one," Aldashir told them, a mournful tone entering his voice.

"You have a new family now," Rihya said, the warmth in her words genuine, yet it only partially seemed to salve the wounds Aldashir suffered when speaking of his family. Yet the prince smiled a wan smile and cupped her hand in his. They were surprisingly tender toward one another. Ell never would have guessed that his sister could be gentle. She was usually just the opposite: fierce and fiery, a quicksilver temper and a mercurial attitude. But with Aldashir she was different. Ell supposed it must be much like he was with Miri. She balanced him out somehow, tempered his anger, soothed his fire, and yet managed to stoke that same fire when needed.

Ell stepped away and let the two share their moment in solitude. He walked toward Miri who was deep in heated conversation with Arendahl. Ell caught the tail end of it.

"He deserves to know the full truth of it," Miri was urging the old elf.

Arendahl sighed gustily. "I suppose so. It's far enough along that the boy won't likely object. Besides, he's grown since we started this."

"Started what?" Ell asked, feeling suspicious as he strode up silently, startling them out of their whispered discussion.

"Oh! Ell, I didn't hear you approaching," Miri said somewhat nervously. Ell narrowed his eyes even more. Something was up.

Arendahl pursed his lips in thought but didn't answer. Miri glanced back and forth between the two Water Callers locked in a staring contest. Finally, Arendahl shrugged. "Fine, we've come far enough, I suppose. There's an army waiting in Legendwood."

"Good!" Ell exclaimed in surprise. "Where's the issue?"

Miri rolled her eyes as the old elf stayed quiet. She spoke, and vexation permeated her words. "What Arendahl isn't saying is that there is an army waiting, yes, but more importantly, it's waiting for you. It is waiting for you to lead."

Ell stared at the two of them in silence for a moment. A year ago—a few months ago, or maybe even a few weeks ago—that information might have frightened him. All that responsibility on his shoulders would be enough to make anybody feel the weight of it. But life had changed. He'd done things, things that defied what he should have been capable of doing. Maybe his father was right: maybe Ell could be a great leader. Besides, with the taint on his consciousness gone, he felt much more fit to make decisions.

"Fine," was all he said.

Both Arendahl and Miri peered at him closely. It was their turn to be suspicious. "He's handling this awfully well, don't you think?" Miri asked the old elf.

"He is," Arendahl allowed slowly. "Surprisingly well."

"Enough, you two. What's done is done. I'm sure you needed someone to rally our people behind. Arendahl no doubt thinks himself too old or some such nonsense and volunteered me for the job. It's fine. I understand and, truth be told, I've been leading and making enough decisions these past months that I'm all right with it now." Ell got it all out in a rush, as if saying the words quickly and forcefully might be enough to push away the tiny bit of doubt that was left in him—the doubt that screamed from a back corner of his mind that leading a few family members into danger was much different than ordering troops of his people into battle.

"Are you sure you're all right, love?" Miri asked tentatively, her eyes searching his face, drinking him in with worry. "I confess, I thought you would be furious when you found out what we'd been doing all summer while you were gone."

Ell shrugged tiredly, a new weariness that came from one battle after another. "It had to be done. We needed an army. It was time to take a stand, and Arendahl did what he had to do to galvanize our people. Besides, I'll have my father, Dacunda, and Iyonei among others to advise me and make decisions with me. Oh, and I suppose I'll also have you to pull on for advice, as well," he joked offhandedly at the old elf.

Arendahl looked put out for a moment by the jest but then guffawed loudly. "Hold onto that spirit boy. It'll help you when things get tough.

As they always do. Well, now that this is settled, I think I'll find a meal." With that, the old elf was off, leaving Ell alone with Miri.

"Truly, you're fine?" she asked again, enfolding him in an embrace.

"Honestly, a part of me expected this," Ell admitted. "He was always going to need a figurehead for the army, a rally point. Who better than a young Water Caller."

"You'll do well, love."

Ell nodded gratefully and then kissed her, tasting the lilywater on her lips, that signature mark she'd managed to maintain even far away from Andalaya. "Thanks, and I really won't be making decisions alone."

"No, you won't. You've a lot of support around you. And anyway, I trust your judgment. You've done what nobody thought could be done on more than one occasion." A note of pride crept into her voice as she spoke, and Ell thought that if only Miri believed in him, if it was just her, it would probably be enough. She was the rock on which his footing in this life rested.

Before he could tell her that, footsteps approached, and Ell's mother, father, and eldest sister approached. The ship inched closer to the shore; it would not be long now.

"We wanted to be with you when it was time to disembark and set foot on home soil again for the first time," Delle said with a smile. "We owe our return to you."

"To all of us," Ell said in slight embarrassment, a flush coloring his cheeks.

"Yes, to everyone, but most of all to you," his mother said. Lliaria grabbed his hand tightly, her worn and callused fingers rough against his own. "I never thought I would see Andalaya again, let alone set foot upon its soil, and yet here I am, surrounded by my family and about to return home." Tears moistened the corners of her eyes, and Adan put an arm around her.

The shore was in close sight now, and Ell heard the anchor drop as they reached the shallows. Shouts of orders to drop skiffs onto the sea echoed from not just their ship but the others nearby in the small fleet.

"Where is your sister?" Adan asked, craning his head to find her.

"Here," Rihya responded, one fair hand holding Aldashir's dark one.

Adan smiled in relief. "We are all together now, as it should be in this moment."

They climbed down the rope ladders to the skiffs, and Ell smelled the scent of the forest brought to them on the wind mixing with the tang of the sea. The rain was a slow drizzle, and it kept the mood relatively calm even in the face of their homecoming. Ell's feet landed on the wood of the skiff, and the rest of them climbed down to accompany him. Departed sailors worked the oars, the steady pull of their muscled arms fighting the small waves and breakers that swelled up and down underneath them as they crept closer and closer.

The skiff finally beached on a rocky strand of coast, and the wind whipped in winter fashion. Ell leaped over and helped pull the boat farther up the beach, his legs getting soaked up to the knee in the salty water. Adan had done the same and strained along with him. When the boat was on dry sand, everyone jumped out. Adan, Lliaria, and Delle knelt. They put the fingers of both hands to their lips, kissed the tips, and then extend them outwards, palms forward in the traditional greeting of the Highest when returning home. It was more often associated with Verdantihya itself, but Ell supposed that returning anywhere on home soil after two decades away from Andalaya was enough to merit the gesture.

"Is that Legendwood?" Aldashir asked almost tentatively as he pointed to the darkened forest that ran all the way up to the rocky shore upon which they stood.

"We aren't far enough north," Adan told him.

"That would be the Lower Forest—the northern reaches of it, anyway," Ell supplied. "A few days journey and we'll be in Legendwood proper. Soon enough, we'll be in the mountains: the heart of Andalaya."

"Is it strange that I'm nervous?" the prince asked, swallowing as he did so.

"You have nothing to fear here. This is home. Your home, too, even if your people don't recall that. Your ability to be healed by Source Water proved that much, even if you don't realize it yet," Adan reassured Aldashir, a fatherly hand placed upon the prince's shoulder.

Aldashir grinned in relief. "Home." He sounded the word out slowly, almost as if tasting it.

"Home," Rihya echoed firmly.

"Home," they all said together as they stared at the forest shadows darkened by winter clouds. More skiffs pulled toward the shore, carrying what was left of the small army they'd taken into the heart of the Enclaves. Dacunda, Ryder, and Brie were no doubt on those skiffs, as were Arendahl, Piripeos, and others. Ell felt a sudden jolt of elation.

He was back in the north. He was home again. He tapped his powers just for the feel of them, felt the power pool in his chest as he tapped into the Creation around him, the familiar, beloved Creation of his homeland.

Ell smiled. He was home.

––––––––

ELL LEANED his back against the bowl of a huge Evergrow Tree, one of the few to have taken root this far south. Most of the Evergrow Trees were in Legendwood, in the heart of Andalaya, their trunks propelling them to twice the height of the forest canopy or sometimes even more. Their seedlings released so high into the air that they drifted far and wide on the wind, accounting for the often long distance between trees of their kind.

It was a midday rest on their trek north. They were just about to leave the northern edge of the Lower Forest. Anticipation had filled Ell and many of the rest of his companions all morning long. It would not be long before the familiar sights, sounds, and scents of his homeland began to truly assail their senses.

Ell and Miri sat shoulder to shoulder, eating in comfortable silence and listening to the quiet rumble of conversation throughout the group. Ell had never traveled by land in such a large company of warriors before. He'd never even been a part of an army, having spent the vast majority of his life fighting from the shadows, loosing darkened arrows unseen by his enemies during raids and ambushes. They were the slash and run, small-force tactics that his people had relied upon for decades. But that was all changing. They had allies to the south now—few, but still some Departed were on their side. According to Miri and Arendahl, they had gathered together more of the Highest than had been seen in one place since the fall of Verdantihya. Most importantly, the human and Departed alliance that had threatened the north for the past twenty years was on its last legs, if it even existed at all anymore. It meant that the contest for the continent was now a three-way conflict and the northern numbers were not at quite such a disadvantage as they had been. Oh, the Highest were still outnumbered, to be sure, but it felt different. There was hope again for the first time in Ell's memory.

"What was that structure?"

"A Pillar. Are you telling me you've never heard of them? They're the tabletop-like fortresses erected by your people and the humans to control the southern edge of Andalaya," Rihya responded incredulously.

"Ah, yes," the prince murmured, "I have heard of them. I guess I just wasn't aware of how oddly shaped they are. Word in the south is that they are impregnable, with their narrow base and series of ladders and pulleys to ascend to the wider, flattened fortress top."

The voices wafted around the trunk of the tree, and Ell felt guilty for a moment for eavesdropping on a conversation that was not his own, but his pointed ears perked at the mention of his name, and he left his sensibilities behind.

"Not for Ell," Rihya said somewhat smugly.

"What? Can he really fly, like the rumors say? I heard a fantastical tale that he flew to the top of one and annihilated an entire cohort of Departed." Aldashir's surprise was clearly tempered by skepticism.

Ell exchanged a smile with Miri as they both listened. Last spring, he had rescued her from a slaver party that had imprisoned her and other elves—the boy Art among them—in the Pillar dungeons, awaiting the right moment to be sent south to Dark Harbor or beyond. It was there that Borian had turned traitor once and for all.

Rihya answered Aldashir, and Ell could hear the grin in her voice as she spoke of his feats. "No, he can't fly. But he did forcibly ride an Icari to the top, a feat which is almost more impressive."

"An Icari?"

Ell imagined his sister shaking her head in dismissal as she responded to the prince's latest question fondly. "You have much to learn, my princeling. An Icari is just one of the many dark creatures that inhabit Andalaya and plague our people. They are controlled by the Unsired— more specifically Spectralists—"

"My brother and father you mean," Aldashir interjected bitterly.

"Your family," Rihya continued smoothly as if his interruption had not changed the course of her miniature lecture, "have control of them. And not just the Icari but also Stone Ogres, Wood Ogres, and last but not least, Ghouls."

"And whatever Silverfist has become. I'm sorry, but I simply cannot think of him as a normal, living elf. He is something worse, something evil." Aldashir's voice was verging on angry.

"We agree on that point," Rihya said before continuing to lecture the prince on what to expect in the north.

Ell let the conversation fade away into the background as he closed his eyes for a lazy moment and leaned his cheek against the top of Miri's head. He smelled the scent of clean sweat from a half-day's travel, the lilywater on her breath, the small flowers with which she had decorated the braids of her golden hair, and felt more at peace than he had in a long time.

Miri breathed in and out next to him, and he felt her breathing slow down until he was almost positive she was asleep. Napping when a moment presented itself was a warrior's right. It wasn't often that they felt safe enough to nap, so often were they in places of danger and risk. So, when the opportunity presented itself, they were loath to allow it to pass.

Ell felt a flicker of regret that he was now forced to think of Miri as a warrior, but it was the truth. She had fought in skirmishes and now an outright battle at the Midnight Cove. She'd killed and nearly *been* killed. That had the potential to harden many an elf, and he hoped beyond hope that it would not do so with her. Somehow, though, he wasn't as worried about her as he might be about another. After all, she had Grafted with him, and that required an immense amount of emotion—of love and caring—to accomplish it. That wasn't conducive with a temperament that was prone to hardening.

"Elliyar." The voice and the gentle hand shaking his shoulder woke him from the doze into which he'd slipped. Lliaria's creased face—worn for an elf's, reflecting her years of hard labor in Lu Fang—was the first thing he saw as he awakened.

"What is it?"

"A small scouting party of our people have come across our path," his mother responded as Miri shifted and awakened beside him.

"Any casualties?" Ell asked, alert with worry now.

His mother saw where his thoughts had gone. "Luckily, no. We've posted our people as sentries instead of our Departed allies, so our people were the first they saw, heading off any misunderstanding."

Ell breathed a sigh of relief. Commanding—or, at the very least, sharing command of—a large force of elves meant that he was constantly worried for their safety. Nothing would be worse than to be welcomed home by deaths due to friendly allies.

"Go," Miri murmured. "I'll wake slowly and catch up with you later." A lazy smile crossed her face and she closed her eyes again, drifting into the half-sleep of newly awakened consciousness.

He kissed her forehead, stood, and picked his way through the scattered bodies and items of the camp, following his mother. Before long, they reached the northern edge of midday camp and Ell saw Dacunda speaking with a member of the Highest, one not in their party.

Arendahl, Adan, and Iyonei were also arriving just as Ell and Lliaria were, runners having been sent to find them all.

Ell approached the leader of the unfamiliar Highest scouts and said, "Report."

The elf looked around the small cluster of the army's leaders strangely, but when none contradicted Ell's order, he spoke. Still, he addressed his report somewhere in between Arendahl and Ell. Ell supposed that would likely never change, and yet, now that he had accomplished his goal of retrieving his family from the south and wasn't facing such opposition from his elders, he felt oddly relieved to have Arendahl alongside him. Their task in Dark Harbor and beyond had been much more difficult without the old elf.

"We are scouting into the Lower Forest," the elf said, "routine reconnaissance."

"I meant, report on the state of our people, of the north, of the conflict," Ell clarified.

The Highest blushed slightly, and Ell realized he was not much older than himself, hardly more than a youth. "Of course. The conflict has escalated. Humans are pushing north and west into the forest from their eastern camps in greater numbers than ever. We see fewer slavers, but the few Departed we've managed to capture speak of a greater force mobilizing to the south. In short, everything seems to be coming to a head."

"Have any of the humans you've managed to capture spoken of anything useful?" Dacunda prompted.

Iyonei snorted and muttered, "I'm still not convinced we should capture any of them, regardless of information. They deserve long and painful deaths for their invasion."

The elf ignored the one-eyed warrior and answered Ell's uncle as Dacunda gave her a reproachful look. "Bits and pieces of useful information. Their leader, the Grand Marshall, is set on pushing inland. Some sort of retribution for a revolt we supposedly started in their land, though how we managed to do that from way over here is beyond me."

"You'd be surprised at what we can accomplish when we put our minds to it," Adan said as an aside, and the scout cocked his head in question. When no answer was forthcoming, he resumed his report.

He relayed more information about the eastern front. "They must be aware we are amassing in greater numbers, since our skirmishes have escalated. We're still raiding and ambushing but in greater numbers and taking out greater targets. Other scouts report that some of their numbers, though, seem to be moving south and west, oddly enough."

"So the rumors of the split are true." Arendahl pursed his lips in thought. "The prince had mentioned that, but this seems even more confirmation."

"That's good. Even if Half-Mask and the King of the South move north, they'll have to leave behind a force to guard their capital," Lliaria ventured.

"But less than you might expect," Adan countered as the conversation opened up. "The Hillforts are strong. A lesser force can hold them against much greater numbers. And even with Aldashir out of the southern seas, the Departed still have warships and longships to ravage any fleet that tries to take them by sea."

"I suspect the human force moving south is just enough to anchor some of the Departed troops there. Etheros is huge, and an ocean of humans are always adding to the ranks of their armies. Even with a revolt on their home soil and a fracture to their alliance with the Departed, they'll still have the numbers, and they know that," Dacunda said.

"But anything is possible in a three-way conflict," Ell murmured. "This is good news on the whole."

Everyone agreed. They questioned the scout some more and then sent him back north to report to his direct commanders with more orders from them. The war had well and truly begun. Ell thought that he'd started it all by leading his force into the Midnight Cove, but the truth was that the war had already been brewing and had begun in the east. Actually, it had begun over twenty years ago when the humans had first invaded, or maybe more accurately it had begun when the Departed and the Highest split. No, this was just a reincarnation of an old war. It had begun in the First Days when the Highest were spun out by Creation to right the wrong of the Unsired and the Spectralists that had polluted the world. This newest war was just an offshoot.

But that didn't change the fact that war was here. It had come to him, to his company and his army. Ell was certain of one thing: before long, war would arrive at the heart of Andalaya.

CHAPTER TWENTY-SIX

Something had changed. The-elf-who-had-once-been-Silverfist stared uncertainly back and forth between his two masters. He'd arrived in Dark Harbor only a short time ago. He had wanted to pursue Wintermoon north, but the speed of their ships would easily outdistance his own. And so logic had compelled him to check in with his masters instead before once again setting off in pursuit.

"What should we do?" the King of the South muttered almost under his breath as he paced, like an elf who was talking more to himself than to those around him. The king had always been half-mad—the Black Water Well liquid had made sure of that—but he'd been cunning and resourceful, as well. Most of all, he had been imposing. Half-Mask had been just as terrifying, just as wily, but there had always been equality between them. Perhaps there was a slight tilt in the king's favor as the elder. That was different now, though. The younger Spectralist was firmly in control.

"Quit pacing," Half-Mask told his father in exasperation. "The boy's escape changes little. What is done is still done. The well is gone, and we cannot change the past. But we *can* modify the future in our favor."

"Yes, yes of course," the king mumbled, clenching and unclenching his hands like a female wringing hers. "May I—may I have some?" Silverfist had noticed the changes between them, but even he hadn't expected to hear the pleading note in the king's voice.

Half-Mask rolled his eyes. "You just had some not even an hour ago."

He flicked his eyes toward the dark corner of the room where a few barrels of leftover opposite source remained.

"But you said we had more in storage rooms deep below the palace," the King of the South pressed with a fevered look, like the addicts Silverfist had seen begging for coin along the alleys of Dark Harbor, hoping for a gift in order to see to their destructive habits.

Silverfist edged away from the king—just a little. The dynamic of power had shifted toward the younger of the two, but that didn't mean the king wasn't still dangerous. Silverfist had seen addicts kill for a single rakka, one coin that could hardly purchase them anything.

A wary look entered Half-Mask's eyes as he appraised his father, and he tensed slightly, making Silverfist edge even more slightly away from the two of them. Silverfist might be able to withstand a blade to the chest and who knew what else, but he doubted he'd survive an encounter with his re-creators. Spectralists had powers he simply could not match.

"Very well, you may have some more," Half-Mask relented and waved a hand toward the barrels. The king dived toward them greedily, landing on his knees before the nearest, uncapped barrel and cupping dark liquid to his mouth, staining his lips and smearing his cheeks.

"Not too much!" Half-Mask's voice cracked like a whip. "We have a finite supply...for now, at least," and Silverfist saw by the clever look on his face that the Prince of Darkness had a plan brewing.

Half-Mask turned his dark face toward Silverfist, his black, form-fitting mask covering the left side of his face from his forehead down to the jaw. The full force of his stare fell upon Silverfist, and the undead elf nodded his head in a bow. He was not too proud to defer to his betters—or, at least, those more powerful than he.

"It seems you are not as useful as we had hoped." Half-Mask peered at him critically as he spoke, sliding forward with graceful steps, slithering like a serpent around Silverfist as he continued, "You failed. I tasked you to kill the boy."

"You never told me he turned your brother to his cause or that he had an army at his disposal," Silverfist retorted boldly—more boldly than he felt.

Half-Mask grimaced at the comment, and all the while slurping sounds echoed across the room from the corner. "I suppose that is true," the Prince of Darkness allowed grudgingly. "Still, I will expect better next time. The time for games is over. I want Wintermoon dead once and for all."

"It should be easier to do so now that he is not threatening to *become*.

The chance of him joining your ranks as a Spectralist winked out with the destruction of the Black Water Well. I am sure you felt it the same as I."

Half-Mask nodded curtly. "A failed experiment. Admittedly, a bad one. No matter. You'll kill him for me—or I will if I see him—when we move north."

"We are mustering the armies?"

"They are already gathered." Half-Mask smirked. "Victory will be delicious." The prince licked his tongue across his needle-sharp teeth— teeth that made him resemble one of the deep-sea fishes oft pulled up in the nets of the Rimmer fisherfolk. Silverfist—even half-dead—shivered unintentionally at the sight. He never planned on crossing Half-Mask. Ever.

"What about the humans? Their Grand Marshall will not enjoy you're breaking the alliance."

"Tsk! What do I care for them? I have powers they do not. I command creatures, armies they know nothing about. Ogres rise at my orders, Icari and Ghouls kill on my command. The time for the alliance is over. I simply needed time to build my army of Unsired. It's finally time to enact my plan."

"And what is that plan?" Silverfist queried.

"I suppose it does not hurt to share it with you now that you are a trusted helper," Half-Mask agreed. Once, that had not been true. Once, Half-Mask had used the living Silverfist but had kept him at arm's length. That was another change. Silverfist was tethered now, tied to his purpose —the destruction of Wintermoon—and tied to his masters, the two elves in the room.

He inclined his head. "So, what shall our armies do?"

Half-Mask's hands clenched into fists as he spoke, his excitement and exultation rising into a crescendo as he spoke. "We march north. We join with our dark brothers—the creatures who do my bidding—adding them to our forces. We kill Wintermoon once and for all. We pay back my brother for his treachery. And finally..." he trailed off somewhat theatrically.

Silverfist bit. "Yes, and then, finally, what?"

"And then, finally, we transport as many barrels of the Black Water Well that I have collected for such a time as this north with us. Once we have laid waste to the Highest and to the humans, we will turn their precious Source against them. They thought to destroy Black Water Well without repercussion?" Spittle flecked around Half-Mask's angry mouth as he spoke. "Well, we shall do one better! We will transform their Source into a newer, more powerful Black Water Well, one that will be carried all across the land as it pumps from its dark spring in Verdantihya."

"You will transform the Source?" Silverfist repeated incredulously. Even as a traitor, the Source was an ever-present fixture in his mind. He couldn't imagine Andalaya without it. "Is that even possible?"

"I know it is. I can and *will* do it," Half-Mask declared.

The king finally pulled himself away from the barrels, his pocked face and pointed ears pricking in attention. "A new Black Water Well?"

"Yes, father. A better, stronger, larger one."

A manic grin spread across the king's face and he danced a mad jig, black royal robes and all. Silverfist watched the king's madness and then looked inquiringly at the prince.

Half-Mask just shrugged, a small smirk streaking across his face. "He still has his powers. He will be useful, but make no mistake; the well's destruction nearly broke him. *I* control my father now, and you would do well to remember that, Silverfist."

The delight mixed with menace in the prince's voice made him swallow a rattling lump in his decaying throat. "I will not forget it, Master."

CHAPTER TWENTY-SEVEN

A week of angling their course northeast since meeting with the scouts had led to this moment. Ell stood poised atop a ridgeline on the western edge of Legendwood not far from the North Crag. His black Dreampine arrow was nocked and ready to draw; a quick motion would be enough to tense the string and loose. This was what he did best, this was what he'd been doing his entire life. This was an ambush.

The small army of humans inched their way closer along the valley floor, the dense tree line pushing them close to the ridge. Ell had an army at his back, as well, waiting and ready to attack. He'd led his company of elves—Highest and Departed—in the direction the scouts had directed them until they met up with one of the small, roving parties that had gathered in Andalaya. A few thousand of the Highest mixed with the company he led north might not equal the sea of numbers available to the humans or even Half-Mask to the south, but it was the biggest force of Highest that Ell had ever seen. And there were more like it scattered throughout the western and southern edges of his homeland.

The humans had been pushing further inland, striking harder, and committing larger numbers now that their alliance with the Departed had capitulated and they could no longer count on the slavers to do their work for them. Also, Ell had an inkling that the humans were bitter about the revolt he'd started in Lu Fang and were eager to exact their revenge. All this led to an increase in the conflict's scale and severity.

Ell sighted his arrow as he drew, waiting for a good portion of the human army to march past, allowing the ambush to take full effect. As one his companions would step from their cover at the ridgeline or from behind trees and loose. This was an entire army of his people and allies waiting for ambush. They still fought with their dark arrows, a relic of a time when slash and run tactics were all that was possible, but that time was changing. Andalaya was about to begin her last stand, and no more hiding was necessary.

"Now!" Ell shouted when the army below had progressed far enough. He stepped from behind the tree that was his cover and loosed his first shaft into the mass below. A war cry erupted from around him, and the elves he led joined him in firing. Arrows streamed down into the small valley, and the humans screamed in anguish and in frantic attempts to raise shields and find cover. There *was* no cover. The forest behind was too dense and full of thickets for retreat, so the only thing to do was attack up the steep ridgeline, a grade that was nearer a small cliff than anything else. Yet charge the humans did, out of desperation. Ell and his elves loosed arrow after arrow until their quivers were empty. They leaped down the ridgeline to meet the enemy in hand-to-hand combat.

The humans were weakened by the ambush, smarting and injured, but they were many. Ell and his army clashed violently with the armored men in their chainmail and helmets. Broad shoulders wielding long swords and heavy, double-bladed axes met lithe elven bodies wielding spears, long-axes, and finer-edged blades. It was a clash of cultures as much as tactics. Bearded faces grimaced in fear or anger as they faced off with the exotic features of the elves.

Ell swept his two dueling daggers to either side of him as he slashed his way through the enemy. He blocked blows with one blade while opening arteries with the other. He was a Water Caller in full might, and the humans stood no chance—well, at least not individually. But enough enemies surrounding even a Water Caller could leave marks. He gained shallow wounds on his arms and legs and a deeper gash on his ribs, but all who came near him died.

Aldashir led The Thousand with green-haired Rihya by his side. His Departed warriors hewed through their opponents like the cutters the humans employed to pillage the forest. Ryder and Brie—who were often found together these days—fought side by side, as well. They made for an odd pair: a giant elf with a diminutive blonde, his long-axe to her hand axes. But they were a good pair all the same. Back-to-back, they covered each other's blind spots and felled enemies left and right.

Ell focused on his immediate surroundings, but his distraction cost him. He ducked an axe swipe but felt a spear enter his calf muscle from behind. He fell to his knees in pain, swiveling on his knees and bringing up a blade to block the downstroke of a sword. Two humans teamed up and, injured as he was, Ell felt his strength ebbing. He managed to fend off a thrust of the spear from one human with a parry of his own, and the same for the sword strike of the other, but it was only a matter of time. The wound to his leg was leaking blood in spurts, and Ell felt his body weakening by the moment. He gritted his teeth and shoved himself up from his knees to his feet, stumbling slightly as he did. This couldn't be how it ended for him. A Water Caller killed in the early phase of the war was unacceptable, at least by Ell's standards. He was forced back by another thrust of the spear and another slash of the sword. Ell grimaced, preparing to throw himself into one last attack with his two immediate enemies when a pair of arrows exploded through their throats from back to front. The two humans crumpled, their glazed eyes unseeing. Ell looked up to the ridgeline and saw Miri and Lliaria staring down at him, already nocking two more arrows to their strings. They had saved him.

Ell stumbled out of the middle of the fray, just barely fighting off another human in the process. He made it to the ridgeline and scrambled weakly up the steep face, grasping rock and bush to get himself to the top. He looked down at his leg and saw just how much blood he was losing. Collapsing on his back when he made the ridgeline, he gasped for air, vision blackening as blood loss threatened to make him lose consciousness. Then a hand was there, supporting the back of his head and tilting it up toward a flask of water held to his mouth.

"Here, drink son. Drink." Lliaria poured the Source Water down his throat in copious amounts, and Ell felt its healing powers take effect immediately. He could feel his wounds close—all but the calf wound, as that was deep, a vicious strike to his muscle and would require a bit more time to heal. Even so, the wound shrunk somewhat, and the blood clotted, aided by the Source Water's mystical properties.

Ell pushed himself up to a sitting position. "Thank you, Mother. My thanks to both of you for saving my life." He directed his comments to Miri and Lliaria.

They smiled, both grateful that he was well enough to sit but clearly still worried, judging by the way they looked ready to reach out and hold him up if necessary.

A few other archers had stayed away from the fray to pick targets. Delle was amongst them, and she focused her volley of arrows to the area around Adan and Dacunda who fought together in the thickest part of the battle. Ell felt his worry ebb as he saw his father—so fluid in defense and even more dangerous in attack—dispatch each foe he faced. Dacunda was only fractionally less strong a swordsmen, and the two of them spearheaded one thrust of the elven army while Aldashir, Rihya and his Thousand took on the other.

The battle raged, and Ell watched, recovering from his vantage point as the humans were mercilessly decimated. The elves lost many, too, but nothing compared to the losses of the ambushed invaders.

And then, on the northern edge of the battle, a small pocket of mayhem appeared. Shrieks from both sides of the conflict pierced the air, and Ell looked on in distress as a band of Ghouls sprinted out of the woods, bounding off boulders and leaping from the trees that their suctions allowed them to climb like humanoid spiders. A Stone Ogre and a few Wood Ogres plodded from the tree line to the north, as well, their red eyes burning angrily. The band of dark creatures set upon elf and human alike. Ogres flailed their powerful fists, decapitating heads and crushing bodies. Elves and men alike stiffened at the touch of Ghouls' suctions as the toxin they released paralyzed their victims. Warriors fell to teeth and claws. And still, both sides battled one another. It was a vicious, three-way contest on the northern side of the battle, and Ell ached to join, to fight the dark creatures as a Water Caller was created to do, but his injuries prevented him. Instead, Arendahl flanked by Adan and Dacunda led the defense against the dark creatures. The three-way melee to the north was a cacophony of sound. Steel ground on claws while guttural bellows and cackles proceeded from the creatures' mouths. Humans, who had never seen such things before, screamed in panic and fought frantically to retreat. Arendahl was too much for them, though. He slew Ghouls and even a Tree Ogre by himself while arrow after arrow peppered the rest before the other creatures were finished off. It had only been a small band of dark creatures, but they had worked cohesively and cost the elves many lives. Ell had been fairly certain he'd seen the dark figure of an Unsired lurking in the shadows behind his minions, commanding them, bending them to his will and into battle. It was a bleak omen, and he couldn't help but feel that it painted an ugly picture of the larger conflict that was to come when Half-Mask made his way north.

On and on the battle raged. Eventually, it was too much, and the humans—even with their numerical advantage—broke and ran, retreating back the way they had come. It was a hasty, desperate retreat, leaving them exposed to arrows loosed into their backs. It was almost sickening how many died as they ran. Or it would have been if Ell didn't know what they had done to his people and how many more of them there were in the Camps on the eastern shore.

Arendahl tasked Iyonei to lead the band of harriers who pressed the humans even in retreat. The one-eyed warrior grinned, and even from the ridgeline Ell could make out the eagerness on her face as she agreed to the old elf's orders.

The battle was over and it was a complete and total victory for the elves. But if that was the case, why did Ell feel so exhausted? There was the usual battle fatigue, and he was recovering from his wounds, but it was more than that.

Arendahl took the ridgeline in a few ability-enhanced bounds. "What, boy, unhappy about something?" the old elf queried as he sat beside the injured Ell. "Sad to be sidelined while the rest get the glory?" He winked to show that he was joking.

Ell shook his head. "This is just the beginning. This doesn't even scratch the surface of what's to come. We thrashed them, but they'll come again and again. So will the Unsired. So many will die before it's over."

Arendahl grunted. "Deep thoughts. Dark musings. But true nonetheless."

Ell stared bleakly over the carnage below. He should feel glad. They'd won a victory and won it strongly, but all he felt was apprehension. Death was in the future, and it felt as though that was all he could envision.

"WHAT WERE THOSE CREATURES?" Aldashir breathed as he sat having his wounds tended to by Rihya.

Ell had propped himself against the trunk of a tree next to the prince. His own wounds were mostly healed except for the gash along his ribs and the deep injury to his calf. Ell was sipping on a flask of Source Water to try and speed up the process. He had tried to heal himself by using his abilities, much like he had in the duel in Dark Harbor, but he was too weak from all the blood he'd lost. When Arendahl finished seeing to the worst of the injured, he'd likely come and see to Ell's annoying—although certainly not mortal—wound.

"Dark creatures," Rihya muttered absently in response to Aldashir's questions, all the while administering her ministrations to little winces of discomfort from the prince. Rihya was deft with healing touches, but she'd never been particularly gentle.

"Specifically?" the prince asked.

"Those were mostly Ghouls—the smaller beings—and they're probably the most common of the dark creatures. They are scavengers and opportunists, but they're still quite dangerous. The poison they release from the stingers in their hands will freeze a person stiff in moments. Usually it's certain death, so you have to avoid their touch," Ell answered instead of his preoccupied sister.

"And the others?"

Miri, who sat slumped against Ell, exhausted from loosing arrow after arrow into the fray, jumped in to answer Aldashir. "Ogres. Stone and Wood. The Stone Ogres are the biggest and probably the more dangerous, but Wood Ogres have a reputation for being nasty. They like to mangle as much as to kill. One nearly got Ell last summer." She slipped a hand into his as she spoke, as if reassuring herself that he was fine.

Aldashir shook his head in disbelief as he stared from the ridge top over the carnage below. They had buried all of their own dead but left the rest for the birds. Perhaps the bones would warn the next human army that advanced this far into Andalaya. And the next, and the next. Ell couldn't help but feel this was only the beginning.

"I had heard stories—myths, really. But I never thought them true," Aldashir said quietly.

"Did you think I was lying?" Rihya grunted, prodding him more forcefully than necessary.

"I...I suppose I thought you might be...*embellishing* a bit. You do have a tendency toward the theatric at times." Aldashir lifted a strand of her dyed-green hair as if to illustrate his point.

Ell's sister made a vexed sound deep in her throat. "The color of my hair has nothing to do with whether you can trust what I say."

Aldashir held up his hands in mock fear. "I'll never disbelieve a word you say again."

Ell smiled at the twinkle in the prince's eye. Rihya needed someone who would occasionally thumb their nose at her. She pursed her lips sourly and went back to tending to Aldashir in a slightly rougher manner than before.

Ell closed his eyes and laid his head against the trunk of the tree, but he'd hardly closed his eyes when footsteps approached, and a voice sounded.

"Water Caller Wintermoon." They still hadn't figured out exactly how to address Ell. He was the youngest elf in a position of command, and 'elder' just didn't feel quite right. "Will you hear a report?" The scout stared at Ell with poorly concealed awe as he spoke. People had been staring at him like that a lot lately. Ell had been around family who had seen his powers in action for so long now that it seemed he'd forgotten what it felt like to be a spectacle to others.

He sighed. "Of course. Report."

The scout nodded swiftly and launched into a report much the way Ell had reported to Dacunda for so many years: all business, brief sentences. Scouts had to get to The Point swiftly in case their news was dire. "A small band of Departed have approached from the south."

Ell interjected in surprise, "What!"

The scout made placating motions with his hands. "Not to worry, Water Caller Wintermoon. They laid down their arms."

Aldashir tilted his head in curiosity as the scout spoke but did not interrupt a report not meant for him.

The scout continued, "They do not seem to be Unsired." The elf stumbled a little as he said the name of an enemy he'd likely thought of as nothing more than a myth for his entire life. "They claim they have come in peace."

"How many?" Ell asked tersely.

"About a hundred. Certainly not more than that."

"Bring the leader to me," Ell said as he shifted his body up from its slumped position to a more upright sitting position. He didn't feel strong enough to stand yet, but neither did he want to appear weak in the face of this Departed whether or not he claimed to be a friend.

The scout disappeared to the south and Ell, Miri, Aldashir, and Rihya sat in tense silence. Only a matter of minutes passed before the scout reappeared leading a swarthy Departed male with the sides of his head shaven in a warrior's manner. His teeth were not filed. The Departed reached them and inclined his head respectfully to Ell. Then he bowed deeply to Aldashir who acknowledged him with a nod.

"Speak," Ell said, indicating that he should sit. It felt strange to have the warrior towering over him as they spoke. The Departed sank into a cross-legged position and directed his words somewhere in between Ell and Aldashir.

"I am Barragan from Dor Khabor—Dark Harbor, as many call it—and I am here to lend my sword."

The statement was short and simple, yet Ell had so many questions. He saw that Aldashir was itching to speak, but he continued to stay silent out of respect for Ell and his place of command here. The prince was growing on him. Ell decided once and for all that he liked Aldashir. He'd been feeling that way for quite some time, but he finalized it in his mind right then and there.

"Why?" Ell asked.

Barragan glanced at the prince, and Aldashir nodded. "Things have come to a head in Dark Harbor. Strange, winged demons parlay with our leaders in the towers of the palace at night. We could see them coming and going by moonlight. The Blackness has spread to all quarters, and not all of us agree with these changes," he finished with a hard tone.

"Icari," Rihya muttered.

Aldashir nodded his approval at Barragan's words, but Ell narrowed his eyes. He had to be careful—he didn't know Barragan. "So you have had enough of the darkness. Enough that you decided to join your longtime enemies." It was a statement more than a question.

"Yes. We could have set sail for the Outer Rim, but the battle is here in the north, and at this point we had to pick a side. I'll never choose the humans! And I cannot side with the Blackness or the vileness it brings and commands. That has left only reconciliation as an option. Besides, we had heard our true prince was already in the north with a thousand of our comrades."

"I am," Aldashir finally spoke, "although it's less than that now, after our assault on the Midnight Cove and this battle today."

"Then we shall replenish your numbers somewhat," Barragan said stoutly.

Ell stared at him. Could he trust him? "You know we are outnumbered, assailed by enemies on all sides. You might have just joined the losing side."

Barragan's face was stone. "It was the only decision left with honor in it."

Now where had Ell heard that sentiment before? He felt like he must have heard Aldashir mention something like that at some point. The prince's look of approval confirmed his suspicions.

"You brought a hundred with you?" Ell asked.

"Just under."

"And you command?" Aldashir ventured. When the Departed nodded, the prince continued, "Do you vouch for them?"

"I do," Barragan replied, reaching to place his hand on the hilt of a sword that wasn't there as he gave his oath.

Ell glanced at Aldashir. The prince read his question. "It is good enough for me."

"I am not sure it is wise to trust them," Ell said quietly.

"I trust his words. There is sincerity in them. I know because I have thought and said the same before. I trust him...do you trust me?"

Ell thought for a minute and stared long and hard at the prince. "I do."

"Good." Aldashir's teeth flashed white in his grin. "Then your numbers have just swelled, and who knows? Maybe more of my people will be courageous enough to join."

"Maybe," Ell said, "maybe."

CHAPTER TWENTY-EIGHT

"I'm fine, Ell." Miri shrugged away his persistent attention.

"You are sure?" Ell asked, suspicious.

"Your sister forced the Source Water down my throat right after it happened. Besides, when have I ever attempted to appear tougher than necessary?" Miri responded, her hand reaching up to lightly finger the thin, white scar on her cheek.

Ell pulled her close, hands on her hips as he stared at her seriously. "It's been three weeks since the war started in earnest, since our ambush of the humans, and at every skirmish—for every stance we've taken— you've insisted on throwing yourself into the thick of things." His disapproving tone would have annoyed her if he didn't look so worried. Well, actually, it still annoyed her—just a little bit.

"As has everyone else, love. You don't see anyone hanging back now."

"Not everyone has your limitations." Ell nodded downward toward her bad leg.

Miri rolled her eyes. "I may not be the swiftest or the sturdiest warrior we have, but I've become a decent shot with a bow. It would be selfish not to fight. Even so, I stay to the back with the other archers. I'm far from the most dangerous parts of the battle."

"Not safe enough, by my opinion." He brushed her cheek gently with his knuckles, touching the scar as if by doing so it might disappear. "I wish you wouldn't insist on fighting."

"We've been over this, Ell," Miri said, pulling him down to the loam in this secluded glen only a few short minutes from the edge of camp. "This war is it. One way or another, this fight will settle things. There's nowhere left to run. The humans are pushing from one end, the Unsired from the south, and the dark creatures are to the north and everywhere in between, harkening to the call of their Spectralist masters. We all have to fight. Every body, every able hand is needed in whatever capacity they can manage if we are to have even a chance at victory."

They lay on their sides on the mossy ground in the shadow of a large Evergrow Tree. A bit of seclusion was necessary from time to time, but Miri wished Ell wouldn't waste their few precious moments together worrying about futile issues. They were propped on their elbows staring at one another. His eyes were so serious. So concerned. She wished she could promise him she'd be safe, but she couldn't. This was war.

Ell sighed and pulled her into a kiss. She gave in to him willingly, let him pull her into the deep pool of bliss for the all-too-short amount of time they had alone. When he broke away, she groaned in mock frustration—well, maybe not so pretend at all.

He grinned. "I'm glad to see I still have that effect on you."

"Always," she murmured, grasping his wavy hair and pulling him back in for one more lingering kiss.

When they broke apart again, he muttered, "I just wish I could keep you safe."

Miri sighed, and this time it really was with frustration. "If we lose this war, I'll never be safe again. I might as well fight and help. Besides, I'm not untrained any more. Arendahl and Brie saw to my skills."

"True," Ell admitted, holding her hand in his to placate her as he went on, "I did not in any way mean to offend you. I know you've practiced much over these last months. But you are my heart, and I don't know what I would do without you."

Miri smiled to show him she forgave him. "Any word from the scouts?" she asked. It appeared Ell couldn't focus on more important things when they were alone, so she might as well give in and talk strategy. The rest could wait for later—maybe that night when the others had fallen asleep. A smirk crept onto her face as she thought of what they might do later.

Ell nodded. "Arendahl is still martialing what is left of our troops to the north in the heart of our homeland. As you know, he left right after the first battle with the humans. Scouts say the forces he's taken command of have fought swarms of dark creatures ranging in from the north and materializing out of the very land around them. They've taken heavy losses." Ell sighed regretfully. "Losses we can't afford. They're being pushed toward Verdantihya."

Miri nodded along as he spoke. It was basically what she'd heard around camp; word traveled fast in an army. "And what of your father and Dacunda?"

"They are still on the eastern front. Messengers report that the fighting is fierce. They take many fewer casualties than the humans, but the enemy has far greater numbers, and they are more cautious now after that first big defeat. My father and uncle are fighting a slow retreat, also being pushed deeper into Andalaya. They could use a Water Caller's powers."

Miri cupped his hands in hers as they sat up to face each other cross-legged. "You did what was right. The north needs Arendahl to continue to rally the last of our support and to keep the dark creatures at bay. He's been doing it for decades. He's the best at it. And you are needed here in the south."

"I just wish I could stand beside my family in battle instead of hear of it from afar."

She touched his cheek. "So tender," she teased.

Ell rolled his eyes. "That's the last time I confide in you!"

Miri laughed, as did Ell. For an instant, the worry and fear faded, and she was glad that in the midst of all this she could still make him laugh. When the laughter died down, she still held onto his hands. She could hold them forever. With her mind—her consciousness—so deeply entwined with his, it only felt right when they were touching, like a physical symbol of their connection.

"What of Aldashir's spies?"

Ell shrugged in a gesture lacking commitment. "His people have infiltrated his brother's army, but they must be careful. Only some of the newer arrivals—the pockets of his people who have fled the south—really fit in as spies. The Thousand do not shave the sides of their heads or file their teeth, so Aldashir is left to rely on only the information provided by the few new arrivals he can persuade to rejoin the southern army."

"And?" Miri prodded.

"Nothing I haven't already told you. We've fought a few skirmishes, and while they are steadily moving north they are moving a lot more slowly than we expected." Ell grimaced.

"What is it?" Miri asked, her heart fluttering for a moment, wondering if he was in pain from some kind of injury she hadn't heard of.

Ever since they'd reunited, she'd been on guard for something awful to happen again. She couldn't take losing Ell again like she had almost done in the weeks leading up to the assault on the Black Water Well. Her access to his mind had made her much more aware than the others of just how far on the brink of darkness Ell had really been teetering. Thankfully, that was over now.

He motioned for her to relax. "Nothing. I haven't picked up any slow-healing injuries in the skirmishes these last few weeks since the big battle. I was just making that face because Half-Mask is cleverer than I thought."

Miri cocked her head. "How so?"

Ell's mouth soured as he spoke of the Prince of Darkness. "He's only sending skirmishers north ahead of his main army, keeping the bulk of it moving very slowly northward. He's letting the humans whittle down our numbers so that he'll have fewer enemies to face when the time comes."

"Can't we do anything about it?"

Ell shook his head in frustration. "Not really. We can't attack his main force because we're not large enough. We've only about a third of our total number of warriors here with us in the south even with Aldashir's warriors and the addition of the Departed who've fled north to join us. Half-Mask has marshaled almost all the warriors he has in the south. If we had all our people to stand with us, maybe, but as it stands..." he trailed off, not needing to finish the rest.

Miri finished it for him. "So even though we're finally fighting in the open, standing tall against the Departed—the Unsired—and the humans, we're still basically fighting a losing battle."

Ell grunted in disgust. "We're outnumbered. We're still setting ambushes and raiding their supply lines, but nothing on the scale of that battle when we ambushed and massacred the human army three weeks ago. Half-Mask is too clever to commit too many troops too early. He's saving them for something else, something later."

Miri saw the worry on Ell's face, that same look he got when he couldn't quite figure out the answer to some riddle. "What are you thinking?" she asked quietly.

Ell shook his head, his blond hair shaking in the chill winter. Grey light pierced the tree canopy above them and cast dark shadows all about. It wouldn't be long before snow set in. "I don't know, love. I just keep trying to figure out what Half-Mask's endgame is. Is it just killing us all? Then why not fully commit to a battle? Even planning for the humans, he'd still have enough to wipe out our army. No, he's got some other plan, and I can't quite figure out what it is."

"Any ideas?" Miri pressed.

"Well, the only thing I can think of is that he wants retribution. We destroyed the Black Water Well, and I can't help but notice that his army is moving along a steady course toward Verdantihya."

Miri's brows rose with sudden concern. "You think he has designs on the Source?"

Ell tilted his head and gave a half-shrug, not needing to say anything more. "I just wish we could do more."

"We are doing all we can. We'll keep slowing them down, giving Arendahl time to gather the last remnants of our fighters and meet up with your family farther north." Miri put a hand on his shoulder. "Your father and uncle will be fine. They have your mother, Delle, and Iyonei to look out for them. Not to mention Ryder and Brie."

Ell grinned half-heartedly. "Of course. It will be good when we're finally all together again, though."

"In the meantime, I'll just have to keep saving your life so you don't miss them so much in these skirmishes," Miri teased.

Ell tackled her with a real grin this time. "Hey, that was one time— how many times have *I* saved *your* life? And technically, you *and* my mother saved my life. Besides, it was weeks ago."

"Whatever you say," Miri breathed. Suddenly, with his weight pressing her to the moist earth, wetness soaking through her clothes, she could care less about who had saved whom and when.

Ell caught the motion of her thoughts and leaned in for a long kiss. When he broke for air, Miri barely gave him time to catch his breath before pulling him back toward her face. "Now, this is a much better use of our time together than talking strategy and tactics," she murmured wickedly between kisses.

"I couldn't agree more."

———

THE SKIRMISH below her was heated. Unsired fought with their blank faces, diseased bodies, and jerky-yet-powerful movements. Ell and Aldashir's allied forces were hard-pressed to keep them at bay. Miri, perched in a tree and loosing arrows as she saw fit—much like a few other archers at Ell's disposal—had the perfect vantage point to watch the conflict unfold. It had been an ambush amongst the flatland woods of the lower forest. Ell and Aldashir had split their army into two forces to hit the enemy like a hammer and anvil. The strategy had worked at first until the Unsired had upped their frantic fury. They fought like caged animals, and their desperate striving to fight their way clear of the vice-like ambush had evened the contest out somewhat.

Miri sighted an enemy Unsired that was in Ell's vicinity and loosed a shaft. Her arrow didn't fly true, only grazing the Unsired's shoulder, inflicting hardly more than a cut. She grunted with exasperation and fit another arrow to her string. She drew and loosed again. This time, the arrow twanged from her bow with angry purpose. It streaked toward her target and struck the creature in the chest. The enemy soldier wobbled and fell. Then, struggling mightily, the Unsired snapped off the arrow and managed to regain its feet only to fall to the vicious downswing of one of Ell's dueling daggers. Well, at least she'd slowed it down for her mate. Miri quickly moved on and began sighting other targets. She drew and loosed until her arm ached, only pausing to breathe. She didn't have an infinite number of arrows, so she picked her targets wisely, focusing on those who might harm Ell, those coming toward him from his blind spots. She liked to think of herself as his silent guardian. A grim smile reached her lips as she feathered yet another Unsired intending to harm Ell, her arrow puncturing its throat.

That done, she paused again, watching the battle unfold beneath her. Aldashir and Rihya pressed hard from the western edge while Ell led the forces at the east. They surged inward toward one another, felling foes. Aldashir and Rihya were partners dealing death, but Ell was something altogether different: he was a hurricane of steel, a natural disaster more than a warrior. Everywhere he went, enemies fell, bodies dropped, and limbs were severed from torsos. Yet there were surprisingly few screams in his wake. The Unsired fought with a measured numbness, and there were very few Departed left in this army's ranks capable of feeling fear.

Still, the two sides of the vice pressed together, butchering Unsired between them. Ell fought with a grimace of mixed eagerness and disgust as he hewed through his enemies. Rihya and Aldashir were back-to-back, fighting with a level of unison that Miri would have credited to years of working together if she hadn't known they'd only met a couple months ago. She wished she could watch their backs like she did Ell's, but they were still too far across the battle for her to pick targets near them.

Just when it seemed the enemy force was about to truly break, a horn blast pierced the cacophony of chaos that already occupied the air. Miri glanced to the south to see a lone Unsired standing on a rise at the back of the battle. He blew the horn again and again, and a waft of air brought the deathly, sickly stench of bonewinds that always accompanied the Unsired. One last blast sounded, and Miri felt a chill unrelated to the winter weather. She had a bad feeling.

As if in reaction to her thoughts, a force of dark creatures answering the command of their masters hit their allied forces from the woods to the north. No advance warning meant that the scouts watching the northern flank were likely already dead. Miri watched as the tide of the battle threatened to turn. Mostly Wood Ogres with one Stone Ogre to lead them, the force of dark creatures was fearsome to watch. They were obdurate warriors, their bark-like skin tougher than some armor. The Stone Ogre especially seemed impervious to arrows, given its granite exterior. Even Miri loosed one of her few remaining arrows at it only to see it clatter off its body like it hadn't been anything worth noticing. Angry, reddish-orange eyes like flames dancing within deep sockets peered out from the dark creature's face. A few Ghouls slunk in from the back of their advance, and Miri sighted her last remaining arrow. She would make it count. Ghouls could be felled by normal weapons just like an elf could. She waited until one sneakily wove its way through the mayhem of battle toward Ell. She sighted and loosed, her arrow pinning the struggling creature to the ground. It had only been a few feet from Ell when it hit. He heard the angry, whining death noise emanating from the Ghouls mouth—a dark hole full of uneven, yellow teeth—and she saw him turn and dispatch the Ghoul without thinking twice. He glanced up and nodded to her in response to what she had done for him. He knew she had his back.

Miri felt a rush of pride that she'd been able to keep him safe again only to watch as Ell turned and engaged a Tree Ogre with oaken arms and a gaping black maw. Fear stilled her heart. A Tree ogre had nearly killed Ell last year, but that had been when he'd still been having difficulty tapping into his abilities. He didn't have the same issue now. The Wood Ogre fought gamely, its lumbering arms taking vicious swipes at Ell, but he danced about it until he was able to duck in close, snakelike and graceful, to put out its eyes. Once that happened, it was only a matter of time before it was swarmed by other elves and put down. And Ell was dancing off through the battle, looking for the next dark creature to put down.

A flash of annoyance pierced Miri's worry. He was down there almost single-handedly keeping the enemy at bay while she was perched on the limb of this tree, out of arrows. She wanted to contribute more. But if she leaped down and joined the fray, at best she'd only draw Ell's attention and at worst she'd probably be dead in moments, encumbered by her lame leg. She sighed with frustration, watching as Aldashir and Rihya continued to hew through Unsired on the southwestern edge of the skirmish.

Even with the addition of the dark creatures, the allied forces of Highest and Departed eventually swung the battle back in their favor. There was no Half-Mask or his father or even Silverfist to lead this expeditionary enemy force, and eventually they succumbed to their opponents. Unsired fell, Ghouls screamed, and Wood Ogres were chopped down until there was only a small pocket of resistance left around the massive Stone Ogre to the north. Twice the height of an elf and with many times the girth, Miri could see why legends of the First Days said that the Unsired had used Stone Ogres to batter down fortress gates and stone walls with just their massive, granite fists. This one was flattening elves left and right, swatting them to death or sending them flying to collide with people and trees. The forest suddenly seemed like an advantage to the dark creature—an added weapon.

Then Ell strode forward to engage. Miri knew his abilities were tapped; today she'd seen him leap higher than an elf normally could, seen him move faster, strike harder, kill more enemies than any one elf should be able to. Yet seeing all the destruction in his wake didn't keep the fear from her as she watched him engage the stone monstrosity. According to what Ell had told her when they were alone, he'd only faced a Stone Ogre once and had barely escaped with his life. Both he and Arendahl—two Water Callers together—had run from it. She watched him dance around this one lithely, striking sparks as his steel clashed with its rocky skin.

As the enemies were slowly disposed of, a ring formed around Ell and his duel with the monster. The rest of the warriors appeared worried to step in and help, almost as if they would cause more distraction than aid were they to attempt moving closer. Ell wove his way around the beast, striking low and leaping high to swing at the creature's face and eyes, but each time his blades clattered off hardened skin. Once, the creature caught Ell with a swat and sent him tumbling painfully to the ground. Even though Miri could see that he was hurting, he leaped up nimbly and resumed the battle. Again she wished she could help, wished she didn't feel so useless. But then an idea formed. Really it was more of a test than an idea, but she thought she'd try it anyway.

Miri sent her consciousness into the Graft she'd forged with Ell's consciousness. She felt his power, the reservoir of strength in his chest swelling, tapped from the water present everywhere in the land, from the smallest droplet of moisture to the streams and creeks and rivers that flowed nearby. She felt his eagerness and the excitement of battle tempered by his wariness while fighting an opponent he knew was just about as dangerous as any he would face short of a Spectralist.

She pushed deeper, pushed herself further into the Graft like she had in the Midnight Cove, and then she wasn't just in him, she *was* Ell. She felt the power inside of her. And then she felt the power swell even more, unexplainably. She didn't have time to ponder why. One massive fist sent one of her daggers clattering from her hand, and she ducked and rolled away from the other fist as it swung downward to collide with the ground where she'd been standing. Her roll took her near a battle axe, and she grabbed it and stood from the roll in one motion. Then she swung.

The battle-axe met the Stone Ogre's wrist and sheared through its rocky skin, sending its huge fist sailing through the air. Black blood fountained from its arm as a howling scream filled the air. She looked up at the beast looming over her, watched as its screaming pain turned to wrath in its angry, red eyes...and yet she felt no fear. She felt only surprise. She was even stronger than she'd realized. She hadn't been aware that she had the strength as a Water Caller to sheer through a Stone Ogre. Even Arendahl had made her run from one when it attacked them just outside the Barren Maze.

Miri twirled the axe lazily through the air in front of her. She dodged one more furious swat from the Stone Ogre's good hand before she swung the axe with a single, powerful stroke and cleaved through its leg at the knee. The beast tumbled, howling again. In one more swift stroke, Miri beheaded the Stone Ogre, wielding the weapon with such strength that it was like a plaything in her hands, wielding it with more power than she'd ever known she possessed. She was brimming with power.

She turned away from the dead creature and stared at herself up in the tree. Wait, at herself? Reality crashed in and she let the connection go, felt herself slithering out of the Graft and back into her own singular consciousness. She gazed down at Ell as he stood over the dead Stone Ogre, looking up at her. He looked at her with excitement and wonder in his eyes. Something had just happened. Something significant. She'd somehow added to his strength.

Ell smiled at her as she scrambled down from the tree. He rushed through the crowd of warriors to reach her side. "That was incredible. I've never felt such power, even as a Water Caller. What did you do?"

"I don't know. I just merged into you as deeply as possible, like when we destroyed the Black Water Well. I think that because you aren't fighting the link anymore I can somehow go deeper. Maybe adding my will to yours magnified your power somewhat?" she finished, her final words coming out more as a question than as a statement.

Ell shrugged and grabbed her hands delightedly. "Well, whatever it was, I am glad of it. I was struggling to finish off the creature, and then I just felt this swell of power, kind of like I do when I tap my abilities, but I was already holding them. It was like a second tapping of my abilities... a swell within a swell."

The excitement in his voice brought a grin to her face, as well. She was useful. Very useful, it seemed. But the thrill was interrupted. A runner came up and addressed Ell respectfully.

"Wintermoon, there is another army approaching from the south. And quickly."

Ell's excitement was tempered by immediate worry. Aldashir and Rihya made it to his side quickly, weaving their way through their warriors.

"My brother and father?" Aldashir asked with grim expectance.

Ell shook his head. "I'm not sure." He looked askance at the scout who nodded almost fearfully.

"There is one who leads the army, the left side of his face covered with a mask. It can only be the Prince of Darkness. He is flanked by a half-dead elf and a cloaked creature."

"They think to catch us unawares," Rihya declared.

"And they almost have," Aldashir responded.

Miri watched them all share worried looks. Finally, Ell spoke. "We must fall back. If their main army is approaching instead of a smaller scouting force, then we cannot face it alone. Not wounded and exhausted as we are. We have to retreat."

"Retreat?" The disgust in Rihya's voice was palpable.

"For now," the prince placated her with a hand upon her shoulder. "Not forever." Aldashir paused a moment before speaking again. "My father hasn't left Dark Harbor or the Midnight Cove in years. If he is with the army, then this must be the final thrust."

"It isn't as if we expected anything less," Ell said darkly. "We knew this was war. Will you be fine to face your own family?" he inquired of the prince.

Miri stared curiously at Aldashir as he briefly thought over the question. He eventually answered, "I suppose they are not family any longer. My old family died long ago, and I have a new family now." His large, dark hand closed over Rihya's smaller one. Miri smiled slightly at the gesture. Rihya blushed, but a light gleamed in her eyes.

"What are we waiting for?" Miri prompted.

Ell nodded. "I said retreat, and we should start on it now." He turned to the scout. "Pass the orders on to the rest. See to the wounded; a larger dose of Source Water than normal is to be given. We need to move quickly and cannot afford to be slowed with an army of that size at our backs." The scout nodded and went off to fulfill his duty.

Miri watched as her mate turned toward Aldashir. "If your brother is finally advancing the full force of his army and pushing north, then it looks like you'll finally be seeing Verdantihya, and sooner than we thought. I only hope that our other forces will be able to meet us there in one piece."

CHAPTER TWENTY-NINE

Ell hefted the battle-axe in his hand. It was human made: heavy and double-bladed like the one he'd used to kill the Stone Ogre. He swung it a few times and had to use two hands to wield it now. That wasn't strange, considering he'd been tapping into his abilities the last time he'd used a weapon this size, but still it reminded him of the amount of power at his fingertips when Miri had merged into him through the Graft, deeply into him like she had when they'd destroyed the Black Water Well together. A part of him wished he didn't need her to access that amplification of his power, but another part of him was glad that so much strength wasn't available to him whenever he wanted. It was a lot of power to have at one's fingertips.

He dropped the axe and began picking his way through the camp looking for his family. Elves not on sentry duty sat and relaxed, fixed evening meals, or caught catnaps where they could. Nobody worked their weapons or held mock duels. There was no need to practice their war craft, not when they'd been fighting their way north day by day. Over a week had passed since Ell had killed the Stone Ogre—the first one, that is. He'd killed another yesterday during a skirmish after it had materialized out of the mountainside into which it had molded itself for its centuries of slumber to wreak havoc on his troops. They had been slowly retreating north, setting traps, ambushes, and generally relying on cut-and-run tactics like they had for so many years. Anything to slow the enemy down and lessen their numbers without losing too many of their own warriors. Ell chafed at being ushered north in such a way by Half-Mask's superior sized army, but he knew that it was necessary. They needed defensible walls to stand against the army pursuing them, and that meant Verdantihya.

He saw his sister and Miri sitting around a small campfire and made his way over toward them. "Where's Aldashir?" he asked out of curiosity.

"How should I know?" Rihya answered in annoyance.

"So sorry to bother you," Ell said just as crossly.

"What? I'm not his keeper!" Rihya muttered and bit viciously into a leg of fowl that she'd pulled from a small spit above the flame. She spat the meat out quickly and breathed in the cold mountain air to soothe her burned tongue, managing to look angry and embarrassed at the same time.

Miri snickered. "Don't be offended, love, she's just frustrated that Aldashir is spending time seeing to his troops instead of her."

"That is not true!" Rihya grumbled, her mouth full of fowl once again now that it had cooled enough to eat. "But we've hardly had a moment to ourselves this past week, what with setting traps, and ambushes, and skirmishes."

"I feel your pain, sister," Miri said with narrowed eyes as she peered at Ell. "Your brother has been wildly inattentive of late." Rihya shifted her gaze to Ell as well, staring daggers at him in place of Aldashir.

"That's enough," Ell said more firmly than he felt. He always grew nervous when Miri and Rihya banded together against him.

"What is?" Miri smirked.

"You know."

She smiled that knowing smile again. "Fine, love. I'll stop. For now."

Ell rolled his eyes. "Besides, Rihya, Aldashir has a lot on his mind. It's not just an army he's attending to. The defectors from the south brought family members, as well. Children. He just wants to make sure they're all fine."

"I know that," Rihya breathed in exasperation. "I know all of that, and I am glad he is so dutiful a leader, but this is war. Neither of us might be here tomorrow. I'd like a little of his attention in the present."

The three of them exchanged silent looks at the grim prospect of Rihya's statement. Ell rolled his shoulders uncomfortably. He'd always been aware of the possibility of death ever since a young age. One couldn't raid and ambush most of his or her life without getting used to the idea. But with Miri and now his family back together, he'd never felt such a strong desire to stay alive. All the old anger still burned below the surface, but there were other emotions there now, too. Joy and happiness, contentment when he was with his family, and excitement and raw passion around Miri. For the first time ever he really didn't want to die, was almost *afraid* to die when for so long he'd been fearless. He understood his sister.

Ell reached over and cupped Rihya's hand in his. She smiled at him gratefully for a second, then narrowed her eyes and grimaced in mock disgust, shaking her hand free. She picked up another greasy wing of fowl.

"Don't coddle me, brother."

Ell smiled. "I wouldn't dream of it, sister."

"I'm the older one, you know. Who has saved your life more times than anyone else, more times than you can count?" Rihya pressed aggressively.

"You have." He covered a small smile.

"Good, and don't you forget it." Rihya punctuated her last statement by taking another bite of meat.

"Any more of that?" Ell asked brightly; hot fowl sounded perfect in this chill weather. He rubbed his hands together and blew on them. It wouldn't be long before full winter cloaks were needed.

Rihya nodded toward the spit, indicating that he was welcome to it. Miri grabbed a piece for him and herself, and they sat eating in comfortable silence.

"How long do you think before we reach Verdantihya?" Miri finally broke the silence, wiping her mouth with the back of her hand after speaking and then finishing her bite.

Rihya shrugged. "A week or so, maybe less. Depends on how much we have to slow down to fight the advance parties Half-Mask sends our way."

"A week is my guess," Ell murmured in agreement. And a long wearying week it would be.

———

THAT WEEK PASSED TERRIBLY by all accounts. The snow finally came and, when it did, it didn't ease them into winter at all—it thrust them full force into the middle of it. Ell's fingers were stiff from the cold and from clutching the hilts of his dueling daggers so tightly as he fought skirmish after skirmish, ambush after ambush, slowly retreating north. The only positive was that the weather affected the southern army even more. According to Aldashir, snow was little more than a myth from old stories or passed along by the few slavers that braved the cold to harry their northern prey during the winter time. People in Dark Harbor and the rest of the Departed territory had no idea how to handle this type of weather. It slowed their progress much more than it did Ell and his army.

Ell crouched low, hunkering down next to Aldashir in a snow drift. They were about to set their latest in a string of raids on yet another expeditionary force sent ahead by the southern army. It appeared Half-Mask had enough warriors to sustain the losses. Ell, on the other hand, did not. Each raid needed to be executed to perfection in order to make sure that no unnecessary loss of life was sustained by his forces.

"How do you do battle in this weather?" Aldashir grumbled bitterly, flexing his hands to fight the cold. Normally, they commanded separate flanks of an attack, but this was a small one. The scout had said the force pushing north was only fifty soldiers strong at most, likely no more than a large scouting party. As such, a simple smash and run would be enough in the way of tactics; they didn't need to operate using different flanks. The small rise to the left of the trail gave them a vantage point over where the ambush would take place. It wouldn't be long now.

Ell looked over at Aldashir and shrugged his shoulders. "The weather hurts them more than us. You said so yourself."

"I did, but that doesn't mean I have to enjoy it."

Ell chuckled, steam leaving his open mouth. The cold was all around; it burrowed deep into his bones, but it felt right. The seasons passed, and no elf should complain about that. Creation had established the seasons for a set purpose. Trees were barren of leaves, and pine needles scattered and dusted across the tops of the snow drifts.

"Don't forget to keep your sword loose," Ell murmured as he shifted his own daggers in their sheaths. "You don't want your steel to stick in the cold."

"I know, I know," Aldashir grumbled again, but he still lifted his sword slightly before letting it fall back into the scabbard.

"Better safe than sorry," Ell told him. "Preparation can make all the difference in a battle in these conditions."

The prince nodded his agreement and they settled back into silence, waiting with the rest of their two hundred soldiers to spring the trap that was waiting for their enemies. Time passed slowly, and Ell began to wonder if the force had turned back to report its findings to the Prince of Darkness or if perhaps his own scout had been wrong. But he stayed quiet and tried to remain patient.

"How did you convince Rihya to let you fight alone?" he asked simply for the sake of making conversation.

Aldashir shrugged slightly and looked away. "I didn't. It was her idea."

"Really?"

Aldashir nodded. "Something about Miriyah's throwing form. Valerihya wanted some last-minute practice with your mate to make sure she's prepared for what is ahead. Besides, I think she trusts you to keep me safe." Aldashir's mouth quirked up into a small smile.

Ell ignored the prince's joke. For what was ahead, for the large-scale conflict—not these small raids and ambushes—that everyone knew was eventually coming, no one was safe. "I see."

"She loves her greatly, as if she were truly her sister," the prince volunteered.

"They *are* sisters," Ell said firmly, "or as good as. In Andalaya these past decades, we've been pressed and harried at every turn. Most family units have been broken through loss or capture. Ours was abnormal to have so much family together. Most people in the north have had to forge their own bonds lately. So, for all intents and purposes, they are sisters."

"Makes sense," Aldashir replied, shifting his sword in his scabbard again to keep it loose. "Our people did a horrible thing to yours." The sorrow in his voice touched Ell.

"Well, you're making up for it now."

Aldashir smiled. "More than making up for it, hopefully. Once we rid the world of my brother and father, perhaps we can end this disease of the Blackness once and for all."

"Perhaps," Ell agreed, "but we'll have to win first."

Aldashir nodded toward the trail with his jaw, hands at the ready on his hilt. "Well then, let's start with these."

About fifty hooded warriors were picking their way up the snow-laden trail that would pass just below the rise on which Ell, Aldashir, and their warriors hid in waiting. It seemed Ell's scout had been right after all.

They waited a few interminable moments before Ell whispered to Aldashir, "Ready?"

"Ready," the prince confirmed.

In one motion, they rose up, drew their bows, and loosed. As they did, their warriors did so with them. The first rain of arrows slammed into the enemy force and elves dropped to the ground, blood painting the snow red. One more volley of arrows was loosed to soften up the enemy, and then Ell and Aldashir charged down the slope into the thick of things.

Ell moved lithely, even with the slippery footing, his abilities as a Water Caller giving him the added agility needed to make sure his stance was solid. He'd been facing off with Ogres lately, so even a few Unsired were easy to dispatch in comparison. His blades struck true time and time again as he danced his way through the midst of his foes. Before long, his steel was dripping as red as the snow upon which he moved.

Aldashir was no Water Caller, but he was only marginally less effective. Armed with his long sword, he inflicted casualty after casualty upon their enemies. Fearless, he stepped into breaches, engaging rivals that were pressing his allies, and it was then that Ell knew what his sister saw in the dark prince.

However, all was not easy. A cloaked figure fought for their foes, hood up, obscuring his face. He moved with a strength, a power, and a reckless abandon that earned him wounds, yet those wounds didn't slow him down. The hooded figure fought as if impervious to pain, relentless in energy. He felled elf after elf, and Ell had just turned to engage him when Aldashir cut him off.

The prince swept in toward the hooded figure, grim faced and steady, his long sword flashing as the light of the wintery sky gleamed down off of it. His sword clashed with the figure's, and Aldashir pressed him, forcing a swift motion of retreat, causing the cowl of his hood to fall back revealing the deathly face of the half-dead Siverfist. The fist itself was still obscured, covered by a drooping sleeve.

"We meet again, my Prince." Silverfist laughed dryly, his throat sounding like dead stalks of grass rattling together on a dry, summer night.

"I am not your prince any longer," Aldashir grunted through gritted teeth as he swung his sword down in a vicious, overhead arch, one that was only barely deflected by the parrying blow of Silverfist's own sword. "I never was."

"Be that as it may, in a moment, you'll never have a chance to be my prince again," the-elf-who-had-once-been-Silverfist taunted as he slashed across Aldashir's chest only to be blocked by his defensive movements.

Ell wished he could duck in and finish the traitor off once and for all, but he feared any interference would cause distraction and result in his friend's death. Rihya would never forgive him. Instead, he dispatched one of the few remaining Unsired that rushed at him with a swift thrust of his dueling dagger through the elf's eye socket. It dropped dead instantly, falling to the ground with the rest of its comrades. Elves all around Ell were finishing off their enemies. His allies had lost warriors, but they'd done their job. Of their foes, only Silverfist was left standing.

Ell stood anxiously, watching his comrade face-off against Silverfist. He'd only barely managed to defeat the living traitor last spring, and now Aldashir faced the half-dead one. But the prince was holding his own, even pressing his advantage. Aldashir worked his sword forms perfectly, executing cuts and slashes, forcing Silverfist back and back again until the half-dead elf wore a grimace of clenched teeth made all the more ghastly by the fact that an entire side of his face was pure bone and rotted flesh, making the inside of his mouth all the more visible. Aldashir fought on in focused silence while Silverfist cursed and taunted, doing anything in his power to throw his opponent off balance. But then it happened.

Aldashir wove his sword in a particularly difficult maneuver and forced the traitor back yet again, but this time Silverfist's footing slipped. Just slightly, but it was enough to afford Aldashir the advantage he needed. The prince pounced and stepped in so quickly that the thrust of his sword was already through Silverfist's belly and out his back before the traitor could even react. It was a killing strike; Ell had fought long enough to know a mortal wound when he saw one. Instead of falling to the ground, though, Silverfist laughed scornfully.

"Did you think it would be that easy, Prince?" Silverfist lashed out with his rusted silver fist, and the ridged knuckles collided with Aldashir's jaw. The prince dropped to the snowy ground, dark clothing and skin a stark contrast to the white and red of the battlefield.

Aldashir stumbled groggily to his knees. "You should be dead," he muttered woozily.

"What I should be is buried in a shallow grave up north. But I'm not. And it will take more than a length of steel to put me back there," Silverfist said as he yanked the blade roughly and unconcernedly from his stomach, a few putrid entrails showing from the wound. The sword fell to the ground, its fall muffled to silence by the snow.

Ell lunged for the half-dead elf, ready to engage, ready to end this once and for all, but Silverfist turned and sprinted away. His voice echoed back over his shoulder, just like his cloak flapping in the breeze. The words arrested Ell in his tracks. "You have a choice, Wintermoon. Follow me or save him. You know what my metal hand can do."

And with that, Silverfist disappeared around a bend in the path, obscured by the leafless trees. Ell was torn. He wanted more than anything to pursue, to finish the traitor—again. But Rihya would kill him if he let Aldashir come to harm. Ell remembered how quickly the poison on Silverfist's metal fist had worked on him those many months ago.

In the end, worry won over fury. He turned back to Aldashir who was already being tended to by a few of their warriors. One poured a mouthful of Source Water down the prince's throat.

"Good, that will help, but it won't be enough," Ell said as he dropped to one knee by the elf tending to Aldashir.

"No?"

"No," he said. "The poison on the traitor's fist is fast-acting—I know from experience—and it took a Water Caller to heal me."

"Can you save him?" a Departed asked, one of the warriors from The Point. The agony in his voice pulled on Ell's conscience. As if he only had Rihya to worry about; Aldashir was more loved by his followers than just about any leader Ell knew.

"I'll try, but I'm not as good as Arendahl at this."

He recalled what Arendahl had told him about healing with his abilities. The litany echoed in his head: *Don't tap generally, don't just focus on drawing the raw power of the land and water around you, you must focus it, hone it down to a knife's edge. Focus, force all that Source Water you can draw from the tiny droplets of water all around you into a concentrated dose of healing power.* Arendahl's voice could be heard even from miles and months away.

Ell did just that. He pulled in on his powers, tapped into the water all around him—the frozen water of the snow, the precipitation-laden air with the clouds above—and he focused that power. Ell touched his friend's bleeding jaw, forcing the concentrated dose of healing power into the wound. His abilities funneled through him and into the prince, purging away the poison. Ell could feel it working, could feel the poison leaving Aldashir, could feel the wound closing. The thrill of doing something other than killing with his abilities was almost intoxicating. It was a good feeling, a sense of balance to all the death he dealt.

Aldashir coughed weakly and his eyes fluttered as he tried to open them. "What happened?"

"Rest," Ell hushed him. "You'll be weak for some time still—I know that I was." Aldashir's eyes closed again.

The Departed looked at Ell, hope and fear mixing on his face. "Did you fix him?"

"I think so," he said wearily, more drained than he normally felt from tapping his abilities. Perhaps it was the strain of exercising a new talent that was underdeveloped, just like how one grew weary from working a new muscle in training. "We should get him back to camp to rest."

Ell glanced over his shoulder back along the path where Silverfist had sprinted away. Departed lifted the prince and carried him in the opposite direction. He could go now. Maybe if he left now he could catch up with Silverfist. But then he wouldn't be there to answer Rihya's questions. Regretfully, Ell turned north and moved with the rest of his company back toward the main camp. Silverfist had escaped yet again. The bitter taste of bile rose in Ell's throat as he realized he wanted the traitor dead almost as much as he wanted Half-Mask destroyed. Soon. The two armies would eventually have to meet in a full-scale battle, and when they did Silverfist would meet his end. The half-dead elf would return to the grave where he belonged.

———

"What happened to him?" Rihya's voice when she saw Aldashir being carried toward her was shrill with worry. Miri put a comforting hand on her shoulder.

"Silverfist," Ell answered succinctly.

"Did you heal him?" his sister demanded. She knew what his powers were capable of.

"I think so."

"You 'think' so?" Her voice rose an octave.

"I haven't practiced healing as much as Arendahl. I think Aldashir's well enough, but he'll need rest either way. I just sped up the body's healing process. He'll still need time to recover. If he holds steady and isn't worse by tomorrow, then he should be fine."

Rihya narrowed her eyes. "He'd better be."

Miri came into his arms as Rihya followed the Departed who were carrying their leader to lay him down in his tent.

"Don't be hurt. Your sister is just worried. I can't imagine what I'd do if that were you," Miri told him.

Ell nodded. "I know. I hate to see her like this."

"He'll recover, and she'll be fine," Miri said firmly, her voice full of faith.

"How can you be sure?"

"I believe in you, in what you can do, even if *you* are not sure," she said as she smiled and kissed him. "Now, are you hungry? Something hot would be good to warm your bones."

Ell nodded again, flexing his hands. They ached from the cold and from gripping his hilts so tightly in this weather. "I will not say no to that."

They sat, and Ell ate. He wolfed his food down much more quickly than he'd expected. He was hungrier than he had realized. As he ate, he couldn't help but let his mind drift to the hot and spicy stews of Dark Harbor and, even though he was thoroughly enjoying the meat and grain cakes he was eating, he still was forced to admit to himself that there were some things he missed about the south. As good as it was to be back in his homeland, not everything southern was terrible. Strange, just a year ago he would have never imagined he'd think such a thing. But, then again, a year ago he hadn't had his abilities as a Water Caller, hadn't been Joined with Miri—hadn't even met her yet, actually—hadn't made friends with a smuggler and his pirate acquaintances, and, most of all, had not been friends with Half-Mask's own brother. A lot had changed in a short time, and most of it for the better. If only the extinction of his people wasn't looming in the battle to come...if not for that, he might even feel hopeful and content.

Ell finished eating and licked his fingers clean. Miri was finishing up her meal in silence. She, too, licked her fingers and then said, "Will we break camp soon?"

"At first light tomorrow," Ell responded. "I want to move more quickly. Also, with Aldashir injured, I'd like to get him under Arendahl's watchful eye."

Miri nodded. "That is a sound plan."

"I'll leave a few soldiers behind to set some smaller traps—annoyances, really—to slow down our enemies, but generally I'd like to quit skirmishing and reach Verdantihya. We can only slow the enemy down for so long before the attrition begins to affect our numbers more than theirs. We have to save them for the final confrontation." Ell scratched his head idly, loosening the leather cord he used to tie his hair up in battle. He let it fall around his shoulders comfortably.

"You look worried, love," Miri said quietly.

Ell took a deep breath—smelling pine even though most of the needles had already fallen—and then exhaled in a reluctant sigh.

"You don't need to keep anything from me. We've come this far, and I know the odds are stacked against us."

Ell shrugged. "It's nothing you don't know, it's just a concerning subject, that's all. We'll no doubt make our last stand in Verdantihya where it all began, but the city is in ruins now. And that includes most of the walls. Arendahl will have had workers striving to repair them as best they can, but they would need months to get the walls ready to withstand a siege assault, not mere weeks."

Miri smiled bleakly. "Long odds have never stood in our way before."

"Fortune runs out eventually."

"Not for us," Miri said, and her words were like a promise. She pulled him close to kiss him passionately, as if defying him to disagree.

Ell smiled when they parted. "Well, that may be true, but still, there will be gaps in the wall, weak points we will have to be aware of. Pressure points that I'm sure Half-Mask, his father, and Silverfist will be keen enough to assess."

"A problem for another day, a day when we can actually do something about it." Miri reclined against the bowl of the tree behind her and let her eyes droop lazily shut.

Maybe she had the right idea. When was the last time he had let his mind go? When had he last slept peacefully? Ell wasn't sure, but now was as good a time as any to try. He squirmed in beside Miri, jostling her enough to make her mouth quirk into a small smile even if her eyes didn't open. He held her hand and closed his eyes. Sleep just might be the best thing for him right now.

CHAPTER THIRTY

Aldashir healed slowly but steadily. The poison Silverfist had employed was dangerous and sapped its victims of life and energy even when they had been tended to by a supernatural healer. And so Aldashir, even as he improved, spent the first few days of his convalescence being carried in a litter. Rihya never moved far from his side. Day and night she was there, and Ell saw in her much the same things he felt when he tended to Miri's needs and she to his.

The next few days of his recovery were a struggle, not because he wasn't improving but because as soon as possible he demanded to be out of the litter and walking on his own two feet. This would have been fine except for the fact that Ell had ordered the army to move at double the pace in order to finally reach Verdantihya. He left very few soldiers behind to set traps or ambushes of any kind; the time for delay was over. Because of this, Aldashir struggled to keep up with the elves around him. He walked with one arm slung across Rihya's shoulders, gritting his teeth and grimacing with exhaustion nearly every time Ell looked at him. After the first few angry and short retorts, Ell learned to let the prince convalesce in silence and without scrutiny, however well-meaning that scrutiny might have been.

As the week of travel passed, Ell's scouts from the back reported to him, and he was glad to hear that despite his army's lack of real delay tactics Half-Mask and his army of Unsired still moved at barely a glacial pace. Half-Mask had many more warriors and was still martialling more up from the south. The growing number of dark creatures materializing out of the forests and hills around his army joined his ranks, as well. It made for a fearsome host, but it also made them slow. Ell didn't enjoy hearing of how his enemy's army was growing, but its pace of movement was welcome.

By the time Ell and his army were a day's journey out from Verdantihya, scouts from the city began to encounter them and go through the formalities of announcing themselves. It was a fiction of sorts—Ell's face and name were well-known across Andalaya ever since Arendahl had begun spreading word of him and especially since Ell had returned from the human continent, Etheros—but Ell had learned that fictions helped armies, kept the warriors feeling safe and secure in the manner of things. The company pushed onward, doubling the double-time Ell had already instated. He was eager to see what Arendahl had been able to make of it over the last month or so. Fortunately, Aldashir was just barely healed enough to keep the time.

Nevertheless, Ell checked in on him. "How are you, my friend?"

"I'll keep up, if that's what you're worried about," Aldashir grunted wearily.

"That's only part of what I was wondering," Ell replied, laying a concerned hand on the prince's shoulder. "I was inquiring about your health."

Aldashir grunted again but otherwise did not respond. Instead, Rihya, who'd shadowed him at every turn this week, answered on his behalf. "He's weak still but growing stronger by the day. He'll benefit from a steady diet of Source Water in his system, something which we don't have the luxury to do while away from Verdantihya. But we won't have any need to conserve our supply by tomorrow, and I plan on force feeding him Source Water until he's close to drowning in it. He'll be ready for the battle when it comes."

"Good. We'll be arriving shortly, so you will not have to wait long to begin the extra treatment." Ell gazed north into the distance, toward where he knew Verdantihya was located, toward his people's ancestral home. It was where the giant spring, the Source from which Source Water flowed, created a small river that split and merged with other streams until it eventually became the five main rivers in Andalaya.

"I look forward to it," Aldashir said and, for the first time, Ell saw something other than tiredness on his friend's face. He saw an eagerness resembling excitement. Ell understood; he felt the same after being away for so long from the heart of his homeland, its spiritual center. He could only imagine what someone might feel when approaching it for the first time.

They pressed onward and, as the army approached from the south, they eventually funneled into the valley leading up to the ruins of Verdantihya. Verdantihya was situated against a mountain backdrop, its entire northern wall essentially a mountain, nature itself providing the bulwark for its resistance. The slopes to the east and west were not nearly so impregnable, but they were still rocky and uneven, making it difficult to mount a successful assault. That left this valley as the southern corridor—the only real corridor an army could use to approach Verdantihya. Ell looked on with pride at his ancestral home, yet he looked on with a grim reality. Even though only one passable approach existed to assail the city, that had clearly not been an issue twenty years ago. No matter that Silverfist had betrayed them and opened the gates from within, loosing the reservoir of Source water at the high point in the city to flow out like a raging river and burst the gates open from the inside out. It didn't matter. The fact was that Verdantihya had fallen, and now it had multiple armies advancing on it again. The city was in ruins this time without even a fully functioning wall.

Ell led the army into the valley and some way forward before all of his people had gained eyesight of Verdantihya. Then he stopped, lifting his hand for all those behind to see. The Departed allies looked around in confusion as the Highest milled to a halt. As one, the Highest all dropped to their knees, placed the fingertips of each hand to their mouths in a kiss, and then spread their hands out wide, palms forward and tilted slightly up in the ancient greeting for home. Every elf did it when they returned to Verdantihya after some time away, only Ell had never seen so many elves do it at once. He glanced behind him at the scene, and a shiver ran down his spine. They might be fewer than their enemies, but they were one of the largest forces of Andalayans assembled since the city had fallen, and they could still be mighty. For a moment, he was buoyed by hope. Perhaps they *could* win this—or, at the very least, make the enemy pay so dearly that they couldn't enjoy the victory. Perhaps, perhaps, perhaps...it was all a game of what-ifs until the battle actually commenced.

Ell and Rihya rose to their feet simultaneously. "What was that about?" Aldashir asked curiously.

"Home," Rihya said simply.

"Home," Ell echoed with a softer smile than normal.

"This is our people's birthplace, where Creation spun into existence in order to combat the evil plaguing the land. It is customary for an elf to greet it in such a manner when he or she has been away for quite some time," Miri provided.

Aldashir looked at them thoughtfully for a moment, the rustling of the rest of the highest as they rose from their knees sounding quietly behind them. "Very well," Aldashir said. He knelt and pressed both fingertips to his lips, mimicking the gesture he'd just witnessed.

Rihya tugged on his tunic. "You don't have to do that. No one expects you to conform to our traditions."

Aldashir looked up from his knees. "I'm not. It just feels...right. This was our people's home once, too, before the rift occurred, before the troubles between north and south. I have been healed by Source Water —that proves I'm still one of you, right? Well, I may never have been here before, but I'm going to greet home the way it should be greeted. All right?" he finished firmly, resolutely.

Rihya stared down at him with an indecipherable look in her eyes, like she was seeing him for the first time. "All right." Her mouth quirked into a small smile.

Another rustling sound could be heard, and all of the Highest looked around in surprise as their Departed allies copied their leader. To an elf, they dropped to their knees and greeted Verdantihya, greeted home for the very first time.

"It's true, love, this feels right," Miri said, slipping her hand into Ell's. He nodded.

And then a great shout echoed over the valley. Watchers on the wall had seen the spectacle, had witnessed southerners reunited with their roots again for the first time in recorded history. Ululating cries washed out over the valley from the watchers gathered in the ruins of Verdantihya. The Highest in the valley lifted their voices to join with the rest, and cries of joy and rightness echoed over the snowy landscape.

"Come what may in the days ahead, at least we are one again," Aldashir said, reaching his hand out to clasp forearms with Ell. He gripped the Departed prince's arm tightly.

"Live together—" Ell began.

"Fight together—" Rihya and Miri echoed the old catechism.

"And, if need be, die together," Aldashir finished with a feral grin.

———

VERDANTIHYA WAS MOSTLY as Ell remembered it. Its interior was in ruins. Buildings had collapsed under the weight of time, cobblestone streets had plants springing from the cracks, and palaces on the hill toward the center and back of the city had darkened windows like eyeless ghosts staring out over a once vibrant and now abandoned realm. Only it wasn't abandoned—not anymore. More elves than Ell had seen in his entire nomadic life as a raider flitted this way and that as they attended to various duties. Even a few humans—former slaves who had no doubt been liberated in some of the fighting to the east—were scattered through the crowds and, oddly enough, they did not seem at all out of place.

There was a desperation to the work, the grim understanding that what needed to be done had to be accomplished quickly, yet there was also a strange cheer in the air—almost a festival sense. Like Ell, many of the younger generation had likely seen only small gatherings of their kind in one place, so this was new to them, as well. For the elder Highest, no doubt it reminded them of past days of glory, the years gone but not forgotten.

The only other real difference to Verdantihya was the walls. While most of the interior still lay in ruins, the Highest had been directing the bulk of their energy to reinforcing parts of the city's walls, completely rebuilding them in other places. The sight was welcome and encouraging compared to what Ell recalled of Verdantihya from his last visit, yet there were some worrying gaps still to be filled. Despite the hard labor, Ell was not sure they'd be able to fill them in time. Half-Mask's army might be behind them, but it wasn't *that* far behind.

As they walked through the now-repaired city gate, Ell watched Aldashir—mostly recovered and walking under his own power—stare in awe at the sights around him. Ell was reminded of his visit as a small boy and the wonder he'd felt that first time when taking in the ruins under Dacunda's watchful gaze.

"It's incredible," Aldashir said breathlessly as he drank in the sights. His head moved continually as if he were worried that if he left it facing one direction too long he might miss some other spectacular sight. His warriors were no different.

"This is home," Rihya said with a slight smile.

"You lived here?" the prince asked.

"Well, no. We traveled and raided mostly, but this is our people's home. It's our birthplace. You can't get much more of a home than that."

"We heard stories in the south. Slavers sometimes spoke of Verdantihya in muffled whispers, afraid that a spy might tell Half-Mask or his underlings that they were speaking well of the north. The slavers whispered of the marvels of Verdantihya, as if the northern city was crafted out of the land itself. How it was somehow a mixture of nature and elf-made architecture all blended together, blended so closely that it that it was difficult to tell where nature ended and architecture began."

Ell gazed around him, trying to see everything again with new eyes. Trees wrapped themselves around pillars, vines covered walls, streams trickled down stairs and crisscrossed cobbled streets. The city itself protruded from the shelter of the rock wall of mountainside to the north, as if the mountain was a hulking older brother protecting the younger.

His eyes trailed up as he followed Aldashir's gaze to the citadel at the top of the hill toward the back of the city. A small river streamed out through an opening partway up the face of the domed structure. The stream of water ran down through the city, the streets acting as its natural riverbed, until it gently coursed out under the gates and gradually gained speed to become a fully-fledged river. Then, as that river grew in power from other streams and creeks and snowmelt, it broke into the five main rivers of Andalaya.

"What's that?" Aldashir asked as they continued to walk toward the citadel.

"That, my friend, is the Source," Ell answered.

"It's a spring that is held in a reservoir inside the citadel," Miri volunteered. "The spring builds up, and the release valves part way up the citadel's face allow enough to run out to form the stream you see. If the lower valve were to be released—the one near the bottom of the building—then all of the Source Water would flood out at once."

"That's what Silverfist did, isn't it? How he broke down the gates of your capital from within." The prince sounded irate.

The three nodded in response. There was no need to entertain memories of that fateful day. They were here now, in these dire times, largely because of the Traitor's actions on that day all those years before. Ell gritted his teeth. And to think, he'd nearly had the chance to face off with Silverfist again not so long ago. Maybe he could have finally killed him, finished him off for good if he hadn't needed to attend to Aldashir.

A voice sounded from their side, startling them out of their talk and thoughts of the reservoir of Source Water and of Silverfist. "It's about damn time, boy! I thought you'd have been back days ago."

"Arendahl," Ell responded with a sigh before he'd even turned to face the old elf. "Good to see you."

"Oh, spare me the pleasantries, I'm in no mood. I've been hip deep in Ghouls for the last month—fighting to the north has intensified—and when I haven't, I've been back here playing master mason, something which is definitely not what I was meant to do." The old elf ran a hand through his lank, grey hair. For once, he actually seemed tired, seemed his age instead of just looking it.

Ell nodded. "Well, the preparations are advanced, yet I notice some gaps."

Arendahl grimaced. "Nothing to be done about it. We can only rebuild so quickly, especially if we want the rebuilt walls to hold and not crumble at the first touch. Quality takes time."

"True enough, but *something* will have to be done," Miri said, "otherwise the enemy will swarm to those gaps like maggots to a wound."

The old elf pursed his lips and looked at her in annoyance. "A few months firing a bow and all of a sudden you're an expert strategist?" He waved a gnarled hand in apology at his terse response almost immediately. "I know, I know, girl. I have a plan. Not a good one, maybe, but a plan nonetheless. We'll plug the gaps somehow."

"How?" Rihya enquired, tagging onto Miri's question. Rihya was never one to allow for vague responses.

Arendahl flicked his gaze uncomfortably toward Ell, and then just sort of shrugged as he tapped his own chest, as well. Ell's three companions stared at the old elf with incomprehension, but Ell already understood. He thought he did, anyway.

"We'll be the wall," Ell answered for his companions' understanding.

Arendahl nodded his head once in agreement, and the look he shot Ell was surprisingly proud, as if he were glad that Ell had understood his meaning immediately and hadn't even thought of shirking from it.

"What?" Rihya asked.

At the same time, Miri exclaimed, "That's insane! You're elves, not walls."

"There are two large holes, and you're right, they'll be targeted," Ell murmured to his mate, hoping to calm her. "We'll fortify the rest, make it strong, and then Arendahl and I can plug the gaps as best we can. We Water Callers are worth thousands of warriors. We can hold. Did I miss anything?" Ell glanced at Arendahl.

The old elf shook his head a bit regretfully. "Nope, that's about the extent of the plan. I never said it was a good one."

"You may be worth a thousand elves, but you aren't immune to arrows," Rihya said, her voice growing shrill. "It's *suicide*."

"Archers on our walls will have to focus on their archers to minimize that risk," Arendahl agreed.

"It'll be fine," Ell consoled Miri as she slipped her trembling hand into his. "Besides, you'll be on those walls looking out for me, won't you?" he asked in a half-joking tone.

"You better believe I will," Miri answered resolutely and pulled his face down for a passionate kiss.

"Good, I'll feel better for it."

Aldashir cleared his throat and finally spoke. "You can't plug the gap alone, Elliyar. You'll need warriors beside you. I'll stand with you in the hole."

Ell looked at him and felt a rush of feeling. For the first time, he realized just how much of a friend Aldashir had become. "Thank you," he said sincerely. Sometimes the simplest words were the best. Aldashir nodded gravely in response.

"As will I," Rihya proclaimed. When Ell looked at her, she added with a toss of her green hair and a raise of her eyebrows, "What, did you think I wouldn't be by your side through this? You'll never be free of me watching your back."

"I never for a moment thought otherwise," Ell told her with a smile.

"Your father and Dacunda will no doubt stand with me," Arendahl said. "And probably Iyonei, since Creation knows she's rarely found far from young Dac these days."

"So they're back from the eastern campaign, then?" Ell asked, a brightness returning to his voice.

"For almost a week now. Your forces are the last to arrive in Verdantihya," Arendahl answered. "We should find them. It would be good to share information."

Ell nodded, although he was thinking less about strategy and more about simply seeing his father again. Twenty years without him and of course there had been a hole in his life, but it was different being separated from his parents now that he knew they were alive. The past month or so had been difficult. Ell was fairly certain Rihya felt similarly, since more than once he'd caught her gazing vacantly to the east as if wondering what their mother, father, and sister were doing.

"Lead the way," Rihya said eagerly, a hand ushering Arendahl forward.

———

"ADAN, Dacunda, Ryder, Iyonei, and her cohort will stand in the gap with me," Arendahl proclaimed, "while Valerihya and Aldashir will join with Elliyar. Lliaria, Delle, and Miriyah will be placed with the archers on the wall." He outlined his basic idea of strategy for the key people and placements during the battle to come.

The elves present nodded their heads in agreement. "Any objections?" Adan asked the group who would be involved in the old elf's plan.

"None from me and mine," Iynoei said firmly.

"Nor mine," Aldashir confirmed. "Some of my captains will stand with me, as well, and surprisingly the pirates have bonded rather well with my company. I would not be surprised if a few of them join."

Heads bobbed up and down all around again. Ell remained quiet even though Arendahl and the others looked to him for disagreement from time to time. He felt none. It was a solid setup, maximizing assets and setting people who had strong ties next to one another. Every tiny bit of incentive helped in battle, and Ell knew that with Miri on the walls there was nobody he would fight harder beside than his sister.

"The question is, which group will stand in which gap?" Lliaria asked astutely.

Again Arendahl shared a glance with Ell before responding, "I'll take the easternmost gap for now while Ell and his group take the other. The boy has the most experience with Half-Mask out of all of us—other than Aldashir—so it makes sense that way. Me and mine will hold the gap against the humans."

"At some point, you'll have to leave it and join with me," Ell finally put in.

Heads turned and looked at him curiously. "Why?" Adan asked.

"Father, I'm just one Water Caller standing against two Spectralists, and who knows what manner of undead elf they have wrought by bringing Silverfist back from the grave? I can stand for a time—and, of course, the eastern gap must hold in the beginning. It wouldn't do to be overrun by the human numbers right at the start. But at some point, we'll have to gamble and shift the focus south. Bloody the humans' noses early and hard enough, and perhaps they'll retreat. But we cannot ignore the Unsired and what they command on our southern edge." Ell sighed as he finished. Once Arendahl left the eastern front of the imminent battle, that side would be greatly weakened. All the better that it had his father, uncle, and Iyonei's strong band of fighters.

Arendahl cleared his throat. "He's right. There's truth there. It'll be so when the time is right. Looks like you've got a mind to match your brawn now, boy."

Ell nodded and felt a rush of warmth at the pride on Arendahl's face. Maybe he was better at this than he thought.

"Humans are about two days out to the east and pushing hard, my scouts tell me," Iyonei said eagerly, relishing the thought of the coming fight.

"My sources say that the Unsired aren't far behind that schedule," Aldashir murmured.

"Then we'll likely be looking for the battle to begin in earnest at first light on the third day," Arendahl surmised.

Dacunda spoke up. "Sounds about right." There were a few other mutters of agreement. "But we'll be ready sooner, just in case."

"Good, let's make sure of it," Ell told him. Those decisions made, there wasn't a lot that needed to be finalized right at that moment and, surprisingly enough, the conversation turned back to mundane topics and the typical jesting that occurred in the prelude to a battle when warriors sensed the impending chaos and danger and sought a modicum of respite beforehand.

It was a time for family and friendships. The group stayed relatively close over the next days, huddling in their cloaks near to cook fires, eating and gaining strength for what was to come. They sharpened weapons and tended to their gear, but mostly they enjoyed one another's company. In particular, Ell made sure to soak up every last moment he could with his once lost family. With Miri close beside him, he memorized their faces, traced their outlines in his mind. Battles always brought death, and he'd only known them for such a short while. He wanted to make sure that if something happened he would not forget them. That is, if *he* survived the battle himself.

Snow piled in drifts, and small bits of ice traveled along the streams flowing through Verdantihya. It felt right that the deadest time of year was coinciding with the culmination of this war. Even with the preparations taking place around the camps in and throughout the city which was filled with more elves than Ell could imagine, there was nevertheless a wintery stillness in the air—a calm before the storm. And when that storm hit, it was bound to be cataclysmic. Everything would be decided one way or another within a few days' time.

Almost the entire population of Andalayan people was there, but as the second day arrived, a few designated elves began leading bands of children out through the sally ports in the side walls. It was a stall tactic;

everyone knew that however this coming battle fared would determine the fate of their people, but it was a necessary precaution nonetheless.

Ell sat on an overturned log next to Miri and listened to his friends and family speak. Dacunda could be overheard telling Iyonei that his one wish was that Dahranian was by his side for this fight. Surprisingly, the one-eyed warrior elf was calm and gentle in her agreement.

Ell's parents held hands and spoke with Delle, Rihya, and Aldashir while Ryder played some made-up game of wits and blades with the pixie elf Brie. It was a game Ell had never seen before, but it involved guessing, and cutting, and even some food, so all in all it seemed perfectly suited to the two elves of such differing heights but such similar personalities. Only Arendahl was not present. Ever watchful, he was conducting patrols of his own, not fully trusting the scouts they sent out.

Miri snuggled in next to Ell, linking her arm through his and huddling close for warmth. "I wish I wasn't on the wall with the archers. I know, I know," she forestalled his immediate response to repeat again why it was better that way, "my leg and all that entails. I get it. I just wish I was going to be by your side in the fray."

"You will be," Ell comforted her.

"I don't just mean in spirit, love," Miri said in exasperated annoyance.

"Neither do I," he responded.

Miri cocked her head in question. Then understanding lit in her eyes and she smiled.

Ell said aloud what they were both now thinking: "I'll need you to graft into me at some point—deeply inside my consciousness, like you did when I killed the Stone Ogre. I'll need the added strength. I am sure of it. You won't be able to do that if you're in the midst of the fray. On the wall, though, you can."

"When shall I do it?" Miri asked.

"You'll know. I know you'll be watching me—you always do. Your arrows have a habit of finding targets nearby." He smiled at her and got a slightly embarrassed grin in response. "So, when the time is right for you to stop firing and start accessing the Graft, you'll know. It will likely be when I finally confront something more than just an average Unsired or Ghoul."

"I'll keep a close watch. My eyes will never leave you," Miri promised and hugged him tightly with their linked arms.

"I wouldn't have it any other way," Ell responded resolutely.

"ENEMY A FEW MILES OUT!" the voice echoed across camp. Ell was startled from his pre-battle ponderings by the sound of a sentry relaying the information. By that point, everyone knew where they needed to be and when. That *when* had become *now*. It was finally time.

Miri pulled Ell close for one final, lingering kiss. "That is not the last time I will kiss you," she whispered fiercely even as her lips and body screamed that she was terrified that it might be. She yanked him close once more then pulled away.

"Be careful," Ell said, holding her hand until she was too far away and then reluctantly letting it go.

"I will. I'm off to meet Lliaria and Delle. I'll be safe with them. Don't worry."

And then she was gone, disappeared through the milling mass of elves, and Ell was glad she couldn't see the fear on his face, glad he wouldn't have to tell her the truth, that it was just as likely that none of them would be safe again. He'd been separated from Miri before, but this time it felt terrifying. He would no doubt confront at least the Prince of Darkness by day's end, if not the King of the South and maybe the undead Silverfist. The odds of him escaping unscathed were remote. Ell swallowed and clung to her words. That was not the last time he would kiss her.

He turned to make his way to his own post, heading toward the southwestern edge of the wall, looking for his sister and Aldashir who would face the horde of Unsired and dark creatures with him. As Ell walked, he passed by Iyonei and his uncle in passionate conversation. Unable to stave off his curiosity, he paused a moment to watch and listen.

As he stopped, Iyonei pulled Dacunda into a fierce embrace not unlike the one Miri had given him, and then, to Ell's shock, the one-eyed female kissed Dacunda.

"For old time's sake," she murmured, staring relentlessly into his eyes as their lips finally parted.

"Iyonei, we were hardly more than children back then," Dacunda protested, yet he didn't let go of her hands nor break eye contact.

Iyonei rolled her good eye, the other masked by the mossy patch. "Yes, yes, I know. We are different people now. We've both lost things. I have lost—well, I've only lost an eye whereas you've lost much more, a mate...But what are we fighting for if not for the chance to move forward?" There was a hopeful, almost pleading note in her voice, and Ell didn't think he'd ever seen her more vulnerable. Iyonei was one of the sternest people he knew, and this was definitely a new side to her.

Dacunda stared for a moment but then answered her words with a hesitant smile. "You are right, Iyonei." He pulled her back in for another kiss, this time gentle instead of fierce, and Iyonei melted into him.

Ell glanced over and saw through the crowd that Ryder was standing next to Briesom and watching the same spectacle. Ryder nudged the pixie elf in the ribs with his long fingers, a sporting grin on his face as he watched Iyonei and his father kiss.

"It's about time," Ell heard Ryder remark. Brie just rolled her eyes at his comment but, when he wasn't looking, Ell saw the blonde's face soften as she looked at Ell's tall cousin. He couldn't help but think that fast companions often led to more, and a shared battle often forged deep connections.

Ell shook his head to clear his thoughts. He had no time for this. They were on the brink of battle yet he was distracted by the intimate lives of others. He rushed through the milling throng until he reached his gap in the wall. It was a few yards wide. Only he and a handful could fit at once while the others manned the walls.

Rihya and Aldashir were already there along with, amazingly, Piripeos and the pirates Rikiol, Baerg, and the half-mad Kester. Ell shared solemn nods of greeting with the sailors before going to his sister and the prince.

"So glad you could join us," Rihya joked.

Ell could not help but smile. "I couldn't let you fight the enemy all alone—as much as you might want to." He loosened his daggers in his sheaths and tried to force down the jitters.

"You know me," Rihya said with mock eagerness.

Ell glanced up the wall and saw his mate's locks of braided hair gleaming in the winter sun.

"She'll be fine," Aldashir comforted him, putting a hand on his shoulder.

Ell turned back and nodded. He made himself focus on what lay ahead. That's when he heard it. War drums echoed in the air, and the sound of distant marching could be heard. A few screams and otherworldly shrieks sounded, and Icari swooped up and over the forest top. The first enemies had been sighted.

It wasn't long before others followed. The army materialized out of the dark reaches of the forest, and Ell was almost staggered by its size. Elf after elf piled from the woods and into the valley. Ogre stood beside Unsired who stood beside Ghoul, and all the while Icari cried overhead. The First Days had returned, all right, and they had come again in all their nightmarish glory.

Ell chanced a look east and saw a sea of humans. He forced himself to focus back on the army of Unsired before him; the other side of the valley wasn't his concern now. Arendahl, Adan, Dacunda, and Iyonei could deal with it. Ell had other things pressing his attention.

And then he could see them. Three shapes glided out of the forest in long, dark robes. It could only be Half-Mask, his father, and Silverfist. Even from afar, Ell could see the third elf oozing some sort of dark substance, staining its cloak. That could only ever be Silverfist.

Once the entire horde had marshaled itself in the valley and Half-Mask had made his way to the front, the Prince of Darkness lifted a horn to his lips and blew a blast. The horn sounded old and worn, the bone of a long-dead beast. It pierced the sky, and its note was not clear. It was as if death were wrapped in its note. It chilled Ell, and he heard the nervous shuffling of feet as the elves behind him felt the same fear. A chorus of screams and shouts echoed from the army of dark creatures. Ogres of all kinds bellowed, Icari shrieked, Ghouls cackled, and Unsired beat their chests and clanged steel to shields. The cacophony of sounds echoed for what seemed like forever. Then, gradually, it died.

Ell felt a drift of breeze carrying the putrid scent of the Bonewinds to him one last time. It told him what he already knew, that his ancient enemy was but a field away from him. Ell glanced to each side and realized how exposed he really was in this gap. He swallowed. He would hold this hole in the wall. If he caved, then the rest of the wall would mean nothing.

The horn sounded again—its garbled, ugly note was shrill, its sound biting as much as the wintry air bit at exposed skin. And then the call faded away again.

As it faded into nothingness, a roar again erupted from the dark army opposite him.

And then the enemy charged.

CHAPTER THIRTY-ONE

For a moment, Rihya tried to ignore how terrified she really was. There were seconds before that charging enemy army collided with her allies at the wall, just a few moments in which to collect her calm. She would never have admitted the fear to anyone; she'd been a warrior too long to do anything other than adopt her calm façade in the face of danger, but inside she was a seething turmoil. It all came down to the fact that this was, quite simply, like nothing she'd ever faced before.

Arrows darkened the sky—a sky already made tumultuous with northern clouds—and rained down to clatter against the wall, a few spattering the gap in which she stood. She sighted a few and stepped out of their way as they zinged to stick quivering in the ground. All the while, Stone Ogres lumbered toward her, followed by cagey Wood Ogres and the manic leaps and bounds of the agile Ghouls. And, of course, interspersed throughout were the Unsired, corralling their charges and sprinting forward, exhibiting jerky movements and blank gazes upon their diseased faces.

She made a decision. Rihya let the fear in. She let it simmer and boil below the surface. She acknowledged it fully, just like she recognized that there was no other choice but to stand and fight. Flaming-red eyes sprinted her way, yet retreat was not an option. One moment longer and her indulgence was over. She shoved the fear aside, buried that terror deep into a faraway corner of her consciousness. She could revisit it later, if she survived.

"Ready?" Aldashir swallowed as he glanced at her and tightened his grip on his sword. He shifted his feet on the slushy, slippery snow packed down by feet. Rihya was irrationally glad that he didn't seem to be calm, either.

"Ready as I'll ever be," she muttered. Then she added with a wink, "I was born for this." It never hurt to keep up the façade. The wink had the desired effect: Aldashir smiled. Somehow, in the face of battle, he found the humor, and she smiled back.

Screams of rage, wild calls of fury wrenched them back to the present and an army that was a scant few dozen yards away. It was now. The time to live or die was upon them. Rihya noticed movement to her left and turned to see Ell crouch and then burst forward into a sprint, careening toward the charging army. All the while, arrows rained down. One struck an elf just behind her, instant death, a reprieve from the struggle.

Ell's momentum carried him forward, and he collided with the enemy like an avalanche meeting a great wave on the coast. His dueling daggers were already out, firmly in his grasp, and his collision sprayed red droplets high into the air as he drew first blood. A cry went up from the wall as the force of Ell's blow sent a Ghoul flying backward many feet to impale itself upon an Unsired's spear. Ell was incredible. He was delicate with his steel as always—cutting tendons, severing arteries, opening bellies—but when he wished, he could strike with enough brute force to send elf or Ghoul alike clattering tens of yards through their comrades. But the wave of enemies passed him by, leaving him an island in the midst of black, and as magnificent as her brother was, Rihya had to focus on her own fight.

The wave that had passed Ell's charging body struck the gap with a forceful concussion. Steel clashed, and bodies locked together in a seething mass of chaos. Rihya danced lithely from side to side, her bladework impeccable as she diced her enemies into little pieces. She kept one eye on Aldashir, maintaining him at her shoulder. She saw him do the same. Silently, without speaking, they had made the same decision. They would fight side by side, close enough to help one another, watch each other's back, and, if need be, fall together as well.

Aldashir's sword glittered in the stormy air as remnants of light shot down through a gap in the darkened sky. The hole closed, and a grim dimness settled over the battlefield. Blackish blood replaced the gleam on Aldashir's weapon as he struck and cut, parried and thrust over and over again. Rihya was spritely madness, a tiny death dealer sticking her knives in the backs of her enemies, blocking sword strikes and deflecting the spear thrusts of an Unsired. She often found herself face to face with Ghouls as the insidious creatures slunk through the battle like ghosts in the night, grabbing elves and dealing near-instant death with their poisoned toxin.

All the while, the dying wailed and moaned in pain, the dark creatures shrieked in an otherworldly manner, and the crush of bodies pushing closer and closer together made it hard to find space to maneuver. Except for Ell. Glancing in front of her as her brother fought his way back to the gap and closer to her position, Rihya saw a pocket of space around him at all times as he felled creatures and Unsired left and right. Sometimes he worked his dueling daggers, but from time to time he sheathed them and grabbed a battle-axe or long spear from the dead lying on the ground and twirled it menacingly like a staff with blades, its arc of death cutting throats and severing hands as enemies tried to close. He fought his way next to Rihya and Aldashir as they continued to plug the gap.

She breathed in short, pained gasps. Nobody ever talked about how tiring a battle was. It was like a thousand raids conducted in a row, or sprinting from the Fracture to the western sea. It was exhausting, but she pushed through. She fought until a silvery note sounded from behind her. *Fall back.* She shifted her weight, inching backward just as Aldashir did beside her. Even Ell moved back into the gap with them. Just as they entered the narrow passage in the wall, a surge of replacements rushed past them, Highest and Departed, working in unison to spell the defenders.

It was a strategy designed by the elders: fight in shifts, rotate warriors through the gap to keep them fresh. Even Ell needed a break at times. His ability-enhanced speed, strength, and stamina could not last forever. Rihya sheathed her weapons and bent over, her hands on her knees, panting. Aldashir was doing the same. Only Ell paced anxiously. He took a minute's rest before throwing himself back into the fray.

"All right?" her prince asked. *Her* prince. That felt right.

Rihya nodded, not wanting to waste breath talking. He nodded back and slumped down to a crouch. Rihya glanced up at the walls where archers were trading shots with those at the rear of the Unsired army. Miri, her mother, and her sister were up there somewhere, but there were too many heads to tell where exactly. Unsired were raising war ladders in an attempt to scale the wall. Ghouls with their suctioned hands and limber bodies were scampering up the face of the battlement like spiders, their ability to camouflage and blend into their surroundings making them hard to see until they reached the parapet and climbed over. Battle raged atop the wall almost as fiercely as in the gap, but so far the defenders had forced back the enemy. They repelled attack after attack just as the allied forces did in the gap. Yet Stone Ogres had lumbered forward and were now pounding on the walls, causing the stones to shake. Rihya could understand why legends said they had downed fortress walls all by themselves. But these were the walls of Verdantihya. They could hold, couldn't they? They had to.

All too soon came the shout to prepare, and then the silvery note sent Rihya and Aldashir back into the fray as replacements. They surged into the battle to spell the weary defenders. Shoulder to shoulder with Aldashir, she sliced her way forward, taking vindictive pleasure with each drop of enemy blood she spilled. Unsired fell, and Ghouls as well, but no warrior escaped a battle of this magnitude unmarked. A Ghoul bit her shoulder—thankfully, it didn't manage to grab her with its toxin-filled, stinger-laden hands before she jammed her knife up into its skull through the bottom of its jaw. It dropped dead. She turned toward Aldashir and saw him harried on three sides by two Unsired and a Ghoul. One of the Unsired delivered a shallow gash to his ribs. Aldashir fought back and forced the Unsired to retreat before fluidly changing course to attack the dark creature. He dispatched the Ghoul with a broad stroke of his sword but left himself open to an Unsired as he engaged the other. With a practiced cast, one of Rihya's knives left her hand and sailed through the air to bury itself hilt deep in the small of the Unsired's back, dropping it to the ground. She closed the distance quickly and wrenched her blade free, not stopping to wipe off the blade as the black blood dripped down and covered her hand in its sickly color. War was messy.

Aldashir finished off the other Unsired and thanked her with a wolfish grin before thrusting his sword over her shoulder. She turned in surprise to see a Ghoul who had nearly reached her, its hand hovering just out of reach of her unsuspecting back. Aldashir pulled his sword free and let the dead creature fall.

"Even?" Rihya asked with a quirked smile.

"Always," he responded. And they turned back to fight again amidst the continued mayhem.

Notes sounded, and they broke to rest and then replaced the replacements over and over. Only Ell took little in the way of rest, fighting relentlessly to stem the flow of enemies that fought to break through this narrow gap in their defenses. It was like a waterfall of darkness trying to squeeze through a crack in a cliff face. Once it gained purchase, it would all be over. And Ell was the primary reason it hadn't yet. He was the thin line that stood between success and failure.

A runner approached Aldashir during a break, one of his Departed warriors. "Tidings from the other side of the battle, my Prince."

"Report," he said wearily.

Rihya perked up her ears as the runner spoke. "The old Water Caller leads the eastern front, and they fight well. They are still holding, but like us they are hard-pressed. Numbers are not in their favor, and the humans have war machines which do not help matters." A thunderous crash sounded, and Rihya suddenly realized that what she had assumed to be thunder was actually a boulder striking the eastern wall.

"Will they hold?" Aldashir asked.

"I cannot say," the runner said worriedly. "It is not certain."

"They'll hold. If I know Arendahl, that bitter old root won't let his side of the defense fall. He's to prideful and ornery to let that happen," Rihya interjected.

"If you say so, my Princess—" the Departed bit off his words as if they were sour in his mouth, and an embarrassed grimace replaced his voice.

"What?" Rihya asked incredulously.

"It is nothing, I assure you. I'm sorry, it's just habit from how the rest of us soldiers sometimes think of you," the runner placated her.

"I'm not a princess, I'm a warrior, and you damn well better remember that," she huffed.

"Yes, of course," the Departed said with an apologetic bow.

"Don't bow to me!" She looked over and saw that Aldashir was covering a smirk with his hand. She shot an angry look his way. "What? Don't you dare say anything."

"Say what? Something to the effect of you being the first green-haired princess in Departed history?" The smirk was full-blown now.

"We haven't even decided yet if we want to Join. And I'll never be Departed, so don't forget that, Aldashir," Rihya muttered.

"Haven't we decided?" He inquired, suddenly serious. "We may not have actually discussed it, but I had sort of hoped..." he trailed off, and she gave him a blank look. "What I mean is, I had thought my intentions were implied." The nervous look on his face was enough to melt her heart.

"There will be time to talk about it later, after this is all over," Rihya said firmly but gently before pulling him to her in a strong kiss. She could taste the sweat from his brow and blood from a split lip gained fighting, yet somehow it was perhaps the sweetest, fiercest, most passionate kiss she'd ever experienced with him. At some point, the runner must have disappeared, and time lost meaning as they crushed each other together in an embrace that a hurricane could not have dislodged. They grasped one another until another horn blast sounded and it was time to step back into the gap. They held hands until the last moment, regretfully letting go to draw steel and then scream their defiance at the horde as they charged forward to hold the line once again.

Blood sprayed—red from elves and black from the enemy. It spattered faces, stained clothing, and more than anything it painted the snow a slick, blackish-red. It was the color of death and destruction. Footing was hard to find now, and Rihya fought intelligently, trying not to take as many risks. She fought without extending herself. One slip, one moment of unsure footing, and it would all be over.

Aldashir fought beside her, and the feeling of contentment from his continued presence was difficult to describe. Amidst the chaos that reigned, he was a constant counterpoint to the terror that threatened to bubble up and cloud her senses. This scale of conflict was something altogether different than anything she'd ever faced. Bleeding and tired, they fought on and on until the press of the battle forced its way in between them, sweeping her a few yards farther away from Aldashir than normal.

Rihya was engaged with an Unsired, its pocked face and powerful limbs causing her problems, when out of the corner of her eye she saw a giant shape moving forward from the back of the enemy lines, getting closer and closer to Aldashir. A Stone Ogre was making a beeline for him. Rihya didn't know whether Half-Mask had tasked the beast with destroying his brother but, whatever the reason, it seemed intent on the course that would take it right toward the elf she loved most in this world. Rihya fought to keep her focus. She dodged a blow from the Unsired's spear then dodged another thrust and darted in close to deliver a blow herself. She opened him up from groin to chest, his entrails peeking out of the wound. It would have been enough to drop a normal elf and even some Unsired. But not all. Some of the Unsired had the sinister ability to fight on well beyond the threshold of what a normal elf could. This particular Unsired did just that. It slowed, and even its blank, stoic face took on a slight grimace of pain, but it fought on methodically, silently, forcing Rihya to stay engaged with it a minute longer instead of reaching Aldashir's side in aid.

Rihya ducked another swipe and then finally came in close enough to open the Unsired's throat. Black blood spurted onto her face, making her even more of a horrific mess than she had been, but the Unsired finally dropped to the ground. She whirled to find Aldashir. She saw the hulking body of the Stone Ogre taking a swat at the prince as he deftly rolled out of its way, his sword flashing as he rose to strike sparks on its stony body. Nearly impervious to steel, its body was huge, twice as tall as an elf's and nearly four or five times as large. Its red eyes gleamed full of hatred and wrath. It swiped again, nearly taking Aldashir's head off.

Rihya bit her lip in worry and looked for Ell. She found him busily fending off three Tree Ogres at once, barely staying afloat in this madness himself as he dealt with an endless barrage of Unsired and Ghouls. There would be no help from him at the moment. A swat caught Aldashir this time and sent him flying to the ground. He dragged himself to his feet, a painful grimace on his face. He wouldn't sustain another blow like that. He could only be tossed around by so powerful a creature for so long before his body would break. Aldashir circled the Stone Ogre wearily, its hulking shape shifting its back to Rihya as it moved with its prey. It took another swipe, narrowly missing Aldashir, and Rihya bit back a scream. Such a blow with that amount of power behind it surely would have been instant death.

Fear made up her mind. Regardless of the danger, she sprinted forward toward the Ogre's rocky back, a back that seemed impervious to most steel. The sound of fighting and dying echoed in the valley and rebounded against the walls of Verdantihya as she ran. In a swift bound, she leaped onto its giant back and scampered up to its shoulders as quickly as she could. It bucked and rolled its shoulders, swatting above its head, but Rihya dodged, riding the movement like a ship on a stormy sea, feet balanced and light on its shoulders. She heard Aldashir call out to her, but there was no time to think. In another fluid motion, she reached forward with both of her knives, and thrust. Blades sweeping downward and in a circle of sorts, she violently cored out the Stone Ogre's flaming eyes—the one true weak spot on its body.

An otherworldly bellow sounded from deep inside the creature's gut, and it fell to its knees, the earth shaking as it did so. Rihya rode the movement down and leaped clear of the ogre in a graceful roll, grabbing a sword from the mucky ground, a weapon discarded from the hand of its lifeless owner. The roll ended in a crouch, knives sheathed and the sword now in her hands. She stared for a moment at the blind Stone Ogre, empty sockets leaking blood like great black tears. And all the while it shrieked, its pain making it sound like the Icari that cried and swooped dangerously amidst the battle and harried the archers in the ramparts.

Without wasting a moment more, Rihya sprinted forward and rammed the sword through the Stone Ogre's giant, wailing mouth. It burst out the back of the creature's skull, sending crumbling bits of skull falling to the ground more like pebbles than bone. It crumpled in death, and Rihya pulled the now-blunted sword free before dropping it to the snow.

"Well, that was impressive," Aldashir breathed in relief, pride lining his face where worry had once been.

"I'll always be there to deal with your little issues," she mocked him and flicked her eyebrows up in jest. "I'm practically indestructible, you know."

He opened his mouth, whether to thank her or laugh she wasn't sure, because the arrows struck her side without warning—two in quick succession—and with a force that knocked the wind from her. They turned his smile to a look of horror. The impact sent her falling backward, and everything went black. There were a few moments where she could still hear his pleading voice.

"No, my love. Don't go. Stay awake. No!" The anguish in Aldashir's voice was palpable until oblivion welcomed her home.

CHAPTER THIRTY-TWO

The sweep of the battle separated Ell from Rihya and Aldashir. He found himself dodging the deadly, grasping hands of Ghouls and facing off with Ogres aplenty. It was like their dark master had implanted a desire to kill Ell into their consciousness, because they came at him one after another after another, an endless stream of depraved creatures with glowing, red eyes lusting for his destruction. At one point, Ell sheathed his dueling daggers—fine for dispatching elves and men, but less effective against the tough Ogre hides—and picked up two discarded battle-axes from the field. He whirled them effortlessly with his ability-enhanced strength, decapitating Ghouls and Unsired, and lopping off the arms and legs of Wood Ogres to send them tumbling and ineffective to the bloody, snow-soaked earth. Only the Stone Ogres provided any real threat. Yet, as Ell faced his first Stone Ogre, he felt the extra rush of strength, the power that he'd only felt before when Miri had Grafted herself so deeply inside of him. He buried both axes in the Stone Ogre's chest with ease, sending sprays of pebbly skin and spurts of black blood everywhere. Ell knew his mate had joined her consciousness to his in the way he needed to gain power. He said a silent thanks.

One after another, he killed them, Unsired and dark creatures alike. Half-Mask never showed his face, though, nor the King of the South, not even Silverfist, as they preferred to let their underlings do the damage first. And so Ell slew a steady stream of those minions until his arms ached from swinging axes and his fists from clenching so tightly around their moss-covered hafts.

Ell glanced east and vaguely made out the raging battle across the field. Human and elf clashed in horrible conflict. He knew his father and Dacunda were there, Arendahl beside them. They were hard-pressed, as the humans had many more men than the elves. Yet there was one consolation: it was clear that there was no alliance between the humans and the southern elves. The last time Verdantihya was attacked, human and dark elf had joined together to vanquish the north. Not so now. Human and Unsired clashed in the south of the valley, and Icari swooped among the human army, plucking generals and even what looked to be the Grand Marshal from the fray before dropping them to their deaths. It was hectic and bloodthirsty, and it was the only reason the north still stood. If this wasn't a three-way conflict, then Andalaya would have fallen all over again already. As it was, they were still hard-pressed.

Ell looked up in time to see an Icari careening down from the sky toward him. He grinned with eagerness and ducked its initial pass with a diving roll before the beast swooped down again. This time, better prepared, he swept one battle-axe up in a vicious arc, lopping off one of the creature's wings even as its claws raked his shoulder. He ignored the blood from his wound, though it made his grip slippery, and strode over to where the beast had crashed into the ground. It flopped weakly, talons and wing giving it little help on the ground. He buried his axe into the Icari's chest as it screamed one last, terrible shriek of defiance, cut off as the weapon swung home.

He yanked the axe out and kept fighting, wielding both axes like a windmill, twirling them through the air around him in dangerous and continuous arcs. The Unsired fell like mown wheat before him. But it was not enough. The battle raged all day. Hours passed, and even as the Highest and their Departed allies fought bravely and took two or three or four enemies for each of them killed, it was not enough. The numbers were against them, and Ogres were pounding their way through walls. The Gap Ell defended became less important as cracks began to appear in the foundation of Verdantihya's walls. It wouldn't be long before the northern alliance had no walls to defend at all. He had to do something.

Where is Half-Mask, damn it? Ell wanted to at least kill the bastard before the day was done. If his people were going to fall, then he wanted to take their aggressor out, too. He threw one axe in a powerful cast, and the weapon sang sweetly, its steel song screaming as it flew through the air to plunge into the face of a Stone Ogre. The creature fell, and as it did so, it crushed the Ghouls and Unsired in its way.

Ell looked east again and saw the humans pressing in, forcing the elves back, fighting their way toward the gap that Arendahl held. They couldn't hold forever. Eventually, numbers always won out. And then cries of surprise and a commotion at the rear of the human army rippled across the battlefield. Ell fought his way back toward his wall and, with a humongous leap, he jumped up to land on the parapet. He gazed east and saw a fourth army smash into the backs of the humans.

Hope blazed in his chest. *What is happening? Who has come to our aid?* Ell peered toward the center of the army and saw with shock who led them.

Dahranian.

With an army of ex-slaves at his back, Dahranian led the fourth army. Even from afar, Ell could tell they were ragged and tired. They had likely fought their way north and across the Great Bridge to then sweep south fast enough to reach Verdantihya in time for yet another battle. They might be exhausted, but they fought with purpose. Ell could see Dahranian issuing orders and commands, saw him standing side by side with his men, the sores from collars that had chafed their necks all their lives still visible. The ex-slave army had elves, as well, Highest who hadn't held a weapon for decades but still remembered how to fight.

Ell almost felt sorry for the human army. Almost. Caught vice-like between the walls to the north, the Unsired army to the west, and now this army of ex-slaves to the east, they fought desperately to avoid getting ground to bits. But Ell could see from his vantage point that their only hope was escape. Even then, they might not be able to salvage much. The human commanders must have realized the same, as their army began milling around, trying to fight its way south. Their retreat was bloody and ineffectual. Harried on three sides, the humans were slowly being slaughtered.

Ell was startled out of his observations by an echoing crash. He looked down in time to see three Stone Ogres finally pounding their way through the wall near the front gate of Verdantihya. His momentary hope fell. It wouldn't be long before more Ogres would come to make more holes in the walls, and the dark creatures and Unsired would sweep through those holes, laying waste to all within.

He leaped down from the wall and back into the raging battle at the gap. He swung his axe over and over, but no matter how many Unsired and dark creatures he killed others inevitably took their places. It wasn't enough. Elves fell all around him. One by one, his people—his comrades —were being whittled down. Fight as hard as he could, there was no way to prevent it. It drove him wild with anger and desperation.

He grimaced in pain as an arrow grazed his thigh, saying a prayer of thanks that it hadn't found its mark completely. He took a swig of Source Water to seal up his minor wounds and hopefully close off the deeper wound on his shoulder gained from the Icari. As he drank, he could feel the Source working.

That was it!

The thought came to him out of nowhere. He slashed downward with the axe, killing an Unsired before dropping the weapon completely. He didn't need it where he was going. But could it work? The idea was crazy and untested. Besides, he wasn't even sure if it was possible. But his memory flickered back to a year ago, to when he'd touched the face of a dead Unsired and watched it heal before changing back again to its sickly shape. A Water Caller could affect the body of an Unsired with his abilities; *Ell* could do that. If he could heal them, what else might he be able to do? Kill them? He just didn't have time to do it to each one. But there was a place from which he could draw power. A source of great power for him. *The* Source.

The fighting continued to rage around him. Hope to the east, but destruction pressed in from the south and west. Another hole appeared as a Stone Ogre battered its way through a crumbling section of newly built wall. Elves screamed as a few of them fell with the rubble when it caved. Ell made up his mind. He drew his dueling daggers, felt them buzz with energy in his hands. He slashed his way through the enemies around him, but this time he fought toward the wall, toward the city of Verdantihya behind him instead of pushing his fight outward. Ell fought his way into the gap and then, as elves stared at him in surprise, he sprinted away from the front lines. Shouted questions and shocked faces followed him as Highest and their Departed allies couldn't believe that their talisman, their young Water Caller, would run. Ell hated that they thought such things of him, gritting his teeth with frustration, but he ran on. He had a mission to accomplish. Even with Dahranian's army it wouldn't be enough, not with the walls falling and the army of Unsired and dark creatures lying in wait. Ell had to do something. And do something he would.

He sprinted into the city along cobblestoned streets slippery with streams and snow, as fast as his ability-enhanced speed would carry him. Ell headed north through the city, up the hill and toward the reservoir. A young Silverfist had once done the same thing, raced to the Source and used it to bring about his people's doom. Ell was about to replicate that feat, only this time he would ensure that it saved them.

He was going to use the Source to turn the tide of this battle. He was going to tap into the Source and all its might. He was going to break the reservoir and unleash it.

CHAPTER THIRTY-THREE

Miri loosed arrow after arrow, more than she ever had in her entire life, until her shoulders and arms ached. Some of the youths, just old enough not to be hidden away, served as runners, plucking arrows from the ground and bringing them back up to replenish the archers' stores.

While the battle raged furious and frenzied below in the gap and on the walls that were more heavily besieged, it was slower, more methodical for her. She was in a section of the wall that was less heavily attacked, and a large portion of the Highest's warriors had been stationed nearby to make sure that the archers had free rein to pick their targets. She did just that, shooting enemies near Ell. Occasionally, she focused some of her attention toward Rihya and Aldashir who were in the same vicinity as Ell, but eventually her focus always shifted back toward her mate. She couldn't really control it. Nor did she want to. From a personal perspective, he was the most important thing to her, but from a strategic one he was, as well. Even a less studied tactician such as herself could see that he was almost singlehandedly keeping the enemy army in check and preventing them from pouring through the gap in the wall which he defended. So, while other archers tended to target their arrows toward the enemy archers, nullifying that threat, Miri let herself focus on Ell.

She loosed a shaft, and the arrow flew true, striking a Ghoul in the base of its skull. It crumpled to the snowy earth, its deadly hand outstretched only a few feet from Ell's back. He never even turned, had no idea how close to death he had just come. But there was no time to congratulate herself. Miri immediately picked another target in his area. After the first few efforts, she'd realized her arrows had no effect on the Ogres, so she was better off picking Ghouls and Unsired as targets and letting Ell deal with the rest. So that's what she did. She shot until her body ached, and then she shot some more. She would break only briefly for sips of water or to merge her consciousness deeply into Ell's through the Graft whenever she thought it looked like he could use more strength, whenever he looked to be facing some particularly strong or powerful foe like a Stone Ogre.

When she did merge, she made sure to tuck herself back against a corner of the wall, out of range of enemy archers, crouched down as safely as was possible. At those times, she prayed no enemy onslaught would hit her section of the wall, prayed the hand fighting wouldn't reach her. Ell's older sister, Delle, was there too, standing beside her and firing her arrows, but serving as a de facto body guard whenever Miri decided to Graft into Ell—which happened more and more frequently. She could tell by the way the battle was turning that her arrows made less and less a dent in the enemy's strength whereas Ell's ability to kill a Stone Ogre or lay waste to an entire cohort of Unsired all by himself was much more effective. And so she Grafted.

Miri spent more and more time merging her consciousness with Ell's, sending it as deep as she possibly could, wanting to imbue their link—and thereby Ell—with as much added strength as possible. So when the hand shook her out of the merge, it was startling being back in her own body rather than embedded in the mind of an all-powerful Water Caller.

"You must drink. Rest a moment." Delle held a skin of water to Miri's lips.

"He needs me," she protested, but she drank all the same.

Delle smiled. "And we need him, so therefore we need you. But if you wear yourself out, it will do no one any good. Keep up your strength. This battle is not done. A good warrior knows to conserve energy, to hold some in reserve for a final push."

Miri nodded. She lifted the skin back to her lips and drained it. "Speaking of which, how goes the battle?" She saw only what Ell saw when merged so deeply into his consciousness.

A flicker of hope warred with the worry on Delle's face. "The east is practically won!" The hope blossomed as she spoke, a smile on her face. "The humans are crushed—my cousin has arrived with an army of those who were once slaves at his back. They are already trying to run." The satisfaction in her voice was no doubt due to the many years she'd spent as a slave in Etheros.

"And the rest of the battle?"

The hope sputtered out as Delle spoke. "You see it through his eyes, yes? No matter how hard we fight, no matter what he is capable of, it is not enough."

Miri swallowed. What was she saying? That it was over? That there was no hope? "What do you mean?"

Delle sighed. "Stone Ogres have broken through the main wall, Icari sweep elves from the parapet, Ghouls scale the walls with their spider-like fingers. Our lines are breaking."

As if in response to her statement, a thunderous crash sounded followed by an echoing crumble, like a mountainside sliding down into rubble. Miri leaped to her feet and saw a portion of the wall crack and fall as a Stone Ogre bulled its way through, flicking arrows off its rocky hide the way someone would swat at a fly. Where was Ell?"

She looked and saw him surrounded on all sides, just outside the gap —unfortunately, no longer the only gap—doing all he could to beat back his enemies. He fought with an axe, which was odd because he so rarely fought with anything other than his dueling daggers.

"Where is Rihya?" Miri mumbled, the shock at seeing the wall break making it hard to think. She felt like she hadn't seen Rihya's green hair in some time. She could make out Aldashir's tall form, muscled and wielding his sword with equal parts might and skill, but there was no flash of color at his side.

Delle's face clouded. "She fell some time ago, while you were occupied with your Graft."

"What do you mean she fell?"

"I mean she was struck by arrows. I fear my sister is fallen. Dead." Sorrow creased Delle's face.

"No!" Miri shouted, the outburst sounding like denial in her own ears. "We thought her dead once before and she came back."

"Let us pray it is so this time, as well. With Source Water, many things are possible, things to which I have grown unaccustomed so far away from here in the human land of Etheros."

Miri swallowed back another angry denial. It would do no good to debate with Delle. Suddenly, Ell's direction changed. Miri always kept an eye on him, even if just from her peripheral vision, and usually he stayed right near the gap, pushing outward, falling back, but staying in its general vicinity. Not so anymore. He fought desperately, changing his direction to practically sprint back to the gap and then into it. Ell passed through the wall and left his allies under pressure, fighting with everything he had to prevent their lines from falling.

"What is he doing?" Delle asked incredulously. Shouts of alarm from the wall and from below showed that many of their allies echoed her concern.

"He always has a plan," Miri said firmly, imbuing her voice with as much faith as she could muster.

"But he's...running. He's leaving the battle!" Delle said in a shocked, almost distant voice.

"Only because he's decided there's something vital to success that he needs to accomplish," Miri assured her. "Trust me. I *know* him. Whatever he is doing, he's doing it for us."

"You know him better than I, that is true." Delle sighed regretfully. "I choose to trust you."

"With him gone for the moment, the line needs us all the more," Miri told her and strode forward toward the brink, sighting a target near the gap and loosing. Delle nodded and followed suit.

And so they nocked, drew, and fired. And did it again. And again. And again.

———

"THE HUMAN FORCES have all but been extinguished or vacated the field of battle in flight, my Prince. There are a few stalwart pockets of resistance, but they will not hold out for much longer."

Half-Mask flicked a finger in dismissal at the runner who disappeared as quickly as he could. "This battle is coming into its final stages. I had hoped the humans would bloody our northern cousins more than they have—that extra army was unforeseen—but there is no way around it. We still have the advantage," he concluded, staring at the mass of dark creatures and Unsired that seethed before him, swelling to push through the holes in the walls. For now, the Highest and their defector allies were holding on. Just barely. One more strong push and they'd fold like the humans had.

"Is it time?" the king asked, a feverish light in his eyes.

Half-Mask shot his father an annoyed look. "Not yet. We'll convert their precious Source into a new Black Water Well once the battle is finished. Patience, father."

The king's fingers twitched as though he couldn't quite keep them still. "I just need a drink. A sip. Just a bit to tide me over."

Half-Mask shook his head in disbelief. Had his father traveled so far down the rabbit hole of addiction that he couldn't even focus long enough to accomplish the very goal that would give him what he so desired? It was concerning. He needed to keep his father busy. A fight would distract him.

"Soon enough, Father. Soon. You'll drink your fill from a new Black Water Well, but for now we cannot waste a drop. We need it to convert the Source. We must finish what is before us. Would you care to hasten those ends?"

"Anything to speed up this process." The King of the South gnashed his teeth in half-mad frustration over the fact that he had to wait for his thirst to be slaked. Half-Mask knew the pull, was familiar with the ecstasy of drinking the dark liquid from whence they drew their powers, but this was too much. His father was an asset now, a piece to move into position. But once this war was finished, once he had no more need of him...well, perhaps it was time to finally start thinking about sending him into the great, black beyond. The old king's uses were running out. Once the two Water Callers were gone, that use would decline even more rapidly.

"Lead the eastern front," Half-Mask urged, "squash this new army that approaches. It's a rabble of slaves, men, and elves who've hardly fought a day in the last decade. They should be easy to deal with."

"I don't take orders from *you*." The king flashed a glare at his son, showing a hint of the old fire, the wild madness and cunning that made him such a dangerous foe.

Half-Mask gritted his teeth and forced a placating smile. "Of course not. But you do want to convert their Source, don't you?"

The feverish look returned almost immediately, and the king nodded eagerly. "I'll break the eastern edge. Just make sure you do the same here!"

And just like that, he swirled off, his cloak dark as dried blood in the night, his hood pulled up so that only a shadow of his diseased face could be seen. Yet a path cleared before him. He was still the king, still feared by all except Half-Mask. Yes, he still had his uses. For now.

The Prince of Darkness turned to the silent observer of the whole interaction. "Go with him. See that he doesn't...make any untoward decisions. But use subtlety. Don't let him kill you before you've completed your purpose on this earth."

"You don't trust him?" Silverfist rasped, a dry and yet somehow gurgling laugh coming from within his wrecked throat—a courtesy of months spent in the cold ground. "You shouldn't. He's completely mad, can't think of anything other than his next drink."

"That's why you'll accompany him. Whisper in his ear. Make sure his decisions do not cost us. Prime him to meet that old bastard of a Water Caller," Half-Mask instructed. Silverfist cocked his head in question. "You didn't think there was just one of them, that the boy alone was able to raise and accomplish all of this? No, there's an older one, and I haven't seen him on our side of the battle which means he is facing off on the eastern front against the humans."

Silverfist nodded complacently, unfazed by anything since he'd returned from the grave. "Arendahl. It must be him. Well, no matter. I'll prime your father for a fight. The king will be eager to meet his most ancient of enemies by the time I am done with him."

"Good," Half-Mask whispered. Still, a clench of caution struck him once more, the old wariness. "But do not expose your subtle nudging. The king might be more gone to the madness than present, but he is still capable of much."

Silverfist's mouth cracked into a gruesome smile, the exposed jaw and cheekbone creaking upward without flesh to cover them, a dark substance oozing out instead of blood. "I can't be killed, remember? What concerns have I?"

"We can all be killed, Silverfist. Remember that."

Silverfist shrugged and then turned and strode off to follow in the direction the king had gone. A path cleared for him among the Unsired almost as widely as it had for the king. Half-Mask narrowed his eyes. Perhaps he would have to go also, once this was over. Back to the grave would be good. The half-dead elf was growing overly confident for Half-Mask's taste.

The Prince of Darkness turned his attention back to the battle raging before him. He was on the back lines of it, having seen no combat yet. But soon. Soon he would engage. The time would come to thrust his sword into battle for the killing blow, to reach out and wrench the very heart from young Wintermoon's chest. That was, if Silverfist didn't reach the boy before Half-Mask and kill him first.

He looked on with satisfaction as the air shuddered with another quake, a small section of wall caving near the gate courtesy of one of his Stone Ogres. They were quite useful, those creatures. His Unsired pushed forward, but their progress was halted, stemmed at the hole—at great cost to his enemies, no doubt—but stemmed all the same. No matter. It would not be long now. The northerners and their futilely allied Departed would fold once their precious walls crumbled under the onslaught of his Ogres.

As if in answer to his thoughts, he looked on from afar at a commotion near the original gap in the wall where the boy had been fighting and bleeding all day. The commotion turned to worried shouts, and Half-Mask could practically feel his enemies' drop in morale. What was it? He gazed on, straining his eyes to see a blonde-haired shape fleeing the battle, sprinting back into the city.

The Prince of Darkness threw back his head and screamed in joyous laughter. Steam came out of his mouth as he cackled, the winter air still cold at the edges of this heated battle.

The boy was running! He was fleeing. It was over.

He would need to be pursued, of course, but Half-Mask had a certain undead elf for that purpose. More importantly, though, without Wintermoon this northern resistance would fold like a faulty wooden chair. He laughed again, unable to hide the delight in his voice as he spoke.

"Push!" he cried to a nearby runner. "Send word to push all forces forward. Hit the gaps hard, but also hit the gate. Thrust our main force toward the front gate. Once we batter it down, it'll be the largest inroad into the city."

So this was what it felt like. The humans were crushed. Their presence on this continent might never regain the same foothold. He was about to establish a new Black Water Well. And most importantly, that upstart of a youth had turned tail and run. The exultation Half-Mask felt was delicious.

"The game is over," he murmured to himself. "I win."

———

IT DIDN'T TAKE LONG for the-elf-who-had-once-been-Silverfist to catch up to Half-Mask's father. The King of the South turned his head to appraise Silverfist as he heard him approaching through the crowd that scattered around them. Unsired eyed them warily even through their blank gazes.

"Come, let us crush this miserable excuse of an army and get on with our true purpose here," the king said with a manic eagerness that could only be described as frantic. Frantic for this to be done, to get more of the Black Water Well in his veins.

Silverfist nodded in agreement and continued to follow until they reached the front line. As they approached, the clash of steel rang louder and the screams of the injured and moans of the dying increased. It was so different than the quiet of the grave, but Silverfist found he preferred the raucous sounds of war and death to the endless stillness of oblivion.

As they reached the front, Silverfist and the king stepped into immediate action, bolstering their troops and galvanizing them into greater action. The king was a one-elf massacre, slaying any who got in his way. He was stronger, faster, and possessed the ability to flicker partially into smoky insubstantiality that made it nearly impossible for his foes to land a blow. Silverfist was beginning to understand the title 'Spectralist', since they were spectral in their existence *and* powers.

The king fought with a frenzied force that pushed their line forward and crushed the Highest and their allied army of slaves back toward their own crumbling walls. The king dealt the sharp of his sword to his enemies and laid the flat of it to any of his troops that he felt were flagging. It was a brutal approach to battle, but effective.

Silverfist was right beside him, fighting in his ragged cloak, half-disintegrated from enduring the cold of a shallow burial. He swirled among the battle, stronger than he ever had been before, immune to the touch of steel on his skin. He felt no pain when a blade bit, only a slight tug as he freed himself and delivered a killing blow to the foe—his former Highest kin—who pretended to think they were a match for Silverfist, the elf who'd risen from the grave. It was a drunken feeling of mad joy as he killed, impervious to harm. This was what *real* power felt like. He'd do like his current master had said: he'd make sure the mad king was fulfilling his purpose, and then he'd go fulfill his own. When steel couldn't kill him, what match was a Water Caller?

He dodged a thrust and then skewered his opponent on the end of his rusty blade, the tendons and veins on his ropey, un-fleshed arm flexing as he ran his opponent through. He threw back his head and cackled. This was what joy must feel like. Silverfist fought on, the press and chaos of battle separating him from his project, from the King of the South who was decimating northern troops left and right. He could barely hear anything from the mayhem that surrounded him. Snow slushed and crunched underfoot, steel scraped on metal, and shrieks of the dying pierced the air. He looked up to see a flock of Icari descend upon the ramparts of the eastern wall of Verdantihya, saw a pack of

Ghouls flooding the battlefield around the King of the South as Ogres of all kinds stalked and killed. The sounds of battle and death and victory surrounded him. This army of Unsired was unstoppable, and he was at its head—well, nearly.

When the stillness hit the battlefield, it was so strange that it almost stopped the entire fight for a moment, beasts and terrified men and determined elves pausing to appraise the duel that was about to take place.

The old one, the one who'd always ignored Silverfist or looked down on him in his youth, had cut his way to the fore. Arendahl. The Water Caller. The two senior warriors in this battle would finally meet. Silverfist thought for moment. He could help. He could join the duel, but what purpose would that serve? A Spectralist could take care of itself, could it not?

Silverfist watched as the two ancient enemies stalked each other in wary silence, circling for a moment more of stillness before the battle could wait on them no longer and erupted back into life. As he stood there, he was struck with an arrow loosed from the wall, the impact sending him to the bloody muck of snow on the ground. He gritted his teeth in annoyance rather than pain and yanked the arrow out as sludgy, black ooze leaked from his wound. It wouldn't slow him down.

He stood and clashed weapons with a man, an ex-slave by the chafed line around his neck where a collar had once been. Silverfist opened him from throat to groin with one powerful slash. It was too easy killing these men. They didn't stand a chance against the army before it, one of Unsired, dark creatures, Spectralists, and an undead elf such as himself. He grinned his gruesome smile and continued to kill.

He spared one glance back toward the dueling supernatural fighters before making a decision. Silverfist considered his options. Half-Mask had tasked him to make sure the king did what was needed, and wasn't facing the Water Caller exactly what Half-Mask meant by 'what was needed'? His task was now completed, freeing Silverfist to pursue the true purpose for which he'd been recreated. Wintermoon. It was time to find him and finish it.

Mind made up, Silverfist began fighting his way toward the gate that was quivering under the press of bodies of Unsired and Ogres trying to force their way through. Once, the old version of himself had burst the gate wide open, shattering the kingdom as he'd splintered the gates, starting the course which the rest of his life—lives—would take. He fought his way closer to the walls, slaying any elf that stood in his path, angling to the east. The gates weren't broken yet which meant the gap abandoned by the old elf would be the easiest to slip through. He could feel the young Wintermoon, his prize, his purpose, somewhere past the wall, somewhere high up in the city beyond.

"Silverfist, you abominable bastard of a half-elf!" The cry rang out through the cacophony of battlefield sounds to arrest Silverfist in his tracks. There was so much pain and fury in the voice—it was sweetness to his ears. He turned around and looked back toward the raging battle behind him, back from where he'd come. And there he was. The elder of the two. Adan the Green, once-great defender of the walls of Verdantihya.

Adan fought his way through two Unsired, slaying them with a practiced ease that belied the decades he'd spent enslaved, working a pick instead of a blade. Silverfist stood still, staring, thinking. His purpose was in the city, but still, he could put that on pause for a moment more, couldn't he? He watched as Adan Wintermoon cut his way through a couple of Ghouls. He looked up again and shouted, but this time his words were lost in the screams of the dying. Yet Silverfist waited.

Adan drew ever-closer, and the-elf-who-had-once-been-Silverfist felt an eagerness wash over him. He could indulge, couldn't he? How sweet it would be to tell the boy that he had robbed him of his father yet again just before finally killing him and completing his purpose. He could make time for that deliciousness. The eagerness was stronger than any desire he'd felt since his recreation, more powerful than anything other than his purpose—and he was now convinced that could wait. He was invincible. Silverfist would slay Adan and then kill the boy Water Caller. Who knew what could happen then? His purpose completed, he could turn his eyes to a bigger prize. Once he'd proved a Water Caller was no match for his invincible new self, perhaps he would turn his sights to a Spectralist or two. Yes, the thought slid across his mind slyly. He had always been cunning—no need to stop that now. He could be the greatest being alive, and it all started here!

Silverfist hacked his way through the intervening space between himself and Adan Wintermoon, slaying ally and foe alike, not caring who his blade bit into, until the two of them were only a few feet apart. They paused, as Arendahl and the king had done.

"I've been waiting for this moment for twenty long years," the elder Wintermoon said through furiously gritted teeth as he hefted his sword in anticipation. Mayhem still reigned around them, but they were the eye of the storm.

"Wait for it no longer, then," Silverfist rasped, finally standing across the field of battle from his old foe for the first time since they were young.

They shared one more long look, and then, before the tide of battle could sweep them apart again, they lunged toward one another, swords at the ready, muscles tight with controlled aggression. The blades clashed in a shower of sparks, Silverfist's rusty, disentombed blade screeching down the edge of Adan's cleaner, newer weapon. Their momentum carried them apart. They swung back around to face off again, and Adan pressed the initial advantage. He stepped in, closing the distance and launching into a quick series of strokes that made Silverfist step back and back, set himself, defend, and then retreat a few steps again.

Silverfist barred his teeth in annoyance, the cold air dancing against his boney jaw. He parried a vicious overhand stroke and pushed Adan back.

"Always were the best, weren't you?" Silverfist muttered.

Adan smiled and inclined his head in agreement. "You said it, not I."

"Well not any more. I'm different now. Better—" but he was cut off before he could finish.

"You're dead now, Silverfist. That is what you are. Walking death. I need to put you back where you belong."

"I don't feel...dead." He grinned and took a swipe at Adan with his metal fist, but the Highest ducked his attack and swept in with a stroke of his own. The swipe opened Silverfist's arm, but no blood flowed, no pain came, and his grin only widened as he saw the surprise on Adan's face.

"What—?" Adan choked out.

"You see? I'm different now. I'll not be easy to put back in the grave." Silverfist laughed in joyful delirium. How sweet this was! To defeat Adan Wintermoon again would be delight beyond belief.

Adan stalked him in a silent circle, verbal jabs gone now, all focus. Silverfist did the same, a smile playing on his gruesome face. *He* pressed the advantage now, stepping forward, wielding his sword in a series of connected maneuvers that put Adan on the back foot. The retreating elf grimaced before a look of steely determination grew on his face. Silverfist chuckled to himself. He would disabuse Adan the Green of that determination once and for all. He pressed forward again, and his attack was deliberately wild and overzealous, not because he was out of control but because it didn't matter. He couldn't be harmed. He hacked and cut and forced his way closer to Adan. Wintermoon's blade flickered in the half-light of the stormy sky and inflicted shallow wounds all over Silverfist's body and face—wounds he ignored with a toothy grin, pressing ever onwards as Adan fought in a desperate retreat to stem the wild onslaught.

One more strong push. One more and he'd wear his opponent down enough to finish it and move on to his true purpose.

Silverfist lunged in again and got within Wintermoon's defenses. His sword bit deeply into his foe's left arm, the one not holding the sword. But instead of crying out in pain, Adan smiled through it, grinned back at Silverfist with a smile that said the predator had caught the prey. Before Silverfist could react, before he could correct whatever mistake he'd made, Adan hacked downward with his sword arm. The blade bit into Silverfist and, although he felt no pain, the blade sheared through his leg at the thigh, and his weight collapsed him to the ground. He screamed in fury.

"You are not invincible," Adan said firmly. "I refuse to believe that."

"I am!" Silverfist screamed, almost incoherent with rage as his body failed him, as he struggled to rise on his one good leg but could not. Instead, he was slumped on his knees before Wintermoon, one dismembered leg laying a few feet away.

"You are not," Adan said again with as much determination as Silverfist had ever seen on an elf's face. Not wasting any more time with talk, Adan's sword arm cocked backward, and Silverfist tried to raise his own blade to parry, but in his state he wasn't quick enough.

Adan's sword swung rapidly downward, and just as the vicious backhand stroke hit Silverfist's neck, cleaving his head from his body, the-elf-who-had-once-been-Silverfist couldn't help but feel like he might have overestimated. He realized that he had miscalculated his own power, and it was a bitter realization.

Then it all went black as cold oblivion welcomed him once more.

———

THEY DANCED A DEADLY, silent dance, a duet of blades singing in the crisp winter air. Arendahl focused, he pushed away all sound of the battle raging around them, ignored the heat rising from dead and bleeding bodies that were fresh enough to still steam in the cold. He gracefully shuffled his feet sideways, parrying a thrust as he heard the clang of steel ring out, and it was all he heard, all he *allowed* himself to hear.

The warriors fighting around them on both sides of the conflict gave Arendahl and the king a wide berth; nobody wanted to interrupt a duel between a Water Caller and a Spectralist.

Arendahl flashed forward, lithely skipping over a dead Ghoul as he moved, pressing the King of the South with his attack. They fought in silence, Arendahl a study of attention and focus, the king with his diseased face locked in a snarl of hate. The king whispered to himself as they fought, the manic meanderings of a mad royal, but Arendahl couldn't quite make out his words and wouldn't allow himself to lose focus to try and discern his mutterings. The only thing he could make out were the occasional phrases: "No, you won't keep me from it," and "I must have it." Just what exactly the Spectralist needed so badly that it turned him into a furious addict Arendahl wasn't sure, but he could guess. In truth, he had no desire to find out if his guess was correct. And so they fought on.

It was a titanic clash of warriors. Arendahl would lunge forward and press his attack, seeming to gain a half step on his foe, the end appearing to draw close, only for the Spectralist to momentarily flick a body part or his entire self into a smoky apparition, long enough for the sword to pass through without causing harm. Arendahl gritted his teeth in frustration and then would leap to defense as the king would take the attack to him.

Arendahl made sure not to underestimate the king. This was an elf—if he could still be called that—who had faced down two Water Callers at one time at the battle of the Midnight Cove and had escaped to tell the tail. He'd run, of course, but even two on one, the boy and Arendahl had found it difficult to deal with the King of the South. And so Arendahl fought on, aggressively, passionately, but oh-so-very carefully. He measured his every move, weighed his attacks. He inflicted shallow wounds, wounds the king seemed willing to take—perhaps it cost too much energy to flicker out of existence for every minor injury—but the Spectralist doled out his own damage. Before long, there was a score of small wounds crisscrossing Arendahl's body from cheek to thigh. Nothing to end him, but enough to slow him down just slightly.

Again the king muttered, "You'll not keep me from it. I need it...it's mine."

Arendahl shook his head. "What are you talking about, Spectralist?" he asked as he stepped forward into attack, once again locking blades with the leader of the Unsired.

The king spun away, a maneuver of his wrist twisting his blade and hooking Arendahl's, nearly yanking his sword from his hand. It was all Arendahl could do to hold on to his own blade, but he managed to do so just barely, grasping it by the fingertips, retreating a few steps to regroup.

"Nothing you would understand, Water Caller," the king responded with a fixed sneer. "Ecstasy you'll never taste."

"I don't think I want to," Arendahl said as he tightened his grip and moved back in to engage.

"You would if you knew its pleasures. And we'll make another one, recreate it from the ashes of yours. Better, bigger, stronger, flowing freely to all corners of the land," the Spectralist's voice rose into a fevered shout and his black eyes had a vacant look to them.

Arendahl's blood chilled. He couldn't possibly mean what Arendahl thought he meant, could he? The Source was impregnable, everlasting. Its waters perennially flooded out into Andalaya and beyond. Nothing could change that. Yet, they had destroyed Black Water Well, so who was to say what was or wasn't possible? This had to end now. Arendahl grimly sought to pull on whatever grit, whatever determination he had left after such a wearying day. He couldn't allow whatever it was the king was muttering about to come to pass. Losing the battle but killing the king was still a preferable option to allowing whatever plans he and Half-Mask had come to pass.

Angrily, Arendahl leaped forward into a vicious attack. He rained a series of blows down upon the king's body, but each one was parried or passed through smoke. He practically screamed his frustration, the noise coming out like a wild war cry even though it felt like vexation and fear as much as anything else. The king thrust back, but Arendahl refused to back down. This had to *end*. He'd spent too many years fighting Ghouls in the north, trying to stave off the end of Andalaya to allow it to end in such inglorious fashion.

He fought on, frenzied now, his energy matching that of the mad king's manic movements. Arendahl tightened his gnarled knuckles along the worn hilt of his trusty sword, the sword he'd fought with for longer than any elf alive—north or south—the sword he'd held when the humans invaded, when Verdantihya had fallen, when the Ghouls and Icari and Ogres plagued the north, the sword he'd held when he was young, the first day he'd realized he was something different, something special. A Water Caller.

Arendahl screamed another furious battle cry, and this time he drew close, coming into the king's guard, swinging his aged fist as often as his sword. He struck blows with both fist and blade, kept his enemy close, drew black blood. But he took more wounds himself. That kind of reckless fighting ended duels, but often with both opponents dead. He didn't care. Arendahl pressed the attack, landing a fist to the king's face and feeling teeth crunch beneath it, but at the same time a kick from his enemy sent Arendahl to his knees as his legs went out from under him.

The ground was a soggy mess of snow and blood and mud as Arendahl tried to roll away from the downward swing of the King of the South's blade. He barely avoided it, but even as he managed to roll away, his reckless fighting caught up to him. The king recovered from his missed strike, slithering closer, snaking the tip of his sword up to kiss Arendahl's throat even as Arendahl knelt and tried to rise.

Arendahl froze. Was it really over? Was this how it ended—in defeat? After all these years, a half-mad dark source addict was to be the end of him?

"I told you, you will not keep me from it." Spittle flecked from the king's sickly lips as his eyes gleamed with frantic excitement. He laughed in an ugly manner. "Two of you were trouble at the Well, but one of you...well, one is not quite enough to best me," he gloated, and Arendahl saw his arm tense to strike, to deliver the killing blow. Arendahl was just about to move, about to hope against hope that he was fast enough to avoid the tip of that sword opening his throat even though he knew he wasn't, when the unexpected happened.

A shape flew out of nowhere and tackled the king away from Arendahl, and the old elf seized the moment. He burst to his feet and followed the motion of the two fighters as their momentum carried them a few feet away. The two bodies rolled apart and bounced to their feet the way only two seasoned warriors know how to do.

The king gnashed his teeth in anger, and the madness took hold even further, its roots burying deep in his mind, shining out through his eyes. He screamed his rage, echoing the still-furious battle consuming the field around them. Ogres and Icari took up his call, reacting to their master's anger.

Arendahl glanced over and saw his rescuer. Adan Wintermoon stepped forward to engage again, and Arendahl's heart sank. He'd surprised the king, saved Arendahl, but he was just a normal warrior—albeit an excellent one—and no match for a Spectralist. Arendahl closed the gap between them but couldn't reach the fighters before his old protégé locked blades with the King of the South. They traded blows as Arendahl approached, and Adan fought bravely, one majestic pass drawing a screech of pain as he scored a black wound across the king's chest before the Spectralist could flicker into insubstantiality to avoid it. But it wasn't enough. No regular elf could face a Spectralist one-on-one and hope to prevail.

It all happened fast. The tackle, their rising, Arendahl closing the distance, the traded blows—all within a matter of moments. Arendahl sent out a prayer on Adan's behalf, a hope he knew wouldn't matter. Adan delivered a well-executed attacking combination, one that would have ended an average opponent, but he couldn't account for the king's supernatural speed. The Spectralist parried and parried again, and then after a quick shift of his feet and a burst of speed and he was inside Adan's guard, all while Arendahl was still closing the distance. Seconds stretched as the old elf saw what was coming.

The sword entered Adan's belly, shock opening his eyes wide, and then enduring pain as the king twisted his blade viciously, wild rage giving him a dark delight in the agony he was causing. His sword cored Adan out as Arendahl finally drew close enough to give aid. Through fading eyes, Adan saw Arendahl coming from behind, and he dropped his own blade, hands grasping the King of the South's hilt, keeping it locked in place. A last colossal effort to help end his enemy.

It was too late. Too late for Adan Wintermoon, Adan the Green, Defender of the Walls of Verdantihya. But it was not too late for his sacrifice to count.

Arendahl plunged his own blade into the Spectralist's unsuspecting back, and this time the King of the South didn't see it coming, couldn't free his sword, couldn't tap his own dark powers to avoid it. Arendahl's weapon punched through cloak and bone and flesh to erupt from the other side in a shower of black blood. He pulled it out and thrust again and again and again until his face, and hands, and blade were covered in the inky substance.

The king's body crumpled into a worthless heap on the ground. Arendahl flipped him over with his toe, checking to make sure he was dead. The glassy eyes said he was, but Arendahl opened his throat just for good measure. Then he knelt beside Adan.

"Adan, my boy, you saved me," Arendahl said as tears streaked his weathered face.

"You'd have done the same for me," Adan choked out with a feeble grin.

Arendahl examined the ugly wound, hoping there was something he could do. The boy would be crushed when he learned of this—if they even survived. But not even a Water Caller's healing powers could prevent death in those most vicious of wounds. The king had practically hollowed Adan out. Arendahl sent a thread of his healing ability into the wounded area, hoping to at least stave off the inevitable for a time. Perhaps Adan could last long enough to say his goodbyes. That was the best he could hope for now. That done, Arendahl gently picked up the mangled body of his old friend, one of his best pupils ever, and headed for the city, for whatever cover might still be found. He couldn't just leave the great Adan Wintermoon on the battle field to be trampled.

Arendahl used his powers to cover the distance in great leaping bounds, skying over Ghouls and Unsired alike to reach the walls. He climbed the nearest one and laid Adan's weak body down.

He would go find Lliaria, but then he'd have to return to the fight again himself. Adan Wintermoon's fight might be over, but this battle wasn't.

———

RIHYA AWOKE A BIT GROGGILY. She felt the cold stone beneath her, felt the flakes of snow on her face. The clouds had well and truly rolled in, and soft, white flakes were sifting down onto the battlefield and the ruined city.

She sat up and looked around. She was at a healing station on the wall. The last thing she remembered were arrows striking her, and then everything had gone black. Rihya felt her side where the wounds were and found that they had shrunk considerably.

"They're not healed yet," a healer said from just a few bodies over—whether they were living or dead bodies, Rihya couldn't tell.

"No?" she mumbled thickly, still feeling woozy, likely from losing blood.

The healer shook his head in answer. "Source Water was enough to stem the blood flow and close the injuries up somewhat, but they were deep punctures, and pulling the shafts out opened the wounds up badly before we could administer the Source, so you were lucky to simply survive."

Rihya forced herself to stand, simultaneously checking to feel if all her weapons were in place—various knives and blades hung or cached about her body. Most were there, a few were gone, likely lost in the belly of some Ghoul or Ogre.

"I have to get back to the fight," she declared and started to walk toward the nearest stair only to trip clumsily over a body—this one she was pretty sure was dead due to the fact it didn't stir at all when her foot collided with it.

The healer gave her a pointed look but then sighed grimly. "I can't argue. Under any other circumstances, I'd advise you under no uncertain terms to rest and stay flat on your back, but this being the end of the world and all..." he trailed off.

"It's not the end yet," Rihya declared forcefully, "not while I'm alive to say anything about it.

She paused at the crenellated edge of the wall near the stairwell, staring out over the battlefield in all directions. The fray had condensed, an army of humans and elves together led by Dahranian—which she was surprised to see—had pinched the field in from the north and east, all but annihilating the previous army of humans or putting them to flight. Dacunda, flanked by Iyonei, Brie, and Ryder among many other elves under their command, had joined with Dahranian's determined but ragged force of ex-slaves, many still wearing their collars from captivity. They were fighting hard but making little headway.

Arendahl could be seen nearby with his blade in the middle of the battle, a circle of angry beasts and Unsired trying their best to get a piece of him. He slew many in the few moments she was watching, but a buzzing arrow struck his shoulder. He snapped it off and kept fighting ferociously, but Rihya had seen enough of war to know when even an immaculate warrior had lost a step. Arendahl's movements came just a fraction slower than usual; it took him a moment longer to dispatch his enemies. He wouldn't last forever.

Rihya tore her eyes away from the old elf, her gaze roving, roving, until finally it settled on the one person she was really searching for. There he was, clothed in black, spearheading the attack on the southwestern side of the battle which, for some reason, was vacant of Ell. Rihya's heart simultaneously lifted as she saw Aldashir while dropping into her stomach at the realization that Ell was nowhere to be found. Her brother couldn't be dead, could he? A Water Caller of his strength, it would take Half-Mask to even have a chance of killing him, wouldn't it? *But that could have happened*, a voice in her head whispered. She shoved it away. No! There had to be another explanation. Either way, she wasn't going to learn of his fate up here. She raced down the stairs, taking them in twos in her haste to return to the fighting. Weariness receded—it didn't disappear, but it diminished through the rush of energy she felt at the prospect of battle again.

She reached the ground and immediately threw herself into the nearby gap in the wall. A Ghoul's toxin-filled fingers reached toward her, and she fended them off with a slice of her blade, sending digits flying to a screech of pain. The next thrust silenced that screech, her knife slitting the creature's throat, and Rihya danced onward through the masses. She ducked and dived, rolled and dodged. She aided fellow elves facing off against foes, she hamstrung creatures, she bloodied Unsired, but all the while she kept a direct course toward where she had last seen Aldashir. Her wound ached in her side and blood started to flow freely from it again. Source Water was mystical and practically a miracle, but it couldn't heal all wounds. The pain returned as her initial blood rush faded. If this was the end, she was damn sure going to go out side by side with Aldashir.

And so she fought on.

A spear was thrust at her face, and she only barely avoided it. Actually, she did not even come away entirely unscathed, as an Unsired's blade tip grazed her cheek, leaving a streak of pain in its wake. She gathered herself to attack when Kester, the half-mad sailor Rihya only vaguely remembered from the ship leaving Dark Harbor, skewered the Unsired on her cutlass. The sailor winked at Rihya in typical fashion and then pivoted, swept her sword low, and left another opponent in a writhing heap on the bloody, snowy slush.

If the sailors were nearby, perhaps she was close to Aldashir! Rihya fought on but kept her eyes peeled for the only love she'd ever known. A break in the masses and Rihya glimpsed him through a gap. Surprisingly, he was flanked by more of Ell's pirate friends—Baerg and Rikiol and the smuggler Captain Piripeos. She forced her way through and shouted his name.

"Aldashir!"

"Rihya?" he roared in response, even though he didn't turn to look. He kept his eyes focused on the enemy and, with a heaving, angry slash, he brought his sword downward, cleaving the arm from an Unsired. "Rihya!" he called again, and this time he did turn.

His dark eyes peered around the chaos, searching, searching. They found her, and his gaze lightened for a moment until another enemy got between them, obstructing their view. Rihya pressed forward, dispatching another Ghoul in the process, and finally she was right by his side. Shoulder to shoulder they stood, as it should be, in the way that felt more right than anything had ever felt.

"Miss me?" she grunted jokingly between blows.

He threw back his head and laughed, his raven hair cascading behind him. The laughter was all the answer she needed, yet he responded all the same. "Never leave me again, my love. Not in this reality or the next."

"Done," she promised with a smile, somehow finding joy in the midst of the bleakness all around. "How goes the battle?" she panted in question. "I've been unconscious for a while."

He grunted in response, parrying an axe. Rihya seized the opening he'd created and cast one of her knives into the Unsired's throat, causing Aldashir to grin his thanks and then move on to the next opponent. Between strokes and slashes, he shouted over the din to fill her in. "The battle goes poorly. Something happened a while ago in our favor, I believe. At least, I heard a great shout and a swell on the eastern flank from our troops a while back, but that faded quickly. Their numbers are greater than ours. The humans abandoning the field is the only reason we still exist. We're barely holding on." Aldashir stole a sidelong glance at her before continuing, "And your brother has vanished."

Rihya swallowed. *Vanished*. That meant he wasn't dead, right? "He'll be back. Ell always has a plan. Mad plans, idiotic ones, but plans all the same."

Aldashir shrugged his shoulders as if to say, *if you say so*, but he didn't bother to voice it. Instead, they both fell into silence, breathing heavily as they let the clash of blades and screams of anguish, the shouts of exuberant victory roll over them. The battle's cacophony drowned out all other noise. Then a familiar face appeared in the nearby fray: a blond, fair-skinned elf with two red tears tattooed on his cheeks. He fought angrily, desperately, and Rihya saw blood streaking his many battle wounds. There was just as much blood on his blade—her people's blood, *his* people's blood, the people he'd forsaken.

Borian.

They locked eyes as the swell of the battle swept them together, and Rihya could tell he recognized her. Yet there was a dullness to his eyes, a dreadfully bleak desperation, the look of an elf haunted by his choices. Rihya didn't feel an ounce of pity for him. He'd chosen his path. He didn't seek her out, but neither did he avoid her.

As the battle closed the distance between them, he locked blades with her just as viciously as he did with any other elf, a grimace forming on his face as he slashed and cut, danced away, and then darted back into the attack. He was more dangerous than Rihya remembered from the petulant youth who'd vied with Ell for Miri's attention in Little Vale, what felt like so long ago. She supposed that close to a year spent in Dark Harbor would harden an elf. Borian fought with the kind of animal desperation any elf gets in the heart of battle, just as Rihya did. They clashed and came apart, they bloodied one another and parried, until Rihya flung a knife. She let it go quickly and forcefully, and as it left her hand, she knew it was a good toss. It cleared his guard and buried itself in his gut. The impact knocked the wind from his lungs, and he doubled over, the shock causing his fingers to drop his sword.

Rihya was about to dart in and finish the job when a random elf she didn't recognize thrust a spear upward through Borian's chest. The force raised him slightly, and Rihya saw the life go from his eyes, the true blankness set in. For an instant, she wished the kill had been hers. She hated northern traitors, but the battle swept her attention away soon enough, back toward another opponent, and in some ways, that was fitting. Borian had been an annoyance, nothing more. And now he was gone. By her hand or another's it mattered not.

Rihya slid back a few feet, placing her back to Aldashir's, and they fought on. Cut, slash. Cut, slash. *Move your feet*, she told herself, *ignore the pain, ignore the exhaustion, or you'll be dead instead of tired.* The litany of self-instruction went on in her head. And so she did.

They fought on until time blended and warped, until she couldn't decide if she'd been in battle an hour, a day, or her entire life. Everything blurred, and all she knew was steel and blood.

ELL STOOD waist-deep in the crystal clear reservoir of Source Water. The domed cathedral arched high above him, ornately carved walls and pillars supporting the exterior while in the center of the building was a giant lake of water. A small amount of spring water trickled from the upper hatch to run steadily and slowly down the outer face of the cathedral, just enough released to keep the reservoir at full capacity. That release of water turned into streams that trickled down through Verdantihya, running along cobblestoned streets, trickling under the raised roots of trees that were woven into the city's tapestry. The streams and creeks eventually combined and proceeded out under the front gate to gain strength and momentum as they ran through the valley and eventually were swelled by snowmelt and other streams to then split into the five major rivers of the continent.

But releasing the dam would cause havoc. It was how Silverfist had turned the tide of the battle twenty years ago. The walls of Verdantihya had had a chance of holding until the traitor opened the lower hatch on the reservoir partway up the outer face of the dome housing the Source. The sudden force of water had run down from the high point of the city to crash with such force that it burst the front gates open from within.

Ell hoped to replicate that feat.

A small voice in the back of his head whispered caution. This could harm his people, as well. The force of the water would strike them, too. He swallowed his fears and thought tactically. They couldn't hold out forever, not against the forces that were arrayed against them. Already, their meager walls were crumbling in sections. It wouldn't be long until the gaps could no longer be held, and the full tide of enemies would wash over them. Besides, Ell was hoping that inundating the battlefield in Source Water would have an adverse effect on the Unsired, possibly even the dark creatures due to the properties that it possessed more than the strength of its motion. It was a gamble based on intuition. It was a last hope, one he was clinging to out of desperation.

Ell waded just a little bit deeper until he was chest-deep in the water and began pulling deep. He sent his consciousness out as far as possible into the water, felt the incredible swell of power as he tapped into the very Source Water around him. He needed to do more than just release the dam. He needed to release it with incredible force, and quickly. Ell drank deep of his abilities and hoped Miri was buried just as deeply within his consciousness to give him the added strength he needed. He felt the Source hurtling up through the spring at an unprecedented pace, felt the water rise around him. He'd do more than break the lower hatch to the reservoir; he would unleash the Source, dragging it upward to form a raging flood.

He tapped deep within his abilities and pulled. The battle would be won or lost by the outcome of this decision, and he prayed again for extra strength, willing Miri to hear him. He needed her now more than ever. The water rose. The volume built. He heard stone crack, and the hatch burst. Ell helped the water. He did more than unleash it: he grasped it, wielded it somehow, like a liquid club against the interior of the reservoir wall, and the resounding crash as the southern face of the dome broke was more satisfying than Ell could ever have imagined.

Source Water poured forth from the destroyed reservoir in more volume and with more power than had ever been seen before in the history of his people. It coursed wildly downward and through the city. It was wild, beautiful, and untamed. A Water Caller had called it forth to set it free.

———

IT WAS INNATE, indescribable. Without knowing how she knew, Miri felt it. She felt his need. Something told her to put down her bow, that wherever Ell had run off to he needed her now, needed her within his mind, aiding him with her strength, her will, her spirit. She set the weapon down, and Delle only gave her a strange look for a moment before glancing up toward where Ell had gone and then back at Miri. Delle was clever. She didn't need to have it explained to understand. Ell's oldest sister nodded tersely and backed herself up against Miri to get as close as possible, shielding her from any harm.

Miri closed her eyes and sent her consciousness into Ell's. She merged through the Graft she had forged into his mind, pushed herself so far into his consciousness that she couldn't tell where she existed apart from him anymore. She *was* him. She felt his thoughts, his feelings, saw through his eyes, and she knew what he was planning. Miri pulled out. In an instant, she was back in her own mind, her eyes snapping open.

"Delle, get as many of our people away from the gate and the gaps as possible! Get as many up on the wall as you can!"

Delle turned to look at her in confusion. "That's madness! If we abandon the gaps, the enemy will overrun us."

"Trust me," Miri pleaded, "you must get them on the wall." Without waiting for another argument, Miri closed her eyes, praying that Delle would listen, and sent her consciousness back into the Graft, embedded it once again so far into her mate's consciousness that they were unified.

She felt the immense power, power even she—a Water Caller—had never felt before, as she tapped not only into the land and water in Creation all around but into the very Source itself. Miri pulled it deep within, gathering strength as she tapped into the core of the land. She did something new then, something that surprised even her. She somehow wielded the water like a weapon. It was fluid still, but in some strange way the water had form, a form she gave it and she used to batter through the walls of the dome like a ram at a gate.

Stone cracked, water raced, and the flood was on. It would only be a matter of seconds before it reached the walls.

———

THE WAVE TOOK the battlefield by surprise. It struck the wall, pouring through the gaps and shattering the gates of Verdantihya from within with enough force to echo like thunder through the mountains of Andalaya. The water smashed into the warriors on the field—north and south, human and elf, Unsired or beast—with the kind of magnitude Rihya had never experienced in her entire life. The deluge inundated the valley, sending bodies of all kinds spraying everywhere.

Luckily, Rihya had turned just as the water was about to sweep over her. She grabbed Aldashir, locked arms with him, and held on for dear life. Whatever insane plan Ell had concocted this time—and unleashing a giant tidal wave of water on the battlefield certainly qualified as one of his maddest ideas ever—she prayed it would work to their benefit. Insane as her brother might be, he didn't do things unless he believed they would gain him success and, by extension, success for his people. *Have faith*, she told herself.

The wall of water hit Rihya and Aldashir, swirling over them, tumbling them head over heels in the surging mass until up and down were only memories and she wouldn't have known which way to swim even if she could have. It was everything she could do to stay locked in a desperate embrace with Aldashir. They were underwater long enough for her lungs to burn, long enough that Rihya began to wonder if they'd ever surface.

Eventually, though, the water dispersed. The wave subsided as it washed through the field, flooded the valley, carrying people with it as it flowed. Rihya gasped for air, bobbing in the cold water, finally allowing herself to let go of Aldashir. She noticed sore spots and bruises that hadn't been there moments earlier, whether they were from the impact of the water or from crushing her dark prince in such a tight embrace she wasn't sure.

"All right?" Aldashir panted.

"Fine," she spluttered in response, treading water as best she could, thankful she wasn't weighed down by chain mail like that which so many of the human invaders wore into battle. Many of them would likely have drowned in the onslaught of water if they hadn't already fled the field.

When it was finally shallow enough for Rihya to touch ground, she planted her feet beneath her as firmly as possible and felt for her weapons, making sure the knives were in place. Not all were there; some were gone from being cast in battle, others displaced during the momentary flood. But she had a few, enough to fight on.

"What was your brother thinking!" Aldashir exclaimed. "He was as likely to injure his own in such a flood as he was to hurt the enemy!"

"But we're fine, aren't we?" Rihya puzzled. And despite her burning lungs, despite her soreness, somehow it was true. She did feel better than a few minutes earlier. She reached down and felt along her ribs. The wound was almost entirely gone. "My arrow wounds...they are practically healed!"

"That means..." Aldashir began, trying to follow her train of thought.

"Check your body. How are your injuries?" she prodded.

Aldashir complied, a look of astonishment blooming on his face. "How?"

"My brother just flooded the battlefield with Source Water!" Rihya crowed with delight. "I don't know how he did it, but he did. And the Source will revitalize us and those of your kind who are our allies, just like it healed you."

"A master stroke," Aldashir murmured.

"And not just to help heal our people but to harm our foes." Rihya pointed to an Unsired who was clawing at its flesh as if the water he was soaked with was burning him. He flailed against it for a moment longer before succumbing and sinking beneath the waist-deep water that permeated the field.

"Somehow Ell knew it would hurt them—the Unsired." Aldashir grinned. "Good elf, your brother."

"He is that," Rihya responded with a grin of her own.

They were shaken from their excited distraction by an arrow whizzing past Aldashir's cheek. It grazed him, leaving a red smudge of blood.

"Apparently, Ell's ploy wasn't enough to kill every Unsired," Rihya muttered as she looked in the direction from which the arrow had come to see a weakened but determined Unsired holding a bow.

"It evened the battle field, though—tilted it in our favor, even."

Rihya nodded. She looked around, elves and Unsired, humans and dark creatures, everyone was slowly returning to their senses. The enemy was diminished—she could see Unsired wilting and withering under the weight of Source Water, sinking beneath the ripples—but it wasn't gone. There was still a fight to be had. Enemies of all kinds eyed each other as the storm of battle picked up again. Blows were traded as foes waded and fought, chunks of ice and snow drifting lazily around the wintery-wet battlefield.

"Come on, let them taste our steel," Rihya urged Aldashir alongside her as she turned to face an approaching pair of Ghouls who were skittering through the water practically effortlessly, as if the liquid had no bearing on their speed or agility. She gripped the hilts of her soaked weapons, tensing for combat. Regardless of what had just occurred, despite how incredible it had been, it was time to focus again.

She was Valerihya Wintermoon, and there was still a battle to be fought.

———

As soon as the water broke the wall of the dome and raced torrentially down through the city, Ell gave in and let the raging flood carry him with it. He plummeted through streets and buildings, the water urging him onward. Only his fortified strength as a Water Caller allowed him to survive the beating he took from his path downward. He prayed this had been the right decision, hoped against hope that his actions taken to flood the city and the battlefield with Source Water would accomplish his aims.

Ell coursed out through the shattered gates of the city, wooden frames splintered at their seams. He plunged into the swirling chaos of the battlefield just as every other creature and being in the valley had been. When his head finally broke the surface, he gathered a huge gulp of air and gazed around. Even the sturdy Stone and Wood Ogres had been impacted by the water; they bobbed and floated just as powerlessly as everyone else. Only the Icari seemed unaffected. They swooped low, picking off a few of the elves who breached the surface first. Ell swore. Had he just condemned his people to a quick death? But no, the water soon subsided enough to stand, although there was enough of it that it remained waist or thigh deep on most of the field depending on where one stood.

He gazed around. His hopes were not unfounded. Unsired writhed and sank beneath the water, scratching and clawing at their bodies as they tried to rid themselves of the Source Water that clung to them in every nook and cranny. There was no escape. Not all succumbed, but most did. Ell watched with satisfaction as Half-Mask's Unsired army faded before him. Inexplicably, some Unsired remained, and most of the dark creatures resumed their attack, but the odds were now even, or possibly in their favor. Andalaya had a chance!

Ell fought through the water, slashing a Ghoul across the throat with one dueling dagger. His mind was muddled. Why had the Source Water destroyed most of the Unsired but not the dark creatures? Did it have something to do with their origin? Either way, it was a question for Arendahl when this was all over. Ell fought on, hope buoying him as he dispatched creature after creature. He picked up a spear that was floating in the water, braced himself, and then slung it upward to skewer an Icari out of the sky. It crashed to the shallow water with a screech of agony. Ell pushed ever onward, fighting amongst his people as they regained their senses after the flood and engaged the enemy once again. Ell noticed that many of his people were clambering down the walls and the stairs from where they had escaped the wave in a place of relative safety. They looked eager to rejoin the fight.

A few Unsired fought on, but they grew weaker as they tried to sluice their way through the Source Water that was soaking many of them to the hips. Yet the dark creatures fought on unencumbered. Stone Ogres were so strong that stepping through water didn't slow them down at all, and the Wood Ogres seemed more or less able to maneuver through the flooded field without much difficulty.

On cue, he saw a Tree Ogre stepping his way, oaken arms and red eyes looking like fiery vengeance. Ell sheathed one dagger and grabbed an axe that was stuck into the muddy ground beneath the water, its haft protruding into the wintery air. His fingers closed around it, and he wrenched upward and back, cocking his arm to throw even as he freed the weapon from the mud. In one more motion, he cast the weapon forward with all his might, and the great battle-axe flew true. It sailed end over end, covering the distance between Ell and the charging Wood Ogre in a moment. He threw it with such strength that the axe split the Ogre in two, the body folding apart, black blood oozing from its insides like dark sap. Ell grinned in vicious satisfaction. There might still be dark creatures aplenty on this field, but he had enough strength to defeat them.

He thanked Miri silently, hoping that somehow she could hear him, sense his gratitude through the Graft. There was no doubt in his mind that he had been given a boost of energy and power since reaching the battlefield—splitting an Ogre in two with one throw of an axe was proof of that—and the added strength could only be down to the fact that Miri was likely nestled in his consciousness somewhere, buried so deep that her mind and will had melded into his. Ell rolled his shoulders, looking for another beast to destroy. He felt strong right now, confident. Then a thought crossed his mind. Why look for another Ogre? There was a much greater quarry to pursue.

Ell scanned the battlefield, searching for the one he wanted. It was time to face Half-Mask once and for all. It was time to kill the Prince of Darkness.

———

"I AM the Prince of Darkness! I gave you life—I transformed you! And this is how you repay me?" Half-Mask raged at the lifeless body of an Unsired. He gripped the pitiful creature, fists grasping its leather vest so that he could hold it up to his face, all the closer to scream at. But it was dead. Like so many of his minions, it had died when that boy flooded the field with Source Water. Who would have thought he had the nerve to devise such a gambit, let alone the power to release the Source with such force? That had been more than just a reservoir breaking. Half-Mask could tell that the boy had delved deep, had yanked his precious Source up out of the earth with more power and force than ever before.

Half-Mask let go of the dead Unsired and watched it slip back beneath the water to hover still and lifeless just above the muck of the ground. It couldn't hear his scream of fury, yet Half-Mask screamed all the same. His army was practically disintegrating around him. Oh, his dark creatures still lived and fought, but the Unsired were near to gone, destroyed by the water, and what few were left were locked in deadly struggle with the Andalayan forces. Not to mention his father and Silverfist—Half-Mask hadn't seen those two since long before Wintermoon's masterstroke. Half-Mask was the Prince of Darkness. He was vengeful, cunning, and powerful beyond measure. But he was also intelligent enough to realize when he was alone. And he was alone now. His allies were gone, or wilting around him, while the boy thrashed his way through his army.

He looked across the field and saw Wintermoon engage a Stone Ogre and quite literally rip its head from its body with his bare hands. Something had given the boy strength. He had found some way to add to his power. He hadn't been that strong when they'd faced each other in Dark Harbor.

No matter, stronger or not, Half-Mask would finish him off. The battle might have turned from landslide odds in his favor to now being a more evenly balanced affair, but he cared not. He'd kill the boy and prove once and for all who was strongest, who was best. No more playing games with him like an eagle toying with a hare. No, he would put the boy in his place and then rally the southern troops to victory. Without Wintermoon, the north would still fall. Half-Mask's plans still had a chance. He could yet snatch victory from the shambles of what had become of his army.

And so the Prince of Darkness set out wading across the field, the hem of his black cloak floating on the water as he slashed through elves, Unsired, and dark creatures alike in his haste. He moved toward the boy. It was time. *Sometimes, to accomplish something, you have to do it yourself.* All others had failed him on this account. He would show him what a Spectralist could *really* do.

Once and for all, it was time to kill Elliyar Wintermoon.

———

FINALLY, Ell saw him. And it looked like Half-Mask had already seen Ell, because the Spectralist was fighting his way toward him in a straight line with no elf able to stand against him. The Source didn't have any noticeable effect on the Spectralist, at least not like how it had affected the Unsired. Perhaps it was a matter of strength.

It had come to this. Somehow, Ell had always known that it would. He picked up the pace, his ability-enhanced strength and speed allowing him to sprint through the water with more ease than the rest of his companions. Half-Mask sped up as well, and as they drew closer, Ell could see the crazed eagerness on the Spectralist's face. The Prince of Darkness meant to kill him and planned to enjoy it.

They came together in a ferocious concussion—Water Caller meeting Spectralist, each buoyed by their supernatural powers. The noise of their meeting was like a thunderclap, and the battle around them paused for a moment, but only for a moment before it resumed its natural course. The collision of such force sent them both spinning and tumbling past one another into the murky, muddy, bloody waters of the flooded valley. Ell felt the chill water roll over his head as his body submerged, and then he fought his way back to an upright position as quickly as he could. Half-Mask had done the same, although the look of revulsion on the Spectralist's face conveyed just how disgusting he found being submerged in Source Water to be.

"Filthy," he muttered through his permanent sneer. "It would be just so, that I'd have to finish this once and for all amidst this revolting substance. It's positively nauseating!" His lip curled up even farther in disgust, revealing rows of his needle-point teeth.

Ell managed a short bark of laughter. "We agree to differ, I guess. I find it...refreshing." He even cupped a handful of the Source Water to his mouth and took a small sip, regardless of the fact that it was clouded with debris. It probably wasn't the cleanest water, but he couldn't pass up the opportunity to taunt the Spectralist.

"You were so close," Half-Mask said as they stepped carefully near and around one another in a cautious circle, trading a few blows with their blades in a testing exchange. "You could have been one of us, could have ruled with us, just below me, eternally!" The Spectralist was practically frothing at the mouth in his anger.

Ell hefted his two dueling daggers in his hands, felt their familiar buzzing kinship adding just a fraction more speed to his strikes, and answered. "I passed then, and I'll do it again now. I never wanted to be on the path to joining you. You forced that on me—I was just lucky enough to have someone to help free me from the mess you made of my insides." Ell was grateful for Miri's help then and could feel the extra strength of her buried deep within his consciousness, making him doubly grateful to her now. To defeat Half-Mask, he would need every ounce of strength, speed, and power he possessed.

The prince sneered again scornfully. "No vision. No ambition. You could have been great. All you'll be remembered for now is for being the last person of note to fall beneath my blade before the ever-present darkness sets in and the First Days return once more!" the Spectralist finished with a roar of fury and anticipation. He launched himself into a flurry of attack. Apparently, the time for talk was over. It was just as well, for Ell was growing weary of hearing the Spectralist's rants.

Ell raised his dueling daggers and blocked the first few slashes of the Prince of Darkness' silvery blade. Ell was wary as he fought, utilizing extra caution. He remembered what it felt like to taste the Spectralist's steel, to feel it pinning him to the city wall. He wouldn't fail again, not when everything was on the line. His people depended on him. He blocked, retreated, took a nick on his shoulder, blood bright and red beginning to seep out, then he blocked and blocked again. Ell moved ever backward, defending desperately against the litany of furious attacks, Half-Mask's continual onslaught. He would not fail. Ell repeated that mantra in his head as he fought, grinding his teeth into a grimace of effort.

Sounds of the battle around them faded away, and all there was were the two of them locked in an endless conflict, a battle that stretched back months to their first meeting in Dark Harbor and the intervening time between when Ell's poisoned body and mind had struggled to free itself of the Spectralist's spidery control. It was a conflict that stretched back decades to when Half-Mask and his father had first sided with the human invaders, sentencing Andalaya to its current plight. Most of all, this was a conflict between Spectralist and Water Caller, a conflict that went back eons to the beginning of time, to the First Days when dark and light had first entered combat for the spirit and soul of this world and its various peoples. Ell gritted his teeth and fought.

He would not fail. Not this time. He could not. Too much was at stake.

So he fought on, but this time he pushed the attack. Ell dug deep inside for that reserve of energy that Miri had buried within him, tapped it, felt it. He pushed himself and took the attack to Half-Mask. The Prince of Darkness snarled with wrath, as it was now Ell's dancing blades that attacked, his dueling daggers whirling with deadly motion in the bitter air.

They stepped in unison, Ell advancing, Half-Mask retreating, each taking cautious steps, searching the slippery muck for safe footing. The Spectralist lost his balance for a moment and Ell pounced, dealing a startlingly quick strike to the uncovered side of Half-Mask's face—a blow that the Spectralist only barely recovered from in time to avoid. As it was, Ell delivered a shallow cut before Half-Mask could spin away, lifting his hand to feel the black blood welling up in shock.

"I'm better than before. Stronger," Ell said with confidence, projecting more than he truly felt. He had to do anything he could to unbalance the Spectralist not just physically but emotionally.

"So I see," Half-Mask responded, but his voice held none of the fear or self-doubt that Ell had hoped to plant. On the prince's face there was only an added excitement, the thrill of combat, and the potential destruction of a mortal enemy. A mad light lit his eyes, and for a moment Half-Mask looked much like his father had in the few moments Ell had faced him in front of the Black Water Well. "I'll kill you and transform your precious Source," he spat, his words full of glee. "I'll make your Source *my* Source."

"You're lying," Ell muttered through gritted teeth as their blades locked and a contest of strength and will had them face to face, straining, bearing all their might down upon one another. His arms and lungs burned. But he would not fail.

"Am I?" Half-Mask taunted. "I've brought enough barrels of the Black Water Well that I had stashed in Dark Harbor to convert your Source into a *new* Black Water Well, one that will flow from a spring. Instead of just spreading its glory across a small cove it will now infect an entire land with rivers of its glorious might!" The Spectralist's voice was now roused with dark conviction.

Suddenly, it was Ell who felt doubtful. The lack of self-belief crept in and weakened him, both his body and his mind. He spun out of their locked blades, and Half-Mask pressed quickly into another attack, sensing an advantage. The Spectralist fought with precision and power. Each move Ell made was just a hair too slow, as if the Prince of Darkness could see his choices just a moment before he made them. It was impossible, Ell knew that, but he couldn't help how he felt. And right now he felt shaken.

A dark light lit up the Spectralist's eyes as he pressed forward, and the two of them waded and sloshed their duel through the muck of the field, through the water. Something tugged at Ell's mind at that thought, but it wasn't enough to fully take root. A furious assault by Half-Mask distracted him anyway, and it was all he could do to survive the Spectralist's concentrated attack. As it was, for all his agility and speed, Ell still took a nasty wound to his upper thigh, slowing him even further. Half-Mask grinned with eagerness, sensing Ell's weakening state. The Source Water didn't quite reach the wound and therefore offered no advantage, and there wasn't time to dunk himself beneath its surface. He had to focus.

Ell tried to press forward, and for a time he put the Spectralist on the back foot. Yet every time Ell came close to delivering a crippling blow Half-Mask utilized his powers. Like his father, Half-Mask's entire torso and legs would flicker into insubstantiality, a smoky haze of an apparition that was impossible to strike.

Half-Mask cackled. "Don't you see? Do you see yet? It is impossible for you to win. I am too strong. I am all-powerful!" As if to punctuate that sentence, the Spectralist delivered a crushing, overhand blow. Ell crossed his dueling daggers above his head and, as he locked them, it was just barely enough to catch the force of the blow and stave it off, but the impact still sent him to one knee in the murky water, bits of ice as well as the bloated bodies of the dead floating all around him.

On one knee, blades crossed over his head, Ell strained to hold up under the weight of strength and purpose as Half-Mask bore down on him. Submerged as it was, his thigh wound began to heal, but even so his strength wouldn't return quickly enough. He felt himself weakening, felt his arms losing strength. If his strength gave out now, the force of that pressure would send Half-Mask's sword straight down into his neck, opening him wide enough that no amount of Source Water would stem the flow. It couldn't end like this, could it?

———

MIRI, lost somewhere deep within Ell's consciousness, buried deep enough to lend him her strength, fought with every ounce of power she possessed. Yet she feared that her efforts were in vain. Half-Mask was too strong. He was too cunning and clever. Every time she was about to deal a wound to him, he would flicker in and out of existence. He was a ghostly warrior, a shadow serpent waiting to strike.

She fought on until a blow from the Spectralist brought her to her knee. She couldn't die like this, could she? After all this effort it couldn't end like this—in defeat.

Her mind rebelled but her body wouldn't follow. She was so tired, tired from fighting everything from Ogres to Ghouls to Unsired. Tired from unleashing the Source, from tapping her Water Calling abilities for so long that her strength felt almost completely sapped. And yet she fought on.

Miri held her blades above her head, fighting the sword pressure bearing down upon her. But she knew she wasn't there, knew that she had split her consciousness between her two bodies—her real body and the one she inhabited by extension, by way of the Graft. It was strange: usually, when she was this deep within her mate, she had no recollection of her own self, yet somehow this time she did.

"You will not fail, my love. You will not fail." Her real body whispered the words, but she felt them echo across the Graft. She prayed he'd hear them and find strength.

And still she fought on.

———

YOU WILL NOT FAIL.

The determined voice coursed through Ell's mind. He'd never heard her before. It shouldn't be possible—the Graft was a one-way path, a road for Miri to enter and see through his eyes, not for him to hear her. But hear her he did. He knew that was the only explanation.

You will not fail. The voice echoed again through his straining mind, whispering to him of success, charging him with faith and belief. Suddenly, he knew that it was true. He knew that he would not, could not, let it end like this.

Still on his knee in the cold, cold water, Ell gathered his strength. Wait...the water. That feeling played at the back of his mind again, fighting to push forward. Water. What had he done only a short time ago in the reservoir when he broke the dome to free the Source? He'd wielded *water*. And once, not too long ago, he'd run on the waves next to Piripeo's ship after being tossed overboard. He was waist-deep in water, and only now was he realizing what use it could be; he was a Water Caller and could manipulate it. Somehow, instinctively, he knew it was true, that it could turn the tide of this duel in his favor.

Gathering for one last push, Ell burst upward with all his remaining strength and sent Half-Mask stumbling backward. Ell rose to his feet and staggered slightly with the exhaustion and effort. Half-Mask hadn't had to fight and exert himself all day like he had done.

The Spectralist sneered his familiar sneer. "Just give in, boy. I'll finish you quickly."

"Never," Ell said firmly as he balanced himself. He stretched out his consciousness, tapping the water around him, feeling its familiar strength and power infuse him. Yet, this time, he also honed his focus—like when Arendahl had taught him to heal and he'd subsequently done so in his first duel with Half-Mask—and willed the water around him to take shape.

Half-Mask leaped into attack, not willing to give up the advantage he saw in Ell's tired state. As the Spectralist attacked, though, silvery sword whirling like a shining tooth of darkness, Ell wrapped his abilities around the water surrounding him and gave it life, gave it shape. The Prince of Darkness swung his blade downward in a vicious arc, and Ell didn't raise a blade in defense. Half-Mask's face lit with dark glee as he tasted his enemy's demise, but at the last moment Ell stole that joy from his face. At the last second, a shield of water rose up swiftly and strongly, armoring itself to Ell's forearm, allowing Ell to raise it and fend off the deadly strike.

Consternation filled the Spectralists face. "What...?" his voice started in surprise then trailed off as rage clouded his features. "Charlatan's tricks won't save you, boy. I'll still end you, Wintermoon!" Half-Mask shrieked as he attacked again.

Ell raised his arm again and fended off another blow and then another as Half-Mask raged endlessly against the watery shield he brandished. The Spectralist took a step back, panting after his furious assault. Ell glanced around and saw that the battle had paused around them. As if involuntarily, weapons lowered, and eyes stared on with sick fascination as elves and beasts watched a duel the likes of which hadn't been seen since the First Days.

Ell smiled grimly. He would not fail. Especially not with his people watching.

He let the shield splash back into the water at his feet and turned from defense to attack. He sheathed one dueling dagger for just a moment and instead formed a spear out of the water. He lifted and threw it with all his might. Half-Mask flicked into insubstantiality with a startled reaction. Yet this time the Spectralist drew no joy from his evasion. *This* time he looked shaken. The prince's masked face darkened with the doubt Ell had been trying to plant there for their entire duel. Ell formed another spear and threw. Half-Mask again flickered and avoided it. Ell formed another and another, casting watery spear after water spear, and it was all Half-Mask could do to keep from being skewered.

It was Ell's turn to gain the upper hand, and he pressed his advantage on the shaken Spectralist. Vaguely, Ell thought he could hear the cheers of his people as he sought to end Half-Mask once and for all. He leaped forward, drawing his dueling dagger once again, fighting with all of the strength and speed he could muster. But this time he attacked with more. Ell pressed Half-Mask from the front as usual, but now weapons raised out of the water on all sides. They were a clear, bluish color even though the water itself was murky, as if to show that in the midst of war the Source was still pure. Spears harried Half-Mask from all sides as water whips lashed at his face and arms like the sharp tentacles of a deadly sea beast. Half-Mask flickered and flickered, avoiding, ever avoiding. But he slowed. Ell remembered how the king had weakened as a result of too many flickers into insubstantiality when they had fought in the Midnight Cove, and apparently his son was no different.

A small cut here as he couldn't quite avoid a blow, a flick of black blood raising on his good cheek from the tip of a watery lash. Half-Mask fought on like a cornered wild animal, frantic and desperate with a frozen snarl plastered onto his face. The longer they fought the calmer

Ell became. He was exhausted. His body was close to giving out—manipulating the water surrounding their duel into weapons was sapping his energy at a furious rate. All the same, he was winning and he knew it.

I will not fail.

He pushed forward with one last onslaught, hoping to finally end the Spectralist, to kill the Prince of Darkness once and for all. He stepped up, and his blades flashed in the stormy sky, steel on steel, as they clashed with Half-Mask's sword. Ell pressed and harried the Spectralist with a watery spear at his back. This time, the prince lacked the requisite energy to flicker. Half-Mask tried—he went smoky for a second—but not for long enough, as his body rebelled against his powers out of pure exhaustion, turning him back to normal. The watery spear skewered him through the fleshy side of his abdomen, cutting through him from front to back.

It wasn't a mortal wound, but it was clearly painful, as it was enough to make the Spectralist scream. Ell pounced. He pushed onward, striking with his daggers. Half-Mask tried to parry his attack but, in his weakened state, Ell swept his sword out of the way with a clever maneuver and just like that the Spectralist was exposed. For a split second, their eyes met, and Ell could tell that Half-Mask knew—could tell the Spectralist knew he'd lost, that his time was over, that he was about to die. Rage, fear, desperation, and pain among other emotions flickered over the prince's enraged face as Ell swept the sword away.

Ell then thrust upward with both of his dueling daggers, feeling their buzzing energy carrying them forward with a vengeful fury. His weapons entered Half-Mask's throat just below the jaw and traveled upward with all the strength he possessed. The blades sliced in and up through the Spectralist's skull, the tips of them protruding through the top of Half-Mask's skull. Then Ell wrenched them back down and out as black blood gushed all over his hands and arms. Half-Mask hung, skewered on the spear, until Ell let the manipulation go and the watery weapon splashed to nothingness. The Spectralist sank into the flooded field.

A frenzied moan echoed from the remaining few Unsired and their creature companions, but it was quickly suppressed by the roaring, wild cheers of his people alongside their southern and human allies.

Ell took a moment to let it all sink in. It was over. It was done. Sweet relief passed through him. He hadn't failed. It had been done by his hand: by his might, the battle was won. Ell had done it.

The Prince of Darkness was dead.

CHAPTER THIRTY-FOUR

The battle lasted a short while longer, but the bite had gone out of the enemy forces. With no Spectralists left to guide them and their immediate masters—the Unsired—all but completely dead, the dark creatures lost all cohesion. Ghouls continued to fight elves, but they also turned on each other. Icari swooped down to harry Ogres as often as elves and humans, and the tail end of the battle turned into a melee free-for-all where dark creatures died in droves. It didn't take long for them to scatter as the invading human army had done earlier. A few companies of the Highest pursued half-heartedly, but most simply sloshed wearily back to the walls of Verdantihya toward healing outposts at different increments along its face. Luckily, the whole valley was still soaked with Source Water, and although it aided the wounded even now the water was gradually dispersing. It was only shin-deep in most parts now and barely over ankle-deep in others.

Dead and dying scattered the battlefield. No longer floating, the dead lay lodged in the muck, heaped upon one another, having lain where they had fallen. It was a grisly sight. The only note of interest was that the thousands of Unsired who had died as a result of the immersion to the Source were now changed. They were still dead, but their diseased appearance was gone, returning them to the Departed they had once been. Ell watched as a sickly Unsired changed to a Departed right before his eyes, and he was transported back to a dead Unsired he'd touched a year ago in a raid to the east, how it had changed under his own hand. It had been the first inclination of the powers he possessed. He'd burned the body then, thinking it plagued. How little he'd known. How little he still knew or understood.

Ell sighed wearily as the last Ogre faded into the woods to the west of the battlefield, a few Ghouls hot on its trail, snapping at each other as they followed, hoping for an easy meal. They'd reverted to their old ways now that their masters were dead.

"That was quite a performance," Arendahl grunted, coming up behind him as Ell gazed after the departing Wood Ogre.

"No show, Elder, just doing my duty to our people," Ell answered, not bothering to cover his exhaustion. Manipulating water and breaking the dome had tired him much more than tapping into his abilities usually did.

Arendahl nodded soberly, a hint of pride in his eyes as he looked at Ell. "Interesting, isn't it?" The old elf jutted his chin toward a once-Unsired and now Departed elf. The dead elf gazed sightlessly at them, but at least there was a measure of peace to its countenance. "Seems like they were affected while the dark creatures were not, maybe because they were elves first, transformed from one thing to another—something the Source ended and then reversed—while the dark creatures were just acting true to their vile natures. I suppose even such an inundation of the Source couldn't undo the dark creatures' origins."

"It's like in death, they have been absolved," Ell murmured without thinking while staring at the corpse.

"Heh, intriguing line of thought. Never really thought of Creation as quite capable of forgiveness, exactly, but I suppose it's a fitting enough idea. We'll never really know."

"I suppose not," Ell said. He was just glad it had happened. Most of those Unsired had been transformed against their will. Not that they'd all been good, necessarily—plenty of the Departed had been thoroughly evil, his people being hounded for decades was proof of that. Still, to be formed into something against your will was a horrible thing. He knew that from personal experience. At least in death they were themselves again: their true selves. He even found himself wishing them peace in the next Reality. It was easier to forgive them in death.

"Boy." Arendahl's voice startled him out of his deep thoughts.

"What?"

A pained look on the old elf's face said it all. "We don't have much time. We might be too late as it is. No more time for deep thoughts or possibilities."

"Who? Ell asked as his heart dropped. He knew of battle and war. He knew that tone. He turned to follow Arendahl back toward the wall and, presumably, to a healing center.

Arendahl shot him a sad, sidelong glance but did not answer. "Come on."

"Who is it?" Ell pressed, fear clutching his belly at the thought of something having happened to Miri. Would he have felt it if it had? No, the Graft didn't work that way. But he'd been strong, stronger than usual at the end, suggesting she'd still been fine and Grafted deeply into his consciousness when he'd fought Half-Mask not long ago.

They reached the wall, and Ell took the steps to the top two at a time, reaching the landing ahead of his old mentor in his worried eagerness. A group of his family lay clustered around the body of his father. Adan's eyes were closed, and Ell's heart lurched at the sight. A terrible, selfish part of him was relieved to see Miri standing nearby, tears streaking her face as she looked on at the scene of mourning.

"He killed Silverfist, you know," Arendahl said in Ell's ear. They hadn't taken a step beyond the head of the stairs. Ell had frozen at the sight of his father. "He's also the reason I managed to kill the King of the South. The old bastard had me at a disadvantage before Adan stepped in, the gallant fool. But a necessary fool all the same. I'd have fallen, and who knows what turn the eastern front might have taken with me gone and a Spectralist still in command."

"So he saved us, in a way," Ell whispered.

"Go to him." Arendahl placed a hand in the center of Ell's back and nudged him forward.

"Is he...?" Ell couldn't bring himself to finish the sentence.

"Almost. He's barely hanging on at this point," Arendahl told him, again urging him forward with a push. Ell followed his direction this time.

He pushed his way through his family members to kneel at his father's side. Lliaria sat cradling Adan's head in her lap, and Delle and Rihya crouched nearby.

"Go on, son, we've already said our goodbyes," Lliaria said. "He's been holding on for one more."

Adan's eyes opened weakly, fluttering like the wings of a tired butterfly. "Elliyar..." he mumbled, barely intelligible.

"Yes, father, I'm here." Ell grasped his father's hand tightly, fearing to let go lest he drift away by the simple act of breaking physical contact.

"I'm proud of you," Adan whispered, a smile on his face as he gazed in a dreamy half-stupor at his son. His clouded eyes drifted lazily around the crowd. "I'm proud of all of you," Adan said, and his gaze locked with Dacunda's. "I'll look after Dahranian for you, like you tended to mine."

Ell's heart clenched again. He glanced and saw another body laid out near the crenelated wall, a shroud draped over the already dead elf. Dacunda's eyes moistened, but he forced a strong smile for his older brother. "I'd expect nothing less of Adan Wintermoon, Defender of the Walls of Verdantihya, Slayer of Silverfist." He spoke the titles, and they echoed hollowly in Ell's ears. What did titles matter in the afterlife? Adan smiled at his brother.

Ell pressed his forehead against his father's, and everyone faded away but the two of them. "I am going to miss you, Father. I've missed you most of my life, but that was just an idea of you. You're better than I could have imagined, and now I am going to miss you all the more." Tears leaked out the corner of Ell's eyes, and he made no move to wipe them away.

Adan reached up and cupped the back of Ell's head. The motion looked like it cost him the last of his energy, his face paling noticeably as he moved. Amidst the joyful cheers of victory, Ell heard the sorrowful keening of elves crying and mourning for their dead. The noise permeated all the valley, all the city.

"Son, you gave me back my life. For that I will always be grateful. You gave me another chance to fight for and defend those and that which I love. You gave me back my life, and a chance to see you, my son, and all that you have become is the greatest gift I could ask for." He paused then summoned energy for one last sentence: "Look after each other. I love you." Adan's hand fell weakly back to the stone of the parapet as his strength finally failed.

Ell looked into his father's eyes and, as the light faded, he didn't see fear. He saw a warrior's courage, and a faithful spirit's belief in a battle well fought and a life well lived. The group knelt around him and, as his last breaths exhaled, Ell saw a peace in his father's countenance that he'd never quite seen in life.

Lliaria let out a mournful wail to join her voice with the many others of their people doing the same on the wall and the valley all around. Victory hadn't come without a cost. Ell wept silently as he looked around. He was glad when, as he stood, Miri pressed herself quickly into his arms, buried her face in his chest, and held him tightly. He held her just as close, and they cried together. Shock hadn't subsided. His father was dead. He looked at the shrouded body next to Adan's. His cousin was dead—Dahranian was gone. After he'd practically saved them all, after he'd lead so many tortured souls to freedom, it had all ended for him with such unfair finality.

Ell glanced over and saw Rihya and Aldashir sharing the same such embrace as his and Miri's. Dacunda was bent over his son, Ryder at his side and Iyonei crouched down behind him, a hand on his shoulder, comforting him as he cried. Brie had somehow managed to find herself in Arendahl's gnarled old arms. Ell didn't think he'd seen the old elf ever hug anyone. Brie broke from the embrace and went to sit, crying, beside Ryder. Arendahl's cheeks were wet, and Ell watched his mentor weep. Ell felt the crush of another body wrapping arms around him and Miri, and he saw that Delle had joined them.

In all the many hours, days, and months that Ell had spent thinking of this day, the day when the threat to the south was gone, his people were reunited together, and the human invaders were on the run, he'd never once imagined it would feel so terrible.

Ell forced himself to try and reach for hope. Dahranian and Adan were dead. They were gone. But their deaths had accomplished something. Without them, Ell might never have even had the chance to face Half-Mask and finish him off. The entire scope of the battle would have been different—and hence their people's future would have been different. He swallowed. They were heroes. There was no question there. Ell wasn't much of a bard himself, but he would do everything in his power to make sure their memories were immortalized, that no one would ever forget what they had accomplished, that nobody would forget their sacrifice.

And yet as he held his love, crying into her straw-blonde hair, he felt hollow. He should feel proud and relieved at what they had accomplished, at the freedom they had earned. But he didn't. The price was high enough that all he felt was grief. Ell had a feeling that every day for quite some time he would have to fight to feel anything else.

For now, there was still much to do. In the short term, the last barrels of the dark source from the Midnight cove would need to be destroyed, the bodies of the dead would need to be cleared from the field and prepared for burial, and the enemies' bodies burned. Long term, Ell couldn't wait to see the walls of Verdantihya rebuilt once more, to stand proudly for all to see.

However, right now, he just let himself breathe, let himself feel the grief and mourn the dead a little while longer. Everything else could wait.

CHAPTER THIRTY-FIVE

Miri tucked a flower into the braid that wound behind her head to meet with the one from the other side. Flowers adorned them like a woodland crown made of her own hair and petals. The scent was pleasant and that didn't hurt, either. She bent over and picked another from the grass. Somehow, they had managed to bloom in the winter. Miri was almost certain their growth had something to do with the flood of Source Water that had inundated the valley. She glanced over at Ell, still slightly in awe of him. She'd seen others casting careful glances his way when he wasn't looking, just as she was now. Even Arendahl appraised him when he thought his one-time pupil wasn't watching. Miri had never seen anything like the rush of water that had burst the gates wide open and turned the tide of the battle in their favor. She caught people whispering about him the moment they thought he couldn't hear them.

"I wish you wouldn't do that," Ell said.

"Do what, love?"

"You know what—stare at me."

Miri sighed. "I try not to, but it's hard sometimes. You're kind of incredible."

"It's just that everyone is looking at me, all the time. People are always asking me what to do, and it makes me uncomfortable. I couldn't bare it if you did that, too."

"Oh don't worry, I won't ask your advice on anything," she teased.

Her remark amazingly managed to elicit a small smile from her mate, the first she'd seen in two days.

Lliaria approached the two of them. "It was a nice celebration, wasn't it?"

Ell let go of Miri's hand to embrace his mother. "It was. I'm just sorry we had to have it."

Lliaria pulled her face back to look at her son. "Don't be sorry. None of this is your fault. You gave us back our lives—gave us what could only be described as stolen months together. Those months were something none of us ever thought we would have."

Ell nodded sadly. "I know, it's just..." he trailed off.

"I know, son. But your father wouldn't want your misery. He'd want you to celebrate him, to remember him with joy in the way we just did. You gave him the chance to fight for his people, to fight for freedom one last time. That's all he could have ever asked for."

Miri smiled as she listened to Ell and his mother. Lliaria was quickly growing to become one of her favorite people in the whole world—the mother she'd never known. Lliaria was wise and strong and loyal. Miri glanced back to the mounds of earth beneath the abnormally large oak tree, its spreading limbs blanketing the sky in a way that most trees could only hope to accomplish. Oaks were rare this far north, near Verdantihya, let alone ones that large. The two burials beneath it were marked. The celebration of Dahranian and Adan's passing had just finished. Dancing, songs, stories, memories, all had been shared as one by those who had loved them.

Dacunda approached as Lliaria and Ell broke their embrace. "Nephew," he said somberly.

"Uncle," Ell responded, equally stoic. The two of them could best granite in a contest of stoniness when they wished, but it was their way. Often the two of them fought harder than most to conceal their emotions. Although, lately, she'd seen their façades crack somewhat. Grief could do that to a person.

Dacunda cleared his throat and, to Miri's surprise, said something emotional which was the exact opposite of what she had just been expecting. "Dahranian is gone. Adan is gone. You've lost a father and I a son. But then, I've always rather thought of you as more of a son anyway."

"And I you as a father," Ell responded gruffly, doing his best to wipe the moisture from his eyes.

Dacunda nodded brusquely. "We'll never replace them, but at least we'll still have each other to do our best to fill that void."

"To help remember them and what they fought and died for," Ell finished. He smiled wanly and pulled his uncle into a rough hug. Miri's heart ached for Ell, to have found his father after so long only to have him taken away. But for all Ell and Dacunda's ups and downs this past year, what they meant to one another could not be summed up in mere words. What could they call someone who was blood, family, friend, companion, leader, and war comrade all rolled into one?

They broke the embrace, and Dacunda smiled before walking over to speak softly with Iyonei who was spending as much or more time alone with Dacunda these days as she was with Satiri, Yendil, and the other survivors from her original party. Ell turned back to Miri and they strolled away from the rest. She knew when her mate wanted some solitude. They spent the afternoon alone in the woods, a forest that had been reinvigorated by the recent inundation of Source Water. This little pocket of Andalaya was like spring in the midst of winter, all blossoms and sprigs surrounded by barren branches. By the time they returned to their camp outside the city walls near the burial sites, crackling fires were already cooking meat. They spent the evening sharing more stories about the fallen, hopes for the future, and crying and smiling and laughing in equal measure. The night fell, and Ell crawled into his blankets, holding Miri close for warmth.

That embrace was full of enough love to salve over at least some of their wounds, and Miri knew that it would continue to do so for as many years as they had left.

EPILOGUE

The day before, all Ell could think of was a desire to be free of responsibility, at least for a while. He had dreamed of himself and Miri escaping the world, of just packing up and leaving, of finding some peace and respite. However, when Ell awakened, he realized that while they might be able to leave soon, that time was not quite yet. There were things to be done before they could do so. Someone—likely he and Arendahl with their heads together—had to figure out a way to dispose of the extra barrels of the opposite source that Half-Mask had carried with his army. Over the next weeks, Ell and the old elf set their minds endlessly to the task while Iyonei and Dacunda led joint bands of elves and ex-slave humans to harry the retreating human forces east and then north. Before too long, the humans were holed up in their final stronghold near the Great Bridge: the fortress known as Hope's End. It wouldn't be easy dislodging them from that last foothold on the continent, but that was a battle for another day.

Aldashir's Departed forces—or, Ell wasn't entirely sure he could even call them that any longer seeing as they'd allied themselves to the north and because many of them could actually experience the benefits of Source Water—joined with many of the Highest to help track the various dark creatures to the corners of the land. They couldn't kill every single one, but it would be a long time before they could do any lasting harm to Andalaya again. Oh, elves and men would still have to watch their backs on occasion during the night, but what land was completely free of dangers?

When Ell and Arendahl reached an impasse regarding how to dispose of the darker source, the old elf finally made a proposition that Ell felt somewhat sheepish for not thinking of sooner. And so Miri was asked to help, to push her consciousness into his and amplify his strength, and they repeated a similar process to the one they'd used in the Midnight Cove to destroy the Black Water Well, seeing comparable effects to these last left over barrels.

"What is it, boy?"

"I just can't believe we didn't think of it before now," Ell muttered, slightly embarrassed.

"You don't see me looking ashamed, do you? I've been working on this, same as you, and the answer didn't come to me until today. Battle— war in general—saps an elf's energy, makes them focus their thoughts on one thing to the exclusion of many others. We just had to remember to really *think* again."

Ell nodded. "It's not just that, though. I've been distracted." His pause pause was laden with pain, not wanting to speak of Dahranian's loss, and especially not his father. "I think it's clouded my thinking."

"I miss them too, you know. It'll hurt for a while. And then it'll hurt some more. I remember that from when my Kelssari died. But eventually it hurts a tiny bit less." Arendahl leaned nonchalantly against the trunk of a tree as he finished speaking.

"You knew him so much better than I did. I guess that's one of the things that saddens me the most—all the years I missed and will miss with him," Ell said, a strained look on his face.

Arendahl paused thoughtfully. "I could tell you some stories if you like." The old elf raised his eyebrow at the proposition.

Ell smiled a real smile, at long last. "I'd like that. But not now. Maybe in a while."

Arendahl's eyes narrowed. "What do you mean, 'in a while'?"

Ell shrugged. "I think I need a break. I want to spend some time— just me and Miri. I'm tired, Arendahl. Tired of fighting, of leading. I just need some rest."

His friend's wizened face softened. "That you do. But don't be gone too long."

Ell nodded gratefully. "Thank you for everything."

Arendahl's eyes narrowed. "Take a little while, but boy, you had better get yourself back here soon. There are still battles to be fought and things to be done. The dark creatures are broken and scattered, but there are still a few of them left. The humans are bloodied but not fully broken. We'll need more than just one ancient and decrepit Water Caller at the forefront of our people."

Ell somehow managed a laugh. "Decrepit? Please, Arendahl, now I know you're stretching. Bands of our people are already out harrying them. And the humans Dahranian led from Etheros are mixing well with our people. They've already given insights that will help us in the future. Besides, Aldashir has aligned us with what's left of the Departed, effectively nullifying the threat to the south. No, I think you can handle things without me well enough for me and Miri to take a quick break." As he spoke, Ell grabbed Miri's hand and tugged her away, toward the grove of trees at the edge of camp. "I want some time alone with my mate. We've been Joined half a year now, and we've spent as much time apart as together."

"Sacrifices of war, boy," Arendahl grunted.

"But we aren't at war anymore, are we, Arendahl?" Miri chimed in sweetly, making Ell grin again.

The old elf grimaced. "Just don't be gone too long is all I am saying."

"We'll be gone as long as we please," Miri said and stepped up on her tiptoes to kiss the old elf's cheek.

"I won't forget our people, Arendahl. I promise," Ell said solemnly. The only thing ruining his delivery was the almost giddy smile that threatened to bubble up at the prospect of seeing the land and traveling just for enjoyment's sake.

Arendahl grumbled something unintelligible to himself, and Ell thought he heard the words 'ungrateful' and 'hardheaded' among them, but he wasn't sure. Even for Arendahl, his words sounded half-hearted, like he didn't believe them himself. The glow of pride in his eyes as he looked at them proved it. Ell grinned. With so much sorrow even after victory, it felt good to smile and laugh. Maybe some time alone would be just what they needed to remind themselves of that.

Ell smiled and tugged Miri into the forest for a day of peace. They only returned at nightfall to find their blankets and get some sleep.

———

WHEN MORNING CAME, the crisp, winter air awakened Ell, and somehow, he knew that now was the time. Today was the day. Miri stirred, and he whispered his plan in her ear. She giggled as his breath and hair tickled her neck as he lay curled behind her, and she nodded her agreement. They rose and began packing their things. They didn't need much, just enough to see them through a few days. Ell and Miri could hunt and gather what food they needed for the rest of their time away. Hand in hand, they said their goodbyes, some full of smiles like with Lliaria and Delle, others gruff as with Dacunda, Iyonei, and Arendahl, and still others joking as with Brie and Ryder.

When it came time to bid farewell to Rihya and Aldashir, the two of them walked a ways with Ell and Miri. When it finally came time to part, Ell let go of Miri's hand and hugged his sister close. Her warmth was reassuring. She was full of more life than just about anyone he'd ever met.

"You're sure about this?" Rihya asked.

He nodded. "It's just for a little while. There's nothing happening here that you all can't handle for now. We'll be back soon enough—before you've even had time to miss me, probably," he joked.

Rihya raised an eyebrow as she glanced between Miri and Ell, making him blush. "Just the two of you, all alone next to a campfire each night. No, brother, I don't expect you'll be back as soon as you think," she laughed as she finished and pulled him into one more hug. Ell could hear Miri giggling and as he pulled out of his sister's arms. Miri wormed her way in and the two of them embraced, as if they'd been sisters since the day they were born.

They whispered something in each other's ears, and as Ell clasped forearms with Aldashir, the dark prince said, "What do you think they're talking about?"

Ell laughed ruefully. "I learned a while ago to stop asking."

Aldashir laughed, as well, and then let go of Ell's forearm. "Take care of yourselves."

"We will. You look after my sister. She isn't half as tough as she acts. Well, actually, she's probably tougher," Ell amended truthfully, "but that doesn't mean she still doesn't deserve to have someone watch her back. Most of our lives that's been me. Now I guess it'll be you."

Aldashir nodded seriously. "We've been talking of heading south again. My people will need someone strong to lead them. She'll be by my side from this day forward. It will be the greatest honor of my life."

"You know, I like you a whole lot more than I expected to," he said with a grin.

"Really?" Aldashir replied, cracking a smile. "I like you a whole lot less. You aren't nearly the elf your sister said you were." He winked, and they both laughed.

"What?" Rihya asked.

"Yes, what's so funny?" Miri echoed.

Ell and Aldashir looked at one another before chuckling again. "Nothing," they said in unison.

Rihya rolled her eyes and pulled Ell into a third and final embrace. "Be careful, Elliyar Wintermoon. If you go and get yourself killed after all that we've been through, I will never forgive you," she said fiercely.

"I love you to, Valerihya Wintermoon. See you soon, sister." And with that, Ell grasped Miri's hand and they turned and walked away, heading south into the forest.

They walked only a short way before stopping again. Miri turned to look at him. "So, it's just the two of us now. Where do you want to go?"

"I don't know. I've never been on a journey before that didn't have a purpose," Ell answered thoughtfully.

"We could go back to Akan Deraiya. It was beautiful there when the sun rose and sparkled off the walls," she volunteered.

"Or we could go west. Piripeos said I'm always welcome in the Outer Rim. I doubt he'll stick around the north very long before heading back to the western ocean to find a new ship and crew. We could go see where the world ends and beyond, places nobody's ever been before," Ell said, excitement beginning to infect him. Maybe everyone was right; maybe he wouldn't be back as soon as he'd thought.

"I like how that sounds," Miri said brightly, pulling his head down for a kiss. "To the great western ocean and whatever lies beyond."

Ell's mind was skittering from place to place now, a happy diversion from so many of his grim thoughts over these past few days. "Or, I know —we could head south to Riora. It was the greatest site of learning in all the ancient land. Stories say its libraries are still partially intact. That would be spectacular to see!"

"So south and then west," Miri agreed eagerly, her hand gripping his tightly with excitement. "Ready?" she asked.

Ell set his feet to start walking south and answered more decisively than he'd felt in quite some time, "I'm ready."

The End

THANK YOU FOR READING

Did you enjoy this book?

We invite you to leave a review at the website of your choice, such as Goodreads, Amazon, Barnes & Noble, etc.

DID YOU KNOW THAT LEAVING A REVIEW...

- Helps other readers find books they may enjoy.
- Gives you a chance to let your voice be heard.
- Gives authors recognition for their hard work.
- Doesn't have to be long. A sentence or two about why you liked the book will do.

Don't miss out on your next favorite book!

Join the Melange Books mailing list at
www.melange-books.com/mail.html

Subscriber Perks Include:

- First peeks at upcoming releases.
- Exclusive giveaways.
- News of book sales and freebies right in your inbox.
- And more!

The Collector
by Mathias G. B. Colwell

Book 1 of The Collector series

The world was nearly consumed by chaos and madness during The Great Transformation, a time when myth and legend were given form overnight. Nearly half a century later, The Collectors Guild, a sect of humans tasked to search and control the supernatural, are still trying to clean up the mess that was made of society. Vampires, werewolves and so much more come to life in this darkly gripping tale of love, friendship, betrayal, and most of all freedom.

Philip is someone who is known as a Collector. He travels around the world pursuing evil/dangerous creatures or beings and capturing or killing them to protect society.

He is in New York when his ship full of captured creatures is attacked and the whole cargo hold full of them are set loose. He is forced to try and piece together the mystery of who killed his partner and attacked his ship, and what the villain's motives are.

Philip discovers that there is something more sinister than usual afoot as he realizes a dark magic is being used to leech the different creatures strength and supernatural powers away. Philip is on the task of fixing this situation when the villain kidnaps Philip's love, Alayna. Philip must go try and fix the problem and save the love of his life all at the same time.

READ ON FOR A PREVIEW OF THE FIRST CHAPTER

THE COLLECTOR

CHAPTER ONE

A knife thudded into the wooden doorframe near his head just as Philip started to peer around the corner. Coattails swirled behind the knife thrower as he ducked into the next room. Watching the weapon quiver from impact so close to his head, he told himself he'd be more careful next time. If that was ever possible! Ripping the blade out of the wood, he hefted it in the palm of his hand before following the youth inside, ducking instinctively at the low ceiling. This dingy apartment was not unlike the usual places where he pursued riffraff. He'd seen places like it hundreds of times.

As he moved inside he traded the foul night air, smelling of refuse and chamber pots emptied from second story windows, for a somewhat different, but no less abhorrent, scent of spoiled food and stale sweat. Philip paced quickly across what was a barren living room and followed the lad through the next doorway.

The skinny youth stood at the other end of a hallway. The lad called out with an odd grin and dangerous glint in his eye, "I'd stop right there if I was you, that first knife was just a warning. The next one I throw will be far more deadly." He wore a mismatched set of clothing with a mess of necklaces and bracelets of all varieties. His faded red tunic, although it had once been bright, now bore the marks of greasy fingerprints. The tight fitting velvet coat appeared a decade or two out of style, flaring out slightly over narrow black trousers. A hooknose and thin features were sheltered, under a shock of unkempt brown hair. All in all, a typical gypsy lad, come to America from the Isles. Only he must be so much more since Philip had orders to bring him in.

Philip raised his hands in a peaceful gesture and didn't make a move down the hall towards his prey. "I just want to talk." The lie rang as false on his lips as it sounded in his head.

The young man threw back his head fearlessly and laughed in derision, then spoke in what sounded like an Irish brogue. "You Collectors never want to just talk. Your definition o' talk always comes with a heavy price and we both know that's the truth." It was true. As much as Philip wished it were not, talking to his quarries just never seemed to accomplish anything. Besides, by the time he was pursuing them, they'd almost always crossed a line too far past the restrictions of society to make talking even an option.

"Surrender quietly and it'll go much easier on you." Philip patted the small cord of rope coiled on his belt as he abandoned the ruse of wanting to talk to the lad. "There are no windows in this piece of dirt apartment and there's no back door. You're trapped." He tried to make his voice sound more reasonable, less harsh.

His foe laughed again. "You think that rope can hold me?"

"It will if I feed you some Nightsleep." Philip patted a small jar of the sleep-inducing substance he kept holstered on his other hip. For the first time Philip saw a flicker of fear dance across the lad's eyes. But quick as it had been there it was gone, with only a smirking face left in its wake. The kid was brave and confident. It would be wise to go carefully at this one since his abilities were somewhat of an unknown.

The youth began advancing slowly down the hall towards Philip. "We both know I'm not coming in peacefully, so let's drop the charade." All trace of friendliness had vanished from his face and only a focused expression remained. Without warning, he rushed along the narrow corridor toward Philip in a clatter of bracelets, necklaces, and earrings. The lad was fast! Philip tucked the extra knife he'd just acquired behind his belt and made ready for a take-down.

The youth dodged one way then the other, quick as lightning, and tried to squirm his way between Philip's right side and the wall. Philip jerked his right arm up in a clothesline action and knocked the lad clean off his feet with one blow. He took a step back as the gypsy-boy popped back up, wiping blood from the corner of his mouth and looking at Philip with a newfound respect.

A fight appeared inevitable and Philip cracked his knuckles in his best menacing fashion. Unphased, the youth rushed him again, this time whipping out a new knife from somewhere on his body, and slashed left and right with swift, sure movements.

Philip leaned from side to side, trying to avoid the blade, and then swung his fist. When his opponent ducked, Philip's hand went through the wall to his left leaving splinters on the floor as he ripped it back out. Gasping, Philip realized his chest and shoulder were bleeding from a few shallow nicks. He could see the blood dripping from the knife as his opponent danced out of the way of Philip's fists.

The fellow's eyes were bright with battle, and Philip knew his type, the kind that got a feverish excitement from the heat of conflict. Philip wasn't immune to this sensation himself; he'd been in enough fights to feel the rush of blood to the head. Not an altogether unpleasant sensation.

But he had no more time to think as the fight blurred thick and fast. The youth pulled a third knife, which had been hidden in some part of his apparel, and forced Philip to yank out his own knife to deprive his opponent of an advantage. He preferred fighting with his fists whenever possible but that wasn't always a good idea. Some situations called for different tactics.

Blade clashed on blade as the boy danced in close and slashed again, leaving a slightly deeper gash on Philip's left thigh and sending a thin flow of blood onto his brown, form-fitting trousers. But for all his dazzling speed, the lad had underestimated Philip's strength. The Collector finally landed a massive blow to the lad's chest and sent him sliding back ten feet along the dusty wood floor as he fell.

In this pause, like the eye of the storm, he watched warily as the gypsy picked himself up yet again, appearing only a bit dazed from the impact of Philip's fist, yet nonetheless not too worse for wear after receiving such a blow. He grinned again, with a look that implied some hidden knowledge, as if he had just been toying with his opponent.

"You're stronger than ya' look, Collector." He whistled a catchy little tune, waiting for Philip to close the distance between them, "but I'm faster than you are strong."

Then, with an unfathomable burst of speed, he feinted one way before wriggling under Philip's attempt to collar him and racing down the hallway into the living room and out into the dark night beyond.

Calling out a parting taunt, "Best o'luck next time!" he disappeared, leaving only the jangle of his trinkets. Philip followed out of the apartment, more out of principle than any real hope of catching his quarry. He saw no one, only the dark street. Where was Philip's partner with the wagon when he needed him? These wounds, although none grave, required tending. He considered searching again for the lad but reasoned it would most likely just be fruitless wandering. Instead, Philip made his way back to the port where he could take care of his wounds on their ship and catch a wink of sleep on one of the hammocks before the morning came, instead of being left to fulfill his duties without a night's sleep.

The streets of New York City passed uneventful as he strode purposefully towards the wharf. At times his boots thudded on cobblestones, but other streets were hardly more than mud in this winter weather and left his calf-high black boots caked and brown. His trousers and even his pale linen shirt tucked loosely into his trousers became speckled with dirt.

He'd opted to leave his coat behind at the start of the night, preferring freedom and mobility in a fight, to the added restriction a coat would offer. He had begun to regret that decision by the time he reached his ship. The wind whipped forcefully around some corners and not at others as if nature herself couldn't decide upon her mood.

Upon reaching his destination, Philip went aboard silently, as was habit for a Collector. Once on deck, he made his way to the ship's small medical closet and gathered the materials needed to stitch up the shallow knife wounds he bore from the fight. He sewed himself up as deftly as possible for a man whose only experience with a needle and thread was in situations such as this. When he finished, the cuts had closed and would stay that way as he wound bandages around the stitches.

It was time for some rest. Thankful to have left the windy city streets behind, he strode across the deck. The wind seemed to die down enough that by the time Philip made his way into the hammock, the creaking of his ship and those around him provided only the normal amount of noise created by sailing vessels rocking gently on a night tide.

Philip fell asleep almost immediately. Yet it felt like he awakened quickly when morning's dull grey light fluttered across his eyelids. He opened his eyes, and thought of closing them again only for the briefest of moments before the rumbling of his stomach won out over the gritty feeling under his eyelids.

Philip rolled out of the hammock, for once grateful that he didn't have to pull on his clothes and boots since he hadn't disrobed at all when he went to bed. He stomped down to the galley to grab a bite for breakfast. As he entered, the ship's cook greeted him with a scowl, pointing out that all they had for breakfast was porridge and milk. "If I had more money, I could buy us some fresh provisions instead of having to live off these army rations you force me to use," the cook complained in a tired voice. It appeared someone else might not have had a full night's sleep either.

The man always griped about the lack of resources. However, food didn't matter much to Philip. He was a plain man, with plain tastes. If the offering filled his belly, it was good enough for him, and he wasn't about to spend extravagantly on unnecessary supplies when more necessary items cost so dear. Holding some of his prey often required a variety of concoctions and the herbs needed for those substances were not always common. Many apothecaries and herb women around the country would charge a man an arm and a leg to procure them.

Philip finished his meal quickly and in silence, and then decided to inspect his cargo holds. Their departure had been scheduled for today, if all went according to plan, and he wanted to make certain that everything was in order.

The ship's timbers creaked eerily as the vessel swayed on the morning tide. The Salt-Spray was a solid ship, built to withstand the transatlantic passage, as she'd done so many times in the ten years Phillip had owned her. The upper cargo area was packed with merchandise to be sold as a front for his occupation in London, Liverpool, or wherever he desired. He descended all the way down the last ladder. Here in the deepest hold in the belly of the ship, he carried an altogether different cargo than your typical merchandise.

A voice, cracked and thin with age, cackled hysterically in the cage to his left, setting off a chorus of grunts and whistles from the wooden box to his right. He turned to the person in the cage and shook his head warningly.

"It will go better for you if you stay silent," he cautioned sternly. The face that before had mirrored madness now contorted into a malevolent mask of rage. It was a different kind of madness he supposed, and he couldn't blame the thing's emotions. *Person*, he reminded himself. She was a person. Twenty-five years officially in the guild, and a childhood spent learning its every rule and protocol, yet Philip promised himself that he wouldn't forget that his quarries were still human. Well, some of them at least. He would never let himself become so indoctrinated into the system that he couldn't hold onto that one shred of decency in a line of work that was either dangerous, dirty, or downright depressing. The witch's eyes took on a shade of red, as the blood rushed to her face, and she tried to mutter an incantation through the muzzle covering her mouth. Philip blinked and then stared steadily at her as she attempted futilely to summon to memory the simple phrase that could free her.

"I wouldn't do that if I were you," he warned. "The mixture of Brainstone and fennel I feed you every morning and night prevents your mind from being able to process thoughts and produce sentences." He shrugged. "If you try to force yourself, you'll only rupture blood vessels in that tired old head of yours, and if too many burst I don't think I'll be able to save you."

The haggard old lady snorted and jerked her head backwards, as if she somehow thought that by doing so she would be able to free herself from the muzzle that prevented her from opening her mouth more than a crack. It covered the lower half of her face, complimenting the stringy, once-white, hair that hung limply to the sides of her head. All of her thrashing wore her out and her body slumped back against the wooden chair to which she was chained. The chair was nailed to the ground so all of her efforts had availed her not a single sentence, nor one inch of shift in her circumstances.

Philip should have felt pleased; she was a threat after all. A vicious killer, and user of men and women alike, the kind of subject that once apprehended, was best when locked away in the deepest vault at St. Thomas's. He knew it was truth, but sometimes it was hard to see the look in their eyes when he carted them away. He and his partner had collected her in Massachusetts nearly two weeks ago, before sailing south, and she was definitely one of their more dangerous acquisitions. He watched a moment more to make sure she was truly mollified. Satisfied that the witch was sufficiently subdued, he turned and made his way back along the narrow aisle that was created by the various boxes, cages and contrivances for keeping things contained that held the rest of his cargo.

He held the lantern aloft as high above his head as he could, illuminating only a fraction of the hold around him. Outside the air would be sharp and wintery, with possibly a fresh morning breeze to waft the smell of fish, unwashed sailors, and the salt and brine of the sea across a person's nose. Compared to the aromas that assailed his nostrils down here, the thought of outside air was a veritable luxury. Bodily waste and urine mixed with the smell of bilge, blood, and strangely even the scent of a swamp, formed a pungent odor, worse than any he had ever imagined. Well, until he had joined the guild that is. After his first assignment he had rather quickly rethought all of his romanticized versions of the career he had chosen. Falling into a Changeling's latrine would do that to you.

The orange glow his light source emitted illuminated boxes briefly as he strode by them, working his way through the maze of crates towards the ladder entrance from the primary hold above him. He wormed his way past a particularly wobbly coffin that was propped up against a large box to his left, as he turned the corner into the few yards of open space surrounding the ladder. He lowered the lantern as he twisted his body to turn, and then he brought it back up to shine on the open area as he continued on his way. As the light came up, he found himself face to face with a snarling mouth. The attack was instantaneous.

Hands closed about his throat and squeezed to kill. He jammed his own fingers into the eyes and neck of his assailant in an attempt to keep him at bay. The creature flexed powerful muscles and flung him against the wall of the cargo hold. Philip crashed to the floor with a painful thud and struggled up to his hands and knees only for the thing to fling itself upon him once more. It landed upon him, a mass of dirty skin, ragged, and torn clothes, and the smell of unwashed blood. This time it was Philip's turn to grasp his attacker's throat and hold the thing at bay. Saliva dripped onto his face as the thing closed in, straining for a bite of his flesh with blackened human teeth.

Philip recognized the half-man as one of his nastier captives. Leaning towards him, it forced its mouth a mere inch or so from his face before Philip remembered the silver dagger he kept at his waist. He risked letting go of the beast with his right hand to snatch the knife out of his belt and then brought it up with vicious speed into his opponent's side. His thrust was not a killing blow, but the thing gave an anguished howl until Philip smashed his left hand into its face and sent it twitching to the floor.

Not many creatures could match Philip for strength and it had been some time since he'd been so hard pressed to defend himself. It did not surprise him, however, every guild member knew that a werewolf's first and most well planned assault was accompanied by an extreme rush of strength, even one that was still in human form due to it not being a full moon.

One of the well-documented characteristics of a werewolf. If you were strong enough to fight it off and resist that first onslaught as he had just now, then its following attempts weakened until you either defeated it or it ran off. Assuming, however, you were strong enough to fend off even a less than full power werewolf. It wasn't as easy as it sounded. Luckily, Philip had a physical trait of his own that not many people knew about. The thing, *the man*, he reminded himself yet again, lay unconscious from his final blow. It wouldn't stay that way for long.

Philip realized that the trap door above his head was open, and he glanced up into the wide-eyed stare of a twelve-year-old boy looking down at him. Philip grunted as he pushed himself up from the ground and grabbed the ankle of the werewolf and began dragging it back towards its confinement.

"Stephen, come down here," he commanded the boy in a quiet but authoritative tone.

The boy gulped and proceeded to shuffle his way down the ladder from one hold to the next. "Yes, sir?"

Philip almost snorted at the boy's attempt at innocence. He would have if he had not just found himself in such a precarious situation. Lucky his mouth had been closed and none of the werewolf's saliva had found its way inside, otherwise things might have been far worse. He doubted that the venom would have changed his physical form, as his own biological quirks would probably nullify that mutation, but he still might have become a carrier, capable of infecting others. Carriers sometimes became more dangerous than the real thing since they often had no idea they might be transmitting the curse even through the simplest of interactions such as a kiss.

"How many times have I told you to check all of the cages while I am out on a night's mission?" He fought for patience he didn't feel. "Is being a guild apprentice important to you or not? You must pay attention to details."

The boy dropped his head and muttered, "Yes, sir."

"How did the beast escape?" Philip already had an idea how, but it didn't hurt to let the boy find his own way to the proper conclusions.

Stephen squirmed uncomfortably. "I don't know, sir."

"Guess then, if you have not a clue," Philip retorted, keeping his exasperation as far from his voice as possible, and repeating over and over to himself that all was well that ended well, and nothing had come of this latest lapse in the boy's attention to detail.

"Well, sir," the boy answered in the accent he had acquired on the rough alleys of London's backstreets, "I suppose, if I had to speculate, there might possibly have been something I did wrong..." he trailed off.

Philip shook his head, his patience nearly at an end. "Just answer the question truthfully, you're not in too much trouble. Yet."

Stephen steeled himself and appeared to finally give up his worthless attempt to hide the truth. "I must have forgotten to douse his chains in the Wolfsbane water last night," he muttered in embarrassment.

Philip patted the boy on the shoulder before turning a corner in the cargo hold as he hauled the captive back along one of the aisles toward its cage. "There, Stephen, was that so hard to answer me plainly?"

The boy seemed encouraged that his overseer didn't appear too angry, and so he shook his head in relief.

"But how many times have I told you that you must take extra care to monitor our captives with the most extreme caution? This is the biggest load we have ever taken, and another unfortunate occurrence such as this could have disastrous consequences." Philip shuddered inwardly to imagine what might happen should a creature break loose and decide to free its fellow captives. He inclined his head at Stephen and raised his furry eyebrows, trying to instill a mite of worry into his apprentice. "You do know that this werewolf isn't even the most dangerous thing we're carrying, don't you?"

"Yes, Master Philip," Stephen responded in the meekest of tones.

Philip dragged the body behind him and proceeded to test the boy. "What is the best way to keep a werewolf confined?" He stared directly at Stephen, his face demanding an answer.

"A cage made of pure silver, of course, sir," the boy fired back.

"And if one isn't available?" he followed up just as quickly. Silver cages were rarely used due to difficultly in procuring them. The Guild had access to the treasuries of many governments, but still, an entire silver cage would cost a fortune. Not many people were willing to go to that length when there were other ways to keep a werewolf locked up.

The lad answered promptly yet again. "Exactly what we are doing, or supposed to be doing." He eyed the body they were hauling back to its cage a bit apprehensibly; as if still unsure he wouldn't be punished for his failure to comply with caging regulations from their guild-provided handbook. "Chains doused morning and night in Wolfsbane water, is enough to hold the creature fast."

Philip nodded his agreement and approval. But this was all information his apprentice should know by now. He continued to question his helper as he soaked the captive's chains in the Wolfsbane water and locked him up with the chains hanging from the iron ring attached to the top of his crate. The man hung limply, still unconscious with his arms stretched above his head. It was easier to remember he was part human when his eyes and mouth were closed. Right now he looked more like the tired, beaten down prisoner he was rather than a dangerous, mythological creature.

As Philip closed the large wooden box sealing the werewolf inside, he looked at the boy again. "And what about a faun, should we happen to have one on board, what does its safe confinement require?"

Stephen rattled off the correct response. "Muzzle over the mouth to prevent it tricking you with its lies, and a blindfold as well over the eyes so it cannot see its captors. And chains, of course, like all the others."

Fauns were certainly clever creatures, and their sharp wit and crafty tongues could spin a web of deception to which even the most experienced Collector could fall prey.

"How about a vampire?" Philip wasn't done yet.

"Locked in a wooden coffin, and pierced through the heart with a wooden stake." Stephen sent a nervous glance at the coffin propped up down the aisle. He didn't seem fully comfortable with his apprenticeship just yet. Philip understood, as it took time to adjust to the extraordinary, especially when it was extraordinarily dangerous.

"A witch?" He continued to regale the boy with questions about various creatures as they climbed the ladder and entered the primary hold full of their cover goods to sell upon return to England.

The boy answered, recounting just how they were holding their witch below for transport, and smiled when Philip gave him a nod of encouragement at all of his correct responses. Stephen was full of knowledge without a doubt, but forgetfulness would get you killed in this line of work, as certain as the snow that fell on a cold winter's night in the mountains. Something had to be done to help the lad not only retain the useful information but utilize it as well. In a job where your primary concern was escaping with your life, information had to be implemented or it died with its owner.

They clambered up the second ladder onto the deck. The morning light stabbed a welcome pain in Philip's eyes after the dark, grim holds beneath. A grey haze coated the sky, but some light shone through. Winter, mixed with the smoke coming from nearly every chimney in the city, created a smog and soot filled painting overhead. The ugliness overhead was still better than what lay below his feet though. He had been at this job of collecting creatures causing harm for nearly twenty-five years now, but he harbored no real affection for it. It was just something that needed doing and he was trained to do it.

"Oy, Philip," a voice called out from the captain's deck.

Turning his gaze from the sky, he saw his partner striding towards him down the steps to the deck where Philip stood. The newcomer was sturdily built in comparison to Philip's deceptively lean frame, with a layer of skin and fat over the thick muscles hidden below. Anyone or anything that thought James soft, however, would be in for a surprise if they decided to attack him. The man was strong, and had some nasty weapons at his belt to go with the arsenal of tricks he kept up his proverbial sleeve as well.

"We should make sail on the evening tide. I fancy the winds will be just right by then."

James functioned as the captain when they were on the ship. His previous experience of working in shipping yards and as a sailor prior to joining the Guild gave him the knowledge of how to steer their course correctly. Whereas Philip tended to take the lead when they left the sea and set foot on solid ground.

He nodded to his partner and friend of ten years. "We'll finish up this morning. I meet with Mr. Astori not long from now to see if he has any final instructions for us before we sail back to England and make a deposit in St Thomas."

Philip suppressed a shudder at the thought of the location to which they were transporting their cargo. It masqueraded as an insane asylum located on a small, remote port on the southeast corner of the English coast, but only those who belonged to the Guild knew what it truly was; a prison for the kind of things most people only saw in their nightmares.

Call them mythological creatures, monsters, legends, half-human or simply magical, it mattered not, they were a menace to society. Well, most anyway. He knew this because every Guild member was trained in the history and code of the Guild when they joined. Creatures who stayed quiet and didn't draw attention to themselves lived out their lives in relative peace, but if those same creatures succumbed to their baser natures and began terrorizing the regions in which they lived, then it fell to the worthy men and women of the Guild of Collectors to go deal with the situation by removing the threat and covering it up, if possible.

He shook off his musings. "I'm headed there right now. Shouldn't be too long I don't think, unless Mr. Astori gives us one last assignment before we leave."

James sucked on his teeth and spat a glob of phlegm over the rail into the filthy port water lapping at the hull of the ship. "Say hello to your old friend for me," he said, his expression sour as he turned back to whatever task had been occupying him on the captain's deck before Philip and Stephen had exited the cargo hold.

"I will," Philip fixed a cool stare on his partner, "Martin Astori is my friend, James, and a senior member of the Collector's Guild. I have known him for years. Is there a problem?"

James paused and then spat again. "Nope, no problem." For a moment he appraised Philip, mouth pinched as if not sure whether or not to speak his mind. "It's just that there's something strange about that man. I can't put my finger on it, but mark my words, I can sense it."

He showed his yellowed teeth in an amiable grin and changed his tone. "Look, he'll probably send us on another bloody mission. Just watch." And with that James was back to his usual lighthearted self and began describing a serving girl at one of the bars downtown who had the roundest hips imaginable.

Apparently, he had gone there for a drink once and recommended Philip visit and procure her services. James told Philip that since he was going into town on business anyways, he might as well have some fun while he was at it.

Philip snorted and waved his partner's suggestions away. He had a far more respectable woman on his mind these days. But she lived on the outskirts of the city and he had already said his goodbyes to her for the coming voyage. He wasn't going to risk her safety by visiting her again so soon. Collectors tended to curry danger wherever they went, and he wanted to limit that element with her as much as possible. She was his secret and he meant to keep it that way.

He hadn't even told James about Alayna. The less people knew of her, the safer she would remain, and keeping her safe had become his goal. He sometimes wondered if that meant he loved her, but he wasn't fully ready to admit that to himself. As a sign, whenever they wished to see one another, they would send a small bouquet of pale blue Morning Glories. The bouquet came alone, without a note, but the message was clear. Philip believed James had guessed that a girl had caught his eye, but his partner never asked. He respected Philip's privacy.

Philip left his thoughts of Alayna and went back to pondering his partner's odd hesitation at the mention of Mr. Astori. In the end he shrugged it off and prepared to leave the ship. James was a Guild member through and through, but he had chosen to enter the Guild at a later stage of life, as opposed to being practically born into it the way Philip had been. At times James found it hard to dedicate his every waking moment to the job. Philip guessed he was probably ready to go home to England to see his wife and daughter. Philip, on the other hand, had never known anything but the Guild life, and had no wife or children awaiting his return, so the length or duration of a mission did not matter. In fact, the closest thing he had to a wife was here in America, so he was more than happy to knock his boots around these streets for as long as the Guild officials deemed necessary.

He turned towards the gangplank connecting the ship to the wharf and left his partner and apprentice behind him. It was time to go. He had a meeting with Mr. Astori, and when one was meeting with a higher-ranking member of the Guild, it did not pay to be tardy.

ABOUT THE AUTHOR

Mathias Colwell grew up in far Northern California exploring redwood forests and cloudy beaches. He loves God, his family, and friends. Mathias has been a writer for most of his life, drafting his first stories as young as eight years of age. His desire to write fantasy was inspired by such authors as J.R.R. Tolkien, David Eddings and the late Robert Jordan. He is an avid traveler and all-around adventurer, having visited or lived in 27 countries. His travels have led him around the world to five continents including stays in Siberia, Spain, and Chile, and he attributes many of his passions and goals in life to these experiences. In his free time, he enjoys reading, outdoor activities such as soccer, snowboarding and water sports. Mathias has a passion for issues pertaining to social justice and human rights and hopes to influence these areas in the future.

facebook.com/Mathias-GB-Colwell-225647397579547

twitter.com/MathiasColwell

ALSO BY MATHIAS G. B. COLWELL

with Melange Books

The Collector Series

The Collector

Blood Loss

Menagerie of Shadow

Dark Arrow Trilogy

Dusk Runner

Entrance to Dark Harbor

Black Water Well

Novellas

An Age of Mist

A Burning Hope